Frederick Martin

The Life of John Clare

Frederick Martin

The Life of John Clare

ISBN/EAN: 9783337416393

Printed in Europe, USA, Canada, Australia, Japan

Cover: Foto ©Raphael Reischuk / pixelio.de

More available books at **www.hansebooks.com**

LIFE OF JOHN CLARE.

BY

FREDERICK MARTIN.

London and Cambridge:

MACMILLAN AND CO.

1865.

LONDON:
R. CLAY, SON, AND TAYLOR, PRINTERS,
BREAD STREET HILL.

PREFACE.

SOME forty years ago, the literary world rapturously hailed the appearance of a new poet, brought forward as 'the Northamptonshire Peasant' and 'the English Burns.' There was no limit to the applause bestowed upon him. Rossini set his verses to music; Madame Vestris recited them before crowded audiences; William Gifford sang his praises in the 'Quarterly Review;' and all the critical journals, reviews, and magazines of the day were unanimous in their admiration of poetical genius coming before them in the humble garb of a farm labourer. The 'Northamptonshire Peasant' was duly petted, flattered, lionized, and caressed—and, of course, as duly forgotten when his nine days were passed. It was the old tale, all over. In this case, flattery did not spoil the 'peasant;' but poverty, neglect, and suffering broke his heart. After writing some exquisite poetry, and struggling for years with fierce want, he sank at last under the burthen of his sorrows, and in the spring of 1864 died at the North-ampton Lunatic Asylum. It is a very old tale, no doubt, but which may bear being told once more, brimful as it is of human interest.

The narrative has been drawn from a vast mass of letters and other original documents, including some very curious autobiographical memoirs. The possession of all these papers, kindly furnished by friends and admirers of the poet, has enabled the writer to give more detail to his description than is usual in short biographies—at least in biographies of men born, like John Clare, in what may truly be called the very lowest rank of the people.

LONDON, *May*, 1865.

b

CONTENTS.

THE LIFE OF JOHN CLARE.

HELPSTON.

On the borders of the Lincolnshire fens, half-way between Stamford and Peterborough, stands the little village of Helpston. One Helpo, a so-called 'stipendiary knight,' but of whom the old chronicles know nothing beyond the bare title, exercised his craft here in the Norman age, and left his name sticking to the marshy soil. But the ground was alive with human craft and industry long before the Norman knights came prancing into the British Isles. A thousand years before the time of stipendiary Helpo, the Romans built in this neighbourhood their Durobrivæ, which station must have been of great importance, judging from the remains, not crushed by the wreck of twenty centuries. Old urns, and coins bearing the impress of many emperors, from Trajan to Valens, are found everywhere below ground, while above the Romans left a yet nobler memento of their sojourn in the shape of good roads. Except the modern iron highways, these old Roman roads form still the chief means of inter-communication at this border of the fen regions. For many generations after Durobrivæ had been deserted by the impe-rial legions, the country went downward in the scale of civil-ization. Stipendiary and other unhappy knights came in

B

shoals ; monks and nuns settled in swarms, like crows, upon
the fertile marsh lands ; but the number of labouring hands
began to decrease as acre after acre got into the possession
of mail-clad barons and mitred abbots. The monks, too,
vanished in time, as well as the fighting knights ; yet the
face of the land remained silent and deserted, and has remained so to the present moment. The traveller from the
north can see, for thirty miles over the bleak and desolate fen
regions, the stately towers of Burleigh Hall—but can see
little else beside. All the country, as far as eye can reach,
is the property of two or three noble families, dwelling
in turreted halls ; while the bulk of the population, the
wretched tillers of the soil, live, as of old, in mud hovels, in
the depth of human ignorance and misery. An aggregate of
about a hundred of these hovels, each containing, on the
average, some four living beings, forms the village of Helpston.
The place, in all probability, is still very much of the same
outer aspect which it bore in the time of Helpo, the mystic
stipendiary knight.

Helpston consists of two streets, meeting at right angles,
the main thoroughfare being formed by the old Roman road
from Durobrivæ to the north, now full of English mud, and
passing by the name of Long Ditch, or High Street. At the
meeting of the two streets stands an ancient cross, of oct-
angular form, with crocketed pinnacles, and not far from it,
on slightly rising ground, is the parish church, a somewhat
unsightly structure, of all styles of architecture, dedicated to
St. Botolph. Further down stretch, in unbroken line, the
low huts of the farm labourers, in one of which, lying on the
High Street, John Clare was born, on the 13th July, 1793.
John Clare's parents were among the poorest of the village,
as their little cottage was among the narrowest and most
wretched of the hundred mud hovels. Originally, at the
time when the race of peasant-proprietors had not become
quite extinct, a rather roomy tenement, it was broken up into

meaner quarters by subsequent landlords, until at last the
one house formed a rookery of not less than four human
dwellings. In this fourth part of a hut lived the father
and mother of John, old Parker Clare and his wife. Poor
as were their neighbours, they were poorer than the rest,
being both weak and in ill health, and partly dependent
upon charity. The very origin of Parker Clare's family was
founded in misery and wretchedness. Some thirty years
previous to the birth of John, there came into Helpston a
big, swaggering fellow, of no particular home, and, as far as
could be ascertained, of no particular name : a wanderer over
the earth, passing himself off, now for an Irishman, and now
for a Scotchman. He had tramped over the greater part of
Europe, alternately fighting and playing the fiddle ; and being
tired awhile of tramping, and footsore and thirsty withal, he
resolved to settle for a few weeks, or months, at the quiet
little village. The place of schoolmaster happened to be
vacant, perhaps had been vacant for years ; and the villagers
were overjoyed when they heard that this noble stranger, able
to play the fiddle, and to drink a gallon of beer at a sitting,
would condescend to teach the A B C to their children. So
'Master Parker,' as the great unknown called himself for
the nonce, was duly installed schoolmaster of Helpston.
The event, taking place sometime about the commencement
of the reign of King George the Third, marks the first dawn
of the family history of John Clare.

The tramping schoolmaster had not been many days in the
village before he made the acquaintance of a pretty young
damsel, daughter of the parish-clerk. She came daily to
wind the church clock, and for this purpose had to pass
through the schoolroom, where sat Master Parker, teaching
the A B C and playing the fiddle at intervals. He was as
clever with his tongue as with his fiddlestick, the big schoolmaster ; and while helping the sweet little maiden to wind
the clock in the belfry, he told her wonderful tales of his

doings in foreign lands, and of his travels through many
countries. And now the old, old story, as ancient as the
hills, was played over again once more. It was no very
difficult task for the clever tramp to win the heart of the
poor village girl; and the rest followed as may be imagined.
When spring and summer was gone, and the cold wind came
blowing over the fen, the poor little thing told her lover that
she was in the way of becoming a mother, and, with tears in
her eyes, entreated him to make her his wife. He promised
to do so, the tramping schoolmaster; but early the next day
he left the village, never to return. Then there was bitter
lamentation in the cottage of the parish-clerk; and before
the winter was gone, the poor man's daughter brought into
the world a little boy, whom she gave her own family name,
together with the prefixed one of the unworthy father.
Such was the origin of Parker Clare.

What sort of existence this poor son of a poor mother
went through, is easily told. Education he had none; of
joys of childhood he knew nothing; even his daily allowance
of coarse food was insufficient. He thus grew up, weak and
in ill-health; but with a cheerful spirit nevertheless. Parker
Clare knew more songs than any boy in the village, and his
stock of ghost stories and fairy tales was quite inexhaustible.
When grown into manhood, and yet not feeling sufficiently
strong for the harder labours of the field, he took service as
a shepherd, and was employed by his masters to tend their
flocks in the neighbourhood, chiefly in the plains north of the
village, known as Helpston Heath. In this way, he became
acquainted with the herdsman of the adjoining township
of Castor, a man named John Stimson, whose cattle was
grazing right over the walls of ancient Durobrivæ. John
Stimson's place was taken, now and then, by his daughter
Ann—an occurrence not unwelcome to Parker Clare; and
while the sheep were grazing on the borders of Helpo's Heath,
and the cattle seeking for sorrel and clover over the graves

of Trajan's warriors, the young shepherd and shepherdess talked sweet things to each other, careless of flocks and herds, of English knights and Roman emperors. So it came that one morning Ann told her father that she had promised to marry Parker Clare. Old John Stimson thought it a bad match : 'when poverty comes in at the door, love flies out of the window,' he said, fortified by the wisdom of two score ten. But when was ever such wisdom listened to at eighteen?

The girl resolved to marry her lover with or without leave ; and as for Parker Clare, he needed no permission, his mother, dependent for years upon the cold charity of the workhouse, having long ceased to control his doings. Thus it followed that in the autumn of 1792, when Robespierre was ruling France, and William Pitt England, young Parker Clare was married to Ann Stimson, of Castor. Seven months after, on the 13th day of July, 1793, Parker Clare's wife was delivered, prematurely, of twins, a boy and a girl. The girl was healthy and strong ; but the boy looked weak and sickly in the extreme. It seemed not possible that the boy could live, therefore the mother had him baptized immediately, calling him John, after her father. However, human expectations were not verified in the twin children ; the strong girl died in early infancy, while the sickly boy lived—lived to be a poet.

Of *Poeta nascitur non fit* there never was a truer instance than in the case of John Clare. Impossible to imagine circumstances and scenes apparently more adverse to poetic inspiration than those amidst which John Clare was placed at his birth. His parents were the poorest of the poor ; their whole aim of life being engrossed by the one all-absorbing desire to gain food for their daily sustenance. They lived in a narrow wretched hut, low and dark, more like a prison than a human dwelling ; and the hut stood in a dark, gloomy plain, covered with stagnant pools of water, and overhung by mists during the greater part of the year. Yet from out these surroundings sprang a being to whom all life was golden, and all nature a breath of paradise. John Clare was a poet almost as soon as he awoke to consciousness. His young mind marvelled at all the wonderful things visible in the wide world : the misty sky, the green trees, the fish in the water, and the birds in the air. In all the things around him the boy saw nothing but endless, glorious beauty ; his whole mind was filled with a deep sense of the infinite marvels of the living world. Though but in poor health, the parents were never able to keep little John at home. He trotted the lifelong day among the meadows and fields, watching the growth of herbs and flowers, the chirping of insects, the singing of birds, and the rustling of leaves in the air. One day, when still very young, the sight of the distant horizon, more than usually defined in sharp outline, brought on a train of contemplation. A wild yearning to see what was to be seen yonder, where the sky was touching the earth, took hold of him, and he resolved to explore the distant, unknown region. He could not sleep a wink all night for eager expectation, and at the dawn of the day the next morning started on his journey, without saying a word to either father or mother. It was a hot day in June, the air close and sultry, with gossamer mists hanging thick over the stagnant pools and lakes. The little fellow set out without food on his long trip, fearful of being retained by his watchful parents. Onward he trotted, mile after mile, towards where the horizon seemed nearest ; and it was a long while before he found that the sky receded the further he went. At last he sank down from sheer exhaustion, hungry and thirsty, and utterly perplexed as to where he should go. Some labourers in the fields, commiserating the forlorn little wanderer, gave him a crust of bread, and started him on his home journey. It was late at night when he returned to Helpston, where he found his parents in the greatest anxiety, and had to endure a severe punishment for his romantic excursion. Little John Clare did not mind the beating ; but a long while after felt sad and sore at heart to have been unable to find the hoped-for country where heaven met earth.

The fare of agricultural labourers in these early days of John Clare was much worse than at the present time. Potatoes and water-porridge constituted the ordinary daily food of people in the position of Clare's parents, and they thought themselves happy when able to get a piece of wheaten bread, with perhaps a small morsel of pork, on Sundays. At this height of comfort, however, Parker Clare and his wife seldom arrived. Sickly from his earliest childhood, Parker Clare had never been really able to perform the work required of him, though using his greatest efforts to do so. A few years after marriage, his infirmities increased to such an extent that he was compelled to seek relief from the parish, and henceforth he remained more or less a pauper for life. Notwithstanding this low position, Parker Clare did not cease to care for the well-being of his family, and, by the greatest privations on his own part, managed to send his son to an infant school. The school in question was kept by a Mrs. Bullimore, and of the most primitive kind. In the winter time, all the little ones were crowded together in a narrow room ; but as soon as the weather got warm, the old dame turned them out into the yard, where the whole troop squatted down on the ground. The teaching of Mrs. Bullimore did not make much impression upon little John, except a slight fact which she accidentally told him, and which took such firm hold of his imagination that he remembered it all his life. There was a white-thorn tree in the school-yard, of rather large size, and the ancient schoolmistress told John that she herself, when young, had planted the tree, having carried the root from the fields in her pocket. The story struck the boy as something marvellous ; it was to him a sort of revelation of nature, a peep into the mysteries of creation

at the works of which he looked with feelings of unutterable amazement, not unmixed with awe. But there was
little else that Mrs. Bullimore could teach John Clare, either
in her schoolroom or in the yard. The instruction of the
good old woman was, in the main, confined to two things—
the initiation into the difficulties of A B C, and the reading
from two books, of which she was the happy possessor.
These books were 'The Death of Abel' and Bunyan's 'Pil-
grim's Progress.' Their contents did not stir any thoughts
or imaginings in little John, whose mind was filled entirely
with the pictures of nature.

When John Clare had reached his seventh year, he was
taken away from the dame-school, and sent out to tend sheep
and geese on Helpston Heath. The change was a welcome
one to him, for, save the mysterious white-thorn tree, there
was nothing at school to attract him. Helpston Heath, on
the other hand, furnished what seemed to him a real teacher.
While tending his geese, John came into daily contact with
Mary Bains, an ancient lady, filling the dignified post of
cowherd of the village, and driving her cattle into the pas-
tures annually from May-day unto Michaelmas. She was
an extraordinary old creature, this Mary Bains, commonly
known as Granny Bains. Having spent almost her whole
life out of doors, in heat and cold, storm and rain, she had
come to be intimately acquainted with all the signs fore-
boding change of weather, and was looked upon by her
acquaintances as a perfect oracle. She had also a most reten-
tive memory, and being of a joyous nature, with a bodily
frame that never knew illness, had learnt every verse or
melody that was sung within her hearing, until her mind
became a very storehouse of songs. To John, old Granny
Bains soon took a great liking, he being a devout listener,
ready to sit at her feet for hours and hours while she
was warbling her little ditties, alternately merry and plain-
tive. Sometimes the singing had such an effect that

both the ancient songstress and her young admirer forgot their duties over it. Then, when the cattle went straying into the pond, and the geese were getting through the corn, Granny Bains would suddenly cease singing, and snatching up her snuff-box, hobble across the fields in wild haste, with her two dogs at her side as respectful aides-de-camp, and little John bringing up the rear. But though often disturbed in the enjoyment of those delightful recitations, they nevertheless sunk deep into John Clare's mind, until he found himself repeating all day long the songs he had heard, and even in his dreams kept humming—

> ' There sat two ravens upon a tree,
> Heigh down, derry, O !
> There sat two ravens upon a tree,
> As deep in love as he and she.'

It was thus that the admiration of poetry first awoke in Parker Clare's son, roused by the songs of Granny Bains, the cowherd of Helpston.

JOHN CLARE LEARNS THRESHING, AND MAKES AN ATTEMPT
TO BECOME A LAWYER'S CLERK.

The extreme poverty of Parker Clare and his wife compelled them to put their son to hard work earlier than is usual even in country places. John was their only son ; of four children born to them, only he and a little sister, some six years younger, having remained alive ; and it was necessary, therefore, that he should contribute to the maintenance of the family, otherwise dependent upon parish relief. Consequently, John was sent to the farmer's to thrash before he was twelve years old, his father making him a small flail suited to his weak arms. The boy was not only willing, but most eager to work, his anxious desire being to assist his poor

parents in procuring the daily bread. However, his bodily
strength was not equal to his will. After a few months' work
in the barn, and another few months behind the plough, he
came home very ill, having caught the tertiary ague in the
damp, ill-drained fields. Then there was anxious consulting
in the little cottage what to do next. The miserable allowance from ' the union' was insufficient to purchase even the
necessary quantity of potatoes and rye-bread for the household,
and, to escape starvation, it was absolutely necessary that
John should go to work again, whatever his strength. So he
dragged himself from his bed of sickness, and took once
more to the plough, the kind farmer consenting to his leading the horses on the least heavy ground. The weather was
dry for a season, and John rallied wonderfully, so as to be
able to do some extra-work, and earn a few pence, which he
saved carefully for educational purposes. And when the
winter came round, and there was little work in the fields, he
made arrangements with the schoolmaster at Glinton, a man
famed far and wide, to become his pupil for five evenings in
the week, and for as many more days as he might be out of
employment. The trial of education was carried on to John
Clare's highest satisfaction, as well as that of his parents, who
proclaimed aloud that their son was going to be a scholar.

Glinton, a small village of about three hundred inhabitants, stands some four or five miles east of Helpston,
bordering on the Peterborough Great Fen. It was famous in
Clare's time, and is famous still, for its educational establishments, there being three daily schools in the place, one of
them endowed. The school to which John went, was presided
over by a Mr. James Merrishaw. He was a thin, tall old
man, with long white hair hanging down his coat-collar, in
the fashion of bygone days. It was his habit to take extensive walks, for miles around the country, moving forward
with long strides, and either talking to himself or humming
soft tunes ; on which account his pupils styled him ' the

humble-bee.' The old man was passionately fond of music, and devoted every minute spared from school duties and his long walks, to his violin. To the more promising of his pupils Mr. James Merrishaw showed great kindness, allowing them, among other things, the run of his library, somewhat larger than that of ordinary village schoolmasters. John Clare had not been many times to Glinton, before he was enrolled among these favourites of Mr. Merrishaw. Being able already to read, through his own exertions, based on the fundamental principles instilled by Dame Bullimore, little John dived with delight into the treasures opened at the Glinton school, never tired to go through the somewhat miscellaneous book stores of Mr. Merrishaw. In a short while, the young student was seized with a real hunger for knowledge. He toiled day and night to perfect himself, not only in reading and writing, but in some impossible things which he had taken into his head to learn, such as algebra and mathematics. Coming home late at night, from his long walk to school, he astonished and not a little perplexed his poor parents by crouching down before the fire, and tracing, in the faint glimmer of a burning log, incomprehensible signs upon bits of paper, or sometimes pieces of wood. Far too poor to buy even the commonest kind of writing paper, John was in the habit of picking up shreds of the same material, such as used by grocers and other village shopkeepers, and to scratch thereon his signs and figures, sometimes with a pencil, but oftener with a piece of charcoal. Perhaps there never was a more unfavourable study of mathematics and algebra.

For two winters and part of a wet summer, John Clare went to Mr. Merrishaw's school at Glinton, during short intervals of hard labour in the fields. At the end of this period a curious accident seemed to give a sudden turn to his prospects in life. A maternal uncle, called Morris Stimson, one day made his appearance at Helpston, having been previously on a visit to his father and sisters at Castor. Uncle

Morris was looked upon as a very grand personage, he holding the post of footman to a lawyer at Wisbeach, and as
such clad in the finest plush and broadcloth. Being duly
reverenced, the splendid uncle in his turn thought it his
duty to patronize his humble friends, and accordingly was
kind enough to offer little John a situation in his master's
office. There was a vacancy for a clerk at Wisbeach, and
Uncle Morris was sure his nephew was just the man to fill
it. John himself thought otherwise; but was immediately
overruled in his opinion by father, mother, and uncle. A
boy who had been to Mr. Merrishaw's for ever so many
evenings; who could read a chapter from the Bible as well
as the parson, and who was drawing figures upon paper night
after night : why, he was fit enough to be not only a lawyer's
clerk, but, if need be, a minister of the church. So they
argued, and it was settled that John should go to Wisbeach,
and be duly installed as a clerk in the office just above the
pantry in which dwelt Uncle Morris. Mr. Morris Stimson
did not stop at Helpston longer than a day; but, before
leaving, made careful arrangements that his nephew should
follow him to Wisbeach precisely at the end of seven days.

Those were stirring seven days in the little hut of Parker
Clare. The poor mother, anxious to assist to the best of her
power in her son's rise in life, ransacked her scanty ward-
robe to the utmost, to put John in what she deemed a proper
dress. She mended all his clothes as neatly as possible;
she made him a pair of breeches out of an old dress, and a
waistcoat from a shawl; and then ran up and down the
village to get a few more necessary things, including an old
white necktie, and a pair of black woollen gloves. Thus
equipped, John Clare started for Wisbeach one Friday morning in spring—date not discoverable, but supposed to be somewhere about the year 1807. The poor mother cried bitterly
when John shook hands for the last time at the bottom of
the village; the father tried hard to hide his tears, but did

not succeed ; and John himself, light-hearted at first, had a good cry when he turned his face at Elton, and got a final glimpse of the steeple of Helpston church. Beyond Elton John Clare had never been in his life, and it was with some sort of trembling, mixed with a strong feeling of home-sickness, that he inquired his way to Peterborough. His confusion was great when he found that the people stared at him on the road ; and stared the more the nearer he approached the episcopal city. No doubt, a thin, pale, little boy, stuck in a threadbare coat which he had long outgrown, and the sleeves of which were at his elbows ; with a pair of breeches a world too large for his slender legs ; with a many-coloured waistcoat, an immense pair of woollen gloves, a white necktie, and a hat half a century old, was a rare sight, even in the fen country. Poor John, therefore, had to march into Peterborough followed by the curious eyes of a hundred male and female idlers, who opened doors and windows to see him pass along. Happily the trial was not a long one, for, having discovered his way to the Wisbeach boat, he ran to it as fast as his legs would carry him, and, fairly on board, ensconced himself behind a bale of goods. Oh, how he repented having ever left Helpston, in the fatal ambition of becoming a lawyer's clerk !

The journey from Peterborough to Wisbeach, in those days, was by a Dutch canal boat—a long narrow kind of barge, drawn by one horse, with a large saloon in front for common passengers, and a little room for a possible select company behind, near the steersman. The boat only ran once a week, on Friday, from Peterborough to Wisbeach, returning the following Sunday ; and, as far as it went, the passage was cheap as well as convenient—the charge for the whole distance of twenty-one miles being but eighteen-pence. But John Clare, fond though he was of water, and trees, and green fields, did not much enjoy the river journey, his heart being big with thoughts of the future. What the great

lawyer to whom he was going would say, and what replies
he should make, were matters uppermost in his mind. To
prepare for the dreaded interview John at last set himself to
compose an elaborate speech, on the model of one which
he had seen in the 'Royal Magazine' at Mr. Merrishaw's
school. The speech, however, was not quite ready when the
boat stopped at Wisbeach, landing John Clare, together with
the other passengers. One more source of trouble had to be
overcome here. When the young traveller inquired for the
house of Mr. Councillor Bellamy, the people, instead of replying, stared at him. ' Mr. Councillor Bellamy ? *You* are not
going to Mr. Bellamy's house ?' said more than one of the
Wisbeach citizens, until poor John got fairly frightened.
He was still more frightened when he at last arrived before
the house of Mr. Councillor, and found that it was a stately
building, bigger and nobler-looking than any he had ever
entered in his life. He had not courage enough to ring the
bell or knock at the door, but stood irresolute at the threshold.
At last John ventured a faint tap at the door ; and, luckily,
Uncle Morris appeared in answer to the summons, and
welcomed the visitor by leading him down into the kitchen,
where the board was spread. ' I have told master about
your arrival,' said Uncle Morris ; ' and meanwhile sit down
to a cup of tea. Do not hang your head, but look up boldly,
and tell him what you can do.' John sat down to the table,
yet was unable to eat anything, in fear and trembling of the
things to come. It was not long before Mr. Councillor
Bellamy made his appearance. Poor John tried hard to keep
his head erect as ordered, and made a convulsive effort to
deliver himself of the first sentences of his prepared speech.
But the words stuck in his throat. ' Aye, aye ; so this is
your nephew, Morris?' now said Mr. Councillor Bellamy,
addressing his footman. ' Yes, sir,' replied the faithful
servant ; ' and a capital scholar he is, sir.' Mr. Councillor
glanced at the 'scholar' from the country—at his white

necktie, his little coat, and his large breeches. 'Aye, aye;
so this is your nephew,' Mr. Councillor repeated, rubbing his
hands; 'well, I *may* see him again.' With this Uncle
Morris's master left the room. He left it not to return; and
John Clare had never in his life the honour of seeing Mr.
Councillor Bellamy again. There next came an order from
the upper regions to make Morris's nephew comfortable till
Sunday morning, and to put him, at that time, on board the
Peterborough boat for the return journey. The behest of
Mr. Councillor was duly executed, and John Clare, on the
following Sunday evening, after three days' absence, again
walked into his father's cottage at Helpston, a happier and a
wiser lad. He had discovered the great truth that he was
not fit for the profession of the law.

JOHN CLARE CONTINUES TO STUDY ALGEBRA,
AND FALLS IN LOVE.

The mother cried for joy when her John again entered the
little cottage; but the father welcomed him with a melancholy
smile. John himself, though with a little mortified vanity,
felt rather pleased than otherwise. His good sense told him
that this journey to Wisbeach had been but a fool's errand,
and that, in order to rise in the world, he had to look into
other directions than to a lawyer's office. He therefore fell
back with a strong feeling of contentment into his old occupation, holding the plough, carting manure to the field, and
studying algebra. In the latter favourite labour he was
much assisted by a young friend, whose acquaintance he had
made at Glinton school, named John Turnill, the son of a
small farmer. The latter, having a little more money at his
command than his humble companion, was able to purchase
the necessary books, as well as a modest allowance of
paper and pencils, the gift of which threw John Clare into

ecstasies of delight.　With Master Turnill, the attachment to mathematics and algebra was a real love, though it was otherwise with Clare, who pursued these studies solely out of ambition, and with a hope of raising himself in the world.　The desire to improve his position became stronger than ever after his return from Wisbeach.　The sneers of the people who met him during the journey had sunk deep into his sensitive mind, and he determined to make a struggle for a better position.　How far mathematics and the pure sciences would help him on the road he did not trouble himself to consider ; he only had a vague notion that they would lead him to be a ' scholar.'　So he toiled with great energy through the algebraic and mathematical handbooks purchased by friend Turnill, often getting so warm on the subject as to neglect his dinner-hour, in brown studies over the *plus* and *minus*, squares, cubes, and conic sections.　Every evening that he could possibly spare he walked over to Turnill's house, near Elton, regardless of wind, rain, and snow, and regardless even of the reproaches of his kind parents, who began to be afraid of his continued dabbling in the occult arts.　However, little John stuck to his algebra, and it was nearly two years before he discovered that he was as little fit to be a mathematician as a lawyer's clerk.

Meanwhile, and before the algebraic studies came to an end, there occurred a somewhat favourable change in the circumstances of John Clare.　Among the few well-to-do inhabitants of Helpston was a person named Francis Gregory, who owned a small public-house, under the sign of the ' Blue Bell,' and rented, besides, a few acres of land.　Francis Gregory, a most kind and amiable man, was unmarried, and kept house with his old mother, a female servant, and a lad, the latter half groom and half gardener.　This situation, a yearly ' hiring,' being vacant, it was offered to John, and eagerly accepted, on the understanding that he should have sufficient time of his own to continue his studies.　It was a promise abundantly kept, for John Clare had never more leisure, and, perhaps, was never happier in his life than during the year that he stayed at the 'Blue Bell.' Mr. Francis Gregory, suffering under constant illness, treated the pale little boy, who was always hanging over his books, more like a son than a servant, and this feeling was fully shared by Mr. Gregory's mother. John's chief labours were to attend to a horse and a couple of cows, and occasionally to do some light work in the garden or the potato field ; and as these occupations seldom filled more than part of the day or the week, he had all the rest of the time to himself. A characteristic part of Clare's nature began to reveal itself now. While he had little leisure to himself, and much hard work, he was not averse to the society of friends and companions, either, as in the case of Turnill, for study, or, as with others, for recreation ; but as soon as he found himself, to a certain extent, his own master, he forsook the company of his former acquaintances, and began to lead a sort of hermit's life. He took long strolls into the woods, along the meres, and to other lonely places, and got into the habit of remaining whole hours at some favourite spot, lying flat on the ground, with his face toward the sky. The flickering shadows of the sun ; the rustling of the leaves on the trees ; the sailing of the fitful clouds over the horizon, and the golden blaze of the sky at morn and eventide, were to him spectacles of which his eye never tired, with which his heart never got satiated. And as he grew more and more the constant worshipper of nature, in any of her aspects, so his mind gradually became indifferent to almost all other objects. What men did, what they had done, or what they were going to do, he did not seem to care for, or had the least curiosity to know. In the midst of these solitary rambles from his 'Blue Bell' home, the news was brought of some extraordinary discoveries at Castor, his mother's native village. It was news which, one might have thought, would fire

C

the imagination of any man gifted with the most ordinary understanding. In a part of the township of Castor called Dormanton Fields, the greater part of the vast ruins of Durobrivæ were discovered : temples and arches crumbled into dust ; many-coloured tiles and brickwork ; urns and antique earthen vessels ; and coins, with the images of many emperors—so numerous that it looked as if they had been sown there. To reconstruct the ancient Roman city, to people it anew with the conquerors of the world, was a task at once undertaken by zealous antiquarians ; yet Clare, though he heard the matter mentioned by numerous visitors to the ' Blue Bell,' and had plenty of time for investigation, took so little interest in it as not even to attempt a walk to the city of ruins, on the borders of which he was feeding his cattle. Now, as up to a late period of his life, a bunch of sweet violets was worth to John Clare more than all the ruins of antiquity.

While at the ' Blue Bell ' John gradually dropped his algebra and mathematics, and began to read ghost-stories. The reason of his leaving the ' sciences called pure ' was the discovery that the further he proceeded on the road the more he saw his utter incapacity to understand and to master the subjects. His friend and guide, John Turnill,—subsequently promoted to a post in the excise—was equally unable to throw light into the darkness of *plus* and *minus*. and after a few last convulsive struggles to get through the ' known quantities ' into the unknown regions of x, y, and z, he gave it up as a hopeless effort. The spare hours henceforth were devoted to studies of a very different kind, namely, fairy tales and ghost stories. Under the roof of the ' Blue Bell ' no other literature was within his reach. and he was quite content to draw temporary nourishment from it. Scarcely any books but these highly spiced ones, stuffed in the pack of travelling pedlars, ever found their way to Helpston. There was ' Little Red Riding-hood,' ' Valentine and Orson,' ' Sinbad the Sailor,' 'The Seven Sleepers,' 'Mother Shipton,' 'Johnny Armstrong,' 'Old Nixon's Prophecy,' and a whole host of similar 'sensation' stories, printed on coarse paper, with a flaming picture on the title-page. John Clare scarcely knew that there were any other books than these and the few he had seen at Glinton school in existence; he had never heard of Shakespeare and Milton, Thompson and Cowper, Spenser and Dryden; and, therefore, with the natural eagerness of the young mind just awoke to its day dreams, eagerly plunged into the new realm of fancy. The effect soon made itself felt upon the ardent reader, fresh from his undigested algebraic studies. He saw ghosts and hobgoblins wherever he went, and after a time began to look upon himself as a sort of enchanted prince in a world of magic. He had no doubt whatever about the literal truth of the stories he read; the thought of their being mere pictures of the imagination not entering his mind for a moment. It was natural, therefore, that he should come to the conclusion that, as the earth had been, so it was still peopled with fairies, dwarfs, and giants, with whom it would be his fate to come into contact some time or other. So he buckled his armour tight, ready to do battle with the visible and invisible world.

Opportunity came before long. Among his regular duties at the 'Blue Bell' was that of fetching once a week flour from Maxey, a village some three miles north of Helpston, near the Welland river. The road to Maxey was a very lonely one, part of it a narrow footpath along the mere, and the superstition of the neighbourhood connected strange tales of horror and weird fancy with the locality. In the long days of summer, John Clare, who had to start on his errand to the mill late in the afternoon, managed to get home before dark, thus avoiding unpleasant meetings; but when the autumn came, the sun set before he left Maxey, and then the ghosts were upon him. They always attacked him half . way between the two villages, in a low swampy spot, over-

hung by the heavy mist of the fens. Poor John battled
hard, but the spirits nearly always got the upper hand.
They pulled his hair, pinched his legs, twisted his nose, and
played other tricks with him, until he sank to the ground in
sheer exhaustion. Recovering himself after a while, the
fairies then let him alone, and he staggered home to the
'Blue Bell,' pale and trembling, and like one in a dream.
His good friend and master, Francis Gregory, wondering at
the haggard look of the lad, thought he was going to have
another attack of the tertiary ague, and spoke to his parents ;
but John, in his silent mood, said it was nothing, and begged
to be left alone. So they let him have his way, and he
continued his weekly errands to Maxey, with the same result
as before. At last, when thoroughly wearied of this repetition of supernatural terrors, he hit upon an ingenious plan
for breaking the chain connecting him with the invisible
world. The plan consisted in concocting, on his own part,
a story of wonders ; a story, however, ' with no ghost in it.'
Now a king, and now a prince—in turn a sailor, a soldier,
and a traveller in unknown lands—John himself was always
the hero of his own story, and, of course, always the lucky
hero. With his vast power of imagination, this calling
up of a new world of bright fancies to destroy the lawless
apparitions of the air had the desired effect, and the ghosts
troubled John Clare no more on his way to and from the
mill.

Nevertheless, his constant reading of fairy tales, with
incessant play on the imagination and surexcitation of the
mind, was not without leaving its ill effect upon the bodily
frame. John sickened and weakened visibly, and his general
appearance became the talk of the village. His long solitary
roamings through the woods and fields, his habits of reading
even when tending the cattle, and his apparent dislike to
hold converse with any one, were things which the poor

labourers, young and old, could not understand ; and when,
as it happened, people met him on the road to Maxey in the
dark, and heard that he was talking to himself in a loud
excited manner, they set him down as a lunatic. Some few
of the coarsest among the youngsters went so far as to greet
him with volleys of abuse when he happened to come near
them, while the old people drew back from him as in disgust.
His sensitive feelings suffered deep under this treatment of
his neighbours, which might have had the worst consequences
but for one great event which suddenly broke in upon him.
John Clare fell in love.

' Love took up the glass of Time, and turned it in his glow-
    ing hands ;
 Every moment, lightly shaken, ran itself in golden sands.
 Love took up the harp of Life, and smote on all the chords
    with might ;
 Smote the chord of Self, that, trembling, pass'd in music out
    of sight.'

John Clare's first love—the deepest, noblest, and purest
love of his whole life—was for ' Mary,' the Mary of all his
future songs, ballads, and sonnets. Petrarch himself did
not worship his Laura with a more idealized spirit of affection than John Clare did his Mary. To him she was nothing
less than an angel, with no other name than that of Mary ;
though vulgar mortals called her Mary Joyce, holding her
to be the daughter of a well-to-do farmer at Glinton. John
Clare made her acquaintance—if so it can be called what
was the merest dream-life intercourse—on one of his periodical journeyings to and from the Maxey mills. She sat on a
style weaving herself a garland of flowers, and the sight so
enchanted him that he crouched down at a distance, afraid
to stir and to disturb the beautiful apparition. But she continuing to sit and to weave her flowers, he drew nearer, and

at last found courage to speak to her.   Mary did not reply;
but her deep blue eyes smiled upon him, lifting the humble
worshipper of beauty into the seventh heaven of bliss.   And
when he met her again, she again smiled; and he sat down
at her feet once more, and opened the long pent-up rivers of
his heart.   Mute to all the world around him, he to her for
the first time spoke of all he felt, and dreamt, and hoped.
He told her how he loved the trees and flowers, and the
singing nightingales, and the lark rising into the skies, and
the humming insects, and the sailing clouds, and all the
grand and beautiful works of nature.   But he never told her
that he thought her more beautiful than ought else in God's
great world.   This he never said in words, but his eyes
expressed it; and Mary, perhaps, understood the language
of his eyes.   Mary always listened attentively, yet seldom
said anything.   Her eyes hung upon his lips, and his lips
hung upon her eyes, and thus both worshipped the god of
love.

The sweet dream lasted full six months—six glorious sunlit months of spring and summer.   Then the father of Mary
Joyce heard of the frequent meetings of his daughter with
John Clare, and though looking upon both as mere children,
he sternly forbid her to see 'the beggar-boy' again.   His
heart of well-to-do farmer revolted at the bare idea of his
offspring talking with the son of one who was not even a
farm-labourer, but had to be maintained as a pauper by the
parish.   Explaining this great fact to his blue-eyed daughter,
he deeply impressed its terrible importance upon her soft
little heart, making her think with a sort of shudder of the
pale boy who told her such pretty stories.   Perhaps Mary
nevertheless preserved a lingering fondness for her little
lover's memory, for though many wooed her in after life, she
never wedded, and died a spinster.   As for John Clare, he
fretted long and deeply, and all his life thought of Mary
Joyce as the symbol, ideal, and incarnation of love.   With

the exception of a few verses addressed to ' Patty,' his future
wife, the whole of Clare's love poetry came to be a dedication and worship of Mary. As yet, in these youthful days
of grief and affection, he wrote no verses, though he felt a
burning desire to give vent to his feelings in some shape or
other. Having lost his Mary, he carved her name into a
hundred trees, and traced it, with trembling hand, on stones,
and walls, and monuments. There still stands engraven on
the porch of Glinton churchyard—or stood till within a
recent time—a circular inscription, consisting of the letters,
' J. C. 1808,' cut in bold hand, and underneath, in fainter
outline, the name ' Mary.'

TRAVELS IN SEARCH OF A BOOK.

Just before quitting the ' Blue Bell,' at the end of his
twelve months' service, another important event took place
in the life of John Clare. One morning, while tending his
master's cattle in the field, a farmer's big boy, with whom he
had but a slight acquaintance, showed him a copy of Thomson's ' Seasons.' Examining the book, he got excited beyond
measure. It was the first real poem he had ever seen, and
in harmony as it was with all his feelings, it made upon him
the most powerful and lasting impression. Looking upon
the book as a priceless treasure, he expressed his admiration
in warm words, asking, nay, imploring the possessor to lend
it him, if only for an hour. But the loutish boy, swollen
with pride, absolutely refused to do so ; it was but a trumpery
book, he said, and could be bought for eighteen-pence, and
he did not see why people who wanted it should not buy it.
The words sunk deep into John Clare's heart ; ' Only eighteen-
pence ? ' he inquired again and again, doubting his own ears.
The big boy was quite sure the book cost no more than
eighteen-pence ; he had himself bought it at Stamford for
the money, and could give the name and address of the

bookseller. It was information eagerly accepted by John, who determined on the spot to get the coveted poem at the earliest opportunity. His wages not being due at the moment, he hurried home to his father in the evening, entreating the loan of a shilling, as he himself possessed but sixpence. But Parker Clare, willing though he was to gratify his son, was unable to render help on this occasion. A spare shilling was not often seen in the hut of the poor old man, dependent chiefly upon alms, and in want, not unfrequently, of the bare necessaries of life. But the loving mother could not listen to her son's anxious entreaty without trying to assist him, and by dint of superhuman exertions she managed to get him sevenpence. The fraction still wanting to complete the purchase-money of the book was raised by sundry loans at the 'Blue Bell,' and John waited with eagerness for the coming Sunday, when he would have time to run to Stamford. The Sunday came—a Sunday in spring; and he was up soon after midnight, and stood before the bookseller's shop in Stamford when the eastern clouds assumed their first purple hue. John Clare patiently waited one hour, two hours, three hours, yet the treasure store which contained Thomson's 'Seasons' remained closed. Tremblingly he asked a boy who came along the street at what time the shop would be opened: ' It will not be open at all to-day, for it is Sunday,' rejoined the other. Then John went home in bitter sorrow to Helpston, not knowing how to get the much-coveted book. On the way, a bright thought struck him. If he could but raise twopence, in addition to the capital already acquired, he thought he could manage the matter. So by making extraordinary efforts, he got his twopence, and then held a long conversation with the cowherd of a neighbouring farmer. Clare's occupation on the following morning was to take his master's horses to the pasture, and he offered the cowherd the sum of one penny to look after the horses for him, and one more penny for 'keeping the secret.' The bargain was struck, after an animated discussion, in which the conscientious cowherd strove hard to get a total reward of threepence, so as to be able to keep the secret for any length of time. But John was inflexible, for strong reasons of his own, and thus gained the victory.

During the night from Sunday to Monday, John Clare could not shut his eyes for sheer anxiety. The questions whether the bookseller would have any copies left of the wonderful poem ; whether it could really be bought for eighteen-pence ; and whether the big farmer's boy did not mean the whole story as a hoax, occupied his mind all night long. It seemed so improbable to him, on reflection, that a book containing the most exquisite verses could be bought for little more than the common fairy tales of the hawkers, and it seemed still more improbable that, being sold so cheap, there would be any books left for sale, that he at last inwardly despaired of getting the book. Thereupon he had a good long cry in the silence of the night, when all the village was asleep ; and the crying closed his eyelids, too, for sheer weariness. And when he roused himself again there was a faint glow in the sky ; so he rushed down to the stables, took out his horses, and led them to the pasture, awaiting the arrival of his confederate. The latter came at length, and, having given over his horses, John set off in a sharp trot, skipping over the seven or eight miles to Stamford in little more than an hour. The bookseller's shop, alas, was still closed ; but the people in the streets told the eager inquirer that the shutters would be taken down in about an hour and a half. John, therefore, sat down in quiet resignation on the door-step, counting the quarters of the chiming clock. At last there was a noise inside the house, a rattling of keys and drawing of bolts. The bookseller slowly opened his door, and was immensely astonished to see a little country lad, thin and haggard, with wild gleaming eyes, rush at him with a demand for Thomson's 'Seasons.' Was there ever

such a customer seen at Stamford? The good bookseller was
not accustomed to excitement, for the old ladies who dealt at
his shop bought their hymn-books and manuals of devotion
without any manifestations of impatience, and even the
young ones, though they asked for Aphra Behn's novels in a
whisper, came in very quietly and demurely. Who, then,
was this queer, haggard-looking country boy, who could not
wait for Thomson's 'Seasons' till after breakfast, but was
hovering about the shop like a thief? The good bookseller
questioned him a little, but did not gain much satisfactory
information. That his little customer was servant at the
'Blue Bell;' had hired himself to Master Gregory for a year;
had a father and mother maintained by the parish; and had
seen Thomson's 'Seasons' in the hands of a farmer's boy—
that was all the inquisitive bookseller could get at; and, indeed, there was nothing more to tell. However, the Stamford shopkeeper was a man of compassion, and seeing the
wan little figure before him, resolved upon a tremendous
sacrifice. So he told Clare that he would let him have
Thomson's 'Seasons' for one shilling: 'You may keep the
sixpence, my boy,' he exclaimed, with a lofty wave of the
hand. John Clare heard nothing, saw nothing; he snatched
up his book, and ran away eastward as fast as his legs would
carry him. 'A queer customer,' said the shopkeeper, finishing to take down his shutters.

The sun had risen in all his glory when John Clare was
trotting back from Stamford to Helpston. Every now and
then he paused to have a peep in his book. This went on
for a mile or two, after which he could contain himself no
longer. He was just passing along the wall of the splendid
park surrounding Burghley Hall, the trees of which, filled
with melodious singers, overhung the road. The village of
Barnack in front looked dull and dreary; but the park at
the side was sweet and inviting. With one jump, John was
over the wall, nestling, like a bird, among some thick shrubs

in the hedge. And then and there he read through Thomson's
' Seasons'—read the book through twice over, from beginning
to end. And the larks and linnets kept singing more and
more beautifully; and the golden sun rose higher and higher
on the horizon, illuminating the landscape with a flood of
light, a thousandfold reflected in the green trees and the blue
waters of the lake. John Clare thought he had never before
seen the world so exquisitely beautiful; he thought he had
never before felt so thoroughly happy in all his life. He did
not know how to give vent to his happiness; singing would
not do it, nor even crying. But he had a pencil in his pocket
and a bit of crumpled paper, and, unconscious almost of what
he was doing, with a sort of instinctive movement, he began
to write—began to write poetry. The verses thus composed
were subsequently printed, but with great alterations, under
the title, ' The Morning Walk.' What Clare actually wrote
on his crumpled bit of paper was, probably, very imperfect
in form, and not fit to be seen till thrice distilled in the
crucible of his future ' able editor.'

John Clare felt intensely joyful when returning to
Helpston from his long morning walk. He did not mind
being taken to task by his indulgent employer for having,
for the first time, neglected his duty; did not mind the
reproaches of his fellow-servant as to his having broken his
compact. The cowherd justly argued that, after the solemn
agreement to look after the horses for three hours on payment
of one penny, and to keep the secret for another penny, it
was unfair to burthen him with the responsibility of the
guardianship, as well as the secret, for more than half a day.
Seeing the justice of the claim, John Clare, in the fulness of
his heart, gave his brother cowherd the sixpence, which the
kind bookseller at Stamford had presented him with. However, though generously paid, the cowherding youth was unable to keep the terrible secret for more than a day. The
next morning he told his sweetheart, in strict confidence, that

Clare had got into an immense fortune, and was running up
and down to Stamford to buy books and 'all sorts of things.'
Before it was evening, the whole village knew the story, and
a hundred fingers were pointed at Clare while he walked
down the street.   He was greatly blamed on all sides : blamed,
in the first instance, for allowing himself to be drawn away
by the sprites and their nameless chief, and, as was supposed,
accepting gold and silver from them ; and blamed still more
for not sharing his fortune with his poor parents.   There
were those who had seen him, on the brink of the mere,
holding converse with the Evil One ; they had actually witnessed the passing of the glittering coin, 'which fell into his
hands like rain drops.'   Clare's poor old father and mother
did not believe these stories ; yet even they shuddered when
their son entered the little hut.   It was clear John could not
remain long at Helpston.   There was danger in being a poet
on the borders of the fen regions.

VARIOUS ADVENTURES, INCLUDING THE PURCHASE OF 'LOWE'S CRITICAL SPELLING-BOOK.'

When the yearly engagement at the 'Blue Bell' came to an
end, there was serious consultation between John and his
parents as to his future course of life.   He was too weak to
be a farm labourer ; too proud to remain a potboy in a public-
house ; and too poor to get apprenticed to any trade or handi-
craft.   John himself would have liked to be a mason and
stone-cutter, which trade one Bill Manton, of Market Deeping,
who had a reputation far and wide for setting up gravestones,
was ready to teach him.   Bill Manton was a big swaggering
fellow, who, vibrating constantly to and fro between tavern
and graveyard, hinted to John that in becoming his apprentice
he would have to write the mortuary poetry as well as to
engrave it upon stone ; and the notion was so pleasing that he
made a desperate effort to get initiated into the art and

mysteries of stone-cutting. But the obstacles were insurmountable, for Bill Manton wanted a premium of four pounds, which Clare's parents had no more means of raising than so many millions. There was another chance for learning a trade in the offer of one Jim Farrow, a hunchback, who proposed to teach John the art of cobbling gratis, the sole condition being that the apprentice should provide his own tools. The few pence necessary for this purpose might have been obtained, and the poet might have taken to the calling of St. Crispin, but that he showed a great aversion to the trade. The prospect of passing his whole life in a narrow cabin, mending hobnailed boots, was one he could not face, and he strongly expressed his wish of rather remaining servant in a public-house than submitting to this necessity. One more resource remained, which was to become a gardener's apprentice at Burghley Park, the seat of the Marquis of Exeter, where such a place happened to be vacant. The mere mentioning of the name Burghley Park had charms of its own to John Clare; and although the situation was but a poor one as regarded pay, he eagerly expressed his willingness to apply for it. To make success more sure, old Parker Clare resolved to accompany John in making the application. Accordingly, one morning, father and son, dressed in their very best, made their appearance at the park gates, inquiring for the head gardener of the noble Marquis. After a long delay they were ushered into the presence of the great man. Parker Clare, in whose eyes a head-gardener was quite as important a personage as a prince, took off his hat and bowed to the ground, and the example was followed, in great trepidation of mind, by John. This evidently pleased the high functionary, and he condescended to engage John Clare on the spot. The terms were that John should serve an apprenticeship of three years, receiving wages at the rate of eight shillings per week for the first year, and a shilling more each successive year, out of which sum he would have to

provide his board and all other necessaries except lodgings.
The arrangement seemed a most advantageous one both to
John and his father, and poor old Parker wept tears of joy
when returning to Helpston, and informing his wife of the
brilliant future in store for their offspring. He was now,
they thought, on the high road to fortune.

However, it was an evil day for John when entering upon
his service at Burghley Park. The visions of poetry which
swept across his mind when first lying under the trees of the
park, and, with Thomson's ' Seasons ' in hand, surveying the
beautiful scenery, soon took flight, to give way to a reality
more dreary and more corrupt than any he had yet witnessed.
John Clare had not been many weeks in his new place, before
he found that his master, the head-gardener, was but a low,
foul-mouthed drunkard, while his fellow-apprentices and the
other workmen sought pride in rivalling their chief in intemperance and dissipation.   It was the custom at Burghley
Park to lock up all the workmen and apprentices employed
under the head-gardener during the night, to prevent them
robbing the orchards.   The men did not much relish the
confinement in a narrow house, and therefore got into the
regular habit of making their escape, at certain days in the
week, to a neighbouring public-house, which they reached by
getting out of the window of their garden-house prison, and
climbing over the park fence.   The tavern at which the jolly
gardeners held their carousals was kept by one 'Tant Baker,'
formerly a servant at Burghley Park, and now retailing
fermented liquors under the sign of ' The Hole-in-the-Wall.'
To go to the ' Hole-in-the-Wall ' was one of the first proposals
made to John after he had entered upon his service, and though
he at first showed some reluctance, his scruples were soon
overcome by the persuasion of his companions, who made the
greater effort for this purpose, as they were afraid that by
leaving him behind he would become a tell-tale.   The young
apprentice, in consequence, paid his regular visits with the

others to the public-house; and it was not long before he came to like Tant Baker's strong ale as well, if not better, than his companions. Thus John Clare became accustomed, in some measure, to intemperate habits. Not unfrequently he took such a quantity of drink at the 'Hole-in-the-Wall' as to be completely stupified, and disabled to reach his sleeping-place for the night. He would then lie down under any hedge or tree, sleeping off his intoxication, and creeping home, in the early morning, to Burghley Park. Debasing as were the moral effects of this course of life, the physical consequences were not less disastrous. Several times, after having made his bed on the cold ground, John Clare found on awaking his whole body covered as with a white sheet, the result of the cold dews of the night. Rheumatic complaints followed, permanently enfeebling a body weak from infancy.

The unhappy course of Clare's life was aggravated by the conduct of those under whom he served. The head gardener, a confirmed drunkard, thought it nevertheless beneath his dignity to get intoxicated at the 'Hole-in-the-Wall,' but sought his alcoholic refreshments at a more aristocratic public-house in the neighbouring town. He often caroused at Stamford so long and so late, that his spouse got impatient at her lonely residence, and despatched one messenger after the other to bring her truant lord home. The policy of the wife, however, was defeated by her drunken husband. He made it a rule of keeping the envoys sent to him, and plying them with strong drink till they were more unable to report their own than his movements. Poor little John, unfortunately, was often sent on these errands, which led to his being made drunk one night at Stamford, by his master, and the next evening, by his fellow-workers, at the way-side 'Hole-in-the-Wall.' What would have become of him had this wretched career been pursued long, is easy to imagine; but, happily, the state of things was brought to an end shorter than at first calculated upon. The drunken master was likewise a brutal master, and, to escape his insults and occasional violence, one of the gardeners, bound by a long engagement, resolved to run away; and, having taken a certain liking to John, persuaded him to become a companion in the flight. This was when John Clare had been about eleven months at Burghley Park, and, by the terms of his agreement with the head gardener, would have had to remain an apprentice for above two years longer. However, he did not think himself bound by the contract, and early one morning in autumn—date again uncertain, but probably about the year 1809, Clare now full sixteen—he scrambled through the window with his companion, and furtively quitted Burghley Park and the service of the Marquis of Exeter. Already on the evening of the same day he repented his rash act. His companion in the flight took him on a long trot to Grantham, a distance of twenty-two miles, where the two lodged at a small beerhouse, and Clare fancied that he was fairly out of the world. Having not the slightest notions about geography, or topography either, he believed he had now arrived at the confines of the habitable earth, and with but little chance of ever seeing his parents again. The thought brought forth tears, and he wept the whole night. On the next morning, the two fugitives tried to find work at Grantham, but did not succeed, so that they were compelled to tramp still further, towards Newark-upon-Trent. Here they were fortunate enough to obtain employment with a nurseryman named Withers, who gave them kind treatment, but very small wages. John, meanwhile, had got thoroughly home-sick, and the idea of being an immense distance away from his father and mother did not let him rest day or night. Not daring to speak to his companion, for fear of being retained by force, he at last made up his mind again to run away from his employer, this time alone. It was beginning to get winter; the roads were partially covered with snow, and swollen streams and rivers interrupted on many points the communication. Nevertheless, John Clare started on his home journey full of courage, though absolutely destitute of money and clothing, leaving part of the latter, together with his tools, at his master's house. During the two or three days that it took him to reach Helpston, he subsisted upon a crust of bread and an occasional draught of water from the nearest stream, while his lodgings were in haystacks on the roadside. His heart beat with tumultuous joy when at last he beheld the loved fields again, and the village where he was born. And when the door swung back which led into the little thatched hut, and he saw his mother and father sitting by the fire, he rushed into their arms, and fairly frightened them with the outburst of his affection.

There now remained nothing for John Clare but to fall back upon his old way of living, and to seek a precarious existence as farm-labourer. This was what he resigned himself to accordingly, only changing his occupation now and then, as circumstances permitted, by doing odd jobs as a shepherd or gardener. It was a very humble mode of life, and its remuneration scarce sufficient to purchase the coarsest food and the scantiest clothing; but it was, after all, the kind of existence which seemed most suited to the habits and inclinations of the strange youth, now growing into manhood. His intense admiration and worship of nature could not brook confinement of any sort, even such as suffered within the vast domain of Burghley Park. While gardener at the latter place, his poetical vein lay entirely dormant; he was never for a moment in the mood of writing nor even of reading verses. Perhaps the habits of dissipation into which he had fallen had something to do with this; yet it was owing still more to the position in which he was placed. The same scenery which had inspired him to his first poetical composition, when viewed in the glowing light of a beautiful morning in spring, left him cold and uninspired ever after. He often complained to his fellow-labourers, that he could

not 'see far enough :' it was as if he felt the rattling of the
chain which bound him to the spot. A yearning after
absolute freedom, mental as well as physical, was one of his
strongest instincts through life, and not possessing this, he
appeared to value little else. It was a desire, or a passion,
which nearly approached the morbid, and gave rise to much
that was painful in the subsequent part of his existence.

Once more a farm-labourer at Helpston, John Clare was
all his own again. Thomson's 'Seasons' never left his
pocket; he read the book when going to the fields in the
morning, and read it again when eating his humble meal
at noonday under a hedge. The evenings he invariably
spent in writing verses, on any slips and bits of paper he
could lay hold of. Soon he accumulated a considerable
quantity of these fugitive pieces of poetry, and wishing to
preserve them, yet ashamed to let it be known that he was
writing verses, he hid the whole at the bottom of an old
cupboard in his bedroom. What made him more timid than
ever to confess his doings to either friends or acquaintances,
was their entire want of sympathy, manifested to him on
more than one occasion. It sometimes happened, on a Sunday, that he would take a walk through the fields, in company
with his father and mother, or a neighbour; and seeing
something particularly beautiful, an early rose, or a little
insect, or the many-hued sky, John Clare would break forth
into ecstasies, declaiming, in his own enthusiastic way, on
what he deemed the marvellous things upon this marvellous
earth. His voice rose; his eyes sparkled; his heart bounded
within him in intense love and admiration of this grand, this
incomprehensible, this ever-wonderful realm of the Creator
which men call the world. But whenever his companions
happened to listen to this involuntary outburst of enthusiasm,
they broke out in mocking laughter. A rose was to them a
rose, and nothing more; an apple they valued higher, as
something eatable; and, perhaps, over plum-pudding they

would have got enthusiastic, too. As it was, poor John was a constant butt for all the shafts of coarse ridicule; even his own parents, to whom he was attached with the tenderest affection, and who fully returned his love, did not spare him. Old Parker Clare shook his head when he heard his son descanting upon the beauties of nature, and reproved him on many occasions for not using his spare time to better purpose than scribbling upon little bits of paper. Parker Clare's whole notion of poetry was confined to the halfpenny ballads which the hawkers sold at fairs, and it struck him, not unnaturally, that the things being so cheap, it could not be a paying business. This important fact he lost no occasion to impress upon his son, though with no result whatever.

While the father was not sparing in his attacks upon John's poetical manifestations, the mother, on her part, was active in the same direction. She had discovered her son's hiding-place of the curious slips of paper which engrossed his nightly attention, and, to make an end of the matter at once, the good woman swept up the whole lot one morning, and threw it in the chimney. Very likely there was in her mind some intuitive perception of the fact that her son's poems 'wanted fire.' John was greatly distressed when he found his verses gone; and more still when he discovered how the destruction happened. To prevent the recurrence of a similar event, he conceived the desperate plan of instilling into his parents a love of poetry. He boldly told them, what he had hitherto not so much as hinted at, that he was writing verses 'such as are found in books,' coupling it with the assertion that he could produce songs and ballads as good as those sold at fairs, so much admired by his father. Parker Clare again shook his head in a doubting mood, expressing a strong disbelief of his offspring's abilities in writing poetry. Thus put upon his mettle, John resolved to do his best to change the scepticism of his father, and having written some verses which he liked, and corrected them over and over again into desirable smoothness, he one evening read them to his astonished parents. But the result was thoroughly disappointing. So far from admiring his son's poetry, Parker Clare expressed his strong conviction that it was mere rubbish, not to be compared to the half-penny songs of the fairs. John was much humbled to hear this; however, he carried within himself a strong belief that his verses were not quite valueless, and therefore resolved upon one more test. Hearing the constant vaunting of the cheap ballads, he made up his mind to try whether his father was really able to distinguish between his own verses and those in print. Accordingly, when he had finished another composition, he committed it to memory, and rehearsed it to his parents in the evening, pretending to read it from the print. Then his father broke out in the delightful exclamation: 'Ah, John, my boy, if thou couldst make such-like verses, that would do.' This was an immense relief to the poor scribbler of poetry. He now saw clearly that his father's want of confidence was in him, the writer, and not in his writings. Henceforth, he made it his regular habit of reciting his own poetry to his parents as if reading it from a book, or printed sheet of paper. The habit, though it was strictly a dishonest proceeding, proved to him not only a real source of pleasure, in hearing his praises from the lips of those he loved most, but it also served him as a fair critical school. Whenever he found his parents laugh at a sentence which he deemed very pathetic, he set himself at once to correct it to a simpler style; whenever they asked him for an explanation of a word, or line, he noted it down as ill-expressed, or obscure; and whenever either his father or mother asked for a repetition of a song which they had heard before, he marked the slip of poetry so honoured as a success. And all these successful slips of paper John Clare placed in a crevice between his bed and the lath-and-plaster wall; a hole so dark and unfathomable as to be beyond the reach of even his sharp-eyed mother, always on the look-out for manuscript poetry to light the fire.

Having gained the surreptitious approval of his verses by his parents, John Clare began to be moved by a slight and almost unconscious feeling of ambition. Hitherto he had written poetry solely for the sake of pleasing himself, but he now was stirred by anxiety to discover what value others set upon his writings. The crevice in his bed-room, jealously guarded since his mother's grand *auto-da-fé*, and as yet undiscovered by the watchful maternal eye, contained a few dozen songs and ballads, descriptive of favourite trees, and flowers, and bits of scenery, and, after long brooding within himself, John resolved upon showing these pieces to an acquaintance. The person selected for this confidence was one Thomas Porter, a middle-aged man, living at a lonely cottage at Ashton Green, about a mile from Helpston. He was one of those individuals, described, in a class, as ' having seen better days ;' besides, a lover of books, of flowers, and of solitary rambles. Their tastes coinciding so far, John Clare and Thomas Porter had become tolerably intimate friends, the former making it a point to visit, almost every Sunday, the little cottage at Ashton Green. Having wound his courage up to the point, John at last, with much secret fear and trembling, showed to his friend the best specimens of his poetry, asking for his opinion on the same. Mr. Thomas Porter, though a very good-natured man, was somewhat formal in his habits, scrutinizing, with visible astonishment, the little pieces of paper—blue, red, white, and yellow, having served the manifold purposes of the baker and tallow chandler before being helpful to poetry—which were submitted to his judgment. Seeing his young friend's disappointed look at the examination, he promised to give his opinion about the poetry in a week, namely, on the following Sunday. The week seemed a long one to John Clare, and he was almost trembling with excitement when again approaching the door of the small cottage of Ashton Green. He trembled still more at the first question of Mr. Thomas Porter:—'Do you know grammar?' It was useless for John to profess that he did know so much as the meaning of the word grammar; or whether it signified a person or a thing. Then Mr. Thomas Porter began to frown. 'You cannot write poetry before you know grammar!' he sternly exclaimed, handing the many-coloured slips of paper back to his poor friend. John Clare was humiliated beyond measure: he felt like one having committed a dreadful, unpardonable crime. Because the sense of the words was not at all clear to him, he was the deeper impressed with the consciousness of the heinous misdeed of having written verses without knowing grammar. So he resolved to know grammar, even should he perish in the attempt.

To ask Mr. Thomas Porter by what means he could get to know grammar, he had not the courage: the ground was burning under his feet in the little cottage at Ashton Green. John Clare, therefore, took his farewell without seeking further information, and hurried off to the house of a lad with whom he had been at Mr. Merrishaw's school. Did he know where or what grammar was? Yes, the lad knew; he had plunged into grammar at Mr. Merrishaw's, instead of into algebra and the pure sciences. But he could not tell how to learn grammar, except through one very difficult work, bound in leather, and called 'The Critical Spelling-book.' To get this wonderful book now became the all-absorbing thought of John Clare. Penny after penny was hoarded by immense exertions, and the greatest frugality, approaching to a want of the necessaries of life. The two shillings for the 'Critical Spelling-book' were saved at length, and John once more made his way to the Stamford bookseller, as eager as when in quest of Thomson's 'Seasons.' He was lucky enough to get 'Lowe's Critical Spelling-book' at once; but, having got it, underwent a fearful disappointment. Reading

it under the hedge on the roadside, in his anxiety to possess
the contents ; reading it at his noonday meal ; and reading it
again at the evening fireside—the more he read it, the less
could he understand it. Algebra and the pure sciences had
puzzled him infinitely less than this awful grammar. Worthy
Mr. Lowe's 'Critical Spelling-book,' happily forgotten by
the present generation, instilled knowledge on the good old
plan of making it as dark and mysterious as possible. There
was, first, a long preface of twenty-two pages, in which Mr.
Lowe deprecated all other spelling-books whatever, especially
those of his very dear friends and fellow-teachers, Mr. Dixon,
author of the 'English Instructor ;' Mr. Kirkby, the learned
writer of the 'Guide to the English Tongue ;' Mr. New-
berry, creator of the 'Circle of the Sciences ;' Mr. Palairet,
the famous compiler of the 'New English Spelling-book ;'
and Mr. Pardon, author of 'Spelling New - Modelled.'
Having gone through the painful task of deprecating his
friends, with the annexed modest statement that the 'Critical
Spelling-book' would be found superior to any other work
of the kind, past, present, or future, Mr. Lowe proceeded to
give his own rules, distinguished ' by the greatest simplicity.
Through the first chapter, treating of 'monosyllables,' John
Clare made his way, with some trouble ; but the second,
entering the field of 'polysyllables,' brought him to a stop.
Read as he might, poor John could not understand the ever-
changing value of 'oxytones,' 'penacutes,' 'ternacutes,'
'quartacutes,' and 'quintacutes,' and was still more bewildered when he found that even after having got through all
these hard words, there was a still harder tail at the end of
them, in the shape of 'exceptions from the spelling-book-
sounds of letters and syllables, some of which are more
simple, and may conveniently be learnt by a single direction,
others more complex, and may better be explained by being
cast into phrases.' Finding it absolutely impossible to get
over the oxytones, he shrunk back from the quartacutes and

quintacutes as beyond the reach of an ordinary human
being, and gave up the study in despair. He next put
' Lowe's Critical Spelling-book ' into the old cupboard where
his mother used to look after his poems—for culinary
purposes.   But the good housewife never burnt the ' Critical
Spelling-book ;' it being, probably, too tough for her, in all
its hide-bound solidity.   As for John Clare, he entirely failed
in learning grammar and spelling, remaining ignorant of the
sister arts to the end of his days.

FRESH ATTEMPTS TO RISE IN THE WORLD, INCLUDING A SHORT MILITARY CAREER.

The failure of his attempt to learn grammar, and the firm
belief in the words of Mr. Thomas Porter that grammar was
indispensable to poetry, for some time preyed upon the mind of
John Clare.   He lost all his pleasure in scribbling verses,
either at home or in the fields, careless even of the praise
which his parents had got into the habit of bestowing upon
his pretended readings from the poets. This lasted for nearly
a year, at the end of which time his own hopefulness, coupled
with the natural buoyancy of youth, drove him again to his
old pursuits.   His spirits were raised additionally by the
encouragement of a new friend, the parish-clerk of Helpston.
The rumour had spread by this time that John was ' a scholar,'
and was ' writing bits of books on paper,' and though the *vox
populi* of Helpston thought not the better of John for this
acquirement, but rather condemned him as a practically
useless creature, the parish-clerk, being teacher also of the
Sunday-school, and, as such, representative of learning in the
village, held it to be his duty to take notice of and patronize
the young man.   He went so far as to call upon Clare, now
and then, with much condescension, and having glanced, in
a lofty sort of way, at the rainbowed slips of paper, already
submitted, with such unhappy results, to the judgment of

Master Porter, he promised to 'do something' for his young friend and pupil. The something, after a time, turned out to be an introduction to Lord Milton, eldest son of the Earl Fitzwilliam, with whom the worthy Sunday-school teacher professed to be on very intimate terms. John Clare, at first, was very unwilling to thrust himself upon the notice of any such high-born personage; but the united persuasion of his parents and the obliging new friend broke his reluctance. A day was fixed, accordingly, for the visit to the noble lord, residing at Milton Park, half way between Helpston and Peterborough. After infinite trouble of dressing, the memorable waistcoat, with cotton gloves, and white necktie, which had made the journey to Wisbeach, being again put into requisition, John Clare and his patron started one fine morning for Milton Park. The stately porter at the lodge, after some parley, allowed them to pass, and they reached the mansion without further misadventure. His lordship was at home, said the tall footman in the hall; and his lordship would see them immediately, he reported, after having delivered the message of the two strangers. Trusting the 'immediate,' John Clare and his friend waited patiently one hour, two hours, three hours; they saw the sun culminate, and saw the sun set, and still waited with becoming quietness. At last, when it was quite dark, the news came that his lordship could not see them this day, but would be glad to meet them some other time. Thereupon John Clare and the Sunday-school teacher left Milton Park and went back to Helpston, slightly sad, and very hungry.

To John Clare this first attempt to gain high patronage was profoundly discouraging; but not so to the worthy parish-clerk, whose experience of the world was somewhat larger. The latter induced his young friend to make another trial to meet Lord Milton, and, the thing being better planned, they were successful this time—as far, at least, as the mere meeting was concerned. Having discovered that

the noble lord was in the habit of occasionally visiting some
outlying farms, the shrewd clerk waylaid his lordship, and,
together with his young friend, burst upon him like an
apparition.   Breaking out into glowing praise of John Clare,
which made the latter blush like a maiden, the parish-clerk
finished by pulling from his pocket a bit of antique pottery,
unearthed somewhere in the grounds between Helpston
Heath and Castor.   Lord Milton smiled, and handing the
bearer some loose cash, accepted the gift, not forgetting to
state that he would remember the young man thus favourably
introduced to his notice.   John Clare instinctively comprehended the meaning of all this, and went home and made a
silent vow never more to seek patronage in cotton gloves,
with a white necktie, and never more to trust his grandilo-
quent friend and patron, the parish-clerk.

The failure of all his attempts to raise himself from his
low condition, drove John Clare into a desponding mood.
Weak in body, and suffering under continuous ill-health, his
work as a farm-labourer brought him scarce sufficient remuneration to procure the coarsest food and the scantiest
clothing, while it left him without any means whatever to
assist his parents in their great distress, so that they had to
continue recipients of meagre parish relief. Throughout, Clare
had an innate consciousness of being born to a freer and
loftier existence, and thus deeply felt the burthen of being
condemned to the fiercest struggle with poverty and misery.
The bitter feeling engendered by this thought he surmounted,
most frequently, by flying into his favourite realm of poetry ;
but often enough the moral strength failed him for the task,
and he sank back in utter hopelessness.   More and more
was this the case at this period.   He was now verging upon
manhood, and with it came, as nobler aspirations, so baser
passions and desires.   To these he fell a prey as soon as he
threw aside his slips of paper and pencil, in consequence of
Thomas Porter's sharp rebuke, and the utter failure to master

'Lowe's Critical Spelling-book.' For many months after, he neither read, nor made the slightest attempt to write verses, and the idle hours threw him again into evil company, similar to that from which he had escaped at Burghley Park. There were, among the labourers of Helpston, two brothers of the name of John and James Billings, who lived, unmarried, at a ruinous old cottage, nicknamed Bachelors' Hall. Both were given to poaching, hard drinking, and general rowdyism, and fond, besides, of meeting kindred spirits, of the same turn of mind, at the riotous evening assemblies in their little cottage. Hitherto, John Clare's passion for poetry had kept him constantly at home, the nightly companion of his poor parents; but no sooner had he weaned himself from his verses, when he fled to the Hall. To his ardent temper, there was a great charm in the wild, uproarious meetings which took place every evening, accompanied by as much consumption of ale as the purses of the lawless fraternity would allow. Poaching, to most of them, proved a source of considerable gain, not less than a pleasant excitement, and the money thus freely acquired was as freely spent in drink and debauchery. Though pressingly invited, Clare could not be made to join in the stealing of game; he was too deep a lover of all creatures that God had made, to be able to hurt or destroy even the least of them wilfully. But although unwilling to commit slaughter himself, he was not at all disinclined to share in its fruits, and it was not long before he became the leader at the frequent drinking bouts at Bachelors' Hall. Shy and reserved on ordinary occasions, he was at these meetings the loudest of loud talkers and singers, the fumes of vanity, together with those of alcohol, exerting their combined influence. Reciting his verses to merry companions, he earned warm and enthusiastic applause, and for the first time in his life deemed himself fully and justly appreciated. That this fancied road to fame was, after all, the dreariest road to ruin, poor John Clare did not see, and, perhaps, could scarcely be expected to see.

Fortunately, at this critical period of Clare's life an event occurred which, though it drove him for the moment into company almost worse than that of Bachelors' Hall, at the same time afforded the means for his rescue. It was in the spring of 1812, Clare now in his nineteenth year, that great efforts were made throughout the kingdom to raise the local militia of the various counties, in view of getting, through this source, recruits for the regular army. Veterans, with red noses and flying ribbons on their hats, kept tramping from one end of the country to the other, making every pothouse resound with tales of martial glory, and fearful accounts of ' Bony.' Even into remote Helpston the recruiting sergeant penetrated, taking up his quarters at the ' Blue Bell,' and with much political wisdom honouring the convivial meetings at Bachelors' Hall with occasional visits. John Clare's heart was stirred within him when, for the first time, he heard of golden deeds of valour in the field, and how men became great and famous by killing other men. The eloquent re-cruiting sergeant rose to his full height when drawing the accustomed figure of ' Bony,' with horns and tail, swallowing a dozen babies at breakfast. John Clare, with other of his fellows at the Bachelors' Hall, got into a holy rage at the crimes of ' Bony,' vowing to enter the list of avenging angels. The veteran with the red nose took his audience at the word, tendering to each of them a neat silver coin, and enlisting them in the regular militia. John was the foremost to take his shilling, and though his heart misgave him a little when thinking the matter over in the cool of the next morning, he had no choice but to take the red-blue-and-white cockade and follow the sergeant. The latter managed to enlist a score of young fellows from Helpston, and the whole village turned out when he marched them off to Peterborough. Old Parker Clare and his wife shed tears on bidding their son farewell, fearing it might be a farewell for ever. As to John, his pride only prevented him from joining in their lamentation, for his mind was by no means easy regarding the consequences of his rash endeavour to become a hero. He deeply felt his own irresolution to commit acts of heroism, even such inferior ones as the killing of small game ; and he asked himself with terror how he would fare when put face to face with such great tigers as ' Bony' and his men. The thought was anything but pleasant, and he was relieved from it only by joining the horse-play of his riotous companions, and ransacking the stores of the roadside taverns. Having reached Peterborough, the whole troop of aspirant warriors was taken before a magistrate to swear fidelity to King George the Third, after which Clare and his fellow-men had quarters assigned to them at the various beer-houses of the episcopal city. For a week or longer, their daily business, in the service of King George the Third, was to get drunk, to parade the streets singing and shouting, and to fight with the watchmen of the town. John Clare, thinking the matter over in his daily musings, wondered at the curious road laid down for people who wished to become heroes.

The Helpston group of warriors having been joined by other clusters from various parts of the county of Northampton, the whole regiment of raw recruits was marched along, one fine morning, to Oundle. Here they were drawn up in a body, some thirteen hundred strong, and divided into companies, according to size. John Clare, being among the smallest of the young heroes, scarce five feet high, was put into the last company, the fifth in number. These preliminaries being duly arranged, the thirteen hundred had to exchange their smock-frocks, jackets, and blouses, for the regulated red coat and trousers. Unfortunately, the official distributor of these articles paid no attention whatever to the stature and physical conformation of the recipients, nor even to their division into different-sized companies, but threw out

his uniforms like barley among the chickens. The consequences were of the most ludicrous kind. Nearly all the big
men got coats which fitted them like strait-laced jackets,
while the little ones had garments which hung upon their
shoulders in balloon fashion. John Clare was more unlucky
than any of his warrior brethren. His trousers, apparently
made for a giant, were nearly as long as his whole body, and
though he drew them up to close under his arms, they still
fell down, by many inches, over his shoes. To prevent his
tumbling over them, like a clown in the pantomime, he held
up his pantaloons with one hand, while with the other he
kept his helmet from falling in the mud. This wonderful
headpiece was as much too small for the big-brained recruit
as the other parts of the uniform were too large, and it
required the most careful balancing to keep it in a steady
position on the top of the crown in a quiet atmosphere,
while, in any little gust of wind, it was indispensable to
ensure the equilibrium with outstretched arm. All this was
easy enough while John Clare went through his first martial
exercises : nothing more simple, while learning the goose-step,
than to hold his big trousers with one hand and his tight
helmet with the other. But at the end of four weeks, his
superiors gave John Clare a gun, and with it came blank
despair. He did not know in the world how to hold his
trousers, his gun, and his headpiece at one and the same
time. Puzzling over the matter till his brain got dizzy, he
at length resolved upon a notable expedient. He tucked his
nether garments into his shoes, thereby giving the upper
portion of them a bag-like appearance, while he exchanged
his helmet for another of larger dimensions, in the possession
of a thin-headed brother recruit. The new headpiece was
a good deal too large, which, however, was easily remedied
by a stuffing of paper and wood shavings, so that henceforth,
unless the wind blew too strong, the ingenious young soldier
had, at least, one of his two hands to himself. This would

have been an immense benefit under ordinary circumstances; but unfortunately, in the case of John Clare, and as if to damp his military ardour, it also turned out a source of un- qualified regret. The corporal under whose immediate orders he was placed, a prim and lady-like youngster, took an aversion to John, partly on account of the bag-trousers, and partly because of the stuffings of his helmet, a fraction of which not unfrequently escaped its' confinement, and hung down, in stiff wooden ringlets, over his pale cheeks. At this the dandy-corporal sneered, and his sneers growing louder on every occasion, John Clare, at the first favourable opportunity, knocked him down with his unoccupied right hand. The offence, amounting to a crime, was at once reported to the captain, and Clare expected momentarily to be thrust into the black-hole, to be tried by court-martial, and perhaps to be shot. But, singularly enough, nothing, after all, came of the whole affair. The serious breach of military discipline was entirely overlooked by the authorities of the Northamp- tonshire militia, who probably thought the whole body of men not worth looking after, the greater number of them consisting of a mere collection of the lowest rabble. In con- sequence of strong remonstrances made by the good people of Oundle about the insecurity of their property, and even their lives, the thirteen hundred warriors were disbanded soon afterwards, and never called together again. John Clare thereupon left his quarters at the 'Rose and Crown,' where he had been tolerably well treated by the owners, a widow and her two daughters, and, with a joyful heart, returned to Helpston. He came home somewhat richer than he left, for he brought back with him a second-hand copy of Milton's 'Paradise Lost,' an odd volume, with some leaves torn out, of Shakespeare's 'Tempest,' both works purchased at a broker's shop at Oundle, and, over and above these acquisitions, a knowledge of the goose step.

TROUBLES OF LOVE, AND A TRIAL OF GYPSY LIFE.

The few weeks' martial glory which John Clare enjoyed had the one good effect of weaning him from the roisterous company at the Bachelors' Hall, and bringing him once more to his former peaceful studies. While a recruit in the militia, he had seen so much of rioting and debauchery, on the part of the vilest of his companions, as to be cured from all desire to follow in their footsteps, and he now made the firm vow to lead a more respectable life for the future, A change of scenery, too, had cured him of the all-absorbing fear that he should never be able to write poetry, for want of grammar, and the proper understanding of 'Lowe's Critical Spelling-book.' It seemed to him, on reflection, that, as he could make himself understood in speaking to his fellow men without knowing grammar, he would be able to do so likewise in writing. He therefore began, more eagerly than ever, to collect small strips of paper, and to fill them with verses on rural scenery, fields, brooks, birds, and flowers. His daily occupation, as before, consisted in working as an out-door farm labourer, and doing occasional odd jobs in gardening and the like, which, though it was barely sufficient to maintain him, had the to him inestimable advantage of leaving him completely his own master. This was the more valuable to John Clare at the present moment, in consequence of an affair which occurred soon after his return from Oundle, and which was nothing less than his falling in love, for the second time in his life. He met, saw, and was conquered by Elizabeth Newton, the daughter of a wheelwright, at Ashton, a small hamlet close to Helpston. She was but a plain girl, but possessed of all the arts of coquetry; and though John Clare did not care much for her at first, she gradually entangled him into fervent affection, or what he held to be such. It was not Platonic love, by any means, like that for sweet Mary Joyce; and less so on the part of the lass than on that of her lover. John, as always, so at his meetings with Elizabeth Newton, was shy, reserved, and bashful, while she was frank and forward, professing to be deeply in love with him. This had the desired effect upon John Clare, whose easily-touched heart could not withstand the charms and wiles of female enchantment. Having got her lover thus far, Elizabeth began to talk of marriage, at the mentioning of which word John felt somewhat startled. His old studies in arithmetic brought to his mind the difficulties there must be in keeping a matrimonial establishment upon ten shillings a week, the average amount of his income, not only for the time, but in all probability for years to come, if not for his whole life. Elizabeth, on her part, did not share these arithmetical apprehensions, in consequence of which there were quarrels, bickerings, and misunderstandings without end. To please his Elizabeth, John Clare was made to go frequently to the house of father Newton, the wheelwright, a curious old man, who was constantly reading in the Bible and trying to find out the meaning of the Apocalypse. He had quotations upon every subject, none of which, however, showed John clearly how to get over the great difficulty of keeping a wife upon nine, or at the best ten, shillings a week. Seeing that her lover was unwilling to do the one thing she wanted, Elizabeth Newton at last jilted him openly, telling him, before a number of other girls, that he was but a faint-hearted fool. After this, she refused to see him again, although John Clare would have been willing to renew the acquaintance, and even, if necessary, to marry her. He felt, now she had parted from him, and, probably, because she had parted from him, a strong affection for the girl, not to be overcome by many inward struggles. For a short time he sank into melancholy, from which he roused himself, however, by a new resolution.

E

On Helpston Heath and the neighbouring commons there were always some gypsy tribes in encampment, the two largest of them being known by the names of ' Boswell's crew,' and ' Smith's crew.'   While out on his solitary rambles, John Clare made the accidental acquaintance of ' King Boswell,' which acquaintance, after being kept up by the interchange of many little courtesies and acts of kindness, gradually ripened into a sort of friendship.   John Clare thought the dark-eyed gypsies far more intelligent than his own working companions in the fields, and he was attracted to them, besides, by their fondness for and knowledge of plants and herbs, as well as their love of music.   Expressing a wish to learn to play the fiddle, the most expert musicians of King Boswell's crew at once began to teach him the art, in their own wild way, without notes or other scientific aid, but with the net result that he was able to perform to his own satis-faction in the course of a few months.   He now became a constant visitor at King Boswell's tent, which he only neg-lected during his courtship with Elizabeth Newton.   This being broken off, in his grief of unrequited affection John Clare was seized with a real passion for the wild life of his gypsy friends, and resolved to join them in their wanderings. He actually carried out this resolve, and enrolled himself as a member of Boswell's crew for a few days ; but at the end of this period left them with much internal disgust.   The poetry of gypsy life utterly vanished on close examination, giving way to the most disagreeable prose.   Accustomed as John Clare was to humble fare under a poor roof, his nerves could not stand the cookery at King Boswell's court.   To fish odds and ends of bones, bits of cabbage, and stray potatoes from a large iron pot, in partnership with a number of grimy hands, and without so much as a wooden spoon, seemed unpleasant work to him, not to be sweetened by all the charms of black eyes and a tune on the fiddle.   He therefore told his new friends that he could not stop with them ; at which they were not very sorry, seeing in him but a poor hand for making fancy baskets and stealing young geese. Thus King Boswell and his secular friend parted to their mutual satisfaction. John Clare returning once more to his accustomed field and gardening operations. However, the poet, all his life long, did not forget the gypsies; nor did they forget him. Whenever any of 'Boswell's crew,' or, in their absence, their first cousins of 'Smith's crew' happened to be near John Clare, on a Saturday evening, after he had drawn his weekly wages, they did not fail to pay him a friendly visit, singing some new song to the ancient text of 'Auld lang syne.'

LIME BURNING AND LOVE MAKING.

The short trial of gypsy life was not sufficient to make John Clare forget his troubles of love, and he began to think seriously of his further prospects in life. He would have been but too happy to ask Elizabeth Newton to become his wife; but having seen so much of poverty in the case of his parents, he had a natural dread to start in the same career, with the workhouse for ultimate goal. While thus given up to reflections on his life, there came an offer which appeared to be most acceptable. A fellow labourer of the name of Gordon, who had been once working at a lime-kiln, with good wages, proposed to him to seek the same employment, and to act as a guide and instructor in the matter. John Clare consented, and starting with his friend, in the summer of 1817, the two were lucky enough to find work not far off, near the village of Bridge Casterton, in Rutlandshire. By dint of very severe labour, Clare managed to earn about ten shillings a week, a part of which he carefully hoarded, with the firm intention of attempting a new start in life, by the aid of a little capital.

The first investment of the small sum thus acquired led to rather important results. Having collected a considerable quantity of verses, and safely carried them off from the old hiding-place at Helpston, John Clare resolved to copy a selection, comprising the best of them, into a book, so as to preserve his poetry the more easily. With this purpose in view he went to the next fair at Market Deeping, and after having gone, with some friends, through the usual round of merry-makings, called upon a bookseller and stationer, Mr. Henson, to get the required volume of blank paper. Mr. Henson had no such article in stock, but offered to supply it in a given time, which being agreed on, particulars were asked as to the quantity of paper required, and the way in which it should be ruled and bound. In reply to these questions, John Clare, made talkative by a somewhat large consumption of strong ale, for the first time revealed his secret to a stranger. He told the inquirer that he had been writing poetry for years, and having accumulated a great many verses, intended to copy them into a book for better preservation. The bookseller opened his eyes at the widest. He had never seen a live poet at Market Deeping, yet fancied, somehow or other, that the species was of an outward aspect different from that of the tattered, half-tipsy, undersized farm labourer who was standing before him. Though an active tradesman, willing to oblige people at his shop, Mr. Henson could not help hinting some of these sceptic thoughts to his customer, and feelingly inquired of him whether it was 'real poetry' that he was writing. John Clare affirmed that it was real poetry; further explaining that he wrote most of his verses in the fields, on slips of paper, using the crown of his hat as a desk. This was convincing; for the hat, on being inspected, certainly showed abundant marks of having been employed as a writing-desk, and even bore traces of its occasional use as a camp-stool. Doubts as to John Clare being a poet were now impossible; and Mr. Henson willingly agreed to furnish a book of white paper, strongly bound, fit for the insertion of a vast quantity of original poetry, at the

price of eight shillings. When parting, the obliging bookseller begged as a favour to be allowed to inspect one of his
customer's poems, promising to keep the matter as secret
as possible. The flattering request was promptly acceded
to, and in a few days after, there arrived by post at Market
Deeping two sonnets by John Clare, which he had recently
composed. One of these was called 'The Setting Sun;'
and the other 'The Primrose.' Mr. Henson, who was
no particular judge of sonnets, thought them very poor specimens of poetical skill, the more so as they were ill-spelt, and
without any attempts at punctuation. He threw the poems
aside at once, and wrote to the poet that he might have his
blank paper book on paying the stipulated eight shillings.
So the matter rested for the present.

John Clare's labours as a lime-burner at Bridge Casterton
were of the most severe kind. He was in the employ of a
Mr. Wilders, who exacted great toil from all his men, setting
them to work fourteen hours a day, and sometimes all the
night long in addition. Nevertheless, Clare felt thoroughly
contented in his new position, being delighted with the
beautiful scenery in the neighbourhood, and happy, besides,
in being able to earn sufficient money to send occasional
assistance to his parents. When not engaged at work, he
went roaming through the fields far and wide, always with
paper and pencil in his pocket, noting down his feelings in
verse inspired by the moment. It was the time when his
poetical genius began to awaken to full life and consciousness. He began writing verses with great ease and rapidity,
often composing half-a-dozen songs in a day; and though
much of the poetry thus brought forth was but of an
ephemeral kind, and of no great intrinsic value, the exercise, combined with extensive reading of nearly all the old
poets, contributed considerably to his development of taste.
Sometimes he himself was surprised at the facility with
which he committed verses to paper, on the mere spur of

the moment. It was on one of these occasions that the thought flashed through his mind of his being endowed with poetical gifts denied to the majority of men. This was a perfectly new view which he took of himself and his powers, and it helped to give him immense confidence. Timid hitherto and entirely distrustful of his own abilities, he now felt himself imbued with strength never known, and under the impulse of this feeling determined to make another attempt to rise from his low condition. The idea occurred to him of printing his verses, and of coming openly before the world as a poet. Each time he had written a new verse with which he was pleased, his confidence grew; though his hopes fell again when he set himself thinking the matter over, and dwelling upon the difficulties in his way. This inward struggle lasted nearly a year, in the course of which there occurred another notable event, which in its consequences grew to be one of the most important of his whole life.

Every Sunday afternoon, the labourers at Mr. Wilder's lime-kiln were in the habit of visiting a small public-house, at the hamlet of Tickencote, called 'the Flower Pot.' Thirsty, like all of their tribe, they spent hours in carousing; while John Clare, after having had his glass or two, went into the fields, and, sitting by a hedge, or lying down under a tree, surveyed the glories of nature, feasting his eyes upon the thousandfold beauties of earth and sky. It was on one of these Sunday afternoons, in the autumn of 1817—Clare now past twenty-four—that he saw for the first time 'Patty,' his future wife. She was walking on a footpath across the fields, while he was lying in the grass not far off, dreaming worlds of beauty and ethereal bliss. Patty stepped right into his ideal realm, and thus, unknown to herself, became part and parcel of it. She was a fair girl of eighteen, slender, with regular features, and pretty blue eyes; but to Clare, at the moment, she seemed far more than fair, slender, and pretty. He watched her across the field, and when she disappeared from sight, John Clare, almost instinctively, climbed to the top of a tree, to discover the direction in which she was going. His courage failed him to follow and address her, though he would have given all he possessed to have one more glance at the sweet face which so suddenly changed his poetical visions into a still more poetical reality. However, the shades of evening were sinking fast; John Clare could not see far even from the top of his tree, to which he clung with a lover's despair, so that the beautiful apparition was soon lost to him. Sleep did not come to his eyes in the following night; and the slow hours of lime-burning the next day only passed on in making projects how he would go to the field near the 'Flower Pot,' and try to meet his sweet love again. He went to the field, but she came not; not the following day, nor the second, nor the whole week. John Clare began to think the fair face which he had seen, and with which he had fallen in love at first sight, was, after all, but the vision of a dream.

More than two weeks passed, and John Clare, with his fiddle under his arm, one evening made his way to Stamford, to play at a merry meeting of lime-burners the tunes which the gypsies had taught him. While walking along the road, the vision burst upon him a second time in not to be mistaken reality. There again was the fair damsel he had seen walking, or floating, across the greensward on the Sunday eve; as fair and trim as ever, though this time not in her Sunday dress. John Clare, with much good sense, thought it useless to climb again upon a tree; but summing up courage, followed his vision, and, after a while, addressed her in timid, soft words. What gave him some courage for the moment was, that being on a festive excursion, he had donned his very best garments, including a flowery waistcoat and a hat as yet free from the desk service of poetry. The fair damsel, when thus addressed in the road, smiled upon her interlocutor; there could be no doubt, his words, and,

. perhaps, his waistcoat and new hat, found favour in her
eyes. And not only did she allow him to address her, but
permitted him even to accompany her to her father's cottage,
some four miles off. Thither accordingly went John Clare,
in an ecstacy of delight; feeling as if in heaven and playing
merry gypsy-tunes to the winged angels. He wished the
four miles were four hundred; and when arrived at the
paternal door with his fair companion, and she told him that
he must leave her now, it seemed to him as if it had been
but a minute since he met her. He looked utterly dejected;
but brightened up when she told him that her name was
Martha Turner, that her father was a cottage farmer, and that
the place where they were standing was called Walkherd
Lodge—which perhaps, she whispered, he would find again.
It sounded as if the fiddle under his arm was again making
music to the bright angels. John Clare was in heaven; but
the poor lime-burners at Stamford did not think so, that
evening, when they had to dance without a fiddle.

After seeing his sweet companion disappear behind the
garden-gate; after hearing the door of the house open and
shut, and watching the movement of the lights within the
house for an hour or two, John Clare at last turned his back
upon Walkherd Lodge, and went the way he came. The
road he trotted along, with his feet on good Rutlandshire
soil, but his head still somewhat in the clouds, got gradually
more and more narrow, till it ended at a broad ditch, with a
dungheap on the one side and a haystack on the other. It
was now that John perceived for the first time that he had lost
his way. While walking along with Martha Turner, he no
more thought of marking the road than of solving riddles in
algebra, and, besides a faint consciousness that he was coming
somewhere from the east and going to the west, he was
utterly lost in his topography. However, under the circumstances, it seemed no great matter to John to lose his way,
and rather pleasant than otherwise to sleep in a haystack

within a mile of the dwelling of Martha Turner. On the haystack, accordingly, he sat down with great inward satisfaction, and, the moon having just risen, pencil and paper were got out of the pocket, by the help of which, in less than half an hour, another love-song was finished. But though the day was warm and comfortable, John felt too restless to sleep. So he cleared the ditch before him with one jump, and pursued the journey further inland, where lights appeared to be glimmering in the distance. Onward he trotted and leaped, over hedges and drains, across ploughed fields, through underwood and meadows, around stone-quarries and chalk-pits. At last, after a wild race of four or five hours, he sank down from sheer exhaustion. There was soft, mossy grass under his feet, and a sheltering tree above, and he thought it best to stop where he was and to compose himself to sleep. The heavy eyelids sank without further bidding, and for several hours his soul took flight into the land of dreams. When he awoke, the moon was still shining, but not far above the western horizon. Looking around, he perceived something bright and glittering near him, similar to the bare track beaten by the sheep in hot weather. To follow this path was his immediate resolve, as sure to lead to some human habitation, if only a shepherd's hut. He was just going to rise, but still on the ground, when one of his feet slipped a short distance, in the direction of the silvery line, and he heard the clear splash of water under him. At the same moment, the last rays of the moon disappeared from above the horizon. John Clare shuddered as if the hand of death was upon him. Creeping cautiously towards the neighbouring tree, and clasping both his arms around it, he awaited daybreak in this position. At length, after hours which seemed endless, the burning clouds appeared in the east. He once more looked around him, and found that he was lying on the brink of a deep canal, close to the River Gwash. One turn of the body in its restless dreams; one

step towards the tempting silvery road of night, would have
made an end for ever of all the troubles, the love and life
and poetry, of poor John Clare.

ATTEMPTS TO GET UP A PROSPECTUS.

Soon after his first meeting with Martha Turner, at the
beginning of October, 1817, John Clare left Bridge Casterton,
and went to Pickworth, a village four miles off, in a northerly
direction, where he found employment in another lime-kiln,
belonging to a Mr. Clerk. The reason he quitted his old
master was that the latter lowered his wages from nine to
seven shillings per week, which reduction John Clare would
not submit to. Though content, throughout his life, to live
in the humblest way, he had two strong reasons, at this
moment, for wishing to earn moderately good wages, so as to
be able to save some money. The first was that he had set
· his heart on having a new suit of clothes, including an olive-
green coat. As young maidens sigh for a lover, and as
children long for sweetmeats, so John Clare had set his heart
for years on having an olive-green coat. For this wonderful
garment he was 'measured' soon after returning from
Oundle and martial glory, under the agreement, carefully
stipulated with the master tailor, that it was to be delivered
only on cash payment. But he had never yet been able to
raise the necessary fifty shillings, although the olive-green
coat was dearer to his heart than ever before. However,
there was one still dearer object, for the carrying out of which
he wanted to save money, namely, the attempt to get some of
his verses printed. His chief impulse, in this respect, was
not so much literary vanity, but a strong desire to get the
judgment of the world on his own secret labours. As yet,
though with an intuitive perception of the intrinsic worth of
his poetry, he had no real faith in himself. The intimation
of Thomas Porter, respecting the necessity of grammar, still

weighed heavily upon his mind, and the cold reception which his verses met with at the hands of the bookseller of Market Deeping greatly contributed to weaken the belief in the value of his writings. Nevertheless, the old spirit of faith urging him again and again, he had more than once renewed his communications with Mr. Henson, and repeated visits to Market Deeping at last produced a sort of treaty between bookseller and poet. Mr. Henson agreed to print, for the sum of one pound, three hundred prospectuses, inviting subscribers for a small collection of 'Original Trifles by John Clare.' The price of the volume was to be three shillings and sixpence, ' in boards ;' and Mr. Henson promised that, as soon as one hundred subscribers had given in their names, he would begin to print the book, at his own risk. This treaty, the result of several interviews, and much anxiety on the part of John Clare, was settled between the interested parties in the month of December, 1817.

A more excited time than that which now followed, Clare had never seen in his life. He was in love over head and ears, and had to pay frequent visits to his mistress at Walkherd Lodge ; he had to think of saving money for his long-desired olive-green coat—more than ever desired now for presentation at the Lodge ; and, last not least, he had to work overtime to get the one pound sterling required for the printing of the three hundred prospectuses. In short, he had to labour harder than ever, in order to gain more money ; and, yet, at the same time, required more leisure than ever, both for writing verses and love-making. To reconcile these opposite wants, he took to night-work, in addition to daily labour, risking his health and almost his life to gain a few shillings and to have an occasional glimpse at his sweet mistress. His love prospects did not appear to be very promising, at first. As for Martha Turner herself, she rather encouraged than otherwise the attentions of the young lime-burner ; her parents, however, were strongly and energetically opposed to the courtship. Dignified cottage-farmers, renting their half-a-dozen acres of land, with a cow on the common, and a pig or two, they thought their pretty daughter might look higher in the world than to a mere lime-burner with nine shillings a week. Besides, there was another lover in the wind, of decidedly better prospects, who had already gained the ear of the parents, and was backed by all their influence. It was a young shoemaker from Stamford, with a shop of his own ; a townsman dressed in spotless broadcloth on all his visits to Walkherd Lodge, and of manners considered aristocratic. Martha herself wavered slightly between the shoemaker and the lime-burner ; the former was not only well-dressed but good-looking, to neither of which externals John Clare could lay any pretensions. The only advantage possessed by him over his rival was that he pleaded his cause with all the zeal and ardour of a man deeply enamoured, and this, as always, so here, carried the day finally. There was some languid indifference in the addresses of the loving shoemaker, to punish which Martha Turner threw herself into the arms of John Clare. So far, things were looking prosperous at the Pickworth lime-kiln, during the first months of 1818.

Meanwhile, the poetical aspirations of John Clare had made little progress. Mr. Henson, of Market Deeping, insisted that the poet should write his own prospectus, or 'Invitation to Subscribers,' and Clare trembled at the bare idea of undertaking such a formidable work. Easy as it was to him to compose scores of verses every day, in the intervals of the hardest manual labour, he had never attempted, in his whole life, to write a single line in prose, and therefore could not bring himself, by any exertion, to go through the new task. Day after day he tormented his head to find words how to begin the required prospectus, but invariably with the same negative result. Often it happened that, when trying to write down the first line of the 'Invitation,' his thoughts involuntarily lost themselves in rhyme, till, finally, instead of the desired 'Address to the Public,' there stood on paper, much to his own surprise, an address to the primrose or the nightingale. Thus, one morning, when going to his work, in deep thoughts of poetry, prospectuses, love, and lime-burning, the reflection escaped his lips, ' What is life ?' and, as if driven by inspiration, he instantly sat down in a field, and, on a scrap of coarse paper, wrote the first two verses of the poem, subsequently published under the same title. Clare's poetical genius threatened to master even his own will.

At length, however, after infinite trouble and exertion, he managed to get the dreaded prospectus ready. Having saved the pound with which to pay the printer, he firmly determined to make a final attempt to write prose, in some form or other, and to send it off to Market Deeping, in whatever shape it might turn. At this time he was in the habit of working, sometimes at Mr. Clerk's lime-kiln at Pickworth, and sometimes at a branch establishment of the same owner, situated at Ryhall, three miles nearer towards Stamford. Firm in his determination to produce a prospectus, he started one morning for Ryhall, and, arrived at his place of labour, sat down on a lime-scuttle, pencil in hand, with the hat as ever-ready writing-desk. For once, the prose thoughts flowed a little more freely, and after a strong inward effort, the following came to stand upon paper :—

' Proposals for publishing by Subscription a Collection of Original Trifles on miscellaneous subjects, religious and moral, in Verse, by John Clare of Helpston. The Public are requested to observe that the Trifles humbly offered for their candid perusal can lay no claim to eloquence of poetical composition ; whoever thinks so will be deceived, the greater part of them being Juvenile productions, and those of later date offsprings of those leisure intervals which the short remittance from hard and manual labour sparingly afforded

to compose them. It is hoped that the humble situation
which distinguishes their author will be some excuse in their
favour, and serve to make an atonement for the many inaccu-
racies and imperfections that will be found in them. The
least touch from the iron hand of Criticism is able to crush
them to nothing, and sink them at once to utter oblivion.
May they be allowed to live their little day and give satisfaction to those who may choose to honour them with a perusal,
they will gain the end for which they were designed and
their author's wishes will be gratified. Meeting with this
encouragement it will induce him to publish a similar collection of which this is offered as a specimen.'

The writing of this paper—presented here as originally
written, with the correction only of the spelling, and the
insertion of a few stops and commas—took Clare above three
hours, and having finished it, and read it over several times,
he thought he had reason to be pleased with his performance.
A third reading increased this satisfaction, in the fulness of
which he determined to send the prospectus at once to the
printer. Accordingly, he sat down upon his lime-scuttle,
fastened the paper together with a piece of pitch, scraped
from an old barrel, and directed it, in pencil, to ' Mr. Henson,
bookseller, Market Deeping.' This accomplished, he started
off in a trot to the post-office at Stamford. On the road,
new doubts and scruples came fluttering through his mind.
Was it not a foolish act, after all, that he, a poor labourer,
the son of a pauper, should risk a pound of his hard earnings
in the attempt to publish a book? Would not the people
laugh at him? Would they not blame him for spending the
money on such an object, instead of giving it to his half-
starving parents? Such were the doubts that crossed his
mind. But, on the other hand, he considered that success
might possibly attend his efforts ; that, if so, it would be the
means of raising his parents, as well as himself, from their
low situation ; and that, whatever the result, it would show

him the world's estimate of his own doings—either encourage him in writing more verses, or cure him of a silly propensity. This last reflection, and a thought of the fair girl he loved, decided the matter in his own mind. He sprang up from the stone heap, where he had sat buried in reflections, and pursued his way to Stamford. His face was burning with excitement, and, entering the town, he fancied everybody was looking at him, with a full knowledge of his vainglorious errand. The post-office was closed, and the clerk at the wicket demanded one penny as a fee for taking in the late letter. John Clare fumbled in his pockets, and found that he had not so much as a farthing in his possession. In a rueful voice he asked the man at the wicket to take the letter without the penny. The clerk glanced at the singular piece of paper handed to him, the pencilled, ill-spelt address, the coarse pitch, instead of sealing-wax, at the back, and with a contemptuous smile, threw the letter into a box at his side. Without uttering another word, he then shut the door in Clare's face. And the poor poet hurried home, burying his face in his hands.

THE TURN OF FORTUNE.

In about a week after the despatch of the pitch-sealed letter, there came a reply from Mr. Henson, of Market Deeping. It intimated that the prospectuses, with appended specimen poem, were nearly ready, and would be handed over to John Clare, on a given day, at the Dolphin inn, Stamford. Accordingly, on the day named, Clare went over to Stamford, his heart fluttering high with expectations. When Mr. Henson handed him the 'Address to the Public,' with the 'Sonnet to the Setting Sun' on the other side, both neatly corrected and printed in large type, he was beside himself for joy. In its new dress, his poetry looked so charmingly beautiful, that he scarcely knew it again. His hopes rose to the highest pitch when he found that the admiration of his printed verses was shared by others. While they were sitting in the parlour of the Dolphin inn, drinking and talking, there came in a clerical-looking gentleman, who, after having listened a while to the conversation about the forthcoming volume of poetry, politely inquired for the title of the book. Mr. Henson, with business-like anxiety, at once came forward, explaining all the circumstances of the case, not forgetting to praise the verses and the writer to the skies. The gentleman, evidently touched by the recital, at once told Mr. Henson to put his name down as a subscriber, giving his address as the Rev. Mr. Mounsey, Master of the Stamford Grammar-school. John Clare was ready to fall on the neck of the kind subscriber, first admirer of his poetry ; but prudently restraining himself, he only mumbled his thanks, with an ill-suppressed tear in his eye. After having made arrangements for the circulation of the prospectuses, boldly undertaking to distribute a hundred himself, John Clare then went back to his lodgings at Pickworth, dancing more than walking.

The first bright vision of fame and happiness thus engendered was as short as it was intense. It was followed, for a time, by a long array of troubles and misfortune, making the poor poet more wretched than he had ever been before. Soon after his meeting with Mr. Henson at the Dolphin inn, he had a quarrel with his mistress, and a more serious disagreement with her parents, followed by a harsh interdict to set his foot again within the confines of Walkherd Lodge. A few weeks subsequently, his master discharged him, under the probably well-justified accusation that he was neglecting his work, scribbling verses all day long, and running about to distribute his prospectuses. This discharge came in the autumn of 1818, and put Clare to the severest distress. The expenses connected with his poetical speculation had swal-

lowed up all his hoardings, and left him absolutely without a
penny in the world. After several ineffectual efforts to find
work as a lime-burner either at Pickworth or Casterton, he
bethought himself to seek again employment as a farm-
labourer, and for this purpose went back to Helpston. His
parents, now quite reduced to the mercies of the workhouse,
and subsisting entirely upon parish relief, received him with
joy; but nearly all other doors were shut against him. The
wide-spread rumour that he was going to publish a book,
had created a great sensation in the village, but, so far from
gaining him any friends, had raised up a host of jealous
detractors and enemies. Among the most ignorant of the
villagers, the cry prevailed that he was a schemer and im-
postor; while the better-informed people, including the small
farmers of the neighbourhood, set him down as a man who
had taken up pursuits incompatible with his position. Perhaps the latter view was not an altogether unjust one; at
any rate, the farmers, all of them people of small means,
acted upon good precedent in refusing John Clare work,
after he had been discharged, by his last employer, for gross
neglect of duty. It was in vain that Clare offered to do
'jobs,' or work by contract; his very anxiety to get into
employment, of whatever kind it might be, was held to be
presumptuous, and all his offers and promises met with
nothing but distrust. In this frightful state of things, there
was only one resource remaining to John Clare, to escape
starvation—to do as his parents, and beg a dry loaf of bread
from the tender mercies of the parish. His name, accordingly,
was enrolled in the list of paupers.

But as if the cup of his distress was not yet full enough,
John Clare, while reduced to this lowest state of misery, got
a note from Mr. Henson, of Market-Deeping, informing him
that the distributed prospectuses had only brought seven
subscribers, and that the scheme of printing the poems would
have to be dropped entirely, unless he could advance fifteen

F

pounds to meet the necessary expenses. To Clare, this information sounded like mockery. To ask him, while in absolute want of food, to raise fifteen pounds, appeared to him an insult—which probably it was not meant to be. Mr. Henson, the printer and bookseller, had very little knowledge of the actual state of his correspondent, and looking upon the whole scheme of publishing poetry as the driest matter of business, addressed Clare as he would have any other customer. This, however, was not the way in which the deeply-distressed poet viewed the proceedings. He gave way to his feelings in a very angry letter, after despatching which he sank into deep despondency. It seemed to him as if he had now made shipwreck of his life and all his hopes.

Recovering from this sudden access of grief, he made a fresh resolve. At twenty-five, men seldom die of despondency—not even poets. John Clare, too, decided not to give up the battle of life at once, but prolong it a short while by becoming a soldier. However, he was afraid to add to the distress of his father and mother by informing them of this plan, and, therefore, left home under the pretence that he was going to seek work. It was a fine spring morning—year 1819 —when he took once more the road to Stamford. Passing by Burghley Park, he was strongly reminded of that other sunny day in spring when he came the same way with Thomson's 'Seasons' in hand; when he was seized with the sudden passion for poetry, and when he wrote his first verses under the hedge of the gardens, full of joy and happiness. And he pondered upon the sad change which had taken place in these ten years. He had written many more verses—far better verses, he fully believed; and yet was poorer than ever, and more wretched and miserable than he had imagined he could possibly be. Thus ran the flow of his thoughts: sad and gloomy, though not without an undercurrent of more hopeful nature. There was a deep-rooted belief in his heart that the poems he had written were not entirely worthless, and that notwithstanding the coldness and antipathy of the world, notwithstanding his own poverty and wretchedness, the day would come when their value would be appreciated. The new sanguine spirit took more and more hold of him while looking over the hedge into the park, and around on the fields, smiling in their first green of new-born loveliness, and enlivened with the melodious song of birds. Once more, his heart was warmed as of old, and he sat down under a tree, to compose another song. It was a poem in praise of nature, gradually changing into a love-song ; and while writing down the lines, his heart grew melancholy in thoughts of his absent mistress, his sweet ' Patty of the Vale,' separated from him, perhaps, for ever. To see her once more, before enlisting as a soldier, now came to be the most ardent desire of his heart.

The shades of evening were sinking fast, when John Clare reached Bridge Casterton, on his way to Walkherd Cottage. He was just in view of the smiling little garden in front of the house, when a figure, but too well known, crossed his path. It was Patty. She wanted to speak, and she wanted to fly ; her lips moved, but she did not utter a word. Clare, too, was lost, for a minute, in mute embarrassment ; but, recovering himself, he rushed towards her, and with fervent passion pressed her to his heart. Patty was too much a child of nature not to respond to this burst of affection, and for some minutes the lovers held each other in sweet embrace. They might have prolonged their embrace for hours, but were disturbed by calls from the neighbouring lodge. The anxious parent within heard words, and sounds, and stifled kisses, and doubting whether they came from the shoemaker, sent forth shrill cries for Martha to come in without delay. But darkness made Patty bold ; she assured her mother that there was ' nobody,' accompanying the word by another kiss. Then, with loving caress, she tore herself from Clare's arms, flying up the narrow path to the cottage. John Clare was transfixed to the spot for a few minutes, and, having gazed again and again at the rose-embowered dwelling, made his way back to Stamford, joyful, yet sad at heart. On the road, close to Casterton, he met some old acquaintances of the lime-kiln, going to the same destination, intent on an evening's drinking bout. John was asked to join, and after some reluctance, consented. The lime-burners had their pockets well-filled for the night, and the jug of ale went round with much rapidity. When gaiety was at the culminating point, a tall gentleman, in the uniform of the Royal Artillery, joined the merry company. The jug passed to him, and he returned the compliment by ordering a fresh supply of good old ale. Now the talk grew fast and loud, opening the sluices of mutual confidence. John Clare loudly proclaimed his intention of becoming a soldier, ready to fight his way up to generalship.

'Do you mean it?' inquired the tall gentleman in uniform.

'Of course I do,' retorted John, somewhat nettled at the incredulity of his neighbour.

'Well, if you really mean it,' resumed the artilleryman, 'take that shilling.'

John, without hesitation, took the shilling. After which, he fell fast asleep.

When he awoke, the next morning, he found that he was lying on a bench, behind a long table, strewn with jugs, bottles, and glasses. The room was filled with fumes of tobacco and stale beer, through which the sun shone with a dull uncertain light. Rubbing his eyes, Clare jumped from his hard couch, and in a moment was out of doors. The first person he met in the passage was the military gentleman of the previous evening. John Clare was astonished; and so was the man in uniform. John was surprised to find the gentleman so very tall, and the gentleman was surprised to find John so very small—two facts observed by neither of them at the convivial table the evening before. The man in uniform was the first to recover his astonishment, and, approaching Clare with a cordial shake of the hand, expressed his regret that, in the excitement of the previous night, things should have happened which would not have occurred otherwise. But it was not likely that one of his Majesty's officers in the artillery would take an advantage of such an accident, keeping as a recruit a friend who, he was sure, meant the whole only a joke. A burden fell from John's heavily-oppressed heart when he heard these words. Of course, it was only a joke, he muttered forth; and the proof of it was that he kept the shilling intact, just as it had been given to him. With which he handed the potent coin back to the tall gentleman. It was the identical shilling he had received; there could be no mistake, inasmuch as it was the only shilling he had had in his possession for many a day. The man in uniform smiled; smiled still more when John Clare searched in his pockets, withdrawing a much-creased, dirty-looking piece of paper. 'Original Trifles,' exclaimed the tall gentleman; reading the paper; 'Ah, I thank you, thank you very much. Not in my line.' Which saying, he vanished behind the counter of the tap-room. John Clare was lost, as to many other things, so to the Royal Artillery.

In a very uncertain mood, his head still somewhat heavy, John Clare took his way back to Helpston. He congratulated himself of having had a very lucky escape from a kind of servitude for which, of all others, he was most unfit; and yet, notwithstanding this piece of good fortune, he felt by no means easy in his mind. What to do next? was the great question he was unable to solve, and which got more intricate the more he thought of it. While giving the spur to his reflections for the hundredth time, he ran against an old fellow-labourer from Helpston, a man named Coblee. The latter was exactly in the same position as John Clare. He had no work, and wanted very much to get a living; but did not know how to get it. Talking the matter over, the two agreed temporarily to join their efforts, under the supposition that such a part-

nership might possibly be useful to both—as, indeed, it could
not make their position worse. This matter settled, plans
came to be proposed on both sides.   To leave Helpston,
and leave it immediately, was a point at once agreed upon ;
but next came the more difficult matter, as to subsequent
proceedings.   John Clare was in favour of going northward,
into Yorkshire, which county he had heard spoken of as one
of milk and honey ; while friend Coblee was anxious to
seek work in an easterly direction, in the fen-country, where
he had some friends and acquaintances.   There was great
waste of good arguments on both sides, until friend Coblee's
experience suggested to decide the matter by a toss.   Being
the fortunate possessor of a halfpenny, he produced it
forthwith, and chance was called upon for an answer.
It declared in favour of John, whereupon Coblee — a
man seemingly born to be a lawyer—raised various minor
questions.   He argued that as the subject was one of high
importance, it ought not to be left to the decision of a
single toss ; and, moreover, chance itself, and not the winner,
ought to declare in which direction they ought to go.   After
protracted discussion, the final settlement of the question was
postponed to the following day, a Sunday—a very important
Sunday in the life of John Clare.

Early on the Sunday morning, the two friends met, as
agreed upon, at Bachelors' Hall, the general club and meeting
place of the young men of Helpston.   The news that Clare
and Coblee were on the point of leaving the village together,
to seek fortune in distant places, had spread rapidly, and
attracted a large number of old friends and acquaintances.
Clare was not a popular man, but Coblee was ; and to honour
the latter, various bottles were brought in from the neighbouring public-house.   Due justice having been done to the
contents of these flasks, the discussion respecting the final
consultation of Dame Fortune was renewed, and happily
brought to an end.   It was proposed by the brothers Billing,

tenants of the Hall, and adopted by a majority of votes,
that a stick should be put firmly in the ground, in the
middle of the room, and that they should dance around it in
a ring till it fell from its erect position. The way in which
it fell was to indicate the direction in which the two emi-
grants were to go. John Clare and Coblee both promised
to abide by this award, the latter specially agreeing not to
raise any minor questions afterwards. All this having been
duly arranged, the stick was put into the clay, the circle was
formed, and the visitors at Bachelors' Hall began their dance.
They danced fast and furiously; danced like men with a
great object before them, and empty bottles behind. Suddenly a loud knocking was heard at the gate. The stick
stood still upright, and there was a moment's pause in the
dance. 'John Clare must come home at once,' said a shrill
little voice outside ; 'there are two gentlemen waiting for him :
two real gentlemen.' 'Shall I go?' inquired John. 'Go,
by all means,' dictated the elder of the Bachelor Brothers,
'we will wait for you.' They waited long, but John did
not return.

JOHN CLARE'S FIRST PATRON.

The two 'real gentlemen,' who were waiting at the little
cottage, wishing to see John Clare, were Mr. Edward Drury,
bookseller, of Stamford, and Mr. R. Newcomb, a friend of
the latter, proprietor of the *Stamford Mercury*. Mr. Drury,
who had not been long established in business, having but
a short time before bought the 'New Public Library' in
the High Street, from a Mr. Thompson, had heard of John
Clare in a rather singular manner. One day, while still in
treaty about the business, there came into the 'New Public
Library,' a gaunt, awkward-looking man, in the garb of a
labourer, yet with somewhat of the bearing of a country
squire. Addressing Mr. Thompson, he told him, in a haughty

manner, that there would be 'no debts paid at present,' and 'not until the poems are out.' The man who said this was Mr. Thomas Porter, of Ashton, the friend of John Clare, and propounder of the awful question concerning grammar and the spelling-book. Though severe upon his young poetical friend, he nevertheless remained attached to him with true devotion, and latterly had assisted him in the distribution of prospectuses and other errands relating thereto. It was on one of these excursions that he came to the 'New Public Library,' in Stamford High Street. John Clare had been so extravagant, while burning lime at Pickworth, as to take in a number of periodical publications, among them the *Boston Inquirer*, and getting into debt on this account, to the amount of fifteen shillings, which he was unable to pay after his dismissal from the lime-kiln, Mr. Thompson had written several urgent letters demanding payment. In reply to one of these, Clare despatched his friend Thomas Porter to Stamford, instructing him to pacify his angry creditor, and to deliver to him some prospectuses of the 'Original Trifles.' It was in order to be the more effective that Thomas Porter adopted a haughty tone, quite in keeping with his tall gaunt figure ; and, talking in a lofty manner of his friend the poet, almost repudiated the right of the bookseller to ask for payment of his little debt. The proprietor of the 'New Public Library,' a quick-tempered man, got exceedingly irritated on hearing this language. Speaking of John Clare in the most offensive terms, he took the prospectuses and threw them on the floor, at the same time ordering Thomas Porter out of his shop. The long wiry arms of John Clare's tall friend were about reaching across the counter and pulling the little shopkeeper from his seat, when Mr. Drury interfered. He had listened to the dialogue with intense astonishment, being quite bewildered as to the meaning of the terms poet, lime-burner, and swindler, all applied to one person, of whom it was clear only that he

was a friend of the gaunt man. When the latter had taken
his leave, pacified by much politeness and many kind words
from Mr. Drury, an explanation was sought and obtained.
Mr. Thompson, still trembling with rage, informed his suc-
cessor in the business, that the lime-burning rogue had
pretensions to be a poet, and wanted to swindle people out
of their money under pretext of publishing a volume
of verses. Picking up one of the prospectuses, Mr. Drury
saw that this, in a sense, was the case. But examining the
' Address to the Public,' he could not help thinking that it
was a prospectus singularly free from all indications of puff-
ing, and less still of roguery. Indeed, he thought that he had
never seen a more modest invitation to subscribe to a book ;
or one which, in his own opinion, was more unfit to attain
the object with which it was written. The writer evidently
depreciated his work throughout, and took the lowliest and
humblest view of his own doings. That such a very
unbusiness-like address could not possibly secure a dozen
subscribers, Mr. Drury knew but too well ; but this made
him the more anxious to get some further knowledge of
the modest author. He accordingly paid the debt of
fifteen shillings to the delighted Mr. Thompson, and put
Clare's prospectus in his pocket-book ; and, having got
somewhat at home in his new business, settling the most
urgent matters connected with the transferment, started on a
visit to Helpston, in company with a friend.

Entering the little cottage, the two visitors, though they
expected to see poverty, were greatly surprised at the look
of extreme destitution visible everywhere. Old Parker
Clare, now a cripple scarcely able to move, was crouched in
a corner, on what appeared to be a log of wood, covered
with rags ; while his wife, pale and haggard in the extreme,
was warming her thin hands before a little fire of dry sticks.
It was Sunday ; but there was no Sunday meal on the table,
nor preparations for any visible in the low, narrow room,

the whole furniture of which consisted of but a rickety
table and a few broken-down chairs. The astonishment of
Mr. Drury and his friend rose when John Clare appeared on
the threshold of his humble dwelling. A man of short
stature, with keen, eager eyes, high forehead, long hair,
falling down in wild and almost grotesque fashion over his
shoulders, and garments tattered and torn, altogether little
removed from rags—the figure thus presented to view was
strikingly unlike the picture of the rural poet which the
Stamford bookseller had formed in his own mind. John
Clare, shy and awkward as ever, remained standing in the
doorway, without uttering a word ; while Mr. Drury, on his
part, did not know how to address this singular being. The
oppressive silence was broken at last by the remark of Drury's
friend, that they had come to subscribe to the ' Original
Trifles,' a few manuscript specimens of which, he said, they
would be glad to see. John Clare did not like the remark,
nor the patronizing tone in which it was uttered, and
bluntly informed the inquirer that nearly all his verses were
in the possession of Mr. Henson, of Market-Deeping, who
had agreed to print them. The further question as to how
many subscribers he had for his poems,' irritated Clare still
more, eliciting the answer that this was a matter between
him and Mr. Henson. Mr. Drury, with superior tact, now
saw that it was high time to change the conversation, which
he did by asking leave to sit down, and exchange a few
words with ' Mr. Clare ' and his parents. Addressing old
Parker Clare and his wife in a friendly manner, stroking the
cat on the hearth, and sending a little boy, lounging about the
door, for a bottle of ale, he at last succeeded in breaking the ice.

To win confidence, Mr. Drury began giving an account of
himself. He told John Clare that he had taken the shop of
Mr. Thompson, at Stamford, and having found among the
papers some prospectuses of a book of poetry, with a specimen sonnet, he had felt anxious to pay a visit to the author.

After awarding some high praise to the sonnet of the 'Setting Sun,' he next asked Clare whether the publication of the poems had been definitely agreed upon between him and Mr. Henson, of Market-Deeping.

'No,' answered John Clare, beginning to be won over by the frankness of his visitor. To further questions, carefully worded, he replied, that as yet he had only seven subscribers —nominally seven ; in reality only one, the Rev. Mr. Mounsey, of the Stamford Grammar-school—and that Mr. Henson refused to commence printing the poems, unless the sum of fifteen pounds was advanced to him.

There now was a moment's pause, broken by Mr. Drury, who said, addressing Clare, 'Well, if you have made no agreement with Mr. Henson, and will entrust me with your poems, I will undertake to print them without any advance of money, and leave you the profits, after deducting my expenses.'

John Clare's heart rose within him when he heard these words, and but for the pompous man at Mr. Drury's side, he would have run up and pressed the good bookseller to his heart. 'Yes, you shall have all my papers,' he eagerly exclaimed ; 'shall have them as soon as I get them back from Market-Deeping. And I can show you a few verses at once.' Which saying, he left the room, returning in a few minutes with a queer bundle of odd-sized scraps of paper, tied round with a thick rope, and scribbled over, in an almost illegible manner, in all directions. At the top of the bundle was a poem, beginning, 'My love, thou art a nosegay sweet,' which Mr. Drury had no sooner deciphered, than he shook Clare warmly by the hand.

'I think that will do,' he exclaimed, with some enthu- siasm, looking at his companion.

The latter fancied he ought to say something. 'Mr. Clare, I shall be happy to see you to dinner, any of these days,' he exclaimed, with a dignified nod and gracious smile. Thereupon, both Mr. Drury and Mr. Newcomb took their farewell, Clare once more promising that he would take his papers to the 'New Public Library,' as soon as obtained from Market-Deeping.

On the threshold, Mr. Newcomb was seized with a new idea. 'If you get the manuscripts from Deeping, Mr. Clare, we shall be glad to see you,' he exclaimed; 'if not, we can say nothing further about the matter.' Thus the friendly visitor got rid of the overwhelming fear of giving a dinner to a poor man for nothing. However, John Clare never in his life troubled Mr. Newcomb of Stamford for a dinner.

Disagreeable, and almost offensive, as the conversation of one of his visitors had been to John Clare, he was very much pleased with that of the other. For Mr. Edward Drury he felt a real liking, and deeming the proposition which the latter had made exceedingly liberal, he at once set to work carrying the proposal into execution. Fearing that Mr. Henson might, possibly, put obstacles in his way, John persuaded his mother to go to Market-Deeping and fetch his poems. The good old dame gladly fulfilled her son's wish, and the next morning trudged over to the neighbouring town. Clever diplomatist, like all ladies, young or old, she managed to get, with some difficulty, her son's bundle of many-coloured papers, in the midst of which stuck, like the hard kernel in a soft plum, a stout, linen-bound book. John, over-anxious now to possess his verses, awaited the result of the journey half-way between Deeping and Helpston, near the village of Maxey. Here both mother and son sat down in a field, the latter examining his paper bundle with great care. It was all right; nothing was missing, not even the pitch-sealed document containing the prospectus of the 'Original Trifles.' Joyful at heart, the two went back to the little cottage, already expanded, in John's imagination, into a large comfortable house. The first difficulty of getting them printed overcome, the success of his poems was to John Clare a matter of no doubt whatever. His fancy painted to him, in glowing colours, what honour they would bring him, what friends, and what worldly reward. He would be enabled to get a nice dwelling for his old parents, abundance of good cheer for them, and abundance of good books for himself. And then—his heart swelled at the thought—he would be able to carry home his beloved mistress, his 'Patty of the Vale.' The idea made him dance along the road; and he kissed his mother, and the good old dame began dancing, too, all through the green fields, in which the birds were singing, and the flowers bending their faces in the wind.

On the following morning, John Clare walked to Stamford with his papers, handing them over to Mr. Drury. The latter presented him with a guinea, as a sort of purchase-money 'on hand,' encouraging him, at the same time, to write more verses, and to complete all the remaining manuscript poetry in his possession. John went home elated with joy, promising to return to Stamford at the end of a week. To John Clare it was a week of joy, while Mr. Edward Drury, on his part, felt somewhat uneasy in his mind. He was a man of good education, a relative of Mr. John Taylor—head of the formerly eminent publishing firm of Taylor and Hessey, Fleet Street, London—but, though with fair natural gifts, and a lover of poetry, was not exactly a judge of literary productions. John Clare's sonnet 'To the Setting Sun,' which had first attracted his attention, looked well in its printed and corrected form ; but the rest of the manuscript poems, when he came to look over them, appeared to him to possess little or no value. Written on dirty bits of coarse paper, ill-spelt, full of grammatical blunders, and without any punctuation whatever, it required, indeed, a judge of more than ordinary capacity to pronounce on the intrinsic poetical value of these productions. Mr. Drury, having spent a day in scanning over the uncouth papers, began to feel very uneasy, doubting whether he had not promised too much in

agreeing that he would print them, and also whether he had
not paid too dear for them already in giving John Clare
a guinea. Full of these doubts, yet not wishing to make a
mistake in the matter, he resolved to submit the question to
a higher tribunal. One of his customers, the Rev. Mr. Twopenny, incumbent of Little Casterton, had the reputation of
a most learned critic, having published various theological
and other treatises; and he being the only literary man
known to Mr. Drury in or near Stamford, the owner of
the 'New Public Library' resolved to make his appeal to
him. Clare's rough bundle of verses accordingly found its
way to Little Casterton parsonage, to the great surprise of
the learned minister, who, though deep in theology, Hebrew,
and Greek, knew, probably, much less of the value of English
verse than even Mr. Drury. This, however, did not prevent
the learned man from giving an opinion, for having examined
the blurred and somewhat unclean MSS. submitted to him,
and finding them full of many blunders in grammar and
spelling, he expressed himself in a decisive manner to the
effect that the so-called poetry was a mere mass of useless
rubbish. Mr. Edward Drury felt much downcast when he
received this oracular note, which happened to come in on
the very morning of the day arranged for the second visit of
the poet of Helpston.

When John Clare came into the shop in High Street,
joyful and excited, with another large bundle of rope-tied
poetry under his arm, Mr. Drury received him with a somewhat elongated face. Instead of expressing a wish to see the
new manuscripts, he told his visitor, after some hesitation,
that unexpected circumstances prevented him from carrying
out the promised publication of the poems at the moment,
and that he would have to postpone it for some time. John
Clare was ready to burst out crying; the blow came so unexpectedly that he did not know what to think of it. Although
with little experience of the world, he saw perfectly well,

from Mr. Drury's manner, that something unfavourable had
occurred to produce a change respecting the poems. After a
short pause, summoning up courage, he pressed his patron to
explain the matter. Thereupon the letter of the Rev. Mr.
Twopenny was handed to Clare. He read it over; read it
once, twice; and then grasped the counter to prevent himself
from falling to the ground. It was the first harsh literary
criticism the poor poet had to submit to in his life. The
blood rushed to his face; his hands clinched the fatal letter,
as if to annihilate its existence. After a while, he could not
contain himself any longer, but bursting into tears, ran out
of the shop. Good-natured Mr. Drury saw that he had made
a mistake—perhaps a great, and certainly a cruel mistake.
He rushed after his humble friend, and brought him back to
the shop, and into the parlour behind, there soothing him as
best he could. It was easy to persuade John Clare that the
Rev. Mr. Twopenny's opinion was, after all, but the opinion
of one man; that men differed much in almost everything
and in nothing less than the value they set upon poetry.
The remarks were so evidently true, that the much-humbled
poet brightened up visibly; brightened up still more when
Mr. Drury got a bottle of old ale from the cupboard and
began filling two glasses. Viewed through this medium, the
future looked much more cheery to John Clare; the world,
there seemed no doubt, would appreciate good poetry, though
the Rev. Mr. Twopenny did not. Having got his poetical
friend into this happy mood, Mr. Drury talked to him
seriously and sensibly. He advised John Clare to seek work
immediately, either as a farm-labourer or lime-burner, and to
devote only his spare time to the writing of verses. As to
the verses already written, he promised to lay them before
other judges, and to publish them, at any rate, more or less
corrected and altered. This, too, sounded hopeful, and when
John Clare shook hands with the owner of the 'New Public
Library' in the High Street of Stamford, he thought he was

a good deal nearer his long cherished object than he had ever been before.

PREPARING FOR PUBLICATION.

Acting upon Mr. Drury's advice, John Clare, at the end of a few days, visited his former employer, Mr. Wilders, at Bridge Casterton, who, upon his earnest application, set him to work at once, first as a gardener, and, after a while, as labourer in one of his lime-kilns. Here John stayed the whole of the spring and summer of 1819; in many respects one of the most pleasing periods of his whole life. At the end of each day's hard work, he visited his beloved mistress at Walkherd Lodge, with whom he was becoming very intimate—too intimate, alas!—while the spare hours of morning, noon, and evening were devoted to poetry, and the whole of Sunday to reading and music. Mr. Drury, beginning to feel more and more sympathy with his young friend, invited him to spend every Sunday at the shop in the High Street, unrestrained by any forms and ceremonies whatever, and acting entirely as his own master. John Clare accepted the first invitation with some shyness; but before long felt himself fully at home at his friend's house, examining the books, maps, and pictures spread out before him with a blissful enjoyment never before known. The Sunday visits to Stamford, after a while, became to him such an intense delight that he could scarcely await the happy day, and even neglected his love affairs in its expectation. There were no visits to Walkherd Lodge on Saturday evenings, when John went early to bed, in order to rise earlier the next morning. The Sunday found him awake hours before the cock had sounded the alarm, and many a time he had got over the two miles of road from Casterton to Stamford, and stood in front of the 'New Public Library,' before even the sun had risen. Good-natured Mr. Drury now had to get out of bed, let his friend into the shop, and compose himself

as best he could, to sleep again.   John now read for an hour
or two ; but when he thought his friend had slept long
enough, he took up his fiddle, safely kept among the books,
and began playing a merry gypsy tune.   This had the inva-
riable effect of bringing Mr. Edward Drury, passionately
fond of music, down to his books and his friend, and, coffee
having been prepared, the long day of talking, reading, and
fiddling set in for both.

While these proceedings were going on, the fate of Clare's
poems had been decided ; unknown, however, to the poet.
Mr. Drury, after the very unfavourable judgment of the
Rev. Mr. Twopenny, resolved upon sending his odd bundle
of verses to London, to get the final opinion of his experienced relative, Mr. John Taylor, the publisher of Fleet
Street.   Mr. Taylor, a talented author as well as bookseller,
at a glance perceived the true poetic nature of John Clare.
He saw that, under an uncouth garb, there were nameless
beauties in the verses submitted to him ; a wealth of feeling,
and a depth of imagination seldom found in poetic descrip-
tions of the external aspects of nature.   Mr. Taylor saw—
perhaps somewhat dimly, but still he saw—that Clare was
one of the born poets of the earth ; a man who could no
more help singing, than birds can keep from pouring forth
their own harmonious melodies.   But he saw also that John
Clare's works were diamonds which wanted polishing, and
this labour he resolved to undertake.   He informed Mr.
Drury of his intention to bring out the poems under his
own editorship and supervision, telling him to encourage
John Clare to devote himself more and more to the study
of style and grammar, as well as to the improvement of his
general education.   Mr. Drury, who, by this time, knew his
young friend intimately, hesitated to communicate Mr.
Taylor's advice and directions.   Thoroughly acquainted with
the excitable nature of the poet, he feared that, in launching
him again on a sea of expectations, which, after all, might

remain unfulfilled, he would do far more harm than good, and he therefore resolved to keep his imagination in leading-strings. He told John Clare that Messrs. Taylor and Hessey were willing to publish his poems, Mr. Taylor himself making the necessary grammatical and other corrections; but that the success of the publication, as of all other books, being doubtful, he must not, for the present, indulge in too sanguine hopes of gaining either fame or fortune through his book. John was quite content with this information, and kept on steadily in his course; reading and fiddling the first day, and making love and burning lime the other six days of the week.

The love-making, after a while, took a turn not entirely creditable to the interested parties. Having re-established his confidential intercourse with Martha Turner, yet not won the good graces of her parents, who more than ever favoured the suit of the rival shoemaker, John induced his sweetheart to meet him at places where she should not have gone, and made proposals to which she should not have listened. Poor Patty, loving not wisely but too well, did go and did listen to her lover, with the ordinary sad consequences. The sequel was as usual. She got sad and he got cold; and her complaints becoming numerous and frequent, he left her and began flirting with other girls, trying to persuade himself that he was the injured party, inasmuch as Patty's parents treated him with scorn and contempt. An accidental occurrence, in the summer of 1819, contributed much to make him forgetful of his moral obligations. At a convivial meeting of lime-burners, held at a Stamford tavern, Martha Turner, who was present, frequently danced with another man, which so irritated John Clare that he, in his turn, paid his attentions to a young damsel of the neighbourhood, known as Betty Sell, the daughter of a labourer at Southorp. Betty was a lass of sixteen, pretty and unaffected, with dark hair and hazel eyes; and her prattle about green fields, flowers, and sunshine, of which she seemed passionately fond, so intoxicated John that he got enamoured of her on the spot. It was a mere passing fancy; but to revenge himself upon Patty for coquetting, as he thought, with others, he did not go near her, and, at the end of the entertainment, accompanied Betty Sell to her home, some three miles distant. The quarrel, thus commenced, did not end soon. Patty was angry with John; and John, in consequence, renewed his attentions to Betty Sell. Not long, and his first liking increased to a feeling akin to real love. Betty was so sweet and artless in her doings and sayings, and, above all, hung with such evident fondness on every word of her admirer about his life and his struggles, his intense admiration of nature, his poetry, and his hopes of rising in the world through his poetry, that the susceptible heart of John Clare soon got inflamed to ardent devotion of his new mistress. His infatuation rose to such a height that he neglected even his visits to Mr. Drury, preferring, for once in his life, glowing eyes and lips to verses, music, and books. The Stamford bookseller was somewhat surprised on missing his young friend and his fiddle on several subsequent Sundays, and on inquiring the cause, was met by replies more or less unsatisfactory. Taking a real interest in John's welfare, Mr. Drury thereupon determined to get at the bottom of the affair, and succeeded in discovering the secret one evening, after a merry supper. Having taken an unusual quantity of drink, John Clare became confidential, and his friend learnt all that was to be learnt respecting Martha Turner and Betty Sell. Like an honourable man, Mr. Drury was not slow in catechising John, telling him in a severe tone that unless he returned to his old love and gave up all acquaintance with the new, he would withdraw his friendship from him, as a creature unworthy of it. This had a deep effect upon Clare, and though the immediate promise of reform made by him, was not fulfilled to the letter, his life, for the next seven or eight months, was a constant struggle between duty and affection, in which duty at last got the upper hand.

After the severe admonition of his friend and patron, John renewed his frequent visits to the ' New Public Library,' spending not only his Sundays, but many evenings of the week at the shop in Stamford. It was on one of these evenings that he was startled by the appearance of a sedate-looking gentleman, in spectacles, who went up to him with much ceremony, inquiring whether he had the pleasure to address Mr. John Clare. John, very confused, scarcely knew what to answer, until Mr. Drury came up, introducing the visitor as Mr. John Taylor, of London, the editor and publisher of his poems. A lengthened conversation followed, which, though it seemed to delight Mr. Taylor, was not by any means pleasant to the shy and awkward poet. Deeply conscious, as always, of his defective education, his rustic mode of expressing his thoughts, and, most of all, his tattered and dirty garments, he had scarcely the courage to look Mr. Taylor in the face, but kept hiding himself in a corner, looking for an opportunity to escape from the room. The opportunity, however, did not come, and worse afflictions remained behind. After Mr. Taylor was gone, and John had settled down to his favourite books, a servant appeared in the shop, inviting Clare to visit the house of Mr. Octavius Gilchrist, a few doors from the ' New Public Library.' John was fairly inclined to run away, as soon as he heard the message ; but found that escape was not so easy. Mr. Drury told him that it was a matter, not of pleasure, but of duty ; that Mr. Gilchrist was a very influential man in the literary world ; that at the house of Mr. Gilchrist he would meet Mr. Taylor, and that the success of his first volume of poems depended, to a certain extent, upon this interview. This ended all opposition on the part of Clare. He allowed himself to be dragged, like a lamb, into Mr. Gilchrist's house, which, though it was but a grocer's shop on the ground-floor, seemed to him a most magnificent dwelling. The drawing-room was lighted with wax candles, and was full of gilded paintings, carpets and fine furniture, amidst which his dirty clothes, fresh from the lime-kiln, appeared entirely out of place. Nevertheless, he was graciously received by Mr. and Mrs. Gilchrist, and warmly welcomed by his previous acquaintance, Mr. John Taylor.

Mr. Octavius Gilchrist, in whose house John Clare now found himself, and who came to exercise a considerable influence over his future career, was a literary man·of some note in his day. He was born in 1779, the son of a gentleman settled at Twickenham, who had served during the German war as lieutenant and surgeon in the third regiment of Dragoon Guards. Octavius was destined by his parents to be a clergyman, and went to Magdalene College, Oxford; but before taking his degree, or entering holy orders, his means began to fail, upon which he went to Stamford, to assist a well-to-do uncle in the grocery business. The change from the study of the classics at Magdalene College to the weighing-out of halfpenny worths' of soap and sugar to the rustics of Lincolnshire, amounted to a melancholy fall in life; however, Octavius Gilchrist bore it gaily, softening the drudgery by a continuation of his studies in spare hours, and frequent attempts to contribute to the periodical literature of the day. The *Stamford Mercury* having inserted several of his articles, he got bolder, and sent essays to several London Magazines, which met with a like fortunate fate. In 1803, the Stamford uncle died, after willing all his property, including the profitable grocery business, to his nephew. This induced Mr. Gilchrist to devote himself more than ever to literature, leaving the shop to his assistants, and taking to the scales only on Fair days and other solemn occasions. Having married, in 1804, the daughter of Mr. James Nowlan, of London, he was drawn still more into literary society, got acquainted with

William Gifford, and became a contributor to the 'Quarterly Review.' He assisted Gifford in his edition of Ben Jonson's works, and in 1808 published a book of his own, entitled 'Examination of the charges of Ben Jonson's enmity towards Shakspeare.' This was followed, in the same year, by 'Poems of Richard Corbet, Bishop of Norwich, with notes, and a life of the author;' and in 1811, by a 'Letter to William Gifford, Esq., on a late edition of Ford's plays.' On one of his periodical visits to London, Mr. Gilchrist made the casual acquaintance of Mr. John Taylor. The acquaintance soon ripened into friendship, leading to much personal intercourse and a variety of literary schemes. Mr. Gilchrist first started a proposal to publish a 'Select collection of Old Plays,' in fifteen volumes, and on the failure of this scheme, owing to the sudden appearance of a flimsy kind of work called 'Old Plays,' Mr. Taylor and he agreed to launch a new monthly publication, under the revived title of 'The London Magazine.' The negotiations for carrying out this work were pending between writer and publisher, when the first instalment of Clare's manuscripts was sent by Mr. Drury to his relative Mr. John Taylor. The latter read and liked the verses, and being desirous to know something of the writer, requested information from Mr. Gilchrist. 'I know nothing whatever of your poet,' was the reply ; 'never heard his name in my life.' This somewhat surprised the cautious publisher; he thought that Stamford being so near to Helpston, and poets being not quite as plentiful as blackberries in the fen-country, John Clare and his prospectuses ought to be of at least local fame. To clear the matter up, as well as to make some further arrangements respecting the early issue of the 'London Magazine,' Mr. Taylor went down to Stamford, called upon his relative at the 'New Public Library,' where, as accident would have it, he met John Clare, and then went to take up his quarters at the house of Mr. Gilchrist. The latter saw John Clare for the first time when introduced to him in his drawing-room over the grocery shop.

Clare was more than ever shy and awkward when ushered into this drawing-room, and it took a considerable time to make him feel at his ease. To do so, Mr. Gilchrist engaged him in conversation, and with the aid of Mr. Taylor and sundry bottles of wine, succeeded in getting from him a rough account of his life and struggles. Wine and spirits were temptations which John Clare was totally unable to withstand, indulging, on most occasions, far more freely in drink than was warranted by propriety and good sense. Perhaps, at Mr. Gilchrist's house, the host was as much to blame as the guest; the former encouraging Clare's weakness for the purpose of overcoming his extreme shyness and getting at the desired autobiographical information. By the time this was extracted, the poet had taken decidedly too much wine, and when a young lady in the room sat down to the piano and sang 'Auld Robin Gray,' he began crying. The sight was somewhat ludicrous, and Mr. Gilchrist sought to annul it by reading an antiquarian paper on Woodcroft Castle, which had the effect of driving John Clare out of the room and back to his bookshop. Here he sat down, and, still under the influence of the entertainment, wrote some doggerel verses called 'The Invitation,' which Mr. Gilchrist had the cruelty to print in number one of the 'London Magazine,' in which the English public received the first information of the existence of 'John Clare, an agricultural labourer and poet.'

It seems somewhat doubtful whether at this time either Mr. Gilchrist or Mr. John Taylor thoroughly appreciated John Clare. Both, although encouraging his poetical talent, never did justice to the noble and manly, nay lofty heart that beat under the ragged lime-burner's dress. Mr. Taylor, on his part, wanted a hero for his forthcoming monthly magazine, and he seemed to think that John Clare was the best that could be had. He therefore induced Mr. Gilchrist to limn the rustic novelty to the greatest advantage, which was done accordingly in the first number of the 'London Magazine.' A paper headed, 'Some account of John Clare, an agricultural labourer and poet,' intended evidently as a preliminary puff of the poems, and consisting of a rather pompous description of the visit of Clare to Mr. Gilchrist's house, was, on the whole, in the tone in which a *parvenu* might speak of a pauper. The chief fact dwelt upon was the extreme kindness of 'the person who has generously undertaken the charge of giving a selection of Clare's poems to the press,' thus trying to make the world believe that a London publisher should so far forget himself as to neglect his own interest in favour of that of a poor author. Though perhaps well-meant in the first instance, this patronizing manner in speaking of Clare, and attracting public attention to him, less as a poetical genius, but as happening to be a poor man, did infinite mischief in the end. It did more than this—it killed John Clare.

After his first interview with Mr. Gilchrist, John continued to visit at the house, and was openly taken under the great literary man's protection. By his desire, William Hilton, R.A., happening to pass through Stamford, consented to paint Clare's portrait for exhibition in London. The poet was delighted ; and all went on well, until one day when Mr. Gilchrist, desirous of aiding to his utmost power the success of the forthcoming volume, asked, or ordered, Clare to write to Viscount Milton, eldest son of the Earl Fitzwilliam, humbly requesting permission to dedicate the poems to his lordship. John Clare, remembering his former visit to Milton Park, in company with the nimble parish clerk of Helpston, refused the demand, to the great annoyance of Mr. Gilchrist. At length, however, giving way to Mr. Drury's importunities, Clare sat down and penned his humble epistle, which was duly despatched by Mr. Gilchrist. But there never came an answer from Viscount Milton, who, probably, at the time, held it to be a vile conspiracy to extract a five-pound note from his pocket. Mr. Gilchrist was mortified; but John Clare was rather pleased than otherwise. He was more pleased when, a few weeks after, Mr. Drury showed him an advertisement in a London paper, announcing, 'Poems descriptive of rural life and scenery, by John Clare, a Northamptonshire peasant.' It was stated, in capital letters, that the book was 'preparing for publication.'

SUCCESS.

In October, 1819, Clare left the lime-kiln at Bridge-Casterton, where he had been working during the greater part of the year, and returned to Helpston. He did so partly on account of a new reduction of wages, but partly also because suffering from constant ill-health. His old enemy, the fever of the fens, continued its attacks at intervals, and he found that he was less able to withstand the foe in the lime-kiln than when working in the open air. This time he was fortunate enough to find regular work as a farm labourer in the neighbourhood of Helpston, and having got somewhat better, he set with new energy to thrashing and ploughing. His visits to Mr. Drury and Mr. Gilchrist henceforth became somewhat more scarce. Though conscious of being deeply indebted to both these friends, he could not bear being constantly reminded of this indebtedness in the patronizing air which they assumed, and the high tone of superiority which they arrogated to themselves in their intercourse with him. With Mr. Gilchrist, especially, he found fault for attempting to guide him in a manner which, he held, this gentleman had no right to do. John Clare had become acquainted, in the spring of 1819, with the Rev. Mr. Holland, minister of the congregational church at Market-Deeping. Mr. Holland, a well-educated man, with a fine appreciation of poetry, happened to see Clare's prospectus, with the sonnet to the 'Setting Sun,' at a farm-house near Northborough, and

being struck with the verses, as well as with the account
which the farmer, who knew Clare, gave of the author, he at
once went in search of the poet. After some trouble, he
discovered him in the lime-kiln at Bridge-Casterton, just
while Clare was resting from his work, and scribbling poems
upon the usual shreds of paper spread out on the crown of
his hat. Mr. Holland, much astonished at the sight, forthwith entered into conversation, and being a simple man,
with nothing of the patron about him, at once won Clare's
affection. The acquaintance thus begun soon ripened into
friendship, with, however, but scant personal intercourse,
owing to the many occupations of the active dissenting
minister, and the distance of his place of residence from
Casterton. But John Clare did not fail to lay most of the
verses he was writing before his clerical friend, and was
delighted to meet always with hearty encouragement. 'If
this kind of poetry does not succeed,' Mr. Holland said on
one occasion, looking over Clare's shoulder, while the latter
was writing the 'Village Funeral;' 'if this kind of poetry
does not succeed, the world deserves a worse opinion than I
am inclined to give it.' These words made a deep impression
upon Clare, and he kept on repeating them to himself whenever his mind was fluttered with doubts of success and
apprehensions of failure. Very naturally, upon the man who
had cheered him with such hearty and well-timed approval,
Clare looked as one of his best friends, and lost no occasion
to proclaim the fact.

He told the story of his acquaintance with the Rev. Mr.
Holland, as at many other times, so at the first interview
with Mr. Gilchrist. The latter seemed rather displeased
when he heard that the young rustic, presented to his
patronage, was acquainted with a dissenting minister, although
professing to be a member of the Church of England. Mr.
Gilchrist took at once occasion of rebuking him for this conduct, and in the account given of Clare in the 'London

Magazine,' alluded to the subject at some length, explaining
that 'Mr. Holland, a Calvinistic preacher in an adjoining
hamlet, had paid him some attention, but his means of aiding
the needy youth was small, whatever might have been his
wish, and he has now quitted his charge.' The statement
was untrue in several respects ; for Mr. Holland was neither
a 'Calvinistic preacher,' nor stationed in a 'hamlet,' nor had
he 'quitted his charge,' that is, given up his friendship
with Clare. To make at least the ultimate assertion true,
Mr. Gilchrist, after having been acquainted for some time
with John, insisted that he should cease all communication
with the 'Calvinistic preacher.' This Clare refused at once,
looking upon his intercourse with Mr. Holland as an entirely
private matter, not in the least connected with religious
opinions. The refusal brought about a great coldness on the
part of Mr. Gilchrist, which Clare no sooner perceived than
he absented himself from his house. This was very unfortunate ; but could scarcely be helped for the moment. John
Clare was totally unable to understand the orthodox high-
church principles of the former student of Magdalene College,
while Mr. Gilchrist, on his part, was incapacitated from ap-
preciating the lofty feeling of independence that existed in
the breast of the poor lime-burner and farm labourer. In
his account in the 'London Magazine,' Mr. Gilchrist's estimate of the poet's character was expressed in the words :—
'Nothing could exceed the meekness, and simplicity, and
diffidence with which he answered the various inquiries concerning his life and habits ;' and it was upon this supposed
'meekness' that all subsequent treatment of Clare by him
and other friends and patrons was based. But it was an
estimate of character entirely false. Though meek and
humble outwardly, the consequence of early training and
later habit, John Clare had all the towering pride of genius
—more than this, of genius misunderstood.

The year of 1820 broke dull and gloomy upon Clare. He

had expected his poems to be published in the month of
November, or the beginning of December previous; but was
without any information whatever, either from Stamford or
London, and did not know when the long-expected book
would appear, or whether it would appear at all. The little
money he had received from Mr. Drury at various periods—
some twenty pounds altogether—had been spent by this time,
and, being out of work, he was once more face to face with
grim poverty. Day after day passed, yet no news, till, in the
last week of January, the smiling face of a friend suddenly
lighted up the gloom. It was a rainy day, and Clare was
unable to take his usual ramble through the fields, when the
clattering of hoofs was heard outside the little cottage. A
man on horseback alighted at the door, and shaking off the
dripping wet, rushed into the room, where Clare and his
father and mother were sitting round the little fire. It was
the Rev. Mr. Holland. 'Am I not a good prophet?' he
cried, running towards John, and shaking him warmly by
the hand. John looked up in astonishment; he had not the
slightest notion of what his friend meant or alluded to. But
Mr. Holland kept on laughing and dancing, shaking himself
like a wet poodle. 'Am I not a good prophet?' he repeated,
again and again. The long face of his melancholy young
friend at last brought him to a sense of the actual state of
affairs. 'You have had no letter from your publishers?' he
inquired. 'None whatever,' was the reply. 'Then let me
be the first herald of good news,' cried Mr. Holland; 'I can
assure you that your utmost expectations have been realized.
I have had a letter from a friend in London, this morning,
telling me that your poems are talked of by everybody; in
fact, are a great success.' How the words cheered the heart
of John Clare! He fancied he had a slight touch of the
ague in the morning; but it seemed to fall like scales off his
body, and he thought he had never been so well all his life.
Mr. Holland was about getting into his wet saddle again.

'Oh, do stop a little longer,' said John, imploringly; 'have something to eat and drink.' And he looked at his father and mother; and father and mother looked at him. Alas! they all knew too well that there was nothing in the house to eat; and no money wherewith to purchase food. Good Mr. Holland, at a glance, perceived the actual state of affairs. 'Well,' he exclaimed, 'I intended having some dinner at the inn round the corner; but if you will allow me, I will have it sent here, and take it in your company.' And in a twinkling of the eye, he was out of doors, leading his horse, which had been tied to a post, towards the 'Blue Bell.' He was back in ten minutes; and in another ten minutes there appeared the potboy from the 'Blue Bell' carrying a huge tray, smoking hot. Thrice the messenger from the 'Blue Bell' came and returned, each time carrying something heavy in his fat, red hands, and going away with empty trays. When he had turned his back for the third and last time, they all sat down around the little ricketty table, the Rev. Mr. Holland, John, his father and mother. 'Every good gift, and every perfect gift is from above, and cometh down from the Father of lights,' said the minister. 'Amen!' fervently exclaimed John.

The good news of which the Rev. Mr. Holland had been the bearer was soon confirmed on all sides. Early the next morning there came a messenger from Stamford, asking Clare to visit Mr. Drury as well as Mr. Gilchrist. He called first at the house of the latter, and was very graciously received, being informed that his poems were published, and that Mr. William Gifford, editor of the 'Quarterly Review' had taken a great interest in him and his book. John Clare, who had never heard either of Mr. Gifford, or the 'Quarterly,' listened to the news with much indifference, to the evident surprise of his friend. Leaving Mr. Gilchrist, he went next door, to Mr. Drury, and, entering the shop, fell back with astonishment on hearing a tall aristocratic-looking elderly gentleman inquire for 'John Clare's Poems.' It sounded like sweet music to his ear, the cracked voice of the old gentleman. Mr. Drury, not noticing the entrance of Clare, took a small octavo volume from the top of a parcel of similar books lying on his counter, and handed it to the gentleman, informing his customer at the same time that the poems were 'universally applauded both by the critics of London and the public.' John kept firm in his corner near the door ; he thought his friend Drury the most eloquent speaker he had ever heard. 'And, pray, who is this John Clare ?' asked the tall aristocratic-looking gentleman. 'He is . . .' began Mr. Drury, but suddenly stopped short, seeing a whole row of his books tumble to the ground. John Clare, in his terrible excitement, had pressed too close towards an overhanging shelf of heavily-bound folios and quartos, which came down with a tremendous crash. It seemed as if an earthquake was overturning the 'New Public Library ;' and the astonishment of the owner did not subside when he saw his poetical friend creeping out from under the ruins of five-score dictionaries, gazetteers, and account-books. Having somewhat recovered his composure, Mr. Drury, with a grave mien, turned towards the tall gentleman, exclaiming, 'I beg to introduce to you Mr. Clare, the poet.' The gentleman burst out laughing at the intensely ludicrous scene before him ; yet checked himself instantly, seeing the colour mount into Clare's face. 'I beg you a thousand pardons, Mr. Clare,' he exclaimed ; 'I hope you have not been hurt.' And as if to compensate for his rude hilarity, the tall gentleman entered into a conversation with Clare, ending by an invitation to visit him at his residence on the following day : 'Mr. Drury will give you my address ; good morning.' John Clare made no reply, and only bowed ; he did not feel much liking for his new acquaintance. However, when Mr. Drury told him that the stranger was General Birch Reynardson, a gentleman of large property, residing near Stamford, on an estate called

Holywell Park, and that his acquaintance might be of the greatest benefit for the success of his book, if not for himself, Clare consented to pay the desired visit. The allusion to his published poems by Mr. Drury was pleasant to his ears, and Clare eagerly sat down to examine *his* book. It was not by any means a handsome volume in outward appearance, being bound in thick blue cardboard, with a small piece of coarse linen on the back. But the coarseness of the material was relieved by the inscription, 'Clare's Poems,' printed on the back in large letters; and the plain appearance of the book was forgotten over the title-page, 'Poems descriptive of rural life and scenery, by John Clare, a Northamptonshire peasant.' He eagerly ran his eye over the poems, and was more than ever pleased with them in their new dress, with slightly altered spelling, and all the signs of punctuation added. There was only one part of the book with which he was not pleased, which was the part headed 'introduction.' It gave an untrue account of his life, and, what was still more galling to the pride of the poet, spoke of his poverty as the main point deserving public attention. All this deeply hurt his feelings; nevertheless the predominating sentiment of joy and satisfaction prevented him saying anything on the subject to Mr. Drury. He stayed some hours at the shop, and it was arranged that early on the next morning he should call again to get ready for the important visit to General Reynardson. When on the point of leaving, Mr. Drury put a letter in Clare's hands. ' I had almost forgotten it,' he said; ' it has been lying at the shop for several days. I suppose it is from your sweetheart.'

The letter was from the 'sweetheart;' but a very melancholy letter it was nevertheless. Poor Martha Turner told her lover, what he knew long ago, that she was about becoming a mother before being a wife; that her situation was known to her parents; that her father and mother refused to forgive her frailty; and that she was cruelly treated and

on the point of being expelled from under their roof. John
Clare read the letter on the roadside, between Stamford and
Helpston ; he read it over again and again, and his burning
tears fell upon the little sheet of paper. A fierce conflict of
passions and desires arose within his soul. He fancied that
he did not love Martha Turner half so well as the pretty little
lass of Southorp ; he fancied that since his first overwhelming affection for ' Mary,' he had never been devoted, heart and
soul, so much to any one as to Betty Sell. Yet to Martha
Turner, once his sweet ' Patty of the Vale,' he knew he was
bound by even stronger ties than those of affection and love
—he trembled thinking thus, yet held firm to the nobler
element in his breast. The secret struggle, short and intense,
ended with a firm resolve that duty should conquer passion.

Early on the day following, John Clare made his appearance
at Mr. Drury's shop. The busy tradesman had already provided an outfit for his friend, whom he meant to patronize
more than ever, now that his poems promised to be successful.
In the course of half an hour, John found himself clothed in
garments such as he had never before worn. He had a black
coat, waistcoat, and trousers, a silk necktie, and a noble,
though very uncomfortable, high hat ; while his heavy shoes
seemed changed by a covering of brilliant polish. Surveying
his figure, thus altered, in a looking-glass, John was greatly
satisfied with himself, and with a proud step marched off
towards Holywell Park. General Birch Reynardson received
him with great affability ; at once took him by the hand, and
led him into the library. It was the finest collection of
books Clare had ever seen, and he warmly expressed his
admiration of it. After a while, the General took a small
quarto, bound in red morocco, from the shelves, and showing
it to his guest, asked him what he thought of the contents.
They were poems written by the general's father ; and Clare,
seeing the fact stated on the title-page, was polite enough
to declare them to be very beautiful. Another red-morocco

volume thereupon came down from the shelves, full of manuscript poetry of the General's own composition. John Clare began to see that genius was hereditary in the family, and expressing as much to his host, earned a grateful smile, and a warm pressure of the hand. He was asked next to promenade in the gardens till dinner was ready.

The gardens of Holywell Park were laid out with great taste, and John Clare soon lost himself in admiration of the many beautiful views opened before him. While wandering along the banks of an artificial lake, fed by a cascade at the upper end, he was joined by a young lady of extraordinary beauty. He believed it was the wife of the General; yet, though showing the deepest respect to the lady who addressed him while walking at his side, he could not help looking up into her face now and then, in mute admiration of her exquisite loveliness. The General, after a while, joined the promenaders, when John, somewhat to his surprise, learnt that his fair companion was not the hostess of the establishment, but the governess. Notwithstanding the presence of the master of the house, the young lady continued speaking to Clare in the freest and most unrestrained manner, bewitching him alike by the tones of her voice and the soft words of flattering praise she poured into his ear. She told him that she had read twice through the volume of poetry which the General had brought home the preceding evening, having sat up for this purpose the greater part of the night. Clare's face got scarlet when he heard these bewitching words; never before had praise sounded so sweet to his ear; never before had it come to him from such honeyed lips. He was beside himself for joy, when, as a proof of her good memory, she began reciting one of his poems : 'My love, thou art a nosegay sweet.' And when she came to the last line, 'And everlasting love thee,' Clare's eyes and those of the beautiful girl met, and he felt her glances burning into his very soul. The general did not seem to take much notice of his com-

H

panions, being busy picking up stones in the footpath, and
examining the state of the grass on the borders of his flower
beds.   On returning towards the house, he informed Clare
that the servants were about sitting down to their dinner,
and told him to join them in the hall.   The young governess
appeared intensely surprised at the words; she looked up,
first at the General and then at Clare.   Probably it seemed
to her a gross insult that a poet should be sent to take his
meal with the footmen and scullery-maids.   But Clare's face
looked bright and serene; to him, as much as to the master
of the house, it appeared perfectly natural to be returned to
his proper social sphere, after a momentary dream-like rise
into higher social regions.

He walked into the hall, and humbly sat down at the
lower end of the servants' table.   The big lackeys whispered
among themselves, looking with a haughty air upon the base
intruder.   John Clare heeded it not; his soul was far away
in a world of bliss.   Before him, in his imagination still
hovered that sweet beautiful face which he had seen in the
gardens; in his ear still sounded the soft tones of her voice:
' And everlasting love thee.'   Thus he sat at the table, among
the footmen and kitchen wenches, tasting neither food nor
drink—an object of utter contempt to his neighbours.   Before
long, however, there came a message from the housekeeper's
room, inviting Clare to proceed to the select apartments of this
potent lady.   He followed the servant mechanically, careless
where he was going; but was joyfully surprised on entering
the room to see his dream changed into reality.   There, opposite the table, sat his beautiful garden-companion, smiling
more sweetly, and looking more exquisitely enchanting than
ever.   She stretched out her little white hand, and Clare sat
down near her, utterly unmindful of the presence of the
mistress of the apartment, the lady housekeeper.   The latter
felt somewhat offended in her dignity, yet overlooked it for
the moment, being desirous to proffer a request.   Having

succeeded in rousing Clare's attention, she informed her
visitor, with becoming condescension, that she was very fond
of poetry; also that she had a son who was very fond of
poetry. But it so happened that, though very fond of reading verses, neither she nor her son was able to produce any.
Now hearing, from her friend the governess, that there was a
poet in the house, she had taken the liberty to send for him,
to do some trifling work. What she wanted was an address
of filial love, as touching and affectionate as possible; this
she would send to her son, and her dear son would return it
to her, signed by his own name. She hoped it could be done
at once, while she was getting the tea ready. Could it be
done at once? Clare started on hearing himself addressed a
second time by the high-toned lady—he did not remember
a word of all that had been said to him. But he bowed in
silence, and the dignified elderly person left the room to make
the tea, firmly persuaded that her poetry would be got ready
in the meantime. When she was gone, Clare looked up, and
found a pair of burning eyes fixed upon him. He tried to
speak, but could not; the words, rising from his heart, seemed
to perish on his tongue. After a long pause, the young
governess, flushed with emotion, found courage to address her
neighbour: 'I hope to see you again, Mr. Clare; I hope you
will write to me sometimes.' He had no time to reply before
the bell rang and a servant entered the room, reporting that
General Birch Reynardson wished to see John Clare before
leaving. The intimation was understood. John went up to
the library, bowed before his stately host, muttered a few
words of thanks, he knew not exactly for what, and left the
house. When the gate closed after him, he felt as if expelled
from the garden of Eden.

Slowly he walked up the road, when suddenly a white
figure started up on his path. The young governess again
stood before Clare. 'I could not hear of your going,' cried
the beautiful girl, her bright face suffused with blushes, and

her long auburn hair fluttering in the wind; 'I could not hear of your going, without saying good-bye.' Clare again tried to speak, and again the words died upon his lips. But she continued addressing him : 'Oh, do not forget to write to me,' she said earnestly, with a tinge of melancholy in her soft voice. It thrilled through his soul, and opened his lips at last. 'I will write,' he answered, 'and I will send you some new poems.' Thus saying, he bent forward and took both her hands, and their eyes met, full of unspeakable passion. But a sudden noise from the distance startled Clare and his fair companion. There was a man on horseback coming up with full speed, riding in the direction of Holywell Park. The young governess softly loosened her hands, turned a last fond look upon the poet, and fled away like a frightened hind into a neighbouring wood.

John Clare hurried forward, his face flushed, his head trembling; forgetful of all the things around him. At last, feeling exhausted, he sat down on a stone, at the turning of two roads. The one of the roads was leading to Stamford; the other to Bridge Casterton and Walkherd Lodge. Clare felt like one entranced. Joy unutterable was struggling in his bosom together with infinite sadness, and the wild pulsation of his heart seemed to drive his blood, like living fire, to his very soul. And he held his burning head in his hands, sitting at the corner of the two roads. The image of the beautiful girl he had just left, an image more perfect, more sweet and angelic than ever conceived by his imagination, appeared standing in one of the roads, and the picture of a sad, suffering woman, surrounded by angry parents, in the other. Lower sank the sun on the horizon; it was beginning to get dark; but Clare still kept sitting at the corner of the two roads, his throbbing head bent to his knees. The clouds in the west glowed with a fierce purple, when he started up at last. He started up and walked, swiftly and with firm step, towards Walkherd Lodge. The clouds in the west seemed to glow with an unearthly light.

'OPINIONS OF THE PRESS' AND CONSEQUENCES.

The London book-season of 1820 was a dull one. The number of books published was very small, and there were but few extraordinary good or extraordinary bad ones amongst them. All the 'reviewers' were at their wits' end; for wit, sharp as a razor, must get dull over books undeserving of praise, yet incapable of being 'cut up' with due brilliancy of style. Into this mournful critical desert, there fell like manna the 'Poems descriptive of rural life and scenery.' Mr. John Taylor and his literary coadjutors had taken great pains to spread the news far and wide that a new Burns had been discovered on the margin of the Lincolnshire fens, and was to be publicly exhibited before a most discerning public. There were low rumours, besides, that William Gifford intended to place the new Burns on the pedestal of the 'Quarterly,' spreading the fame of the humble poet into the most distant regions. Accordingly, when the first volume of Clare's poems was published, on the 16th of January, 1820, there was an immediate rush to the shop of Messrs. Taylor and Hessey, in Fleet Street. Before many days were over, a first edition was exhausted; and before many weeks were gone, all the critical reviews began singing the praises of the book. The 'Gentleman's Magazine,' leading the van, got eloquent over 'the unmixed and unadulterated impression of the loveliness of nature,' contrasting it with 'the riches, rules, and prejudices of literature;' the latter being in allusion to a quarrel which the learned editor had just had with some learned fellow-editors. Next followed the 'New Monthly Magazine,' the reviewer of which informed a discerning public that 'Clare is strictly a descriptive poet, and his daily occupation in the fields has given him manifest advantages.' This profound remark made great impression, and was quoted by Messrs. Taylor and Hessey in all their prospectuses; not even the deepest thinkers disputing the thesis that if Clare had been born and lived all his life in a cellar in the Seven Dials, his rural poetry might be less truthful. The 'London Magazine,' belonging to the publishers of Clare's poems, came modestly behind in critical praise, contenting itself, in a review of five pages, with giving plentiful extracts from the book. putting forward, at the same time, a somewhat undignified appeal to public charity. The demand for the pence and shillings of the charitable was, as stated in the review, ' made by one who has counselled and superintended this interesting publication,' and the same authority piteously invoked the aid of the nobility and gentry for 'this poor young man.' When Clare came to see this article, some months after its publication, he burst into a fit of indignation, and wrote an angry letter to Mr. Drury; but with the sole result of hearing, on his next visit to the Stamford Public Library, that he was not only a very poor, but a very ungrateful young man.

The ' Eclectic Review,' reviewed Clare in a very flattering article; and the ' Antijacobin Review,' ' Baldwin's London Magazine,' and a host of other periodicals, followed suit, all dwelling upon the luminous aspect of the poems, with pauperism as dark background. Last in the list, but greatest, came the ' Quarterly,' with William Gifford at the helm. The ' Quarterly Review ' of May, 1820, actually devoted nine pages to a description and praise of Clare's poems, speaking of them as the most interesting literary production of the day. The review was supposed to be written by Mr. Gilchrist; but it was generally understood that the editor of the ' Quarterly' himself corrected and altered the article, strengthening its praise, and putting in some hearty, honest words about Clare as a *man*, as well as a poet. Perhaps of all living authors,

William Gifford best understood John Clare, and felt thorough and entire sympathy with the attempt of this noble soul to struggle into light, through all the haze of printers, publishers, and reviewers. Very likely he might have loved Clare as a brother—had the poet not been an author. William Gifford, as Southey truly remarks, ' had a heart full of kindness for all living creatures, except authors; *them* he regarded as a fishmonger regards eels, or as Izaak Walton did slugs, worms, and frogs.' Nevertheless, the 'Quarterly Review' praised Clare in a way which quite astonished the book-makers of the day. After comparing him with Burns and Bloomfield, and dwelling upon the fact that his social position was far lower than that of either these two poets, the writer in the ' Quarterly '— here Mr. Gifford himself—gave some sound advice to Clare. ' We entreat him,' the article ran, ' to continue something of his present occupations; to attach himself to a few in the sincerity of whose friendship he can confide, and to suffer no temptations of the idle and the dissolute to seduce him from the quiet scenes of his youth to the hollow and heartless society of cities; to the haunts of men who would court and flatter him while his name was new, and who, when they had contributed to distract his attention and impair his health, would cast him off unceremoniously to seek some other novelty.' These words of true advice proved almost prophetic in the life of the poet.

The article in the ' Quarterly Review ' had the immediate effect of making John Clare the lion of the day. Rossini set one of his songs to music; Madame Vestris recited others before crowded audiences at Covent Garden, and the chief talk of London for the season was about the verses of the ' Northamptonshire peasant.' His fame descended to North-amptonshire itself, and far into the misty realm of the fen-bound regions. The Right Honourable Charles William, Viscount Milton, was somewhat startled on the waves of this fame reaching Milton Park. The idea that for one five-pound

note he might have secured part of this high renown to
himself, figuring in the 'Quarterly Review' as a noble patron
of literature, and protector of heaven-born genius slumbering
in obscurity, made him feel intensely vexed with himself.
Reflecting upon the subject, it struck his lordship that it
would be best to take Clare still under his protection, in
view of new editions open to dedication. Full of this idea,
a messenger was despatched at once to Helpston, with a
gracious order that the poet should present himself on the
following morning before the noble Viscount. John Clare,
remembering but too keenly the past, was unwilling to obey
his lordship's command; but the tears of his father and
mother made him change his resolution. Consequently, on
the morning appointed, a Sunday, he went to Milton Park,
and having had the honour of lunching with the footmen in
the kitchen, was ushered into the presence of his lordship.
Viscount Milton was exceedingly affable, took Clare by the
hand, sat him down on a stool, and at once explained to him
why his letter respecting the dedication of the poems had not
been answered. His lordship had been excessively busy at the
time, making preparations for a journey, and in the hurry of
these labours had unfortunately forgotten to send a reply. Now
her ladyship entered the room, in turn addressing the poet.
After questioning him on all points, birth, parentage, weekly
income, religion, moral feelings, and state of health, Clare
was finally asked whether he had found already a patron.
His vacant look expressed that he did not know even
the meaning of the word patron. To the plainer question,
whether some nobleman or gentleman of the neighbourhood
had promised him anything, Clare truthfully replied in the
negative. There was nobody who had made offers of assistance, except Mr. Edward Drury, bookseller, of Stamford;
and his promises, John was sorry to say, were rather vague.
Thereupon the noble viscount warned Clare to be on his
guard against all publishers and booksellers; not explaining,

however, how to protect himself, or how to do without them.
Meanwhile the Earl Fitzwilliam had entered the room, and
added his voice to that of his son in a warning against booksellers. After a little more conversation, Lord Milton put
his hand in his pocket, and withdrawing a quantity of
gold, threw it into Clare's lap. John was humbled and
confused beyond measure. His first impulse was to return
the money instantaneously; but a moment's thought convinced him that this would be excessively rude, and he contented himself, therefore, with a feeble protest against his
lordship's kindness. He now left, making an awkward bow,
his pockets heavy under the weight of gold, and his brain
heavier under a feeling of deep humiliation, akin to shame.
However, this feeling was dispelled in the fresh outer air.
He thought of his poor father and mother at home, and the
comfort all his gold would bring them; and getting almost
joyful at the thought, sat down at the roadside to count his
golden sovereigns. There were seventeen pieces, all bright
and new, fresh from the Mint. Clare had not had so much
money in his possession in all his life, and he got frightened
almost in looking at the glittering treasure before him. To
secure it well, he took off his neck-tie, wrapped the sovereigns
in it, and ran home as fast as his legs would carry him.
There were happy faces that night in the little cottage at
Helpston.

John Clare's invitation to Milton Park created much
astonishment in the village; but the wonder increased when,
a few days after, another liveried messenger inquired his way
to Clare's dwelling. The new envoy was of far more gorgeous
aspect than the former one, being the representative of the
greatest lord in the county, the most noble the Marquis of
Exeter. His lordship had seen the ' Quarterly Review,' as
well as Viscount Milton; and his lordship had learnt, moreover, that Clare had been called to Milton Park, for purposes
easily imagined. The chief of the elder line of the Cecils there-

upon determined not to be outdone by his petty Whig rivals,
the Fitzwilliams, with which object in view he summoned the
poet in his turn. The gorgeous scarlet messenger who arrived
at Helpston, to the wonderment of the whole village, brought
a letter from the Hon. Mr. Pierrepont, brother-in-law of the
marquis, desiring Clare to make his appearance on the following morning, precisely at eleven o'clock, at Burghley Hall.
To this summons there was no opposition on the part of Clare,
for to resist the will of the Marquis of Exeter, within twenty
miles of Stamford, was deemed nothing less than treason by
any inhabitant of the district. John was ready to go to
Burghley Hall the next morning; but it rained heavily, and
the cobbler had not returned the shoes entrusted to him for
mending. Could John present himself without shoes on a
rainy morning, before the most noble the Marquis of Exeter?
That was the question gravely debated between Parker Clare,
his wife, and his son. It was decided that John could not
go without shoes; and the village cobbler refusing to return
his trust, because engaged in threshing, the important visit
to Burghley Hall had to be postponed till the day after.
John went quite early, trembling inwardly to show himself
before the great lord, whose very valet was looked upon in
the country as a man of high estate. His fears increased
a thousandfold when arrived at the gate of the palatial
residence, and being told, on giving his name to the porter,
that he ought to have come the day before. On Clare
making his excuse on account of the state of the weather,
the high functionary got very angry. 'The weather?' he
exclaimed, excitedly; 'you mean to say that you have
not obeyed his lordship's commands simply because it was a
wet day! I tell you, you ought to have come if it rained
knives and forks.' This frightened Clare beyond measure;
he turned round upon his heels and was about running away,
when he was stopped by a footman. The arrival of Clare had
just been announced to the marquis, and there was an order

to admit him instantaneously to the presence of his lordship.
So the tall footman, without further ceremony, took Clare
by the arm, and hurried him up a marble staircase, through
innumerable passages, and a maze of halls and corridors which
quite bewildered the poor poet. The sound of his heavy hob-
nailed shoes on the polished floor made him tremble, no less
than the sight of his mud-bespattered garments among all the
splendid upholstery, through which the gorgeous lackey was
guiding his steps. At last, after a transit through painted
halls which seemed endless, Clare stood before the noble
marquis. His lordship received the humble visitor in a quiet,
unaffected manner; and the mind of the poet was relieved
of an immense burthen when he found the great lord to be
a decidedly amiable and cheerful young man of his own
age, with manners pleasantly contrasting with those of the
aristocratic porter at the gate, and the splendid footman who
had shown him the way. The marquis, with great tact,
questioned Clare as to his antecedents; asked to see some of
his manuscript verses—which the Hon. Mr. Pierrepont, in his
summons, had ordered him to bring—and, having inspected
these, informed the astonished poet that he would grant him
an annuity of fifteen guineas for life. John Clare scarcely
believed his own ears; the announcement of this liberality
came so unexpected, and appeared to him so extraordinary,
that he did not know what to say, or how to express his
thanks. Quitting his lordship in utter confusion, he felt
almost giddy on finding himself in the hall outside. There
were immense passages stretching away to right and left,
leading into unknown realms of magnificence, into which the
poor poet was trembling to venture. The marquis, who, with
great politeness, had accompanied his visitor to the door, on
seeing his embarrassment undertook the part of guide, leading Clare to the outskirts of the palatial labyrinth, and here
handing him over to a valet, with instructions to let his guest
partake of the common dinner in the servants' hall. It was

the third dinner in the hall of noble patrons to which Clare
was ushered—clearly showing that, however much differing
on other subjects, the admirers of high literature in Northamptonshire held that the true place of a rural poet was among
the footmen and kitchen-maids.

NEW SIGHTS AND NEW FRIENDS.

The great liberality of the Marquis of Exeter enabled Clare
to carry out, without further delay, the wish of his heart, and
to make 'Patty' his wife. Her parents, under the circumstances, had given up all their old opposition, and were not
only willing, but most anxious, that Clare should cement his
unhappy connexion with their daughter by the sacred ties of
marriage. The due preparations were made accordingly, and
on the 16th of March, 1820, John Clare and Martha Turner
became man and wife. The event stands registered as follows in the records of Great Casterton Church :—

'John Clare of the Parish of Helpston Bachelor and
Martha Turner of this Parish Spinster were married in this
Church by banns this 16th day of March in the year one
thousand eight hundred and twenty by me Richard Lucas.'

And underneath :—

'This marriage was solemnized between us,

JOHN CLARE
her
MARTHA + TURNER
mark.'

Little more than a month after the wedding, a child was
born to Clare; a little girl, baptized Anna Maria. Mrs.
Clare for a while remained at her father's house; but as
soon as she was able to move, went to live with her husband,
at the humble dwelling of his parents at Helpston, which,

though scarcely large enough to contain the aged couple, had now to accommodate two families. Yet Clare felt happy in this narrow cottage, for, humble as it was, it presented to him a thousand cherished associations, and now became dearer than ever to his heart, as sheltering not only his beloved parents, but his dear wife and child. All his life long the Helpston cottage was to Clare his 'home of homes.'

Before removing with his young wife to his native village, the poet had to go through some exciting adventures in a journey to London. When one day at the house of Mr. Gilchrist, at Stamford, there arrived a letter from Mr. John Taylor, speaking in high terms of the success of the 'Poems of Rural Life,' which brought about the question, addressed to Clare : 'Should you like to go with me on a short visit to London ?' John Clare was delighted at the idea, and eagerly expressed his wish to go ; whereupon it was arranged that he and Mr. Gilchrist should set out on the journey at the end of a week. Patty cried when the news was brought to her ; and old Parker Clare and his wife cried still more. In a few hours, the report spread like wildfire through Helpston that John Clare was going to London. There was but one man in the village who had ever been to the big town far away, and his account of it had filled the hearts of all the Helpston people with terror. This man, an old farm-labourer called James Burridge, as soon as he heard of Clare's intention to undertake the dreaded journey, hurried up to entreat him to abandon the plan. To enforce his advice, he gave a vivid description of the horrors awaiting the unwary traveller in the great metropolis, and the fearful dangers that beset his path on every side. One half the houses of London, he said, were inhabited by swindlers, thieves, and murderers, and a good part of the other half by their helpers and confederates, all on the look-out for the good people from the country. To catch their victims with the greater certainty, there were trap-doors in the pavement of the most frequented

streets, which, when touched, let the wayfarer down into a
deep cellar, and into a kettle of boiling water, surrounded by
cut-throats who made all escape from the kettle impossible.
The assassins, having killed the unhappy victim, and taken
all his property, to the very shirt on his back, finally—
culmination of horrors!—sold the body to the doctors.
Such was the account which James Burridge gave of London,
with the effect of striking terror into the hearts of his
hearers.   Parker Clare and his wife, with bitter tears,
entreated their son not to leave them; and John himself,
though slightly incredulous about some of the items in the
tales of his friend Burridge, began to be seriously alarmed.
But he was ashamed to confess his fears to Mr. Gilchrist;
the more so, as a mere casual mentioning of the street-traps
and the kettles of boiling water produced immoderate
laughter.   He therefore made his mind up to start on his
dangerous journey like a hero.   After bidding solemn farewell to wife and parents, and dressing, by the advice of
James Burridge, in his worst clothes, to be the less a mark
for thieves and cut-throats, John Clare very early one morning in April, 1820, started for Stamford, and having met Mr.
Gilchrist, took his seat precisely at seven o'clock in the
'Regent,' a famous four-horse coach, warranted to take
passengers in thirteen hours to London.   There was little
talk on the road; John Clare had enough to do to look out
of the window, marvelling at all the new sights open to his
eyes.   Thus the travellers passed through Stilton, Huntingdon, St. Neot's, Temsford, and Biggleswade, until at last,
soon after dusk, the fiery glow of the horizon announced the
neighbourhood of the big city.   On being told that they
were about to enter London, Clare became much excited; but
there was time for the excitement to cool, for more than two
hours elapsed before the heavy coach rumbled from the soft
high road up to the hard-paved streets.   At last, at nine
o'clock in the evening, the 'Regent' stopped in front of the

'George and Blue Boar,' in Holborn, and John Clare alighted, utterly bewildered with all that he had seen during the day in the greatest journey he had ever made in his life.

Mr. Gilchrist took his friend to the house of his brother-in-law, a German named Burkhardt, proprietor of a jeweller's and watchmaker's shop in the Strand. Herr Burkhardt, a well-to-do tradesman, with a rubicund face and an inexhaustible stock of good humour, was excessively fond of showing strangers the sights of London; and his guests had no sooner arrived, than he wanted to take them to Covent Garden theatre. John Clare was very anxious to go, on hearing that Madam Vestris was reciting one of his poems at this place of entertainment; but finding that Octavius Gilchrist was disinclined to rise from his comfortable arm-chair, and with secret apprehension of the trap-doors and vessels of boiling water, he declared himself likewise in favour of the arm-chair, with hot whiskey and water. Worthy Herr Burkhardt had his full share of satisfaction the next day, when he had the pleasure of taking his brother-in-law and friend to Westminster Abbey, the Tower, Smithfield market, Newgate, and Vauxhall Gardens. John Clare was not so much astonished as disappointed with all that his eyes beheld in the great metropolis. Standing upon Westminster Bridge, he compared the River Thames with Whittlesea Mere, and found it wanting; the sight of the Tower, of Newgate, and of Smithfield, engendered not the least admiration; and as for the Poet's Corner in the Abbey, he loudly declared that he could see no poetry whatever about it. But what hurt the feelings of Herr Burkhardt most of all, was the utter contempt Clare showed for the delights of Vauxhall. The tinsel and the oil-lamps, the wooden bowers and paper flowers, struck Clare as perfectly absurd, and he expressed his astonishment that people should go and stare at such childish things, with a world of wonder and of beauty lying all around it in the green fields. The worthy jeweller of the Strand was amazed, and privately confided to his brother-in-law that he thought his companion ' a very stupid man from the country.'

John Clare stayed a week in London, and during the whole of this time felt painfully uncomfortable in his thread-bare suit of labourer's clothes, patched top and bottom, with leather baffles and gaiters to match. He fancied, when walking along the streets, that everybody was staring and laughing at his smock frock ; and the sound of his heavy hob-nailed shoes startled him whenever he entered a house. What made things worse was, that Mr. Gilchrist wanted to draw him into many fine places and among high and wealthy people, for whose company Clare felt an instinctive dislike. He knew that they could not look upon him otherwise than in the light of a rustic curiosity, and being unwilling to play the part of a newly-discovered monkey or hippopotamus, he absolutely refused to go to parties and meetings to which he had been invited. However, a few of the visits were indispensable, such as presentation to Messrs. Taylor and Hessey, and their friends. Mr. John Taylor, on meeting Clare, perceived at once that one reason of his excessive reluctance to show himself was his scant stock of clothing, and mentioning the matter with great frankness, he offered him a suitable dress. But Clare refused to take anything, except an ancient overcoat somewhat too large for him, but useful as hiding his whole figure from the top of the head down to the heels. In this brigand-like mantle he henceforth made all his visits, unwilling to take it off even at dinner, and in rooms hot to suffocation.

It made a deep impression upon Clare that, with all his awkwardness, homely speech, and ragged clothes, he was, for the first time in his life, treated as an equal by Mr. Taylor's friends, and other gentlemen whom he visited at London. The example of his patrons in the country, who, after praising his talents in the drawing-room, sent him down to the kitchen for his dinner, had already pauperized him to such an extent that he was quite startled when Mr. Taylor, on his second visit to the shop in Fleet Street, asked him to meet several men of rank and talent, among them Lord Radstock, at dinner the same evening. He would gladly have declined, but was not allowed to do so, being told that it would be a thorough breach of good manners to refuse to see his friends, the admirers of his poems. Clare went, with much fear and trembling; but came to be at ease before long. He sat next to Lord Radstock, and this gentleman, with an extreme tact and knowledge of character, at once succeeded in gaining his whole confidence. It proved the beginning of a friendship which lasted for years, and spread its influence over Clare's whole life. William Waldegrave, Baron Radstock, Admiral of the Red, was a gentleman much known at this period in the literary and artistic circles of London. A younger son of the third Earl of Waldegrave, born in 1758, he was bred to the naval profession, became a captain at the age of eighteen, and commander of a fine frigate soon after, so that the way to fame and distinction was marked out for him clearly and forcibly. But not content to be lifted in the world solely by reason of birth, he, from an early age, devoted himself to independent pursuits, and became a scholar and a poet even before he was a captain in the Royal Navy. The scientific and literary tastes of the young nobleman were greatly fostered by his marriage, in 1785, with the second daughter of David Van Lennep, chief of the Dutch factory at Smyrna, a lady of most genial disposition and an education very superior to her age. William Waldegrave was appointed admiral in 1794; distinguishing himself at the naval fight off Cape Lagos, in 1797; and having been advanced, three years after, to the dignity of Baron Radstock, of Castletown, Queen's County, quietly settled with his family in London,

to give himself entirely up to his favourite studies and
pursuits.   On the appearance of Clare's poems, he at once felt
greatly interested in the author, and being acquainted with
Mr. John Taylor, heard of his arrival in London, and arranged
to meet him at dinner.   So it came that John Clare, in his
smock frock, leather gaiters, and brigand mantle, found himself sitting at the right hand of the Right Honourable Lord
Radstock, son of an earl, and admiral in the Royal Navy.

Lord Radstock's simple, sailor-like speech, distant alike
from condescension and studious politeness, had the effect of
at once opening the pent-up affections of John Clare.   For
the first time since his arrival in London, he found somebody
to whom he could speak in full confidence, and he did so
to his heart's desire, prattling like a child about trees and
flowers, fields and meadows, birds and sunshine, and not
at all disguising his dislike to the big town in which he
now found himself.   As the dinner went on, Clare became
still more communicative, tenderly encouraged by the sym-
pathising friend at his side.   He spoke of his struggles,
his aims, and aspirations; his burning desire to soar upward
on the wings of poetry, and his constant battling for the
barest necessities of life, the mere daily bread.   Lord Radstock was deeply touched; he had seen many authors, writers
of prose and of verse, in the course of his life, but never such
a poet as this.   Clare did not in the least complain of his
existence; he merely described it, in simple, graphic utterance, the truth of which was stamped on every word and
look.   The admiral, before meeting John Clare, had admired
him as a poet; he now began to feel far deeper admiration
for him as a man.   He told him in a few kind and affectionate words, speaking as a father would to his son, that he
intended to be his friend, and Clare warmly shook the hand
offered to him.   It was late at night when the party broke
up at Mr. Taylor's, and Lord Radstock and John Clare were
the last to leave the house together.

During the few days that Clare remained in London, he was almost constantly in Lord Radstock's company. The latter, anxious to introduce his young friend to persons who he thought might be useful to him in life, led him to a great number of places, one more uncomfortable than the other. Clare suffered much, but had not the courage to confess it to his noble patron, whose good intentions he fully understood. So he kept on trotting from one drawing-room to the other, with his heavy mud-bespattered shoes, his immense coat, a world too large for his thin, short body, and his long unkempt hair, hanging down in wild confusion over the shoulders. His friends soon got accustomed to the sight, and thought no more of it, and strangers willingly excused the garb as born of the 'eccentricity of genius;' but Clare himself, with his extreme sensibility, felt daily mortification on contrasting his own appearance with that of the people he met, and suffered tortures in thinking himself an object of general ridicule. The feeling was aggravated by the fact that he met but few persons he liked, and in whose conversation he took an interest. Among these few was Mrs. Emmerson, an authoress of some talent, and contributor to the 'London Magazine,' to whom he was introduced by Lord Radstock. John Clare at the first interview was not at all favourably impressed by this lady; for she assumed what he fancied to be a theatrical air; burst out in bitter laments about what she termed the 'desolate appearance' of her visitor, and wept that 'so much genius and so much poverty' should go together. All this was very unpleasant to Clare; particularly the 'desolate appearance,' which he took to be an unmerited allusion to his great coat. In return, the poet, stung to the quick, replied in a few cold and sarcastic words, which irritated Lord Radstock so much that, on leaving the place, he reproached his companion for his apparent want of feeling. Subsequent interviews greatly modified Clare's first impression, for he found Mrs. Emmerson not only a most amiable, kind-hearted lady, but a true and faithful friend, whose advice and assistance often proved of the greatest service to him.

Having stayed a week in London, in a continual round of visits to dinner parties, soirées, and theatrical entertainments —which latter did not impress him very much—John Clare again went, in the company of Mr. Gilchrist, to the 'George and Blue Boar,' Holborn, and took seat for the return journey to Stamford. He was heartily glad to get away from the big town, yearning for his old haunts, the quiet woods, streams, and meadows, and the little cottage among the fields with his wife and darling baby. It seemed to him an immense time since he had left these everyday scenes of his existence; it was as if his whole life had changed in the interval. He felt like one in a dream when the coach went rolling northward along the high road, through fields in which labourers were busy with plough and spade. It was not so very long ago that he had been just such a labourer : how strange that he should now loll upon soft cushions, in a coach drawn by four horses, while others like him kept on digging and ploughing in the sweat of their brow. And would he be ever content to dig and plough again, after having tasted the sweets of a more genial existence, treading upon carpeted floors and dining with lords ? Such were the thoughts and questions that arose tumultuously in his mind, in the long ride from London to Stamford. He had not the courage to face them and think them out, feeling his brain begin to ache, and his heart to throb in wild excitement. Then there flickered before his eye the vision of wife and babe in the little cottage at home, and the tumult of his soul changed into bliss. He determined to be happy, as of yore, in the green fields among his former friends, and to dismiss all thoughts of changing his old course of life. It was late at night when the coach rattled into Stamford ; but John Clare would not hear of stopping at his friend's house, even for a few minutes.

The clouds were dark overhead, and no lights visible any-where; yet through night and darkness he groped his way home, and bursting into his little hut, clasped wife and babe in his arms.

FIRST TROUBLES OF FAME.

The news that a poet had arisen on the borders of the Fens soon spread far and wide, even into Northamptonshire. The 'Quarterly Review' and 'Gentleman's Magazine' carried the report into mansions, villas, and vicarages, and the 'Stamford Mercury' and other local papers spread it among the inmates of farmhouses and humbler dwellings. Much incredulity was manifested at first; but the news being confirmed on all hands, there arose a great and universal desire to behold the new poet. The reign of fame commenced soon after Clare's return from London, when, true to his resolution, he had taken to his old labours in the fields. About the second or third morning after resuming work, there came a message from his father, requesting him to return home in all haste, in order to see some gentlemen waiting for him. Clare ran as fast as he could, and found two elderly men in spectacles, who said they were schoolmasters, had come from Peter-borough, and wished to make his acquaintance. After questioning him closely for two hours, upon all matters, and at the end subjecting him to a rigid cross-examination, they went away, promising to call again. Clare had lost part of a day's work; however, he did not mind it much, for he was somewhat flattered by the visit. The day passed, and the next morning; but on the following afternoon, he was again called away from his labours. This time, there were three aged ladies from Market Deeping, who said that they had bought a copy of his poems between them, and could not rest till they had seen him face to face. One of the ladies was somewhat deaf, and Clare had to answer all questions twice ; first by speaking to two of his visitors in the ordinary key, and then shouting it into the ear of the third old dame. After detaining him for an hour, the elderly individuals said they did not know their way back, and nothing remained but to show them the road for a couple of miles. It was getting late, and Clare, therefore, instead of going to his work again, went into the public-house. Fame threatened to be dangerous.

The tide set in with full force before another week was over. Not a day passed without Clare being called away from his work in the fields, to speak to people he had never seen in his life ; people of all ranks and conditions, farmers, clergymen, horsedealers, dissenting ministers, butchers, schoolmasters, commercial travellers, and half-pay officers. One morning, the inmates of a whole boarding-school, located at Stamford, visited the unhappy poet, and, a shower coming on, the fluttering damsels with their grave monitors crowded every room in the little hut, preventing the baby from sleeping, and Mrs. Clare from doing her weekly washing. Most of the visitors were polite ; some, however, were sarcastic, and a few rude. After having inspected Clare, his person, house, wife and child, father and mother, they wanted further information concerning his daily habits, mode of eating and drinking, quantity of food consumed, and other particulars, and not getting the wished-for replies to all their questions, they told him to his face that he was an ill-bred clown. But there was another class of visitors still more dangerous to the peace of Clare and his little household. Young and middle-aged men came over from Stamford, from Peterborough, and sometimes as far as from London, inviting the poet to conversation and ' a glass ' at the tavern, and keeping him at their carousals for hours and whole days. Already too much inclined by nature and early bad example to habits of intemperance, the good resolutions of Clare fairly gave way under this new temptation. The persons

who invited him to the alehouse were among the most intelligent of his visitors; they talked freely and pleasantly
about subjects interesting to the poet, and often made their
conversation still more attractive by music and song. To
resist the incitement of flying the dull labours of the fields in
favour of such company, required more moral strength than
Clare possessed, or was able to command. Early training he
had none; and even now there was not a soul near to teach
and warn him of the danger. So the unhappy poet kept
gliding down the fatal abyss.

Clare's visits to Stamford were not quite so frequent after
his return from London as before, although he made it a
point to call upon Mr. Gilchrist and Mr. Drury at least once
a week. On one of these occasions he made the acquaintance
of a very eccentric elderly gentleman, who, cold at first and
almost offensive in speech, subsequently proved himself a
warm friend. This was Dr. Bell, a retired army surgeon,
who had long resided near Stamford, and was on good terms
with many of the gentlemen of the neighbourhood. While
serving in His Majesty's forces abroad, Dr. Bell became the
intimate friend of a versatile colleague, Dr. Wolcot, subsequently known as Peter Pindar, who inspired him with a
taste for literature, to which he devoted himself with a real
passion after his retirement from the army. Though not a
writer himself, he brought out several books, among them a
very droll one, made up of quotations of the most curious
kind, and entitled, 'The Canister of the Blue Devils, by
Democritus, junior.' Dr. Bell possessed a very large library,
and spent a good part of his time in extracting, both from
his books and the newspapers and periodicals of the day, all
available paragraphs containing quaint sayings and doings,
which he stuck upon large pieces of pasteboard, for the
inspection of his friends, and subsequent publication in some
'canister' shape. John Clare met Peter Pindar's friend at
the house of Mr. Gilchrist; they did not seem to like each

other at first sight, but got on better terms at the second
meeting, and after a while became attached friends. Dr.
Bell had an instinctive dislike to poets, whom he held to be
'moonstruck.' He was not long, however, in discovering
that John Clare was a great deal more than a mere maker of
verses and apostrophiser of love-sick boys and girls. The
high and manly spirit of the poor labourer of Helpston ; his
yearning after truth, and his constant endeavour to discover,
beneath all the forms and symbols of outward appearances,
the godlike soul of the universe, struck him with something
like wonderment. He first began to look upon Clare as a
sort of phenomenon ; but found that the more he studied
him, the more incomprehensible, yet also the more admirable,
appeared this great and lofty spirit, wrapped in the coarse garb
of a ploughman and lime-burner. The odd, tender-hearted
doctor soon conceived a passionate affection for Clare, and set
him up as a hero at the shrine of his devotion. He thought
of nothing else but advancing his young friend's welfare, and
worked with great zeal to this effect ; to such an extent that
his endeavours frequently overstepped the bounds of prudence.
The first thing he did was to write letters to all the wealthy
inhabitants of the neighbouring district, begging, nay, entreating them to set their name to a subscription list for a
fund, destined to make the poet independent for the rest of
his days. However, the appeal was but faintly responded to,
and most of the persons addressed either declined, or contented themselves by forwarding small sums. But Dr. Bell
was by no means discouraged at this result. With con-
summate worldly experience, he resolved upon attacking his
'patients' from the weakest side, and extract from their
vanity what he could not get from their munificence. He
put himself in communication with Mr. John Taylor, and, by
dint of extreme pressure, succeeded in enlisting him in his
project. It was to make an appeal in favour of John Clare
on the part of the conductors of the 'London Magazine ;'

with delicate hint that any act of liberality would not be condemned to blush unseen. But this scheme, too, did not realize the expectations of Dr. Bell, chiefly because Mr. John Taylor, out of feelings easily comprehended, did not join him in his endeavours with the heartiness he expected. To make the appeal appear as much in favour of poetry as of a single poet, Mr. Taylor, in his letters, asked assistance for Keats as well as for Clare, wording his request in terms more dignified than persuasive. There was only one response to this petition, which came from Earl Fitzwilliam, who forwarded £100 to Clare and £50 to Keats. The liberality of the kind nobleman was scarcely appreciated as it deserved. One of the friends of Keats, in a loud article in the 'London Magazine,' of December, 1820, disclaimed his intention to be beholden to any lord. 'We really do not see,' ran the article, 'what noblemen have to do with the support of poets, more than other people, while the poor rates are in existence. In the present state of society, poetry, as well as agricultural produce, should be left to find its own level.' All this was very fine ; though it looked somewhat inconsequential that the conductors of the very periodical in which this was printed, should go a-begging for poets, and that the poets themselves—Keats not excepted—made no scruple in taking the money. As for poor Clare, he got the news of Earl Fitzwilliam's noble gift together with the 'London Magazine' of December, 1820, and felt utterly ashamed to accept the money with the accompanying reminder of the poor rates being in existence.

John Clare for some time was unaware of all the exertions made by his friends to secure him an independence, and when he heard the whole of it, so far from being pleased, reproached them for what they had done. He told them they were wrong in bringing him forward in the character of a beggar without his consent, and with some energy declined to live upon alms as long as he was able to subsist by the work of his hands. Mr. Taylor was somewhat offended when he got this protest, which seemed to him like ingratitude; but Dr. Bell remained undisturbed, and secretly made up his mind to continue his efforts with more energy than ever for his friend. 'A noble soul, yet altogether unfit for this ignoble world,' he said to Mr. Gilchrist, issuing his circulars for another philanthropic campaign. When Clare learnt that new appeals to assist him had been put forward, he determined to interfere in the matter. Accordingly, he wrote long letters—very pathetic, though ill-spelt—to Earl Fitzwilliam, Earl Spencer, General Birch Reynardson, and other gentlemen, telling them that he had nothing to do with these appeals in his favour, and that he required no assistance whatever. Clare's innate nobility of character was strikingly shown in these epistles; nevertheless, they were very injudicious, and had an effect decidedly contrary to that imagined by the author. The gentlemen to whom the letters were addressed naturally came to the conclusion that Clare, scarcely risen from obscurity, was already quarrelling with those who had helped him to rise, and showed himself ungrateful as well as ill-bred. Besides, the wording of the letters was of a kind not to inspire any admiration of the poet. Though verse flowed as naturally from his pen as music from the throat of the nightingale, Clare, all his life long, was unable to express his thoughts in prose composition. There was not wanting in his letters a certain ruggedness and picturesqueness of style, but it was marred nearly always by ill-expressed and frequently incoherent eruptions, and disquisitions on extraneous matters, marking the absence of a regular chain of thought. It was here that Clare's want of education was most strongly visible. High-soaring like the lark in his poetical flights, yet unable to trot along, step by step, on the grammatical turnpike road of life, Clare's mode of expressing his thoughts, orally or in writing, was not of the ordinary kind, and required some sort of study to be duly appreciated. But it could scarcely be expected that gentlemen like Earl Spencer, and the other exalted personages to whom the poet addressed his pathetic notes, should enter upon such a study. They saw before them nothing but large sheets of paper, of coarse texture, full of ill-spelt and ill-connected sentences, made more obscure by an utter absence of punctuation; and the not unnatural judgment thereupon was that the man who wrote such letters was a thoroughly vulgar and uneducated person. There came doubts into the minds of many, who read these prose compositions, as to whether the author was really the genius exalted by the periodicals of the day. Was it not possible that the 'Quarterly Review' which unduly depreciated poor Keats, had, equally unjustly, raised John Clare upon an unmerited pedestal of fame? This was the question asked by some of the former patrons of Clare, notably Earl Spencer and General Birch Reynardson. The latter spoke to Dr. Bell about it; but was astonished at the burst of indignation which broke from the lips of Peter Pindar's friend. ' What! Clare not a poet?' exclaimed the irate doctor; ' well, if he is not a poet, there never was one in the world.' General Reynardson, having a great respect, somewhat mingled with fear, for the author of the ' Canister,' humbly acquiesced in the decision, promising to put his name down on the Stamford subscription list. But Dr. Bell was ill at ease nevertheless, and rode over the same day to Helpston. ' If you ever again write letters to our friends without showing them to me first, I shall be very angry with you—I shall put you among the Blue Devils.' So spoke the doctor; and John Clare, having heard the whole story of the effect of his epistles, promised obedience. He knew but too well, by this time, that the speech which God had given him was poetry, not prose.

The stream of visitors which set in at Helpston during the spring of 1820, did not cease till late in the summer of the same year. After the flood of schoolmasters, of farmers' wives, and of boarding-school misses, there came a rush of rarer birds of travel, authors and authoresses, writers of unpublished books, and unappreciated geniuses in general. The first of the tribe was an individual of the name of Preston, a native of Cambridge, and author of an immense quantity of poetic, artistic, and scientific works—none of them printed, owing to ignorance of public and publishers. He sent Clare formal notice that he would come on a certain day, and, previous to coming, forwarded a large box full of manuscripts. There was a full description of his life, with sketch of his rare talents and accomplishments; also the greater part of his poetical writings, comprising five epics, three hundred ballads, and countless acrostics, madrigals, and sonnets. John Clare felt greatly flattered when he got the large box, and the same evening, after coming home from his work in the fields, sat down to inspect the manuscripts sent for his perusal. However, he did not get far, but fell asleep over the first dozen pages of the first epic. He honestly tried again the second evening, but with the same result as before; and on the third day relinquished the attempt in despair, accusing himself for his want of intelligence. Soon after, Mr. Preston made his appearance. He was a tall, thin man, with red whiskers and a red nose; dressed in a threadbare black coat, buttoned up to the chin. Introducing himself with some dignity, he at once fell into a familiar strain: 'How do you do, John?' and 'Hope you are glad to see a brother poet.' John was glad, of course; very glad. The tall, thin man then gave a glance at his large box, and John trembled. To allay the coming storm, Clare confessed at once that he had not had time to read through the manuscripts, having been hard at work in the fields. The great man frowned; yet after a while relaxed his features, telling Clare that he would give him two days more to read through his poems. At the end of this term, he intended to ask for a kind of certificate containing the brother poet's appreciation of his works, together with letters of introduction to his patrons and publishers. It seemed cruel to refuse the request of such a dear and determined brother. John Clare, weighing in his mind how poor and friendless he had been himself but a short while ago, felt stirred by compassion, and though he knew he could not read the epics, indited a warm letter of praise and admiration for Mr. Preston. The latter thereupon took his farewell, and went away, accompanied by his large box. Some days after, Dr. Bell came down to Helpston, in greater excitement than ever. 'What do you mean by sending me such a d—— fellow?' he broke forth in a burst of indignation. Poor Clare! he meant nothing, thought of nothing, and knew nothing; and all that he could do was in a few simple words to explain the whole story. The doctor quietly listened to the account of Mr. Preston and his box, and when Clare had finished, delivered another lecture upon practical wisdom, threatening his friend, as penalty for disobedience, with the 'Canister of the Blue Devils.'

PATRONAGE UNDER VARIOUS ASPECTS.

Honours and good news came in fast upon Clare in the autumn of 1820. The poet, at his humble home, was visited, first by Lady Fane, eldest daughter of the Earl of Westmoreland; secondly, by Viscount Milton, coming high on horseback, in the midst of red-coated huntsmen; and, finally, greatest of honours, by the Marquis of Exeter. The villagers were awe-struck when the mighty lord, in his emblazoned coach, with a crowd of glittering lackeys around, came up to the cottage of Parker Clare, the pauper. Mrs. Clare was utterly terrified, for she was standing at the washing-tub, and the baby was crying. Her greatest pride consisted in keeping the little cottage neat and tidy; but, as ill-luck would have it, she was always washing whenever visitors dropped in. The marquis, with aristocratic tact, saved poor Patty from a fresh humiliation. Hearing the loud voice of the baby from afar, his lordship despatched one of his footmen to inquire whether Clare was at home. The man in plush carefully advanced to the cottage door, and holding a silk handkerchief before his fine Roman nose, summoned John before him. Old Parker Clare thereupon hobbled forward, trembling all over, and, in a faint voice, told the great man that his son was mowing corn, in a field close to Helpston Heath. Thither the glittering cavalcade proceeded, and John was soon discovered, in the midst of the other labourers, busy with his sickle. Though somewhat startled on being addressed by his lordship, he was secretly pleased that the interview was taking place in the field instead of in his narrow little hut. It seemed to him that here, among the sheaves of corn, he himself was somewhat taller and the noble marquis somewhat smaller than within the four walls of any cottage or palace; and this feeling encouraged him to speak with less embarrassment to his illustrious visitor. His lordship said he had heard rumours that a new volume of poetry was forthcoming, and wanted to know whether it was true. Clare replied that he was busy writing verses in his spare hours, and that he intended writing still more after the harvest, and during the next winter, which would, probably, result in another book with his name on the title-page. The marquis expressed his satisfaction in hearing this news, and, after a few kind words, and a hint that he would be glad to see some specimens, in manuscript, of the new publication, took his farewell. John Clare was not courtier enough to understand the hint about the manuscripts in all its bearings. For a moment, the thought flashed through his mind of asking his lordship to allow the new volume to be dedicated to him; but the idea was as instantaneously crushed by a remembrance of the fatal article in the 'London Magazine,' in which it was said, 'We really do not see what noblemen have to do with the support of poets more than other people.' The remark had left a deep impression upon his mind, and he felt its truth more than ever while standing face to face with a great lord, sickle in hand, among the yellow corn. He therefore said nothing about the dedication, and the visit of his lordship remained without result—which was not his lordship's fault.

A few days after this interview with the Marquis of Exeter, Clare went to Stamford to see Mr. Drury and Mr. Gilchrist. The latter had important news. He told his friend that he had just received a letter from Mr. John Taylor, stating that the fund collected for his benefit through the exertions of Lord Radstock, Dr. Bell, and others, had now reached the sum of £420 12s. and that this capital had been invested, for his benefit, under trustees, in the 'Navy five per cents.' Mr. Gilchrist, on communicating this information, expected an outburst of gratitude; but was surprised to see that Clare received it with a coldness which he could not understand. Being pressed for an explanation, Clare frankly stated that he was not pleased with the whole affair, both as being personally unwilling to receive alms, and, still more, unwilling to receive them in the aggravated form of helplessness, from 'under trustees.' Clare's remark quite startled Mr. Gilchrist. He had hitherto looked upon the poet as a man who, gifted with considerable talent, was yet little removed from the ordinary hind of the fields; willing not only, but anxious to live upon charity, and kneeling, in all humility of heart, before rank and wealth. The high manliness of Clare now struck him for the first time, and he deeply admired it, though giving no words to his feelings. He even remonstrated about his friend's coldness in receiving gifts offered by real lovers and admirers of his genius. The chord thus struck reverberated freely, and Clare, after warmly shaking Mr. Gilchrist by the hand, returned home to his wife and parents, joyfully communicating the great news that he was now the owner of not less than four hundred and twenty pounds. They fancied it an inexhaustible store of wealth, and great, accordingly, was the joy within the little cottage.

The four hundred and twenty pounds invested for the benefit of Clare, were the gift of twenty donors. Nearly one-half the sum was contributed by two benefactors, namely, the Earl Fitzwilliam, who gave £100, and Clare's publishers, who bestowed the like amount upon him. The remaining two hundred and twenty pounds—accurately, £220 12s.—were made up of sums of five, ten, and twenty pounds, the principal contributors being the Dukes of Bedford and of Devonshire, who gave twenty pounds each; Prince Leopold of Saxe-Coburg—subsequently King Leopold of Belgium—the Duke of Northumberland, the Earl of Cardigan, Lord John Russell, Sir Thomas Baring, and six other noblemen, who subscribed ten pounds; and a few others who gave five pounds each. The sum thus collected was certainly insignificant, taking into account the extraordinary efforts made by Lord Radstock and other friends of Clare to procure him a provision for life. After all the high praise bestowed upon the new poet by the 'Quarterly Review,' and other critical journals, and the loud appeals for aid and assistance, it was found that there were only two patrons of literature in all England who thought him worth a hundred pounds, and of these two, one was a bookselling firm in Fleet Street. It really seemed as if the world at large engrossed the dictum of the 'London Magazine,' of the wealthy having no business to assist poets while the poor rates are in existence. The two hundred and twenty pounds collected for Clare from eighteen patrons of literature, together with the two hundred from Earl Fitzwilliam and Messrs. Taylor and Hessey, served, in the aggregate, to relieve the poet from absolute starvation. Invested in the funds, the capital gave him nearly twenty pounds a year, and, with the annuity already granted by the

Marquis of Exeter, about thirty-five. Dr. Bell, by dint of restless exertions, managed to add another ten pounds to this yearly income. He wrote to Earl Spencer, temporarily residing at Naples, and obtained the promise of his lordship to grant Clare ten pounds per annum for life. So that altogether the poet now was endowed with a regular income of forty-five pounds a year, or rather more than seventeen shillings a week. It was far above the average of what he had ever earned before as a labourer, and, properly regulated, might have been sufficient to make his future career comparatively free from the cares and anxieties of daily subsistence. Unfortunately, this was not the case, and the very aid intended to smoothen his road through life led, almost directly, to his ruin.

The autumn of 1820, together with many gratifying gifts, brought Clare some little mortification. A few of his friends were somewhat too zealous : among them, Captain Sherwell, to whom the poet had been introduced by Lord Radstock, and who lost no opportunity to aid and assist him. Shortly after his meeting with Clare, Captain Sherwell went on a visit to Abbotsford, where he indulged in high praises of the 'Poems of Rural Life and Scenery,' trying hard to gain the sympathies of his distinguished host in favour of the author. But Sir Walter Scott showed little inclination to fraternize with the poet of Northamptonshire, and sternly declined the pressing demand of Captain Sherwell to write a note of approbation to Clare, or even to put his name to the subscription fund. The warm-hearted captain was the more grieved at this refusal as he had already, in a letter to Lord Radstock, held out hopes that the 'Great Unknown' would enter into correspondence with their humble friend; and seeing the probability of this report reaching Clare, he deeply felt the disappointment which it would cause. He, therefore, when on the point of leaving Abbotsford, tried once more to get some token of friendship for Clare; but all he was able to obtain

K

was a copy of the 'Lady of the Lake,' together with a present
of two guineas.   Even the slight favour of writing his name
inside the book, Sir Walter Scott absolutely refused.   Captain
Sherwell, greatly humiliated in finding all his endeavours
fruitless, forwarded the two guineas and the 'Lady of the
Lake' to Messrs. Taylor and Hessey, placing a paper in the
volume, with the inscription : 'Walter Scott presents John
Clare with the " Lady of the Lake," with the modest hope
that he will read it with attention.'   John Clare, in receiving
the book, naturally supposed that this paper was written by
Sir Walter Scott himself.   He therefore pasted it on the
fly-leaf, and having to proceed, a few days after, to Burghley
Park, to receive his quarterly stipend from the Marquis of
Exeter, he took the book with him, and showed it to his
lordship's secretary.   The latter, deeming it an interesting
curiosity, sent the copy to the marquis for inspection ; but
was astonished on getting it returned on the instant, with
the message that the autograph was not that of Sir Walter
Scott, and that the matter seemed to be an imposture.
John Clare, of course, felt terribly mortified on hearing
this message delivered.   He forthwith applied to Captain
Sherwell, for an explanation ; but, before he could expect
an answer, received a note from this gentleman, written,
evidently, before obtaining the request.   The captain's note,
notable in many respects, ran as follows :—

'My dear Clare,—I have forwarded to Mr. Taylor the
long-expected " Lady of the Lake," with an earnest request
that it may be sent to you speedily.   If you have not read
it already I shall be better pleased.   It contains a sweetness
of style, guided by a correctness of language, which no one
of his works surpasses.   All my endeavours, all my efforts of
persuasion proved fruitless in obtaining the fulfilment of the
anxious wish I had expressed to him that he would address a
few lines to you on the blank-leaf.   Sir Walter Scott seemed
bound hand and head.   It was not from any disapprobation

of your talent, or taste ; but occasioned by the high path in which he strides in the literary field of the present day. The paper in the " Lady of the Lake " is placed by me merely as a memorandum.'

This curious letter certainly furnished a confirmation of the fact discovered by the Marquis of Exeter, that the paper in the 'Lady of the Lake' was not in Sir Walter Scott's handwriting ; but it all the more increased the deep humiliation felt by John Clare. To ease his over-burthened heart, he ran to Stamford, and laid both Captain Sherwell's letter and the book before Mr. Gilchrist. The latter had no sooner looked through the note, when he burst out laughing. ' Well,' he exclaimed, ' this is the funniest thing I ever read.' And seeing Clare's melancholy face, he continued, ' Oh, don't be disheartened, my dear fellow ; all this is stuff and nonsense. I know the time when this great Scotch baronet did not stride in the high path into which he has now scrambled, and I will show you something to the effect.' Which saying, he went to his bookcase, and brought forth an elegantly-bound volume, together with a silk-tied note. ' This letter,' Mr. Gilchrist exclaimed, ' and this book, called the " Lay of the Last Minstrel," the author of the " Lady of the Lake " sent me more than ten years ago. He was then simple Mr. Walter Scott : a very humble man as you will see from his letter, in which he gives profuse thanks for a little review of his work which I wrote in a magazine. Therefore, I say again, don't be disheartened, my dear fellow. Keep up your head, and let us have some more of your verses ; some better ones, if possible. Then, if the world applauds you, and applauds you again and again, I give you my word, the great baronet in his high path will be the first to shake hands.' Thus spoke Octavius Gilchrist, grocer of Stamford, and contributor to the ' Quarterly Review.' And his speech set John Clare musing for some time to come.

As soon as the harvest was over, Clare ceased working in

the fields, and during the next six months devoted himself to
literature.   He had arranged with Messrs. Taylor and Hessey
to bring out another volume of poetry in the spring of
1821, and the preparation of this work, together with much
reading, filled up the whole of his time.   Clare now was in
possession of a rather considerable collection of books, chiefly
poems; most of them gifts of friends and admirers, and
the rest added by his own purchases.   Small presents of
money from strangers he invariably invested in books; and
the two guineas of Sir Walter Scott went directly to buy the
works of Burns, Chatterton's poems, and Southey's 'Life
of Nelson.'   The assiduous study of these works necessarily
tended to elevate Clare's taste and to improve his style.   All
his earlier productions bore more or less the stamp of crude-
ness, by no means effaced by the corrections of the editor
in orthography and punctuation; but he now gradually
acquired the skill of handling verse, and shaping it into the
desired smoothness of expression.   He began to compose,
too, with far greater rapidity than before.   Many a day he
completed two, and even three poems, elaborating the plan,
as well as revising them finally.   His mode of composition, likewise, became almost entirely changed at this
period.   While formerly his poetical conceptions were usually
scribbled on little bits of paper, and furtively revised at
intervals of labour, the correction, amounting to entire re-
writing, often extending over weeks and months, he now got
into the regular habit of finishing all his poems in two
sittings, casting them first, and polishing them the second
time.   Almost invariably the first process took place out of
doors.   Inspiration seldom came to him in-doors, within the
walls of any dwelling; but descended upon his soul in
abundant showers whenever he was roaming through the
fields and meadows, the woods and heathery plains around
Helpston.   It mattered not to him whether the earth was
basking in sunshine, or deluged with rain; whether the air

was warm and mild, or ice and snow lying on the ground. At the accustomed hour every morning, he would wander forth, now in one direction, now in another ; only caring to get away from the haunts of men, into the cherished solitude of nature. Then, when full of rapture about the wonderful, ever-beautiful world—wonderful and beautiful to him in all aspects and at all seasons—he would settle down in some quiet nook or corner, and rapidly shape his imagination into words. There were some favourite places where he delighted to sit, and where the hallowed vein of poetry seemed to him to flow more freely than at any others. The chief of these spots was the hollow of an old oak, on the borders of Helpston Heath, called Lea Close Oak—now ruthlessly cut down by 'enclosure' progress—where he had formed himself a seat with something like a table in front. Few human beings ever came near this place, except now and then some wandering gypsies, the sight of whom was not unpleasing to the poet. Inside this old oak Clare used to sit in silent meditation, for many hours together, forgetting everything about him, and unmindful even of the waning day and the mantle of darkness falling over the earth. Having prepared his verses in rough outline, within the oak, or in some other lonely place, he would hurry home without delay. Patty, carefullest of housewives, although little comprehending the erratic ways of her lord, had got into the habit of always keeping a slight meal ready for the hungry poet. He took his broth, or his cup of tea, in silence, and then crept up to the narrow bedroom in the upper part of the hut. Here the day's poetical productions were passed in review. Whatever was not approved, met with immediate destruction ; the rest was carefully corrected and polished, and afterwards copied out into a big book, a sort of ledger, bought at Stamford fair. Clare had laid down the rule for himself to make no further corrections or examination whatever. The poems thus composed were sent to the printer ; and though Mr. Taylor, the editor and publisher of the new work, was anxious to alter and revise some of them, Clare would not allow any change, save orthographical and grammatical corrections. There was at this time an impression on Clare's mind that his verses were the product of intuition; and that the songs came floating from his lips and pen as music from the throat of birds. So he held his own orthodoxy more orthodox than that of the schools. In which view poor John Clare was decidedly wrong, seeing that his music was not offered gratis like that of the skylark and nightingale, but was looking out for the pounds, shillings, and pence of a most discerning public.

PUBLICATION OF THE 'VILLAGE MINSTREL.'

The publication of Clare's new volume, arranged for the spring of 1821, gave rise to some difficulties as the time grew near. It was the intention of his publishers to bring out the work with some artistic embellishments, including a portrait of the author and a sketch of his home; to both which Clare had certain objections, as far as the execution of the task was concerned. On the other hand, Messrs. Taylor and Hessey wished to exclude some of Clare's poems, which they did not think quite as good as the rest, under the pretence that they had already more than sufficient in hand to make a strong volume ; but this again was opposed by the author, who sent in his ultimatum to print all his verses or none. The difficulty might have been easily arranged by Mr. Gilchrist, with his great influence both over Clare and his publishers, but he, unfortunately, was over head and ears in trouble, and had no time to attend to the perplexities of others. Mr. Gilchrist, in the summer of 1820, had the misfortune of being dragged into the great quarrel of the Rev. William Lisle Bowles, the editor of Pope, with Byron, Campbell, and the 'Quarterly Review;' a battle of the

windmills which occupied the literary world of England for
several years. Having despatched the chief of his big foes.
the Rev. Mr. Bowles thought fit to turn round upon Mr.
Gilchrist, whom he held to be the author of a severe article
in the 'Quarterly.' This was not the case; nevertheless,
Mr. Gilchrist took up the cudgels, striking out with all the
impetus so much in vogue among the pen-wielding celebrities
of the time. From the 'Quarterly'—too Jupiter-like to be
long detained by street rows—the quarrel was transferred to
the pages of the 'London Magazine,' where abundant space
was allowed to both Mr. Gilchrist and the Rev. Mr. Bowles
to fight out their battles. The great question was whether
Mr. Bowles had done justice to the character of Pope, or
drawn the figure of his hero in too hard outlines; and as
there was much to be said on either side, the articles grew
longer every month, and the spirit of the combatants became
more and more embittered. The conflagration got general
through a flaring pamphlet, 'by one of the family of the
Bowles's,' and for a year or two the air was filled with squibs.
flysheets, articles, and reviews, for and against Bowles. What
with his grocery business at Stamford, and his multifarious
literary engagements, poor Mr. Gilchrist fairly lost his head
in the midst of this thunderstorm, and was unable to think
of anything else but Bowles and Pope, and Pope and Bowles.
Clare happening to visit him one day, when musing on this
all-absorbing subject, he tried to inspire him with a sense of
the wrongs he had suffered at the hands of the Rev. William
Lisle Bowles; but meeting with utter apathy, Mr. Gilchrist
turned in disgust from his poetic friend, shocked at his
callousness. As a sort of revenge, on being appealed to for
his aid in settling the difficulty between his friend and
Messrs. Taylor and Hessey, he declared that he had no time
to attend to the matter. This was certainly true, for the din
of the great Bowles battles kept raging in the air and the
pages of the 'London Magazine' for nigh another year.

After some lengthened correspondence between Clare and his publishers, it was arranged that the new work should be brought out in two volumes in the summer of 1821. This made it possible to give the whole of the poems, and to finish the engravings with the care desired by the author. In the meanwhile, to keep Clare before the public, specimens of the forthcoming volume were published at intervals in Mr. Taylor's periodical, and, finally, the September number of the 'London Magazine' contained at the head of the list of 'works preparing for publication,' the announcement that 'The Village Minstrel, and other Poems, by John Clare, the Northamptonshire Peasant, with a fine portrait, will be published in a few days.' The work was published accordingly, in the middle of September. In outward appearance, the two new volumes offered a great contrast to Clare's former book. The 'Poems descriptive of Rural Life and Scenery,' were dressed in more than rustic simplicity; stitched in rough cardboard and printed on coarse paper, with no artistic adornments whatever. On the other hand, the 'Village Minstrel' presented itself in beautiful type, with two fine steel engravings, the first a portrait of Clare, from the painting by William Hilton, R.A. and the latter a sketch of his cottage. Notwithstanding all these attractions, the new work met with but a cold reception. It was accounted for by the publishers in the fact that its price, 12s., was too high compared with the former volume, which was sold at 5s. 6d.; but the real cause undoubtedly was that the time of publication was very unfavourable. It was a period when the English book-mart was overstocked with poetry and fiction, and when the world seemed less than ever inclined to devote itself to poetry and fiction. The year 1821, in fact, formed a notable epoch in the annals of literature for the number of productions from celebrated authors. Sir Walter Scott published 'Kenilworth Castle;' Lord Byron issued his tragedy of 'Marino Faliero;' Southey, his 'Vision of Judgment;' Shelley, his 'Prometheus,' and Wordsworth a new edition of his poems. Besides these giants in the field of literature, numerous stars of the second and third magnitude sent forth their light. Charles Lamb, Hazlitt, Barry Cornwall, Tom Moore, Allan Cunningham, Leigh Hunt, and others, were busy writing and publishing, and John Keats sent his swan-song from the tombs of the Eternal City. In the midst of this galaxy of genius and fame, John Clare stood, in a sense, neglected and forlorn. The very reputation of his first book was against him, for most of his friends were unreasoning and uncritical enough to assert that the 'Poems on Rural Life and Scenery,' were less remarkable as poetic works, than as productions of a very poor and illiterate man. This statement was echoed far and wide, with the necessary result of getting 'the Northamptonshire Peasant' looked upon as but a nine-days' wonder. Quite as fatal to Clare's fame as a poet were the loud appeals made on his behalf for pecuniary assistance. There was, and, indeed, is at all times, an instinctive feeling, in the main a just one, among the public, that genius and talent are self-supporting, and that he who cannot live by the exercise of his own hand or brain, does not altogether deserve success. The feeling was even stronger than usual about this period, because of the repeated announcements of fabulous sums earned by book-makers, including the notoriously helpless poets. It was well known that Sir Walter Scott had made a large fortune by his verses and novels; that Moore got £3,000 for his 'Lalla Rookh,' and Crabbe £2,000 for his 'Tales of the Hall;' that Southey had no reason to be dissatisfied with the pecuniary result of his epics and articles, nor Mr. Millman cause to weep over the 'Fall of Jerusalem.' There were rumours even, embodied in sly newspaper paragraphs, that Mr. Murray was paying Lord Byron at the rate of a guinea a word; though this was disputed by others, who asserted that the remuneration was

only five shillings a syllable. However, all these reports
had led the public to the not unjust conclusion, that
booksellers, on the whole, are no bad patrons of literature,
and that the reward of genius might be safely left to them.
As a consequence, from the moment that the begging-box
was sent round for Clare—sent round, too, with a zeal far
surpassing discretion—there arose a latent feeling among
readers of books, that ' the Northamptonshire peasant ' was
not so much a poet as a talented pauper, able to string a few
rhymes together. The feeling, for a time, was not outspoken ;
but nevertheless unmistakeable in its results.

The sale of the ' Village Minstrel and other Poems,' was
not large at the commencement, and the book was scarcely
noticed by the literary periodicals of the day. Though
containing verses far surpassing in beauty anything previously published by Clare, the work passed over the heads
of critics and public alike as unworthy of consideration. It
drew passing notes of praise from a few genuine admirers
of poetry ; but which resulted in nothing but a couple of
letters to the author, and the present of some cheap books.
From one of these letters, it appears that the ballad
commencing ' I love thee, sweet Mary,' printed in the first
volume of the ' Village Minstrel,' was read one evening at
the house of a nobleman at the West End of London,
before the assembled guests. All were in raptures about
the sweetness of the softly-flowing stream of verse, and all
inquired eagerly after the author. But there was but one
person in the room who knew anything about him ; and his
whole knowledge consisted in the fact, told somewhere by
somebody, that Clare was a young ' peasant,' formerly very
poor, but now in a state of affluence through a most liberal
subscription fund, amounting to some twenty thousand
pounds, which had been collected for him and invested
in the Funds. The news gave universal satisfaction to the
distinguished company ; and though none had contributed a

penny to the wonderful subscription list, every guest felt
an inward pride of living in a land offering the bountiful
reward of 'the Funds' to poetic genius, born in obscurity.
After the applause had subsided, the portrait of Clare, prefixed to the 'Village Minstrel,' passed round the circle of
noble West End visitors. All pronounced the face to be
highly *distingué*, and one young lady enthusiastically
declared that John Clare looked 'like a nobleman in
disguise.' In which saying there was a certain amount of
truth.

Notwithstanding many unfavourable circumstances, and
the ill-considered zeal of his patrons, who continued to im-
portune the public with demands for charitable contributions,
the coldness with which Clare's new work was received at
its appearance, was really very extraordinary. The greatest
share of it, in all probability, was due to the period of
publication, which could not well have been more ill-timed.
Besides the natural anxiety of a civilized community to read,
in preference to cheap rural poetry, verses paid for at the
rate of 'a guinea a word,' or at the least 'five shillings a
syllable,' there were many notable matters directing public
attention away from village minstrelsy to other things. The
book was brought out in the same month that the 'injured
Queen of England' died ; that the populace fought for the
honour of participating in the funeral ; and that royal life-
guardsmen killed the loyal people like rabbits in the streets
of London. Political passions soared high, and public
indignation was running still higher in newspapers and
pamphlets. It was not to be expected that, at such a
moment of universal excitement, there should be many
people willing to withdraw to rural poetry. Thus Clare,
'piping low, in shade of lowly grove,' was condemned to
pipe unheard, or very nearly so.

A copy of his 'Village Minstrel' Clare sent to Robert
Bloomfield, for whose poetic genius he felt the most sincere

admiration. In acknowledgment he received, about seven months afterwards, the following characteristic letter :—

'*Shefford, Beds, May* 3d, 1822.

NEIGHBOUR JOHN,—If we were still nearer neighbours I would see you, and thank you personally for the two volumes of your poems sent me so long ago. I write with such labour and difficulty that I cannot venture to praise, or discriminate, like a critic, but must only say that you have given us great pleasure.

I beg your acceptance of my just published little volume ; and, sick and ill as I continually feel, I can join you heartily in your exclamation—"What is Life ?"

With best regards and wishes,

I am yours sincerely,

ROBERT BLOOMFIELD.'

The above letter, as will be seen from the date, was written little more than a year before Bloomfield's death, he living at the time in great retirement, broken in mind and body. The author of the 'Farmer's Boy,' like Clare, felt a noble contempt for punctuation and spelling, and in the original note the word 'vollumn,' twice repeated, stands for volume —representing, no doubt, the way in which he used to pronounce the word.

How entirely free John Clare was from the common failing of literary jealousy, is shown by his admiration of Bloomfield. He not only freely acknowledged the high standard of Bloomfield's works ; but, what was more, held him up to all his friends as a poet far greater than himself. Untrue as was this comparison, it strikingly exhibited the innate nobility of soul of the poor 'Northamptonshire Peasant.' Yet even this humility, the true sign of genius, was ill-construed by some of Clare's lukewarm patrons, who reproached him for being a flatterer when he only wanted to be just.

GLIMPSES OF JOHN CLARE AT HOME.

During the summer of 1821, Clare gave up his agricultural labours almost entirely. The greater part of the time he spent in roaming through woods and fields, planning new poems, and correcting those already made. Visits to Stamford, also, were frequent and of some duration, and he not unfrequently stayed three or four days together at the house of Mr. Gilchrist, or of Mr. Drury. The stream of visitors to Helpston had ceased, to a great extent, and the few that dropped in now and then were mostly of the better class, or at least not belonging to the vulgar-curious element. Among the number was Mr. Chauncey Hare Townsend, a dandyfied poet of some note, particularly gifted in madrigals and pastorals. He came all the way from London to see Clare, and having taken a guide from Stamford to Helpston, was utterly amazed, on his arrival, to find that the cottage, beautifully depicted in the 'Village Minstrel,' was not visible anywhere. His romantic scheme had been to seek Clare in his home, which he thought easy with the picture in his pocket; and having stepped over the flower-clad porch, to rush inside, with tenderly-dignified air, and drop into the arms of the brother poet. However, the scheme threatened to be frustrated, for though the village could easily be surveyed at a glance, such a cottage as that delineated in the 'Minstrel,' with more regard to the ideal than the real, was nowhere to be seen. In his perplexity, Mr. Chauncey Hare Townsend inquired of a passer-by the way to Clare's house. The individual whom he addressed was a short, thick-set man, and, as Mr. Hare Townsend thought, decidedly ferocious-looking; he was bespattered with mud all over, and a thick

knotted stick, which he carried in his hands, gave him something of the air of a highwayman. To the intense surprise
of Mr. Chauncey Hare Townsend, this very vulgar person,
when addressed, declared that he himself was John Clare, and
offered to show the way to his house. Of course, the gentleman from London was too shrewd to be taken in by such
a palpable device for being robbed; so declining the offer
with thanks, and recovering from his fright by inhaling the
perfume of his pocket handkerchief, he retreated on his path,
seeking refuge in the 'Blue Bell' public house. The land-
lord's little girl was ready to show the way to Clare's cottage,
and did so, leaving the stranger at the door. Mr. Townsend,
now fairly prepared to fall into the arms of the brother poet,
though not liking the look of his residence, cautiously opened
the door; but started back immediately on beholding the
highwayman in the middle of the room, sipping a basin of
broth. There seemed a horrible conspiracy for the destruction of a literary gentleman from London in this Northamptonshire village. Mrs. Clare, fortunately, intervened at the
nick of time to keep Mr. Townsend from fainting. Patty,
always neatly dressed—save and except on washing days,—
approached the visitor; and her gentle looks re-assured Mr.
Chauncey Hare Townsend. He wiped his hot brow with his
scented handkerchief, and, not without emotion, introduced
himself to the owner of the house and the neat little wife.
The conversation which followed was short, and somewhat
unsatisfactory on both sides, and the London poet, in the
course of a short half an hour, quitted the Helpston minstrel,
leaving a sonnet, wrapped in a one-pound note, behind him.
Clare frowned when discovering the nature of the envelope;
but he liked the sonnet, and for the sake of it, and on Patty's
petition, consented not to send it back to the giver.

Shortly after this curious visit, there came another, which
gave Clare much more pleasure. Mr. John Taylor, of London,
having been on an excursion to his native place, Retford, in

Nottinghamshire, on his return spent a few days at Stamford, with Mr. Drury; and, while here, could not help looking-in at the home of his 'Northamptonshire Peasant.' His survey of Helpston, Mr. Taylor described in the 'London Magazine' of November, 1821, in a letter 'to the Editor,'—that is, to himself. The sketch thus given furnishes an interesting glimpse of the poet and his quiet home life at this period. Mr. Taylor's letter, dated Oct. 12, 1821, set out as follows:—
'I have just returned from visiting your friend Clare at Helpston, and one of the pleasantest days I ever spent, was passed in wandering with him among the scenes which are the subject of his poems. A flatter country than the immediate neighbourhood can scarcely be imagined, but the grounds rise in the distance clothed with woods, and their gently swelling summits are crowned with village churches; nor can it be called an uninteresting country, even without the poetic spirit which now breathes about the names of many of its most prominent objects, for the ground bears all the traces of having been the residence of some famous people in early days. "The deep sunk moat, the stony mound," are visible in places where modern taste would shrink at erecting a temporary cottage, much less a castellated mansion; fragments of Roman brick are readily found on ridges which still hint the unrecorded history of a far distant period, and the Saxon rampart and the Roman camp are in some places seen mingled together in one common ruin. On the line of a Roman road, which passes within a few hundred yards of the village of Helpston, I met Clare, about a mile from home. He was going to receive his quarter's salary from the steward of the Marquis of Exeter. His wife Patty, and her sister were with him, and it was the intention of the party, I learned, to proceed to their father's house at Casterton, there to meet such of the family as were out in service, on their annual re-assembling together at Michaelmas. I was very unwilling to disturb this arrangement, but Clare insisted

on remaining with me, and the two cheerful girls left their companion with a "good bye, John!" which made the plains echo again.'

Walking along the road, Mr. Taylor, under the guidance of Clare, came to Lolham Brigs, a place sketched in the second volume of the 'Village Minstrel,' in a poem entitled 'The last of March.' The curious publisher and editor, anxious to gather facts for his 'London Magazine,' wanted to know the origin of the poem, and got a full account of it, which, accompanied by some lofty criticisms, he communicated to his readers. 'John Clare,' Mr. Taylor reported, 'was walking in this direction on the last day of March, 1821, when he saw an old acquaintance fishing on the lee side of the bridge. He went to the nearest place for a bottle of ale, and they then sat beneath the screen which the parapet afforded, while a hasty storm passed over, refreshing themselves with the liquor, and moralizing somewhat in the strain of the poem. I question whether Wordsworth's pedlar could have spoken more to the purpose. But all these excitations would, I confess, have spent their artillery in vain against the woolpack of my imagination; and after well considering the scene, I could not help looking at my companion with surprise: to me, the triumph of true genius seemed never more conspicuous, than in the construction of so interesting a poem out of such common-place materials. With your own eyes you see nothing but a dull line of ponds, or rather one continued marsh, over which a succession of arches carries the narrow highway: look again, with the poem in your mind, and the wand of a necromancer seems to have been employed in conjuring up a host of beautiful accompaniments, making the whole waste populous with life, and shedding all around the rich image of a grand and appropriate sentiment. Imagination has, in my opinion, done wonders here.'

From Lolham Brigs, the poet and his publisher turned

towards Helpston, passing by 'Langley Bush,' also sung in
the 'Village Minstrel.' The Bush furnished an opportunity
for some moralizings on the part of Mr. Taylor, interesting
as giving the impressions of an eye-witness as to Clare's
character and the working of his mind. Says Mr. Taylor:—
'The discretion which makes Clare hesitate to receive as
canonical all the accounts he has heard of the former honours
of Langley Bush, is in singular contrast with the enthusiasm
of his poetical faith. As a man, he cannot bear to be
imposed upon,—his good sense revolts at the least attempt
to abuse it ;—but as a poet, he surrenders his imagination
with most happy ease to the allusions which crowd upon it
from stories of fairies and ghosts. The effect of this distinction is soon felt in a conversation with him. From not considering it, many persons express their surprise that Clare
should be so weak on some topics and so wise on others.
But a willing indulgence of what they deem weakness is the
evidence of a strong mind. He feels safe there, and luxuriates
in the abandonment of his sober sense for a time, to be the
sport of all the tricks and fantasies that have been attributed
to preternatural agency. Let them address him on other
subjects, and unless they entrench themselves in forms of
language to which he is unaccustomed, or take no pains to
understand him according to the sense rather than the letter of
his speech, they will confess, that to keep fairly on a level with
him in the depth and tenour of their remarks, is an exercise
requiring more than common effort. He may not have read
the books which they are familiar with, but let them try
him on such as he has read,—and the number is not few,
especially of the modern poets,—and they will find no
reason to undervalue his judgment. His language, it is true,
is provincial, and his choice of words in ordinary conversation is indifferent, because Clare is an unpretending man,
and he speaks in the idiom of his neighbours, who would
ridicule and despise him for using more or better terms than

they are familiar with.   But the philosophic mind will strive
to read his thoughts, rather than catch at the manner of
their utterance ; and will delight to trace the native noble-
ness, strength, and beauty of his conceptions, under the
tattered garb of what may, perhaps, be deemed uncouth and
scanty expressions.'

Arrived at Helpston with his companion, Mr. Taylor was
somewhat surprised at the outer aspect of Clare's humble
home.   Of the inside, he furnished the following neat
sketch :—' On a projecting wall in the inside of the cottage,
which is white-washed, are hung some well engraved portraits,
in gilt frames, with a neat drawing of Helpston Church, and
a sketch of Clare's head which Hilton copied in water
colours, from the large painting, and sent as a present to
Clare's father.   I think that no act of kindness ever touched
him more than this ; and I have remarked, on several
occasions, that the thought of what would be his father's
feelings on any fortunate circumstance occurring, has given
him more visible satisfaction, than all the commendations
which have been bestowed on his genius.   I believe we must
go into low life to know how very much parents can be
beloved by their children.   Perhaps it may be that they do
more for them, or that the affection of the child is concentrated on them the more, from having no other friend on
whom it may fall.   I saw Clare's father in the garden : it
was a fine day, and his rheumatism allowed him just to move
about, but with the aid of two sticks, he could scarcely drag
his feet along ; he can neither kneel nor stoop.   The father,
though so infirm, is only fifty-six years of age ; the mother is
about seven years older.   While I was talking to the old
man, Clare had prepared some refreshment within, and with
the appetite of a thresher we went to our luncheon of bread
and cheese, and capital beer from the Bell.   In the midst of
our operations, his little girl awoke : a fine lively pretty
creature, with a forehead like her father's, of ample promise.

She tottered along the floor, and her father looked after her with the fondest affection, and with a careful twitch of his eyebrow when she seemed in danger. Our meal ended, Clare opened an old oak bookcase, and showed me his library. It contains a very good collection of modern poems, chiefly presents made him since the publication of his first volume; among them the works of Burns, Cowper, Wordsworth, Coleridge, Keats, Crabbe, and other poets. To see so many books handsomely bound, and "flash'd about with golden letters," as he describes it, in so poor a place as Clare's cottage, gave it almost a romantic air, for, except in cleanliness, it is no whit superior to the habitations of the poorest of the peasantry. The hearth has no fire-place on it, which to one accustomed to coal fires looked comfortless, but Clare found it otherwise.'

The idea of a man being happy without a regular fire-place evidently staggered Mr. John Taylor. However, he recovered from his surprise, and having sent his servant—a stately domestic from town, introduced as 'my man'—in front, to prepare the way, the great publisher of Fleet Street solemnly took farewell from his poet, accompanied a proper distance along the road. This duty fulfilled, Clare buttoned up his smock-frock, and trotted away in great haste to meet Patty, and 'such of the family as were out on service.' Very likely, in the company of these 'cheerful girls,' John, for the rest of the evening, felt a great deal more at ease than in the presence of the learned and inquisitive gentleman, his editor and publisher.

SECOND VISIT TO LONDON.

Before Mr. Taylor left Helpston, he gave his client an invitation to come up to London, and spend a few weeks at his house. Perhaps the offer was meant only as a polite phrase, or a 'general invitation;' however, Clare, una-

quainted with the ways of good society, took it to be a
special summons, and, after due reflection, made up his mind
to visit the great metropolis once more. He fixed the journey,
to him a great undertaking, for the spring of 1822, and,
remembering former miseries, decided upon going this time
in a new suit of clothes, expressly ordered at Stamford. The
winter of 1821–2 Clare spent at home, in comparative idleness. Visitors continued to drop in from various places, and
the little cottage being too small to entertain them, he got
into the regular habit of meeting them at the ' Blue Bell.' The
custom, originating in this way, became a fatal one before
long. Clare began to look upon the public house as his
second home, and the corner seat near the fire-place as one
specially appropriated to him, and which he ought to fill
every evening. Fortunately, he was not enabled to indulge
the habit to its utmost extent. Frequent excursions to
Stamford, and sometimes to Peterborough, where he found a
few good friends, drew him away from the ' Blue Bell,'—
though sometimes to places where ale and spirits flowed as
rapidly and were consumed with as much relish as at the
little inn at Helpston. It was altogether a fatal period of
excitement, threatening to the future of the warm-hearted
and but too susceptible poet.

The winter thus passed, and Clare got ready in the spring
to start for London. He had hoped to travel, as before, in
the company of Octavius Gilchrist; but found, at the last
moment, that this was impossible. Poor Mr. Gilchrist was
lying ill at his house at Stamford, the dreadful battle with
the Rev. Mr. Bowles and all the Bowles family having thrown
him on a bed of sickness. Unaccustomed, like his more
hardy brethren of the metropolitan press, to fight with the
windmills of periodical literature, and to throw fire from his
nostrils without burning himself, he had taken the whole
Bowles campaign too much to heart, and was bleeding from
the strokes which he had given as much as the wounds he

had received. His mind was deeply impressed with the
notion that he had suffered defeat on some, if not on many
points, and there being no stout-hearted literary lion within
reach of his grocery store, to cheer his spirits and console
him in his affliction, he began to feel sick and weary. All
entreaties of his friends to come to London he absolutely refused, and there remained nothing for Clare but to set out
alone. The due preparations having been made, he went to
Stamford, one fine morning, in the month of May, mounted
the outside of the coach, and was whirled away, through
Northamptonshire, Huntingdon, and Beds, to the metropolis.
Discharged, once more, at the 'George and Blue Boar,' Holborn, he was bold enough to steer, unaided, through the
intricate thoroughfares of London, and reached the haven
in Fleet Street without accident. Mr. John Taylor looked
somewhat surprised on beholding his poet, carrying a big
stick in one hand, and in the other a large bundle tied in a
coloured pocket handkerchief, with a pair of hob-nailed boots
sticking out on each side. However, a gentleman born and
bred, he smiled pleasantly, helped to unpack Clare's bundle,
and made him welcome to his house. Supper and wine contributed to break the ice, and Mr. John Taylor discovered, for
the first time, that his guest from the country was a very
pleasant companion.

The busy bookseller of Fleet Street had no time to play
the cicerone; therefore, on the morning after Clare's arrival,
he delivered him formally over to Mr. Thomas Hood, sub-
editor of the 'London Magazine.' But Mr. Hood, too—just
rising into fame, thanks to 'Elia' and other friends—thought
he had no time to spare, and left him to Tom Benyon, the
much-respected head-porter of the firm of Taylor and Hessey.
When Thomas Hood came to know John Clare a little better,
he paid more attention to his charge; but this did not happen
till at the end of two or three weeks. Meanwhile Clare amused
himself as best he could, guided wherever he wished to go by

the faithful Tom. One of his first visits was to Mrs. Emmerson, who received him in the most affectionate manner, and invited him to dine daily at her house. The invitation was freely accepted, and Clare for some time spent his afternoon and the early part of the evening regularly at the lady's house at Stratford Place, Oxford Street. Clare here met again his old friend and patron, Lord Radstock, besides a goodly number of the literary and artistic celebrities of the day. He found few friends, or men he liked, among the authors; but more among the painters into whose company he was thrown. With some of them he struck an intimate acquaintance, particularly with Mr. Rippingille, an artist of some note in his day. The latter was very fond of long rambles through London, and very fond of pale ale, too; and Clare sharing both these likings, the two were constantly together. Many an evening, after leaving Mrs. Emmerson's house—which happened, nearly always, immediately after dinner—the artist and poet set out together on a journey of exploration, visiting unknown parts of the metropolis, the haunts of thieves and vagabonds. When getting tired of this amusement, they directed their researches into other quarters, inspecting all the small theatres, exhibitions, and concert rooms, down to the very lowest. The progress of this movement was interrupted by an unexpected event. One evening, when visiting the Regency Theatre, in Tottenham Court Road, both were fascinated by the charms of a beautiful young actress, a native of France, figuring in the play-bills as Mademoiselle Dalia. Clare's susceptible heart took fire at once; and friend Rippingille was not behind in the sudden burst of his affections. They both vowed eternal love to the fair actress, and, as a commencement, Rippingille drew her portrait, after the dictate of his fancy, while Clare added to it a passionate effusion in verse. The artistic-poetical gift was duly despatched to Mademoiselle Dalia, but elicited no reply. Night after night, poet and painter took their seat within the temple of the muses in Tottenham Court Road; but night after night they waited in vain for a glance from the beautiful eyes of Mademoiselle Dalia, although they had taken care to inform her that they were sitting, arm in arm, in front of the pit. The neglect of Mademoiselle preyed upon their minds; they pined away, the two friends, and drank more pale ale than ever.

Clare's excursions with his friend kept him generally till after midnight from his residence, which was a great source of annoyance to the methodical bookseller of Fleet Street. Mr. Thomas Hood thereupon got instructions to tell Clare that early hours would be more acceptable to his host; which instructions were communicated by commission, in due business course, through the faithful Tom, the head-porter. Clare felt offended, and informed Mrs. Emmerson of what had happened; making a full confession of his sorrows, even those concerning the too beautiful Mademoiselle Dalia. Mrs. Emmerson deeply sympathised with her poetical friend, telling him at the same time that he would be welcome to stay at her house if he liked. The offer was accepted, and Clare marched back straightway to Fleet Street, gathered his property, including the boots, within the coloured pocket-handkerchief, and came back in triumph to Stratford Place. That same evening, thinking himself more at liberty in his new quarters, he undertook a somewhat longer excursion with Mr. Rippingille. After staying punctually through the performance in the Tottenham Court Road Theatre, sighing over the enchanting looks of Mademoiselle, the friends adjourned to a neighbouring public-house, and from thence to a tavern known as Offley's, famous for its Burton ale. The ale was unusually good this evening, and the company too was unusually good, which combined attraction made the friends remain in their place till long after their wonted time. Talking about poetry and high art,

and talking still more about Mademoiselle Dalia and her
angelic charms, the hours slipped away like minutes, and the
first rosy clouds of a bright June morning began to appear in
the east before they were able to quit Offley's hospitable roof.
Shaking hands once more at the door, Rippingille took his
way, with somewhat faltering step, to his lodgings in Oxford Street; while Clare, rather more steady in his gait,
went straight to Mrs. Emmerson's residence. He discovered
Stratford Place with the help of a sympathetic watchman;
but was unable to get an entrance into his temporary home.
Mrs. Emmerson, after waiting for her guest till towards the
dawn of day, had gone to bed, thinking that he might have
taken his way back to his old quarters in Fleet Street. The
combined efforts of Clare and the friendly watchman having
proved fruitless to get into the house, nothing remained but
to seek some other shelter. But there were no places open
anywhere, and the poet, beginning to feel very tired, resolved
to take the advice of his companion, and creep into the inside
of a hackney coach, drawn up in a yard. The kind watchman carefully shut the door, and Clare, finding the place un-
commonly snug and comfortable, fell asleep immediately.

Sweet dreams soon filled the mind of the poet. There
came visions of green fields decked with flowers; of large
banqueting rooms thronged with beautiful ladies; and of
theatres crowded by joyous multitudes; and right in the
midst of all these apparitions stood the enchanting fairy of
Tottenham Court Road. She approached him; she pierced
his heart with a smile of her dark eyes; at last she kissed
him. The touch of her lips was like an electric shock, and
he sprang to his feet. But he could not stand; something
was moving under him. He rubbed his eyes; rubbed them
again and again; and at last discovered that he was inside a
square box, drawn along by two horses. Gradually the events
of the past day and night arose from out the mist of his
dreams and fancies, and he began to be conscious that he was

sitting in the identical hackney coach into which his friend, the watchman, had put him. The difficulty settled as to how he got in, there came the more perplexing question as to how he should get out again. The coachman was evidently un-aware of the presence of a poet in his box, and a too sudden revelation of the fact, Clare feared, might produce the worst consequences. Viewed from the back, he seemed a grim, ferocious-looking fellow, the terrible driver of the hackney-coach. He kept whipping his horses continually, and faster and faster the vehicle jolted along, Clare hiding his face in the cushions, in bitter anguish of heart. At last the coach stopped in front of a public-house. A fervent prayer arose in the mind of the traveller that his coachman would go inside and take something to drink. Part of the prayer was fulfilled, for the man did take something to drink, though he did not go inside. A lounger at the gate, with whom he seemed on familiar terms, appeared in a moment with a glass in his hand, containing a steaming liquid, which the man with the whip gulped down in an instant, and then prepared to ascend his seat again. But Clare now began to think that he had travelled far enough, and, in a desperate leap, jumped out of his coach, and nearly overturned the astonished driver. The latter, however, had him by the collar in an instant, crying, 'And who are you?' Clare tried to explain; in-troducing himself as author of 'Poems of Rural Life,' and the 'Village Minstrel,' in two volumes, with engravings. But the hackney man, learning these facts, frowned more grimly than ever, his mind evidently full of grave doubts. After short reflection, he carefully examined the inside of the coach, and giving his victim a good shake, asked him how much money he had in his possession. Clare, trembling all over, took out his purse, and found he had ten shillings and a few pence. The terrible coachman grasped the purse, gave the owner a slap on the back as a receipt, and with a valedictory 'Go along, you scamp!' dismissed the unhappy

poet.   John Clare felt faint and ready to sink to the ground ;
but fear gave him courage, and he ran away as fast as he could.
It was not long before he discovered that he was, after all, not
far from his dwelling in Stratford Place.   Having obtained
entrance, he sank down utterly exhausted in an arm-chair,
to the intense astonishment of Mrs. Emmerson.

When Clare had somewhat recovered himself, the questioning commenced.   Although reluctant to tell his whole
story, his vigilant hostess extracted it piece by piece, and
finally broke out into an immoderate fit of laughter.   Clare
was surprised, and somewhat offended ; but felt too weak
for opposition or remonstrance.   Even his desire that the
affair should be kept as secret as possible was met with
renewed merriment, the reply being that, before saying more,
he should take some refreshment.   A good luncheon, with
liberal supply of sherry, had the effect of bringing Clare's feelings more in accordance with those of Mrs. Emmerson.   He
was himself inclined to laugh at his droll adventure in the
hackney coach, and thought he should be ready almost to
shake hands with the terrible driver.   In this vein of good
humour, Mrs. Emmerson got ready permission to tell his
curious adventure to whomsoever she liked—even in his
presence at the dinner-table.   The stipulation was fulfilled
to the letter.   There was a grand party that evening at Mrs.
Emmerson's house, and, towards the end of the entertainment, when all were in good spirits, the fair hostess told
the story of the poet in the hackney coach.   She told it in
good dramatic style, embellishing it a little, and heightening
the effect of some of the incidents.   But she was not allowed
to tell it uninterruptedly.   There broke forth such a storm
of laughter on all sides as seemed to shake the very table,
and not a few of the guests appeared absolutely convulsed
with merriment.   Clare good-humouredly joined in the
general hilarity, for which he was recompensed by having
his health drunk, with full bumpers, by the whole assembly.

After which, in special honour of Clare's ingenious method of declaring his identity to a hackney coachman, there came, amidst universal delight, another toast to 'The Village Minstrel in London.'

At the house of Mrs. Emmerson, Clare stayed about a week, and then accepted an invitation of the Rev. H. T. Cary, the translator of Dante, who had met him previously at Mr. Taylor's office. Mr. Cary was living at Chiswick, in an old ivy-covered mansion, formerly inhabited by Sir James Thornhill, the painter, and after him by his famous son-in-law, Hogarth. Clare spent some pleasant days here, his kind host pointing out to him various memorials connected with the great satirist and moralist—the window through which Hogarth eloped with old Thornhill's only daughter; the place where he painted the 'Rake's Progress;' and the spot in the garden where he buried his faithful dog, with the inscription, 'Life to the last enjoyed, here Pompey lies.' There were agreeable excursions, too, from Chiswick to the neighbouring places, particularly to Richmond, where Clare visited Thompson's monument on the hill, as well as his tombstone in the old church, which, covered as it was with cobwebs, he thought much less beautiful than that of Hogarth's dog. It was Clare's intention to stop at least a week with his kind host at Chiswick, but an awkward circumstance occasioned his departure at the end of a few days. The reverend translator of Dante's 'Inferno' introduced his guest in a careless sort of way to his house, without presenting the various members of his family, and the consequence was that Clare fell into a grievous mistake from the beginning. Mr. Cary had several grown-up children, and a beautiful young wife, looking of the same age as his daughters. In the round of excitement through which he had gone, and with his head still full of the charming Mademoiselle Dalia, of Tottenham Court Road, Clare thought it incumbent upon him to write verses at the old ivy-covered

mansion, the more so as the owner had emphatically introduced him as author of 'I love thee, sweet Mary.' So he
began by penning delicate sonnets, dedicated to the lady
whom he deemed the fairest of the daughters of the Rev.
Mr. Cary, or, in point of fact, to his wife. Mrs. Cary, on
getting the first poetical epistle, held it to be a declaration
of love, and, very properly, burnt the paper. But getting
a second piece of poetry, somewhat mystic in expression, she
showed it to her husband, who, being an elderly gentleman with a wig, got very excited over the matter. He
took Clare aside on the instant, telling him, with much
warmth, that it was not the custom at Chiswick to make
love to other men's wives, and that, however much he
admired his sonnets, he did not like his mode of distri-
buting them. Clare was thunderstruck on learning that he
had been addressing Mrs. Cary instead of the fair daughter
of the house, and, for a moment, was almost unable to
speak. Recovering himself, he stammered forth his simple
tale, hiding nothing, nor trying to excuse his conduct. It
was impossible to listen and not believe his words. The
Rev. Mr. Cary perceived at once the ridiculous error into
which he had fallen, and shaking Clare's hand in a most
affectionate manner, bade him think no more of the whole
affair, and for the future distribute as many specimens of his
poetry as he liked to his wife and daughters. Clare fully
appreciated the kindness which dictated this offer ; however,
he thought that it was impossible for him to stop any longer
at the house. He insisted upon leaving at once, and Mr. Cary,
finding all his persuasions fruitless, accompanied him back to
London. It was Clare's intention to return to Helpston immediately, but going to the shop of his publishers in Fleet
Street, he heard that Octavius Gilchrist had arrived the
previous day, and wished to see him. He therefore took up
his quarters once more at the house of Mr. Taylor.

The great battle with the Bowles' family and the book-

grinding windmills had made poor Mr. Gilchrist really and
seriously ill.   The doctors of Stamford shook their heads,
talking of nervous affection, of change of air, and of rest from
the cares of grocery and literature.   With every succeeding
day, the men of science got to look more and more mournful,
until the patient felt as if he was going already through the
process of being buried.   One morning, thereupon, he took
a desperate resolution.   Although ordered not to leave his
room on any account, he went to the stage coach, engaged the
box-seat, and bravely rode up to London.   Mr. Gilchrist was
really fond of Clare, and had no sooner arrived than he went
in search of him.   Clare consented to stay a little longer in
town, partly at the house of Mr. John Taylor, and partly at
that of Herr Burkhardt, Mr. Gilchrist's brother-in-law.   The
jolly watchmaker in the Strand was overjoyed on seeing his
rural friend again, fancying to get another opportunity to show
the lions of London.   But Clare soon proved to him that by
this time he knew more about the big metropolis, its theatres
and concert-rooms, its taverns and alehouses, and even its
beggars' and thieves' slums, than many a native of Cockaigne,
and Herr Burkhardt, therefore, was compelled, much against
his wish, to leave him alone.   Mr. Rippingille having meanwhile taken his departure for Bristol, vainly trying to persuade
his friend to follow him thither, Clare was left almost entirely
in the company of Mr. Gilchrist.   The latter introduced him
to a great many of his acquaintances ; first and foremost to
Mr. William Gifford.   Clare felt somewhat abashed when
admitted into the presence of the renowned editor of the
' Quarterly Review,' whose pen had so much contributed to his
rise in the world.   Mr. Gifford, who was sitting on a couch,
surrounded by an immense quantity of books and papers,
received the poet in a very friendly manner, making some
judicious remarks about the ' Village Minstrel,' which he
declared to be vastly superior to the ' Poems of Rural
Life.'   This gave Clare courage, and he freely entered into a

lengthened conversation, in the course of which the editor
of the 'Quarterly' took care to warn him, with much em-
phasis, to be on his guard against booksellers and publishers.
Leaving Mr. Gifford, Octavius Gilchrist, somewhat maliciously,
took his friend direct to one of the dreaded class of publishers
against which he had just been warned. They went to the
house of Mr. Murray, in Albemarle Street, in front of which
stood a number of brilliant carriages. Mr. Gilchrist and his
friend had to wait some time in an anteroom; but, once
admitted, both were received with great cordiality. Clare
was much pleased with the simple, hearty manner of the great
patron of literature; and the pleasure appeared to be mutual,
for Mr. Murray, in his turn, began to converse in a very unrestrained manner, and, on leaving, bade Clare never to come
to London without seeing him. Quitting the house in
Albemarle Street, Clare ran right against Mr. Gifford, who
was coming up the steps. Both apologised, and both felt
somewhat confused concerning the thankless old business of
giving and taking advice.

During the remaining part of his stay in London, Clare
was much in company with Mr. Thomas Hood. The genial
sub-editor of the 'London Magazine' had found out by this
time that Mr. Taylor's guest was something more than a
mere spinner of verses and glorifier of daisies and butter-
cups, and, having made this discovery, he got anxious to
be in Clare's company. The acquaintance soon grew
intimate, and Clare followed his new friend wherever he
chose to take him. First on the list stood the house
of Mr. Charles Lamb, to which they went on a pilgrimage
late one evening. 'Elia' was in splendid good humour;
comfortably ensconced in a large arm-chair, with a huge
decanter at his right hand, and a huge bronze snuff-box,
from which he continually helped himself, on his left.
Clare having been formally introduced, Charles Lamb took
a whole handful of snuff, and falling back in his arm-

chair, stuttered out an atrocious pun concerning rural poets and hackney coaches. Seeing that his guest looked somewhat displeased, he took him under closer treatment at his right hand, and with the help of the big decanter, soon put him into excessive good humour. The conversation now became general, and Clare thought he had never met with such an agreeable companion as the great 'Elia.' Till late at night, the drinking and talking continued, until at last Charles Lamb's sister, the motherly Bridget, came into the room, delivering an eloquent lecture upon the value of sobriety. When Clare looked serious: 'Do ... do ... don't be offended, my boy,' quoth Charles, 'we all know the virtue of rustic swine—I me ... me ... mean of a rustic swain!' Which saying, 'Elia' pushed on his decanter. But it was too much for Clare. 'I must *goo*,' he said. And go he did accordingly.

The return journey to Stamford which Clare and Octavius Gilchrist had arranged to make together, was made impossible, on the part of the latter, by his continued illness. In order to find absolute rest, together with kind attention, Mr. Gilchrist resolved to go on a lengthened visit to two of his brothers at Richmond, in Surrey. Having stayed already more than a month in London, Clare now had to think of returning, which he did after taking solemn farewell from all his old and new friends. Faithful Tom Benyon, on a sunny morning in June, carried the poet's well-stocked handkerchief, with the boots, to the 'George and Blue Boar,' in Holborn, and the streets were just beginning to swarm with life, when the Stamford coach went rolling through them into the green fields. Clare was the only outside passenger, besides a stout elderly gentleman who went as far as Islington. The stout person had seen Clare somewhere before, and, being extremely pleased to meet a famous poet on such a fine morning in June, ordered brandy and water at three successive taverns where the coach stopped for passengers. The effect was such that Clare went to sleep on his seat, and, having been carefully strapped to the cushion by the experienced guard, slept all the way to Stamford—last result of a visit to the great metropolis.

DARKENING CLOUDS.

Clare's second excursion to London was productive of many evil consequences. From the first trip he returned with a renewed love for the simple life of the country, and a renewed desire to spend his days peacefully in his humble cottage, earning bread and health by hard labour in the fields; but from this new visit he came back with wild visions of glory and fame, a restless, fretful, discontented man. A feeling he had never before known now got hold of him—the silent dread of poverty. The month he had stayed in London, sitting down every day at a well-filled table, moving every day and night among bright and genial men, among beautiful and intelligent women, had opened to him a new mode of life of which he had scarcely been conscious before. His vivid imagination painted it even brighter than it was in reality. He did not see, and could not see, the petty cares and miseries hidden behind all the brilliant scenes which met his eyes; and though he discovered the great truth in course of time, he was not aware as yet that real happiness is found distributed with tolerable equality among all ranks and classes. But John Clare was only getting towards thirty, and not yet a philosopher. Returning to his humble home, he fondly kissed his wife and little girl, and fondly embraced his aged father and mother; but the first transport of love gone, he sat down moody and discontented. During his absence large parcels of books, the presents of old and new friends, had arrived at Helpston, and, eagerly as he looked over the volumes, particularly those of poetry, his heart grew sad in thinking that there was nobody near to share his pleasures with him. While in London he had become accustomed to constant conversation on poetical and artistic subjects, his daily routine being to spend his mornings in reading all the new works within his reach, and during the afternoons and evenings to discuss the matters treated in these books. It seemed a terrible want to miss these delights on returning to his narrow home. He felt it, for the first time, as a personal affliction and source of misery that his wife was unable to read and write; that his parents were talking of nothing but their illness and physical sufferings, and that all the inmates of his home alike had no more sympathy with him and his poetical joys and sorrows than if they had been inhabitants of another world. It seemed to him as if he had been banished from the Eden of intellect into a lower and grosser existence, and every letter and every book he received had but the effect of making him more sad and fretful. He had not been long at home when there came a richly-bound volume, inscribed on the title-page, 'The gift of Admiral Lord Radstock to his dear and excellent friend, John Clare, August 1st, 1822.' The gift gave him no pleasure, but, awakening thoughts of the past and the present, only brought tears into his eyes.

The reaction from this unmanly and morbid state of feeling came in time, and Clare's pride and native strength of mind got the better of his sickly yearning after lost pleasures. Nevertheless, one lasting source of unhappiness remained. He found that his regular income of forty-five pounds a year, secured to him by his friends and patrons, was quite insufficient, with his new wants and desires, to cover his expenditure, and the profits derived from his books being fluctuating and altogether inconsiderable, he experienced the worst pangs of poverty in the terrible knowledge of being constantly in debt. To improve his position, he formed a thousand plans, some practicable and some visionary; but

all equally barren as to the net result. The first and most
natural idea that occurred to him was to write as many
verses as possible and to sell them immediately. In order
to effect this, and seeing the very moderate success of his
last published two volumes, he resolved to print his poems
separately, and offer them to readers in this form. Mr.
Drury, to whom he communicated this somewhat singular
plan, approved it, suggesting at the same time to have the
poetry set to music. This struck Clare as exceedingly
appropriate, and he set to work at once to produce a liberal
supply of verses. He began with such eagerness as to
bring forth no less than seventy-six poems in less than
three weeks; and though physically and mentally exhausted
by this effort, he felt exceedingly joyful and buoyed up by
bright anticipations of the future, when handing the whole
of these manuscripts to Mr. Drury. But hard as was the
toil, and prodigal the waste of mental power, it absolutely
came to nothing. Mr. Drury, having entered into arrangements with a small publisher in Paternoster Row, despatched
the poems to London, and a number of them were set to
music by Mr. Crouch, and issued on picturesque sheets of
paper, with flaming dedications to fashionable singers, and
to supposed generous noblemen, patrons of all the arts.
Clare was much surprised on seeing his verses turn up in
this unexpected shape; however, he consoled himself with·
the hope, in which he was strongly backed by Mr. Drury,
that the profits on his poetry would be as bounteous as the
expenditure of gold and colours upon the picturesque sheets.
But, to his utter dismay, he got no payment whatever for his
verses. All applications to Paternoster Row proved ineffectual to secure even the return of the verses not printed,
which were found afterwards coming to the surface in
albums, reviews, and periodicals, in wonderful disguises and
with new names attached. To crown the misfortune, Clare
received a reproachful letter from Mr. John Taylor, com-

plaining of his connexion with Mr. Crouch and the flaming
dedications, and intimating that these dealings with small
composers and publishers would damage his reputation.
Clare felt utterly dejected at the result of the whole speculation, although it gained him the valuable experience that
able as he was to write verses, he was utterly unable to
convert them into money and bread.

Having recovered from this great disappointment, Clare
resolved upon another experiment for getting a living, and,
provisionally, getting out of debt. He thought that if he
could become the possessor of a small farm, not so extensive
as to require the use of valuable stock and cattle, but large
enough to produce food for his family, with something to
sell at the market-town, he should be able, together with his
annuity, to place himself in a respectable and comparatively
independent position. This was an excellent idea, and had
it been realized, might have saved Clare from despondency
and final ruin. Unfortunately, its realization, though easy
at one moment, depended not upon the poet, but upon his
patronizing friends, who proved painfully lukewarm at this
momentous period of his life. It so happened that in the
winter of 1822-3, an opportunity offered itself for acquiring
a piece of freehold land of about seven acres, close to the
poet's cottage, known to the people of Helpston as 'Bachelors'
Hall,' and already noticed as belonging to two brothers of the
name of Billing. The brothers were somewhat improvident,
leading gay bachelors' lives ; and, getting into debt gradually,
they were compelled at last to mortgage their small property
to a Jew for the sum of two hundred pounds. For some
years, the interest was duly paid, but this failing at last, on
account of the growing infirmity of the brothers, the Jew
stepped in, threatening to sell the property. This roused
Clare to a desperate effort for raising the necessary sum to
pay off the mortgage, and, by acquiring the small estate,
benefit both himself and his staunch old friends, the brothers

Billing. The latter agreed to let him have 'Bachelors' Hall' with its seven acres, on condition of discharging the encumbrance, and allowing them a very small sum for the remaining few years of their lives, which they intended spending with some relatives in a neighbouring village. The offer was a very favourable one, and the more so as freehold property was extremely scarce at Helpston, the ground being, as in most agricultural counties, the property of a few large landowners. The more Clare thought upon the subject, the more anxious did he become to enter upon the proposed arrangement, and, in settling on this little piece of ground, shape his whole future career into a more fixed direction. But his boundless anxiety met with no assistance on the part of those who called themselves his friends. Though it was for the first time in his life that he claimed help for himself, he, to his immense distress, found all doors resolutely closed against him.

To get the two hundred pounds required to pay off the mortgage upon 'Bachelors' Hall,' Clare addressed himself first to Lord Radstock, whom he looked upon as one of his warmest and most sincere friends. What he asked was not to lend him the money, but to take it from the sum standing in his name in the funds. To Clare's surprise, Lord Radstock told him that this could not be done, as the four hundred and twenty pounds were invested in the name of trustees, who had no power to withdraw any portion of this amount. Clare looked upon this as a personal humiliation, fancying that he was treated like a child, or like a man not responsible for his own actions, and deeming the refusal a new attempt to keep him in leading strings. For a moment, Clare felt quite angry with his noble patron, who, he thought, might have easily advanced him the small sum of money had he so liked. The explanation was that Lord Radstock, like most other of Clare's patrons, was entirely ignorant of the poet's character, regarding him in the light of a genial infant, full of intellect, but without strength of character. What chiefly produced this impression on his lordship, otherwise decidedly the truest friend of the poet, was that Clare, notwithstanding repeated advice to that effect, had neglected to make a good arrangement, or, in fact, any arrangement at all, with his publishers, so that he stood to them in the position of a helpless client. Probably, Lord Radstock reasoned that as his friend had shown himself thus unable to carry on the ordinary affairs of life, he would not be better qualified to be the manager of a farm, although one of only seven acres. In consequence, he not only refused to get the two hundred pounds, but strongly advised Clare to have nothing to do with the purchase of 'Bachelors' Hall.' The poet saw through the motives which dictated this advice, and keenly felt the distrust and want of appreciation of him whom he held to be one of the best of his friends.

Much downcast, however, as Clare was by Lord Radstock's refusal, he did not give up the struggle for his great object. His next attempt was to get the required sum of two hundred pounds from his publishers, to whom he offered, in return, a sort of mortgage on his writings, for a period to come. He addressed himself to Mr. John Taylor in a very pathetic letter, vehement almost in the anxiety manifested to gain the little plot of land, and thus become an independent man. 'The cottage with land,' he wrote to Mr. Taylor, in a letter bearing date January 31, 1823, 'is a beautiful spot of six or seven acres. There are crowds for it if it be sold; but if I could get hold of the mortgage, it would be mine, and still doing a kindness to a friend. I should like to alter it into Poet's Hall, instead of its old name of Bachelor's Hall, which must soon be extinct if I don't succeed. I'll do this way if you like. I'll sell you my writings for five years for that sum, which can't be dear.' Fervent though this appeal was, it left the great publisher in Fleet Street very cold. Mr. Taylor replied, with some sarcasm, that he could not see what put the ambition into Clare's head to become a 'landed proprietor.' Very likely, Mr. Taylor thought it would raise the cost price of the verses, if they were to be manufactured at a 'Poet's Hall.' Therefore, while declining to advance the two hundred pounds, he told his friend, in a long letter, not to be ambitious, but to remain in the state in which God had placed him. The counsel was seasoned, somewhat unnecessarily, by quotations from the Bible.

'Bachelors' Hall' did not become 'Poet's Hall,' but went to the Jew. Clare, seeing all his efforts vain, sunk into a state of low despondency, followed by a long and serious illness. It was the turning period of the poet's life. His career, hitherto, had been strange and anomalous. Tossed about on the surging waves of existence, now in deepest poverty, and now again amidst wealth and splendour, he was beginning to feel weary and faint-hearted, doubting whether he should ever be able to reach the haven of rest and of ease. At the age of thirty now he fancied he had a glimpse of this blissful haven. He felt, and the feeling was undoubtedly just, that the possession of a small independent property would secure to him the much-wanted support in life, not only as furnishing him with additional means of subsistence, but in raising his mental energies, dependent hitherto upon the fitful accidents connected with his position of farm-labourer. His fancy painted to him, in glowing colours, how happy he should be in his roomy 'Poet's Hall,' standing on his own land, 'a beautiful spot of six or seven acres,' full of flowers and fruit trees, with hedges of roses and laurel, and songbirds nestling under the green leaves. No more necessity, then, to take his visitors to the public-house for entertainment; no more necessity to hide in hollow trees in the wood, seeking poetical inspiration; no more necessity to go about, with downcast look, among the insolent farmers, in that most humiliating of all pursuits, asking for work. A charm to even the coarsest minds, the overwhelming consciousness of being *owner* of a fraction of the surface of great mother earth, had countless allurements to the poet. He knew it would not only raise him in the world, but would make him a better, a nobler, a wiser man. Yet for all that, and though the haven was so near, he was not allowed to reach it. With patrons in abundance, there was not one willing to advance the small sum of two hundred pounds, which, he said, would make him happy for life; with friends who praised his genius to the skies, there were none who thought it safe to entrust him with the means for purchasing independence otherwise than 'under trustees.' The patrons and friends admired the poet's genius, but they never forgot that he was a 'Northamptonshire peasant,' the son of a pauper. As such, even kind Mr. John Taylor thought proper to preach humility, and refer the 'Village Minstrel' to the Bible.

With the failure of all his schemes, the great truth began to dawn upon Clare that he was destined, notwithstanding all his friends and patrons, to remain a farmer's drudge and poetical pauper; destined to plough and thresh for others, and, in his spare hours, to make pretty songs for ladies and gentlemen—something better than a clown, and something less than a lackey in uniform. Clare was meek and accustomed to suffering, yet for a long time he could not reconcile himself to the thought that this was part of 'the eternal fitness of things.' So he chafed and fretted under his new burthen of sorrow, and finding it weigh too heavily upon his heart, again sought forgetfulness in the wretched refuge open at the tavern. He drank not much, for he was too poor to do so, at this moment; but even the small quantity of ale or spirits which he imbibed to drown his mental anguish acted like poison upon a weak and ailing body, now more than usually debilitated by insufficient food. In the winter of 1823, Clare found himself almost penniless; yet with inborn

loftiness of mind, he hid the fact from his family, so as not
to distress them.   His wife and parents, therefore, lived as
well as ever, while he, to save expenditure, got into the habit
of absenting himself at meal-times, pretending to call upon
friends and acquaintances.   Instead of doing so, he went
forth into the fields, munching a dry crust of bread, and,
when breaking down under hunger and fatigue, crept to the
'Blue Bell' for a glass of ale.   Such a diet, always fatal, was
doubly so after the liberal style of living to which he had
got accustomed in London, and which he had kept up for
some time after, as long as his hope lasted to get payment for
the poems delivered to Mr. Drury, as well as for others contributed to the 'London Magazine.'   When these sources failed,
and the succeeding schemes to acquire 'Bachelors' Hall'
broke down one after another, there was bitter want staring
him in the face, to stave off which he resolved to make an
application to one of his first and best friends, Mr. Gilchrist.
It seemed impossible that help, and, what was almost as
precious under the circumstances, good advice, should be
wanting from this quarter.

Mr. Gilchrist had been absent from Stamford for a long
time.   His illness, which first seemed slight, and merely due
to temporary overwork, had taken a more serious turn after
his journey to London, chiefly in consequence of a severe
cold caught on the outside of the coach.   It was for this
reason that he was advised to seek rest and strength at the
house of his brother, living, with some members of his family,
at Richmond.   Retired to this new home, it seemed for a
while as if he was getting better; but the old spirit for jour-
nalistic controversy stirring within him, he took pen in hand
as soon as he felt sufficient strength, which brought on a fresh
attack of the disease.   Hasty and impatient in all his movements, he now refused to submit any longer to the treatment
prescribed by his medical advisers.   He fancied that absolute
quiet did him more harm than good, by weakening his energy

of mind, and, expressing this to his friends, he, notwithstanding their earnest opposition, left Richmond at the
beginning of 1823. It was a severe winter; all the streams
and rivers being thickly frozen, and the roads covered many
feet deep with snow. Under these circumstances, a journey
from Surrey into Lincolnshire was no easy undertaking,
particularly to an invalid; and when Mr. Gilchrist arrived
at his own home, he found that his illness was so much
aggravated that he was scarcely able to move. John Clare,
on the first news of his friend's arrival, hurried up to Stamford. He had long wished to see him and to speak to him,
under the impression that if he could have had his advice,
his own circumstances would have taken a very different turn.
At present, it was his intention to lay before Mr. Gilchrist a
clear statement of his affairs, entreating him to act as a guide
in his difficulties, and, as a beginning, to assist him with a
small loan, so as to enable him to pay off the most pressing
of his debts, and purchase a few necessaries for his family.
Clare had been ill for some weeks when setting out for Stamford; however, he forced himself from his bed of sickness,
and slowly crept along the frozen snow-covered road. He
reached at length the well-known shop in the High Street;
but was surprised, on coming face to face with Mr. Gilchrist,
to see that he was far worse than himself. Mr. Gilchrist
received Clare with a smile, yet was scarcely able to speak,
lying on his couch in utter prostration, physical and mental.
Clare felt moved by infinite compassion, and, forgetting all
his own sufferings, asked what he could do for his friend.
The patient again smiled; he would soon be better, he said;
there was nothing the matter with him, except a slight rheumatic fever and a little overwork. Mr. Gilchrist then inquired
after his friend's circumstances, and got replies similar to his
own. Clare, too, would have it that he was quite well, and,
on being questioned, accounted for his hollow cheeks and
sunken eyes as due to previous attacks of his old enemy, the

ague. Of his embarrassed circumstances he said nothing;
no more than of all the other matters he had come to discuss,
nobly thinking that such a discussion might do harm to his
friend in his feeble state. He even refused some slight
refreshment, in order not to give trouble; but, seeing the
waning day, took his farewell, dragging himself with great
difficulty back to his cottage, along the dark road covered
with snow and ice. It was late when he arrived, his weakness, partly owing to want of nourishment, having compelled
him to sit down, every few minutes, on the lonely high road.
Entering his hut, his mind seemed wandering; he muttered
incoherent words, and crept to his bed, from which he did
not arise for months to come.

There was little intercommunication at this time between
Stamford, Helpston, and London. Mr. Gilchrist's literary
friends scarcely knew of the serious turn his illness had
taken, and as for Clare, his name was scarcely ever mentioned. Entirely ignorant of the great art of 'keeping before
the public,' he had no sooner become known than he fell
again into oblivion, from which even his warmest admirers
did little to rescue him. Clare's correspondence with his
publishers, too, had lapsed after his unsuccessful attempt to
get the small sum of money for the purchase of a freehold;
and they were entirely ignorant that he was lying ill in his
little hut, and almost dying. For a while, Clare's indis-
position seemed quite as serious, if not more so, than that
of Mr. Gilchrist. However, under the tender care of his
wife and his aged mother, the poet rallied gradually, and in
the month of April he was able once more to walk to Stamford, and inquire after the health of his friend. He was not
admitted, this time; but the servant, in reply to his inquiries,
told him that Mr. Gilchrist was getting better. Clare was
still extremely weak, and could not come back till at the end
of a month, when he had the satisfaction of seeing his friend,
and hearing from his own lips that he was gradually advancing

to recovery. Thus reassured, and not willing to intrude himself more than necessary, he remained quietly for another month, and, feeling now almost restored to health, walked with brisk step to Stamford. It was a glorious summer morning—date, the last day of June, 1823. The green fields glistened in the sunshine, and the nightingale sang in Burghley Park; more beautiful, the poet fancied, than he had ever known her sing before. He felt full of joy, in the glow of newly-recovered health, and, while walking along the sunny path, kept revelling in golden day-dreams, in none of which the image of his dear friend Gilchrist was wanting. Thus he got into the old town of Stamford, and before the familiar shop, which, to his surprise, was closed. He knocked, and a female servant opened the door. The girl stared Clare full in the face, and slowly said : 'Mr. Gilchrist died an hour ago.'

PHYSIC AND PHYSICIANS.

The parish doctor of Helpston was called in to see John Clare on the first day of July. Mrs. Clare gave it as her opinion that her husband had worked too hard, by writing verses day and night, and thus had brought on the mysterious illness which confined him to bed. Clare himself could not explain his exact condition ; he only intimated that it was a sort of stupor, which came over him at intervals, like an apoplectic fit. The doctor shook his head, looked very learned, and promised to send something to cure the disease. He was as good as his word ; for a messenger brought the same evening two large bottles, containing a greyish fluid, with directions to take portions of it at stated times. Clare obeyed the order, but did not get better; on the contrary, his fits of stupor became more frequent and his lassitude more overwhelming. He was lying on his bed, almost unconscious, on the fifth day of July, when a visitor entered the cottage. It was

Mr. Taylor, of Fleet Street, who had been to the funeral of
his friend Gilchrist, and, returning, passed through Helpston.
He was surprised and alarmed at the sight which met his
eyes, and set to work immediately to render all the assistance
in his power. Messengers were despatched in various directions for medical aid, and Mr. Taylor himself watched at
the bedside till they returned. The doctors came, but only
repeated what the parish surgeon had said already; they
proposed to send some medicine at once, and afterwards
to 'observe the symptoms.' It required no great penetration
to see that these medicine-men knew less of Clare's disease
than the patient himself; and Mr. Taylor, having come to
this conclusion, looked forth in other directions. He told
Mrs. Clare that he was unable to stay longer, having to
return to London the same day; but that he would take the
road by Peterborough, and send the best medical aid from
that place. The Peterborough physician arrived late at night,
when Clare felt a little better—having left off taking the
greyish concoction—and was able to explain the particulars
of his illness. The new doctor ordered absolute rest, plenty
of fresh air, and some nourishing food; all which being
provided, a visible improvement began to manifest itself.
There was some difficulty in getting the second part of the
prescription, the fresh air, Clare's narrow bedroom having no
ventilation whatever. The energetic doctor, however, got
over the obstacle by the simple expedient of knocking a
brick out of the top of the wall, which furnished a channel
sufficiently large to let in the warm summer air. Perhaps
this thrown-out brick, as much as anything else, saved the
life of the poet.

Under the treatment of the Peterborough physician,
Clare's health improved greatly, though it was a long time
before he was able to leave the room. His brain was haunted
by fantastic visions, reflecting all the scenes of his past life,
and mingling together his doings in the lime-kiln of Cas-

terton, the fields of Helpston, and the gilded saloons of
London. In the midst of this phantom existence there
came the report that Robert Bloomfield had breathed his
last, in utter poverty and misery, broken down alike by
physical want and mental suffering. The news made a deep
impression upon Clare. He had never personally met the
author of the 'Farmer's Boy,' yet looked upon him almost
as a brother, feeling that his career was not unlike his own
in its chief incidents. A shudder came over him now in
reflecting that his end might be as terribly sad as that of the
brother poet. Full of this thought, he composed, on his bed
of sickness, a sonnet, dedicated 'to the memory of Bloomfield,' expressing his conviction that 'the tide of fashion is
a stream too strong for pastoral brooks that gently flow and
sing.' After this sudden effort, there came a relapse, not
without danger for some time. The medical gentleman,
while carefully watching all the symptoms of the disease,
now began to fear that he would be unable to master it, and
wrote to this effect to Mr. Taylor, entreating him to use
his influence to get Clare removed to some hospital, or other
house where he might have the necessary attention. In the
letter it was stated without disguise that the illness of the
poet was mainly the effect of poverty. His dwelling, the
Peterborough physician argued, was altogether unfit for a
human habitation, being dark, damp, and ill ventilated, with
a space so circumscribed as to be worse than a prison for
the two families. He insisted, therefore, that to make
recovery possible a better home should be found for Clare
himself, and, if possible, for his wife and child, pending the
removal of his aged and suffering parents. A copy of this
note the writer sent to Lord Radstock, knowing that his
lordship had taken, from the beginning, a deep interest in
Clare's welfare.

The appeal, energetic and well-meant as it was, had no
result whatever. Mr. Taylor even thought it presumptuous

on the part of the provincial doctor to give his counsel as well
as his medicine, and wrote to Clare an order to dispense with
his attendance, and come up to London to be cured. This
was impossible, under the circumstances, Clare being so weak
as to be unable to leave the room. Fortunately, the good
Samaritan of Peterborough did not leave him at this critical
position, but seeing that neither Mr. Taylor nor Lord
Radstock felt inclined to do anything for his charge, determined to undertake the task himself. Soliciting help from
some wealthy persons in the neighbourhood, he set to to collect a small sum of money, by means of which he procured
a regular supply of strengthening food for his patient. The
winter having set in now, Clare's cottage also was put under
repair, with such improvements as had become necessary.
The help was timely, for Mrs. Clare, too, was now an invalid,
having given birth to a son, baptized Frederick, on the 11th
January, 1824. There was a real affection for the poor
poet in the heart of the Peterborough doctor, which moved
him to incessant labour for his client, and had the effect of
instilling somewhat of the same feeling into others with
whom he came into contact. Lady Milton visited the poet,
and sent welcome presents of game and fowl; and after
her came the wife of the Bishop of Peterborough, her hands
full of warm clothing and victuals. The latter lady, previously acquainted with Clare's writings, was so eager in her
desire to afford assistance as to induce her husband to drive
over into the obscure village, and give Clare his episcopal
blessing, together with half a dozen bottles of good port
wine. The right reverend Dr. Marsh, obedient to the
commands of his active wife, delivered the wine, but reported that he did not like Helpston, nor the poet of
Helpston—the village not being sufficiently clean, nor the
poet sufficiently humble. His lordship's opinion, however,
nowise influenced Mrs. Marsh into discontinuing her visits.

The assistance and sympathy thus shown to Clare had a

visible effect upon his health. Gradually recovering, he was strong enough when the first blossoms of spring came peeping in at the window, to issue forth once more into the open air. To him the first walk was such boundless enjoyment as to be almost overpowering in its intensity. Never seemed the green fields more glorious, the song of the birds more enchanting, and the whole wide world more full of ecstatic bliss. In vain the good Peterborough doctor entreated him not to risk his yet imperfect health in long excursions, but to keep as quiet as possible, and only venture upon short walks during the middle of the day. Clare promised to attend to the injunction, and honestly meant to obey it, yet was lured into forgetfulness whenever the birds sat piping in the trees, and the sun's rays came streaming into his narrow hut. They witched him away almost against his own will, making him creep forth into the fields and woods, heavily leaning on his stick. One day he stayed out longer than usual, and, the doctor arriving, a search was made after him. It was fruitless for some time; at last, however, he was found in his favourite hollow oak, sitting as in a trance, his face illumined by the setting sun. Enraptured joy seemed to pervade his whole being; unutterable bliss to fill his mind. The doctor looked serious, and made an attempt to upbraid his patient, but which was entirely unsuccessful. 'If you loved the sun and flowers as I do,' quietly said Clare, 'you would not blame me.' The words somewhat startled the Peterborough man of science.

Sunshine and the hollow oak, nevertheless, if conducive to his worship of nature, were not beneficial to Clare's health. Again and again the lengthened excursions brought on a relapse, until at last it seemed as if his old illness, a compound of ague and other afflictions, would throw him anew on his bed, perhaps to arise no more. In fear of fatal consequences, Clare's medical friend now advised him to accept the former invitation of Mr. Taylor, and to seek benefit both from a change of air and the consultation of the best physicians of the capital. Clare did not feel much inclined to go to London, oppressed with the idea that he might not be really welcome at the house of his publisher, and looked upon as but an unfortunate alms-seeker. Being pressed, however, to undertake the journey, he frankly stated his case in a note to Mr. Taylor, and receiving a fresh invitation, couched in very friendly terms, resolved to set out on another pilgrimage to the big town. It was the third visit to London, and as such bereft of many of the startling incidents of former journeys. The Stamford coach was no more the mysterious vehicle of olden days, nor the scenery on the road imbued with that charm of novelty so conspicuous on the first, and partly on the second, trip to town. Moreover, he felt very weak and melancholy, and his heart was oppressed by sad thoughts. Even a merry Irishman, a fellow-traveller, could not induce him to open his lips; and it was not until the coach rolled upon the pavement of London that he roused himself from his lethargy, preparing to meet former friends. He found them nearer than he expected, for at the 'George and Blue Boar,' Holborn, there stood faithful Tom Benyon, the head-porter, ready to carry any amount of Helpston luggage, and, if necessary, the owner himself. The latter was unnecessary, though the poor traveller felt rather giddy when dragging himself along the crowded streets, grasping his Tom by the arm. Mr. Taylor's house was soon reached, and being received in the kindest manner, Clare was not long in recovering from his fatigue and depressed spirits.

At this third visit, Clare remained above two months in London, from the beginning of May till the middle of July, 1824. Immediately after his arrival, Mr. Taylor introduced him to Dr. Darling, an eminent Scotch physician, who, in the kindest manner, consented to give his advice without any charge whatever. But Dr. Darling did more than merely give his advice; he attended Clare as if he had been his own son, devoting every hour that could be spared from his extensive practice to intercourse with his patient. He first of all ordered that Clare should be kept absolutely quiet; in cheerful society, if possible, but not allowed to read too many books, or to discuss abstruse subjects. It might have been difficult to carry out these orders; but, fortunately, friend Rippingille, the painter, was drinking pale ale at Bristol for the season, so that Clare, having nobody to lead him through his favourite taverns and concert-rooms, and being still afraid to hazard alone into the whirlpool of London life, was almost compelled to stop at home. For the first few days the sojourn at Mr. Taylor's house in Fleet Street appeared to him somewhat dreary, though it was not long before he came to like it, and at last got into a real enjoyment of his new mode of existence. He spent the whole day, from early morn till dark, at a window on the ground floor, overlooking the street. The endless stream of vehicles and pedestrians which passed before his eyes was to him like a vast panorama, in the contemplation of which he forgot, for the moment, even his beloved fields and woods. Of the life of the majority of human beings, particularly the dwellers in large towns, Clare had as yet but very vague and indistinct notions, and was surprised, therefore, at many of the scenes before him. What struck him most was the feverish anxiety manifested in the countenances of the hurrying crowds, and the restless tumult of the never-ending wave of human life which kept floating up and down the narrow street, without interval and without rest. At his former visits to London he had frequently asked the question what all these thousands of hurried wanderers were doing; and though only laughed at by his friends, he now repeated the query. Mr. Taylor was too busy himself to be able to tell why others were busy, nor was Mr. Hessey, his partner, sufficiently wise or simple to give a clear answer; and John Clare, therefore, in the last instance, addressed himself to Tom Benyon. Tom was a

N

shrewd man, a real Londoner, with not much education, but
plenty of mother-wit. He explained to his friend, in a very
clear manner, the complex organization of the trade of the
great city, together with its result, the universal thirst for
wealth. Clare perfectly understood the short lesson in
political economy; nevertheless, he was yet at a loss to com-
prehend how there could be full a million of men upon earth
willing to relinquish all the charms of fields, and flowers, and
green trees for the mere sake of making money, useful, he
conceived, only for procuring a certain amount of food and
clothing. It was in vain that shrewd Tom, not a little a
philosopher in his own way, explained that the delight consisted, not in possessing wealth, but in hunting after it. The
view was not appreciated by Clare, who still thought that
seven acres of land, with a cottage, a row of trees, and a few
flowers, were worth all the money-bags of the city. Tom
Benyon on his part had a contempt for green trees, and liked
the smell of roasted apples better than that of fresh ones,
so that the interchange of ideas converted none of the dis-
putants.

For full three weeks Clare stuck with his face to the
window in Fleet Street. The hurrying crowds, when once
he understood the object of most of them, ceased to amuse
him, but there remained another interest, deeper than questions of political economy, which preserved its attraction for
him to the end. Clare, passionately fond of every shape of
beauty upon earth, did not get tired of looking at the throng
of fair forms which passed before his eyes in the busy city
thoroughfare. He had never seen so many handsome women
under what he conceived so very favourable circumstances.
Deeply imbued with the consciousness of possessing none of
the attractions which render men agreeable in the eyes of
women of superior rank, he always felt a morbid shyness to
converse with ladies into whose company he was thrown, and
in many instances was not able even to look them in the

face. This feeling was greatly increased by that exalted worship which the poet paid, as to all shapes and symbols of beauty, so to that highest type, the female form. Even to come near a beautiful woman made him tremble, and the touch of so much as the hem of her garment sent his blood coursing through his veins. Thus, though he knew no other enjoyment than the communion with beauty, his very worship of its splendours kept him away from it. At the receptions of Mrs. Emmerson, and other entertainments, at which he was present on his former visits to London, he could never be induced to go into the drawing-room, where the ladies were awaiting him ; or, as he fancied, lying in wait for him. At the risk of being called rude, he always left the room on these occasions, as soon as the dinner was over. Only here, at his Fleet Street window, the poet felt quite at ease in contemplating female beauty. To see and not to be seen was what his heart enjoyed in full delight, and he fervently expressed his opinion to Tom Benyon that the only thing that made the big city endurable, and even money-hunting excusable, was the presence of all these fair women. Tom felt much gratified at this declaration, considering any praise of London as a personal flattery.

Dr. Darling's treatment had such a good effect, that at the end of three weeks the last symptoms of Clare's illness had vanished. He now gave his patient permission to read, of which Clare availed himself to the fullest extent, beginning to feel somewhat satiated with the Fleet Street panorama. The season of June, dull in the book trade, having set in, Mr. Taylor also had more leisure on his hands, and gave frequent evening parties, to which he invited many of the literary stars of the day, particularly those contributing to the lustre of the 'London Magazine.' Clare was invariably present at these entertainments, though he managed to hide his person as much as possible, being occupied in watching the lions at the table, like the fair women in the street, from a convenient bird's-eye view. The view, altogether, was highly attractive, for the lions were numerous, and of a more or less superior kind. Among the first who visited Mr. Taylor's evening parties was Thomas De Quincey. Clare had read with the deepest interest the 'Confessions of an English Opium-eater,' which appeared in the 'London Magazine,' of September and October, 1821; and the picture of the outcast Ann haunted his imagination whenever walking the streets and meeting with any of her frail sisters. Mr. De Quincey being announced one day, just when they were sitting down to dinner, Clare quickly sprang to his feet to behold the extraordinary man; but was much astonished on seeing a little, dark, boyish figure, looking like an overgrown child, oddly dressed in a blue coat, with black necktie, and a small hat in his hand. Clare's astonishment became still greater when this singular-looking little man began to talk, not, as the listener innocently expected, of such abstruse subjects as he was wont to write on in the 'London Magazine,' but in a banter about the most ludicrous and vulgar things. He kept Mr. Taylor and his friends in a roar of laughter, until another guest was announced, in the person of Mr. Charles Lamb. The latter, outwardly friendly to De Quincey, seemed, as Clare observed, not altogether partial to him, but stuttered forth more than one witticism which evidently displeased the 'opium-eater.' Further arrivals, the same evening, continued to enliven the scene. There came the Rev. Mr. Cary, translator of Dante's 'Inferno,' a tall, thin man, with a long face and a vacant stare, not much given to talk; Mr. George Darley, a young Irish poet, afflicted with a stutter worse than that of Charles Lamb; Baron Field, every inch a country gentleman, constantly informing his hearers of the fact of being a magistrate in South Wales, but claiming allegiance to literature as writer of several articles on and about Wales; and, last on the list, Mr. Allan Cunningham, arriving late, and stalking into the room, as Clare fancied to himself, 'like one of Spenser's black knights.' Allan seemed a great favourite of Baron Field and De Quincey, though not of Charles Lamb, who fixed his targets upon him as soon as he had opened his lips, with some remarks upon Scotch poetry. Clare remembered Elia's words : 'I have been trying all my life to like Scotchmen, and am obliged to desist from the experiment in despair.'

There were more lions at a 'London Magazine' dinner which Mr. Taylor gave at the end of another week. It was a kind of state reception, and Clare was put for the occasion in pumps and dress-coat. He would have gladly kept away from the table, but was not allowed to do so, the occasion being deemed favourable as an advertisement of the 'North-amptonshire Peasant.' About three-fourths of the guests were patrons of literature, titled and untitled, and the remaining visitors were called for the purpose of being exhibited. Samuel Taylor Coleridge was the chief lion of the evening. Clare was once more surprised on finding the great philosopher a heavy, stout, phlegmatic-looking man, instead of the pale dreamer pictured by his imagination. He was slightly annoyed, too, on hearing the famous sage talk incessantly, to the exclusion of every one else, notably of William Hazlitt, who sat close to him, and of Charles Elton, the translator of the 'Hesiod,' whom Clare had at his right hand, and whose quiet, sensible conversation he greatly enjoyed. Coleridge left, after having spoken, with little interruption, for nearly three hours, and at his departure the talk became general, and, Clare fancied, much more pleasant. The leader of the conversation was William Reynolds, whose sparkling wit, keen as a sword, extinguished even that of Charles Lamb. He attacked everybody in turn, in a good-humoured manner ; and by setting his brother wits against himself and each other, produced endless fun and amusement. Even William Hazlitt, who at first appeared low-spirited and ill at ease, began to laugh and talk ; and at length Clare himself was drawn into the whirlpool of conversation. When he began to speak, in his broad Northamptonshire dialect, there was a sudden stillness in the room, the whole of the guests feeling startled at the sound of the strange voice, which seemed to come as from another world. Though nerved by sundry glasses of wine, Clare was almost terrified at the sudden quiet around him, his intention having been merely to address his neighbour, and not the entire assembly. He therefore relapsed at once, and somewhat abruptly, into silence, and, not long after, with a nod to his patron at the head of the table, and a quiet 'good bye' to Mr. Elton, quitted the room. It was an immense feeling of relief when, creeping upstairs to his little chamber, he was able to divest himself of his pumps and dress-coat, and march forth, in solid boots and jacket, for a saunter along the Fleet pavement, reflecting, in the cool of the summer evening, on all that he had heard and seen, in the shape of lions, poets, philosophers, wits, booksellers, unfortunate Anns of the Street, and more unfortunate opium-eaters.

Clare's visit to London was now drawing to a close. Dr. Darling counselled that he should quit the town as soon as possible, fearing that the 'London Magazine' entertainments might undo all the good gained by his former exertions. However, Clare felt unwilling to leave before having met his old friend and patron, Admiral Lord Radstock, who was retained at his country seat by a rather serious illness. He waited, week after week, but his lordship did not arrive. Instead of the admiral, there came friend Rippingille, the painter, rushing wildly into Clare's arms, and declaring that he had left Bristol, and the best pale ale in the world, solely for the purpose of seeing him. Clare rejoiced; but Dr. Darling did not. The shrewd Scotch physician insisted upon his patient leaving London immediately, and it was arranged, finally, that Clare should start at the end of a week. Friend Rippingille, or 'Rip,' as his acquaintances used to call him,

was instructed privately not to lead Clare into the old round
of taverns and theatres, and, above all, not to tempt him to
an undue indulgence in drink. The promise was made, and
was kept, too ; nevertheless, Clare and ' Rip,' while giving
up evening visits, remained companions during the daytime.
Clare was introduced by his friend to Sir Thomas Lawrence,
and some other famous artists of the day, which led to much
interchange of compliments, and many promises of support,
but ended, as usual, in nothing. He was likewise taken to
Mr. Deville, a noted professor of the art called phrenology,
who felt his head, carefully measuring all its bumps, and,
having learnt Clare's name, informed him that he possessed
all the swellings necessary to make verses. This so delighted
' Rip,' that he insisted on getting a cast of his friend's
cranium. Clare submitted in meekness of heart ; but found
the operation stifling to such a degree, that he ran away in
the midst of it, with the loss of a portion of his skin. For
the next few days the poet wandered in rather lonely mood
through the streets of London, and in one of these excursions became the involuntary spectator of a striking scene,
which he never forgot in his life.

It was on the 12th of July, a hot summer day, that Clare
went down the Strand, towards Charing Cross, intending to
have a stroll in the parks. When near Parliament Street,
however, he found the way blocked by an immense crowd,
and on inquiry learnt that a great funeral was coming up the
street. Taking his place among the idlers, he did not know
at first whose funeral it was, and only at the last moment
learnt that the body of Lord Byron was being carried to its
last resting-place. A fervent admirer of Byron, he yet had
never heard of his death till this moment, when standing
face to face with his mortal remains. He felt startled and
almost bewildered at the sight, and when the gorgeous procession, with all its mutes, pages, cloakmen on horseback,
and carriers of sable plumes, had come up, he reverently

followed in the rear, amidst a confused mass of people in
carriages and on foot.   The slow and solemn train went up
the Haymarket, Coventry Street, Princes Street, and Oxford
Street, passing thence along into Tottenham Court Road.
At the corner of the latter thoroughfare great confusion was
created by another funeral train which came up in an opposite
direction.   In the tumult that ensued, many were thrown
down, among them the unknown poet, who followed in the
rear of the procession.   Clare fell to the ground, and was
pushed along by the crowd ; but, fortunately, did not suffer
much harm, beyond being rolled over and over in the mud,
and spoiling the only suit of good clothes of which he was
possessed.   Mr. Taylor was surprised on seeing his guest
come home in a state which made it almost impossible to
recognise him.   Clare smiled sadly, and in a somewhat
serious tone told Mr. Taylor that he thought it was his fate,
now as ever, to be a martyr to poetry.

Two days after Byron's funeral, John Clare left London.
Previous to starting, he had a long conversation with Dr. Darling, who had come to rank among his most intimate friends.
The kind-hearted and shrewd Scotch doctor volunteered some
advice, to which Clare listened with great attention.   He
told him, in the first instance, that he ought to give up all
expectations of acquiring either fame or wealth as a poet, but
that it would be wisdom on his part to return forthwith to
his old occupation as a farm-labourer, and write verses only
during his leisure hours.   This seemed hard to Clare ; however, the doctor proceeded to explain the matter to him in
his own prosaic fashion.   It was Dr. Darling's opinion that,
on the whole, there existed no real demand for verses among
the public at large, but that only a few exalted minds were
able to appreciate and enjoy true poetry.   But the masses,
he held, were carried along, now and then, by a kind of
fashionable movement, engendered by the appearance of great
authors, the renown of whose works was so vast as to spread

from the closet of the student, upward and downward, through all ranks and classes. Such a poetical fashion, or poetical fever, Dr. Darling thought England had just gone through, stirred by the almost simultaneous productions of many first-class writers, such as Burns, Byron, and Sir Walter Scott. But as all excitement must be followed by reaction, so, the doctor explained, the reaction was setting in at that moment, proved by the fact that even the works of these famous poets were encumbering the booksellers' shelves, waiting for buyers which did not come. This was a fact which Clare knew to be true, and so far he fully acquiesced in the remarks of his wise Scotch friend. He, therefore, consented to follow the counsel thus tendered, and, at least for a time, return to his old occupation. But Dr. Darling had another piece of advice in store. Taking Clare by both hands, and looking him full in the face, he earnestly exhorted him not to take ale or spirits but in greatest moderation, and, if possible, leave off drinking entirely. Clare promised. An hour after he was on his return to Helpston, feeling happier in his mind than he had been for a long time.

NEW STRUGGLES.

The promise made to Dr. Darling was faithfully kept. For several years to come, Clare never visited the public-house, and even at home drank little else but water, subsisting chiefly upon bread and vegetables, and such decoctions of weak tea and coffee as his wife was in the habit of distilling. The diet, probably, was not quite what Dr. Darling expected; at least, it did not prove very beneficial to Clare's health. For a long time, he felt weak and debilitated, so as scarcely to be able to do the simplest out-door work. This was very unfortunate, as it prevented him from carrying out the other part of the engagement undertaken towards his medical friend, that of devoting himself again to field labour. He earnestly sought work immediately after his return from London, and though sneered at by one or two farmers, who told him that he was too famous a man again to soil his hands, he at last secured employment near Helpston Heath, part of which was being enclosed for the benefit of the great landowners of the neighbourhood. For a few days, he kept working here with all the strength he could muster, which was not sufficient, however, for the demands of the overseer. There were drains and ditches to be made, which required the use of brawny arms and a body untouched by ague, and the work being done by contract, the foreman was exacting, and saw at once that he was not up to the mark. He, consequently, got his discharge, and went home in a very sad mood. Ever since his marriage, his debts had been accumulating, and though altogether small in amount, they now began to press heavily upon him, the more so as his expenditure kept gradually increasing, which was by no means the case with his income. He found that to maintain his aged parents, his wife, two children, and himself, he could not do with less than sixty-five or seventy pounds a year, and his annuity amounting to rather less than forty-five pounds, there was the absolute necessity of gaining the rest, either by his writings, or as a farm-labourer. It was the fear that both sources might fail, which threw him into a deep melancholy.

After a while, he roused himself to another effort in finding work, and this time submitted to what he fancied to be a deep humiliation. When applying for his quarterly pension to the steward of the Marquis of Exeter, he begged for some employment in the gardens, or, if no place should be vacant, as a labourer on any of the estates of his lordship. The steward promised to mention the subject to the marquis, but did not keep his word. Being overwhelmed with business, he probably forgot the matter entirely; otherwise the noble lord, who seemed to take a real interest in Clare, could not have failed to listen to a request the fulfilment of which would have cost him little or nothing, and been the means of securing the welfare of the poet for life. Indeed, a place as gardener at Burghley Hall, or some other similar employment, into which a mere whisper of the noble owner might have installed Clare, would have been greatly preferable to the pension of fifteen guineas granted to the poet, and the quarterly payments of which he never received but with inward humiliation. A place such as this would have removed at once the whole burthen of cares which weighed him to the ground, and, while giving him a maintenance for his family, with a comfortable home, would yet have left him abundant time to attend to the inspirations of the muse. Clare himself perceived this very clearly, and once or twice started with the intention of laying his case before the marquis in person, explaining his whole situation, his hopes, troubles, and fears. But each time he approached the stately gates of Burghley Hall, his courage failed him. He trembled to be looked upon as a beggar, and the apprehension of being refused was constantly before his eyes. There were faint hopes, moreover, that the steward, who seemed a friendly man, would succeed in getting him some employment, without personal application to his lordship. However, the promised message from Burghley Hall did not arrive, and Clare at last gave up all expectation of getting anything else but alms from his greatest patron, the Marquis of Exeter.

Having not much else to do, Clare kept up an active correspondence with his friends in London, during the latter part of the summer and the whole of the autumn of 1824. To Allan Cunningham in particular, with whom he had contracted a close friendship during his last visit to the metropolis, he sent long letters, discussing poetical and other topics. One of these letters, rather characteristic in its way, as showing Clare's opinion of Bloomfield, as well as of his own position in 'the fields of the Muses,' deserves to be given.

It was sent to Allan Cunningham, together with an enclosure containing Bloomfield's short note to 'Neighbour John,' already given.

'To Allan Cunningham,

(Left at Messrs. Taylor and Hessey's)
93, Fleet Street,
London.

Helpston, September 9th, 1824.

Brother Bard and Fellow Labourer,

I beg your acceptance according to promise of this autograph of our English Theocritus, Bloomfield. He is in my opinion our best Pastoral Poet. His " Broken Crutch," " Richard and Kate," &c. are inimitable and above praise. Crabbe writes about the peasantry as much like the Magistrate as the Poet. He is determined to show you their worst side ; and, as to their simple pleasures and pastoral feelings, he knows little or nothing about them compared to the other, who not only lived amongst them, but felt and shared the pastoral pleasures with the peasantry of whom he sung. I had promised that I would visit him this summer at Shefford, but death went before me. He was a warm-hearted friend and an amiable man. His latter poems show that his best days were by. His " Remains" are very trifling, but these have nothing to do with his former fame. I never forgave Lord Byron's sneering mention of him in the " English Bards and Scotch Reviewers ;" but, never mind, he has left a genius behind him that will live as late as his lordship's ; and, though he was but a " Cobler," his poems will meet posterity as green and growing on the bosom of English nature and the muses as those of the Peer. I could hazard a higher opinion for truth, but this is enough. Titles and distinctions of pride have long ago been stript of their dignity by the levellers in genius ; at least they have been convinced that the one is not a certain copyright or inheritance of the other. I should suppose, friend Allan, that "The Ettrick Shepherd," "The Nithsdale Mason," and "The Northamptonshire Peasant," are looked upon as intruders and stray cattle in the fields of the Muses (forgive the classification), and I have no doubt but our reception in that Pinfold of his lordship's "English Bards" would have been as far short of a compliment as Bloomfield's. Well, never mind, we will do our best, and as we never went to Oxford or Cambridge, we have no Latin and Greek to boast of, and no bad translations to hazard (whatever our poems may be), and that's one comfort on our side.

I have talked enough on this string, so I will trouble you a little with something else. I can scarcely tell you how I am, for I keep getting a little better and a little worse, and remaining at last just as I were. I was very bad this morning, but have recovered this evening as I generally do, and I really fear that I shall never entirely overset it. I have written to Hessey for Dr. Darling's assistance again to-day, and I have desired him to forward this letter to you. Drop a line to say that you receive it, and give my kind remembrances to your better half, Mrs. Cunningham. I will try your patience no longer with this gossip, so believe me, friend Allan,

Your hearty friend and well-wisher,
JOHN CLARE.'

Dr. Darling's 'assistance,' in the shape of some medicine, acting as a febrifuge and preservative against the ague, arrived soon; after which Clare felt strong enough to make another attempt towards finding work. Having received no reply to his application to the steward of the Marquis of Exeter, he resolved to address himself to his next greatest patron in the neighbourhood, the Earl Fitzwilliam. The noble earl having been always very kind to him, he summoned courage to obtain an interview with his lordship. But it so happened, unfortunately, that neither the Earl, nor his son, Viscount Milton, was at home at the time ; and although Lady Milton received him very graciously, Clare felt too much shyness to state to her what he intended to say. By the commands of her ladyship, however, Clare was entertained by the upper servants of the house, and finding them to be a very well-educated class of men, quite unlike the domestics of other lordly establishments, he renewed his visits frequently, and after a while became a regular guest at Milton Park. The butler, Edward Artis, was an enthusiastic antiquarian, possessing a large library, always hunting for old coins, medals, and pottery, and an absolute authority on all matters concerning Durobrivæ and the works of the ancient Romans in the neighbourhood. With Mr. Artis, Clare soon got very intimate, and having become acquainted with the pursuits of his friend, imbibed even a slight fondness for antiquarian lore. There were two other servants, named Henderson and West, both distinguished in their way. Henderson was an accomplished botanist, spending whole days in search after plants and flowers, and West was a lover of poetry, as well as a writer of rather indifferent verses. Henderson offered to teach Clare the elements of botany, which proposal was eagerly accepted, though it did not lead to great results. After various attempts to master the hard words of the scientific handbook given to him, John Clare frankly stated to his friend that he could not get on with it, and must continue to love trees and flowers without knowing their Latin names. But eager of knowledge, under whatever form it offered itself, he made, after discarding botany, a new stride towards erudition. The head cook at Milton Park, a Monsieur Grilliot, better known to the servants as 'Grill,' undertook to teach Clare French. He did so in the rational way, not by stuffing his friend with rules and exceptions to rules, but teaching him words and their pronunciation, by which means Clare made rapid progress, and at once acquired a real liking for the study. Nevertheless, he had to relinquish his attempts to learn French in a very short time, being too poor to purchase the few books which Monsieur 'Grill' recommended him to read.

Clare's visits to Milton Park continued all through the autumn of 1824, till late in the spring of 1825, without leading to any advantageous result as far as the chief object was concerned. Having become intimately acquainted with the upper servants, particularly with Artis, Clare learned that there was no place suitable for him vacant in the establishment, and the consequence was that, when the Earl returned, nothing was said about the matter. Clare had an interview with his lordship, and was received in the kindest manner, but not being asked as to his worldly prospects, kept silent on the subject. The Earl probably fancied, as did many others, that Clare made a good income from the sale of his books, and it was not till years afterwards that he learnt the real truth. To his friend Artis, Clare made a confession to some extent, informing him that he was in want of work, and would be glad to get some employment even as a thresher or ploughman. But Mr. Artis would not hear of this, and strongly advised Clare to discard all ideas of hiring himself out as a labourer, as it would stand in the way of his appointment to a more honourable place. It was expected that the managership of a small farm near Helpston Heath, belonging to Viscount Milton, would become vacant before long, and Clare was told that there was no doubt that he could get this post by merely biding his time. So Clare waited ; but, while waiting, got more and more melancholy, his mind overwhelmed by family cares, amidst the incessant struggle of getting the daily bread.

The temporary failure of his hopes to get employment in the fields made Clare now think once more of turning his poetry to account. Though aware that his ' Village Minstrel' had not proved a success, he still cherished the belief that new productions might meet with a better fate, the more so as he was fully conscious that through constant study his mind was being greatly enlarged, leading to an improvement of his writings, in conception as well as outward form. He accordingly wrote to Mr. Taylor, sending specimens of some new poems, and offering sufficient to form a small volume. But Mr. Taylor was unwilling to try another publication, excusing his reluctance by the same arguments already impressed upon Clare by Dr. Darling, namely, that the taste for poetry was on the wane, and that the world was crying for prose. Reflecting on this subject, Clare began thinking of a new scheme, which was to write a novel. He made the proposition instantly, but was answered by a refusal, thinly veiled under a heap of compliments. Clare felt somewhat offended, although Mr. Taylor was certainly right in this case, there being no doubt whatever of the absolute incapacity of his client to write prose. However, in order to soften the hardship of his refusal, he asked him to contribute occasional poems to the 'London Magazine,' which offer was accepted, but proved of little advantage to Clare, the remuneration being uncertain and of the slenderest kind. In his feverish anxiety to work and to gain some additional means of subsistence, Clare committed the mistake of writing too many poems at a time, which naturally lowered the value of the article in the eyes of his publisher. A letter to Mr. Taylor, dated February, 1825, shows the excited state of the poet at this period. 'I fear,' wrote Clare, 'I shall get nothing ready for you this month; at least I fear so now, but may have fifty subjects ready to-morrow. The muse is a fickle hussy with me; she sometimes stirs me up to madness, and then leaves me as a beggar by the wayside, with no more life than what's mortal, and that nearly extinguished by melancholy forebodings.' Further on he breaks out into the exclamation : ' I wish I could live nearer you; at least I wish London could be within twenty miles of Helpston. I live here among the ignorant like a lost man; in fact, like one whom the rest seem unwilling to have anything to do with. They hardly dare talk in my company, for fear I should mention them in my writings, and I feel more pleasure in wandering the fields than in musing among my silent neighbours, who are insensible to anything but toiling and talking of it, and that to no purpose.' This ' living among the ignorant like a lost man' came to be the deep key-note sounding through all the subsequent letters of Clare.

In the summer of 1825, Clare's pecuniary embarrassments grew to a climax. He could not refuse anything to his family; and though living personally worse than a beggar, eating little else than dry bread and potatoes, and drinking nothing but water, his expenditure, including medical attendance and many articles of comfort for his aged parents, averaged considerably more than a pound a-week, while the income from his annuity, on which he now solely depended, was very much less. Repeated new efforts to find employment as a labourer proved fruitless; while his visits to Milton Park had ceased by this time, his stock of clothes being so scanty, and patched all over, that he was ashamed to show himself in the company of his friends, always elegantly dressed. With Artis alone he kept up an acquaintance, the learned butler having a soul above dress, and showing himself on all occasions utterly careless whether the companion with whom he was searching for old medals and pottery was dressed in purple or in rags. For many a day, the two went roaming through the environs of Castor and Helpston Heath, digging for the remains of the ancient inhabitants of Durobrivæ. One afternoon, when thus employed, Clare fainted, to the great consternation of his friend. The latter, fortunately, had a small flask of wine in his pocket, a few drops of which were sufficient to restore

O

Clare to consciousness. He was gently led home by Edward Artis, who was told, in answer to his inquiries, that the illness had been brought on by the sudden heat. This was not true, or, at the best, only partially true. The fainting was caused by hunger.

When Dr. Darling advised Clare to drink no more ale or spirits, he probably was not aware of the nature of his patient's diet, or of that of Helpston labourers generally. Very likely, had he known that dry bread and potatoes, both in limited quantities, were the staple food, the able Scotch physician would have recommended an occasional glass of port wine, or even of stout—if obtainable. As it was, Clare's promise of abstinence, which he kept religiously for several years, was very detrimental to his health. His naturally delicate frame sank under the coarse diet, as soon as the accustomed stimulants were withdrawn, and his stomach getting gradually weakened, he at last began to feel a sort of abhorrence for his daily food. He now took to eating fruit, which still more debilitated his digestive organs, so that finally there took place a process of slow starvation. When fainting at the side of his friend Artis, he had eaten nothing but a few potatoes with milk for twenty-four hours, having left his home in the morning without taking any food whatever. In this case, it was not merely want of appetite, but actual want of bread. Being greatly indebted to the baker, the latter thought fit to withhold the regular supply of bread, and although there were plenty of vegetables for his wife and children, Clare quitted the house without tasting anything, for fear they might want. It thus happened that, while exploring the ruins of the old Roman city, he sank to the ground from sheer want of food.

The learned butler was much absorbed by his antiquarian speculations, and little given to reflections about his fellow-men ; nevertheless, Clare's case struck him as very peculiar. Getting back to Milton Park, he told the particu-

lars to Earl Fitzwilliam, suggesting that a little help might
be welcome to the poor poet. The noble earl, however,
thought otherwise. It was not that he was unwilling to
give; on the contrary, his hand was always open to those in
distress, and his previous liberal present of a hundred pounds
showed that he was particularly well disposed towards
Clare. In all likelihood, had he known the real position of
the poet, he would have further extended his liberality, or
come to his assistance in some other way. But he knew
very little of Clare, and looked upon him as any ordinary
earl would look upon an ordinary farm-labourer. From the
few interviews with the poet, his lordship had come to the
conclusion, true in the main, that Clare was a proud man,
and having a strong feeling that Northamptonshire farm-
labourers had no business to be proud, he did not think him
self justified in giving any further assistance unless specially
asked to do so. The earl told this to his learned butler,
who acquiesced, as in duty bound, in his master's decision.
However, Artis mentioned the subject at the dinner table,
where it was attentively listened to by all assembled,
especially the worthy head-cook. Monsieur Grill had a
secret liking for Clare, based on the fact that the poet was
almost the only one of all the people with whom he came
into contact who did not torment him with sneers and
mocking speeches. Monsieur was endowed with a most
extraordinary visage, much like a full moon, put into a
dripping-pan, and baked before a slow fire; and the aspect
of which was not improved by a pair of ears of very unusual length, and a total absence of hair at the top. To
make matters worse, Monsieur Grill was very susceptible of
criticism concerning his face, having done his best to improve
it, by painting the nose white, the cheeks rosy, and the eyebrows dark. But, whether he liked it or not, the members
of the establishment at Milton Park, together with their
friends, would laugh at him, and, what was almost as bad,

would insist upon calling him 'Mounsear.' Clare alone
never laughed, and, after two lessons, pronounced the word
'Monsieur' to Grill's entire satisfaction. At the end of three,
he said 'Mon chèr ami,' in the best Parisian accent, to the
delight of the head-cook, and the astonishment of the whole
company in the servants' hall. All this went straight to
the heart of Monsieur Grill. When he heard, therefore,
that Clare was unwell, he said nothing, but went quietly
down into his laboratory, put his saucepan on the fire, and
began mixing together a wonderful quantity of groceries,
spices, and other ingredients. Being a conscientious man
withal, he next despatched the valet to Lady Milton, asking
permission to give some strengthening broth to John Clare
of Helpston. 'Give as much as you like,' was the immediate reply of her ladyship. This was satisfactory, and after
an hour's simmering of his saucepans, Monsieur Grill put
on his coat, poured his broth into a stone bottle, took his
stick, and went out at the back of the mansion, and through
the park towards Helpston. Not long, and he stood before
Clare. The latter was amazed on beholding Grill, with the
jar in his hand; having always held Monsieur to be the
vainest of mortals, quite incapable of carrying a stone bottle
across the country. 'Ah, mon chèr ami, voilà quelque
chose pour vous!' exclaimed Monsieur, evidently delighted
to see Clare. And without further ado, he grasped some
sticks, made a fire in an instant, laid hold of an ancient
earthen vessel, and in a few minutes presented, with graceful
bow, a basin of broth to his astonished friend. Clare tasted
it, and found it delicious. He fancied he had not partaken
of anything so nice for months; all the faintness and languor
under which he was suffering seemed to disappear as by enchantment. 'This is much better than medicine,' he said,
with a look of gratitude to the clever head-cook. 'Medicine?
parbleu!' exclaimed Grill; 'do not speak of medicine, mon
chèr ami, or I leave alone my batterie de cuisine.' Monsieur

Grill felt deep contempt, approaching hatred, for all drugs and doctors, labouring under the impression of having lost his beautiful head of hair through some ill-applied medicines. Clare saw the passing cloud, and, with much tact, renewed his praises of the delicious broth, asking his friend to show him the making of it. There was no objection on the part of Monsieur Grill; nevertheless, an hour's teaching was attended with but little success. Though having the manipulation explained to him in the most lucid manner, in terms half French and half English, Clare got more confused the more he listened, till at last his friend told him, with some severity, that his mind seemed incapable of comprehending 'l'art du cuisinier.' Which was true enough. Heaven certainly had not gifted John Clare with a genius for cookery, any more than with the higher faculty of money-making.

PUBLICATION OF 'THE SHEPHERD'S CALENDAR.'

The visit of worthy Monsieur Grill to Helpston had the good result that henceforth Clare's diet and mode of living became greatly improved. Lady Milton, hearing of the illness of the poet, sent him her physician, while, better still, the chef de cuisine at Milton Park continued to supply him with good broth. The physician, a man of sense, soon perceived that his patient required not medicine but food. He told Clare that it was absolutely necessary that he should adopt a most nourishing diet, and even advised him to take some ale, or stout, in moderate quantities. However, Clare refused the latter part of the advice, urging the promise he had given to Dr. Darling. As to his general mode of living, he consented to do as requested, although too proud to state the reasons which had prevented him, and would, probably, continue to prevent him fully adopting the counsel. The physician, being asked by Lady Milton whether Clare

seemed in want, stated that there were no signs of poverty
in Clare's home. Though but a narrow hut, the many
handsome books on the shelves, with a few good paintings,
gave it the appearance of comfort, and thus the informant of
the noble lady, like many of the other acquaintances of
Clare, acquired very erroneous notions concerning his real
means. This was the more the case, as Clare always managed
to let his wife and children, as well as his aged parents, want
none of the necessaries of life, and frequently contrived to
procure them even a few luxuries. Nobody knew that
while Clare's family had a good dinner, he himself was
munching dry bread in some corner in the fields. The fact
was not discovered till long afterwards—when discovery
came too late.

In the autumn of 1825, the sad news reached Clare that
his best friend and patron, Lord Radstock, had succumbed
to a stroke of apoplexy. Admiral Lord Radstock died on
the 20th of August, at his town residence in Portland Place,
in a very sudden manner, after but a few days' illness. The
loss of his noble patron would have been a deep affliction to
Clare at any time, but it was particularly so at this moment.
During the whole of the summer, the admiral had been in
correspondence with Mr. Taylor, trying to induce him to
come to some distinct arrangement with his client, in regard
to the payment for his books and poetical contributions to
the 'London Magazine.' Hitherto, Mr. Taylor had not
treated his 'Northamptonshire Peasant' on the same footing
as other authors, but looked upon him more in the light of a
child under tutelage than of an independent man, desirous of
gaining a living by the exercise of his talents or industry.
When, therefore, Lord Radstock urged him to enter into a
regular business agreement with Clare, he felt somewhat
offended. Replying to his lordship, he stated that he had
given much more to the poet than was due to him, without
even charging for his own labours as editor, and that he had

hitherto acted, not as a mere business agent, but as a real friend to Clare. Lord Radstock was not satisfied with this answer, but rejoined that, admitting Clare had received more than was due to him, it yet would be better to furnish regular accounts to him, and, by paying what was due, and no more, to foster his self-reliance, instead of keeping him in the position of a dependent, living upon alms or friendly gifts. The correspondence continued through several more letters, with a prospect of Mr. Taylor yielding his point, when the death of Lord Radstock brought it to an end. It was a sad misfortune to Clare, affecting his whole life. In Lord Radstock he lost the truest and noblest friend he possessed—the only one of all his patrons who might have been willing as well as able to remove the darkening clouds already visible in the future.

In the autumn of 1825, Clare was fortunate enough to find some employment in harvesting, which continued till the end of October, when he was once more thrown out of work. He now devoted himself with increased ardour to poetry, anxious to excel in the new volume which Mr. Taylor had agreed to publish. The chief poem of the work was to be a pastoral, in twelve cantos, descriptive of the aspects of the months and seasons, under the title, 'The Shepherd's Calendar.' The work required lengthened exertion, which, though he devoted himself with the greatest energy to the task, he could not always muster. Again and again the all-absorbing feeling of poverty broke upon and crushed the mind of the poet. Turn as he might, dire want stared him in the face, and his spirit kept chafing and fretting under the constant exertion of making his small income suffice for the ever-growing wants of his family. Some regular work to perform, or the consciousness of being seated on a few acres of his own ground, with the pleasure of growing his corn and vegetables, would have been sufficient to destroy all these petty cares; but the chance of entering upon such happy existence seemed to grow less and less every year. Liberty, the greatest boon which he desired, he was never able to obtain. To spend half the day in hard out-door work, and the other half in wanderings and poetical musings, would have made him completely happy, as well as, in all likelihood, physically strong; yet this simple wish of his heart not all his great and noble patrons were willing to grant him. They gave him alms, sufficient to lift him from the sphere of labour, but not enough for subsistence, and thus left him in a position as false as hopelessly ruinous. Working at intervals, almost beyond his strength, as a farm labourer, and then again remaining for a long time in forced idleness, writing too much, thinking too much, and ever and ever with the grim phantom of poverty before him, was a form of existence necessarily fatal. It was a life too hard, too cold, too angular, too crystallized—a life which would have broken the heart of any poet under the sun.

In the preparation of his new volume, Clare adopted the sensible plan of correcting and revising his writings constantly, so as to reach the greatest perfection in form. The uninterrupted study of the best poets began to have effect upon his mind by more and more developing his taste, and destroying his former notion that his verses came flowing by a sort of inspiration, and, as such, were not liable to further artificial improvement. Mr. Taylor was much pleased with the new verses which Clare sent him, far more polished than most of the previous ones, and encouraged him by many praises to persevere in the new course. Praise, as to all poets, was sweet to Clare, and he kept on writing with great eagerness during the whole of winter and the coming spring. He expected that his new book would be published early in the summer of 1826, but was disappointed in his expectation. There were poems enough in Mr. Taylor's hands to make at least two volumes; but the careful publisher was not over-anxious to print them. A shrewd man of business, he was fully aware that the tide was running strong against

pastorals, or, indeed, against any form of good poetry, the
fashion being all for jingling rhyme, embodying the least
possible amount of sense. It was the period when annuals
began to flourish, with all merit concentrated in 'toned'
paper, gilded leaves, and morocco bindings. Mr. Taylor
liked John Clare, and held his talent in fair estimation from
the fact that the 'Poems descriptive of Rural Life and
Scenery' had gone through four editions. But against this
fact there was the terrible set-off that the 'Village Minstrel'
had only risen to the second edition, with the larger part of
the second issue still on the shelves in Fleet Street. Mr.
Taylor, therefore, like a sound man of business, resolved to
manipulate his 'Northamptonshire Peasant' with great cau-
tion, for fear of accidents.

John Clare got into a very excited state when he learnt
that his new volume was not to be published in the summer
of 1826, nor during the remaining part of the same year.
He felt the delay as a scorn of his poetical fame; and he felt
it, moreover, as a sad ruin of his financial prospects. The
money which he expected to receive was anxiously awaited
to pay off pressing debts, and its non-arrival involved not
only scanty clothing and short rations, but cares of a pecu-
liarly tender nature. 'Patty' brought her husband a third
child, a little boy, who was christened John on the 18th of
June, 1826; and though there arrived much timely assistance
from Milton Park, the baby, as well as his mother, wanted
many things not to be met with in the little hut at Helpston.
Always a tender and most affectionate father, Clare's heart
was ready to break when he found his poor little son suffering from the absence of those comforts which a few pounds
might have purchased. He wrote a pathetic letter to Mr.
Taylor, entreating him to send his poems to press; but
received a cold answer in return. The sound business man
of Fleet Street told his client that it was the wrong time for
bringing out the 'Shepherds' Calendar.' He informed him,

moreover, that the annuals had got the upper hand, and advised him strongly to write for the annuals. Clare answered that he preferred breaking stones at the workhouse.

But when Clare said so, he was in an angry mood. The baby continued crying, in want of milk and a few yards of flannel, and the mother commenced crying, too; and at length things came to such a pass that Clare determined to write for the annuals. He heard that he should get five shillings per poem, and from some publishers even as much as seven and sixpence. In great haste, therefore, he penned as many verses as he could, sitting up night after night, and on getting a bundle ready despatched them to London. But here again there was terrible disappointment. The annuals, it turned out, did not pay annually, but remunerated their contributors at uncertain periods, varying from two years to ten. When Clare found he could get no payment from the proprietors of the splendid morocco-bound volumes, he complained to Mr. Taylor. The busy publisher was vexed at this, as naturally he might be. He answered that he did not, and could not, hold himself responsible for the liabilities of others, and that it was unfair, after having tendered some general advice, to burthen him with the consequences. Here the matter ended, leaving both parties very dissatisfied. For some time to come there was a great coldness between them, and their correspondence almost entirely ceased.

The failure of his attempt to make money by contributing poems to the gold-edged toy-books had the good result of inciting Clare to renewed exertions to return to his old sphere of labour. He was after a while fortunate enough to find employment at Upton, a village on the southern border of Helpston Heath, where he continued at work during the autumn and winter, and far into the spring of 1827. The labour had the most beneficial effect upon his health, and brought on a fresh desire to leave the allurements of writing, or at least of printing, poetry, and devote himself more to out-door occupation. The great difficulty in carrying out this plan was to find regular employment of a nature suited to his bodily strength, and his somewhat erratic habits. After much pondering on the subject, Clare resolved to try a little farming on his own account, with the help of his friends, and on a very limited scale. A visit to Milton Park settled the matter. The two head servants of Earl Fitzwilliam, the antiquarian and the botanist, were both ready and willing to assist the poet to become a farmer, though they told him frankly that they had small hopes of his success. Like in all agricultural districts, the owners of land at Helpston and throughout the neighbourhood were opposed to small tenants and ' spade husbandry,' and Clare's friends justly feared that, even if there were no other obstacles, this cause alone would prevent him prospering. However, sanguine as he was, Clare held these fears to be exaggerated, and having obtained a small loan from his friends, rented several acres of barren soil at a rent four times as high as that paid by the larger farmers for really good land. The result, not for a moment doubtful from the commencement, did much to accelerate Clare's road to ruin.

During the whole spring and summer of 1827, Clare was so busy and excited in attending to his farming operations as almost to forget his new volume of poems. He scarcely expected to see it published, and was somewhat startled on receiving a copy of the book by post, unaccompanied however by a single line from Mr. Taylor. At any other time, he would have keenly felt the neglect ; but as it was, the potatoes and cabbages on his farm attracted his attention more than even his printed verses, and the slight put upon him by his publisher. It was only when the harvest was over—a harvest very poor and unsatisfactory—that he be-thought himself again of his poetical doings. Conscious that he had been in the wrong, to a great extent, in his quarrel with Mr. Taylor, he determined to be the first to hold out the hand of friendship. Having made his resolutions to this effect, he sat down to pen a long letter, dated, 'Helpston, November 17, 1827.' It ran :—' My dear Taylor,—I expect you will be surprised when you open this to' see from whence it comes, so scarce has our correspondence made itself. Ere it withers into nothing, I will kindle up the expiring spark that remains, and make up a letter by its light, if I can. When you sent me the poems in summer, you never sent a letter with them ; I felt the omission, but murmured not. It was not wont to be thus in days gone by. So I will shake off this ague-warm feeling, and this dead-living lethargy, and ask you how you are, and where you are, and how our friends are.' And much more to the same effect.

Mr. Taylor replied in a bland, dignified manner. The 'friends,' he reported to be well ; but said nothing about what the poet was most desirous of knowing, the fate of his new volume. The truth was, the ' Shepherd's Calendar ' did not sell ; and the volume having come into the world almost unnoticed, was lying in the publisher's shop neglected and forgotten. A few periodicals mentioned the book in terms of faint praise, and one solitary critic, visibly behind his age, spoke of the verses as ' exquisite, and by far the most beautiful that have appeared for a long time ;' but the great majority of the representatives of public opinion utterly ignored John Clare's new work. It soon became clear that, though infinitely superior to the ' Poems of Rural Life and Scenery,' which passed through four editions ; and far better even than the ' Village Minstrel,' issued twice ! the ' Shepherd's Calendar ' was entirely overlooked by the public and the press. And it could not well be otherwise. The book, instead of in morocco, was bound, or rather stitched, in coarse blue cardboard ; the paper was not only not ' toned,' but rough and inelegant in the extreme ; and the edges, which ought to have been smooth and gilded, were rugged and uneven like a ploughed field. It was hopeless to expect that a most discerning public should pay six shillings for a book of pastorals of such clownish appearance, when the sweetest rhymes, jingling like silver bells, and descriptive of angels and cupids, and the whole heaven of Greek and Roman mythology, were offered for a lesser sum, in settings resplendent with all the colours of the rainbow. There was no room for the 'Shepherd's Calendar' at the side of all the gorgeously beautiful annuals of the day, of the Souvenir, Keepsake, and Forget-me-not family.

If this was one reason why the 'Village Minstrel' passed entirely unnoticed, another and still more important cause was the negligent manner in which it was published. Books, like all other earthly objects requiring to be bought and sold, must undergo certain preparations, and run through prescribed channels of trade in their way from the producer to the consumer, and it is well known that the regulation and management of this process may either greatly retard or accelerate the sale of a work. It often happened that really valuable works have met with very little success, owing to want of energy or want of thought on the part of the publishers; while, on the other hand, not a few bad or paltry books, utterly unworthy of public patronage, have, through active commercial management, met with a considerable demand, and brought both profit and fame to the writers. The truth of this was once more proved in the sale of Clare's works. In the first published volume, the 'Poems descriptive of Rural Life and Scenery,' Mr. Taylor took a very great interest, and devoted the whole of his energy to ensure its success with the public. He looked upon Clare's book as a personal property; for it was he who enjoyed the honour of having discovered the poetical genius of the 'Northamptonshire Peasant;' he who brought him out in society; and he who was not merely the publisher but the 'editor' of his works, and who as such could fairly claim a share of the renown accruing to the writer. Accord-

ingly, Mr. Taylor took the greatest trouble in ensuring a
favourable reception to Clare's works, and being a literary
man of some standing, as well as a bookseller—with the
additional advantage of gathering, at stated periods, the
chieftains in the republic of letters around his bachelor's
table, to enjoy the most excellent dinners—he succeeded
in doing what perhaps no other London publisher could
have accomplished at the time. Long before the 'Poems
of Rural Life' were issued from the press their merit was
discussed at Mr. Taylor's dinner-table, under the cheering
influence of exquisite port and madeira, and the persuasive
eloquence of the most charming of hosts. Thus it happened
in the most natural manner that the poems at their appearance were received with a perfect storm of applause, in which
even such stern critics as William Gifford—carefully guided
by Octavius Gilchrist—could not help joining. Mr. Taylor's
own periodical, the 'London Magazine,' marched ahead as
chief drummer, and behind came a long train of daily,
weekly, and monthly 'organs,' with the great 'Quarterly
Review' as commander-in-chief. The result proclaimed itself in four editions of 'the poems of the 'Northamptonshire
Peasant.'

It was in the nature of things that Mr. Taylor should
attach due importance to his own efforts in raising the unknown poet upon a pedestal of fame. That he did so, and
even reminded Clare of his exertions at a subsequent period,
when the poet did not show himself sufficiently grateful,
could scarcely be blamed, although it had the consequence
of leading to a gradual estrangement between author and
publisher. John Clare was not a grateful man, in the ordinary sense of the word. He deeply felt kindness, but
had an equally deep abhorrence of servility, or what he
fancied to be such; and, therefore, while humble as a child
towards those whose real benevolence he appreciated, he
showed himself stiff and proud against all who approached

him as condescending patrons.   Upon Mr. Taylor he looked,
rightly or wrongly, as a mere patron.   That his publisher
refused throughout to give him any accounts, but treated all
payments to him as voluntary presents, was a real grief ; and
that his whole demeanour, though very affable and courteous,
was marked by an air of proud superiority, was a fancied
distress, but which not the less irritated the sensitive poet.
Thus there was, from the first, a want of real attachment
between Clare and his influential friend and protector, which
was looked upon by Mr. Taylor as a kind of ingratitude.
He gradually slackened in his endeavours to spread the fame
of the hero he had raised, when he perceived the hero's
repugnance to be properly saddled and harnessed.   While
using prodigal exertions for the success of the first volume,
he fell back upon the ordinary bookseller's routine when
issuing his second work.   In the publication of the third,
the 'Shepherd's Calendar,' there was not even this ordinary
attention, owing to circumstances of a peculiar kind.   Mr.
Taylor, in the year 1825, dissolved partnership with his
active coadjutor, Mr. Hessey, and, while the latter remained
at the old establishment in Fleet Street, he went to set
up a new but smaller publishing house at Waterloo Place.
It was here he issued the 'Shepherd's Calendar,' under conditions more than usually unfavourable.   Expecting to be
appointed publisher to the new London University—which
expectation was realized not long afterwards—Mr. Taylor had
to devote the greater part of his time to preparations for his
new position, so as almost to be unable to attend to his bookselling business.   Thus Clare's new volume kept lying very
quietly on the shelves of the new shop at Waterloo Place.

The 'Shepherd's Calendar' was dedicated to 'the most
noble the Marquis of Exeter.'   To previous counsel of
putting the name of some great patron to his poems, Clare
had always leant a deaf ear ; but he was persuaded in this
instance by his old friend, Dr. Bell, to act contrary to his

own judgment.   Perhaps there was not much harm in the dedication ; but there came from it not much good either.   The
most noble the marquis, as acknowledgment of the honour,
condescended to order ten copies of the 'Shepherd's Calendar,' for which he paid the sum of three pounds, being at
the ordinary retail price of six shillings the volume.   Clare
asked no further favours from his lordship; and his lordship,
as a rule, did not grant any favour unasked.   Probably, the
noble marquis might have broken through his rule on this
occasion, but that he was not altogether satisfied with the
'Shepherd's Calendar.'   The humble dedication on the title-
page was well enough ; yet, considering that the poet was
enjoying a stipend of fifteen guineas a year, payable quarterly,
it was thought that he might have done something more.
But there being not a page, nor even a line, in the whole
book in praise of the elder branch of the Cecils, showed
a deplorable want of feeling proper to a farm labourer living
on his lordship's estate.   It was clear that the Helpston poet
was, on the whole, a silly, foolish man.   Dwelling under the
very shadow of Burghley Castle, he should have known that
by trimming his poetic course in the right direction, he might
have landed at almost any haven of comfort—might have
become under-gardener in the park, or, if less ambitious,
been sent to the House of Commons as member for Stamford.   But there was a deplorable want of worldly wisdom
in John Clare.   That he was a real poet the noble marquis
was ready to believe, not distrusting the authority of the
'Quarterly Review.'   At the same time, his lordship could
not close his eyes to the fact that the man was, all things
considered, unworthy of high patronage.

The bad news that his 'Shepherd's Calendar' had met with
no success whatever reached Clare in the first days of 1828.
He did not learn it from Mr. Taylor, who, as usual, did not
think it worth while to give a business account of his trans-
action to his 'Peasant,' but contented himself in sending. now

and then, a few pounds as a present to Helpston ; but became
aware of the fact through a communication of his kind friend
Allan Cunningham.   Honest Allan's admiration of Clare
increased, as that of the world decreased ; and having gone
into raptures about some of the poems in the 'Shepherd's
Calendar,' yet seeing that few others shared his delight, or
were aware even of the existence of the book, he went to
the publishing office in Waterloo Place to investigate the
matter, and was informed there of what sounded to him
utterly strange, that the work did not sell.   Exasperated at
this communication, he sat down to pen a long epistle to
Clare, seasoned with strong epithets, and winding-up with an
invitation to his friend to come to London.   While consoling
Clare about the neglect of the public, to which, he said,
'poets must get accustomed,' he told him at the same time
that he was sure that some of his verses in the 'Shepherd's
Calendar,' such as 'The Dream,' and 'Life, Death, and
Eternity,' were worth more than all the sing-song of the
age put together, and, if not at once, could not fail being
appreciated in course of time.   But in the meanwhile, Allan
thought, Clare could not do better than connect himself with
the periodical literature of the day, especially the fashionable
annuals.   John Clare hated the annuals ; but he dearly loved
his kind and honest friend, and thereupon promised once
more to write verses for the pretty toy books, payable by
the cubic foot, or yard, or in any other desirable form.   But
he made it a stipulation that he should be allowed to send
his best productions to 'The Anniversary,' an annual edited
by Allan Cunningham himself.   The proposition was accepted,
and Allan thereupon put his friend into communication with
proprietors of annuals who actually paid their contributors.
Clare, on his part, promised to visit London, at the beginning
of February, to conclude some necessary business arrangements.

Soon   after   Allan's   letter,   there   came   another   from

P

Mrs. Emmerson. The lady, though a very indifferent writer of verses, had a keen appreciation of sterling poetry, and warmly congratulated Clare on his new volume. Having induced some two or three of her friends to purchase copies of the 'Shepherd's Calendar,' she lived under the impression that the book was a great success, and could not fail bringing wealth and fame to the author. In connexion with this, Mrs. Emmerson had planned a neat little project of her own. Her apartments had become somewhat deserted since the death of Lord Radstock, the chief leader of her literary assemblies, and dreading the idea of being forgotten among the rising generation of female sonneteers, she bethought herself of calling her old lion, the 'Northamptonshire Peasant,' to the rescue. John Clare accordingly got a sweet little letter, full of bewitching flattery, ending with an invitation to Stratford Place. He trembled when he opened the note, addressed in the old familiar handwriting, and trembled still more when he read it. There was a time when poor John had been making Platonic love to Mrs. Emmerson; when he wrote to her scores of letters, very passionate and very ill-spelt; when he called her his Laura, and made verses in imitation of Petrarch; and in the end had the courage to ask for her portrait. Mrs. Emmerson graciously smiled upon the poor lover at her feet, and while employing him to correct her verses, even granted his request for her likeness, and sent him a beautiful painting by Behnes, the sculptor. John revelled in an elysium of bliss, and, hanging the picture on the place of honour over the mantelpiece, to the great disgust of Patty, got more and more embedded in tenderness, until his letters became sheer unreadable for passionate love, unassisted by grammar. The thing getting tiresome now, and there being no more verses to correct, Mrs. Emmerson thought fit to drop her Northamptonshire poet, and accordingly wrote him a quiet little note asking for a return of her portrait. John Clare fell from the clouds; but fell on his feet, fortunately. He took the beautiful picture down from over his mantelpiece, wrapped it in straw and brown paper, and sent it to Stratford Place, Oxford Street, by the next carrier. The consciousness came dawning on his mind that he was not quite up to the art of making Platonic love.

But Clare trembled when he read the new letter from Mrs. Emmerson. He had not heard from her for a long time, and could not for a moment understand what brought her to renew a correspondence, broken off in the most abrupt manner. His first impulse was to decline the invitation, which he did on the instant in a very long letter. And when he had written the long letter, he threw it into the fire, and indicted another shorter note, informing Mrs. Emmerson that he had already arranged with Mr. Allan Cunningham to visit London, and would be most happy to accept her hospitality at Stratford Place. Having despatched this note, Clare felt much pleased with himself. It would have been very rude, he thought, and almost offensive, to refuse the invitation of an old friend, given in all kindliness of heart. Perhaps it was he, after all, who was in fault respecting that unhappy affair of the portrait, which he took to be a gift, though it was meant only as a loan. He owed an apology to Mrs. Emmerson, that was quite clear; and for this reason alone, if for no other, ought to become her guest during his stay in town. Thus reasoned the poet, and the more he reasoned, the more impatient he got to set out on his journey. At last he started, earlier than he intended, taking the road by Peterborough, to pay his respects to the inmates of the episcopal palace.

VISITS TO NEW AND OLD FRIENDS.

Lions were rare at Peterborough forty years ago. The wife of the Right Reverend Dr. Herbert Marsh, an elderly lady of much energy, often felt lonesome in her old mansion at the foot of the big cathedral, for which suffering neither the sound doctrinal sermons of her husband nor the saintly gossip of weekly tea-parties offered any remedy. There was a little theatre at the episcopal city, at which performances were given now and then; but the histrionic talent of the strolling players being of the slightest, and the Right Reverend Dr. Marsh objecting, moreover, in a subdued manner, to give his immediate patronage to the Punch and Judy of the stage, the lady often felt time hanging heavy on her hands. In this exigency, Mrs. Marsh heard of the Helpston poet, and lost no time in making his acquaintance. Her kindly help and sympathy during his illness was greatly appreciated by Clare, and left him full of gratitude ever after. Nevertheless, though often invited to become a guest at the episcopal palace, he could not summon resolution to do so. He was afraid, not so much of the stiffness and ceremony which he would have to encounter, as of the stern looks of the high dignitary of the Church, who, when visiting him at home, had cross-questioned him in the most awful manner on all subjects, in particular as to the state of his religion. But pressed again and again to pay a short visit to Peterborough, Clare at length consented, being told that Dr. Marsh would be ' kept in his proper place,' and not be allowed to interfere with him. It was on this understanding that Clare made his appearance at the episcopal palace, at the commencement of February, 1828. Mrs. Marsh rejoiced that her poet had come at last, and at once installed him in a funereal little chamber overlooking the gardens, which she had long selected as fittest for the habitation of genius. Before being led to this room, Clare was informed by the lady that he would find several reams of paper, with stores of pens and ink, for his poetic use, and would be at liberty to write anything he liked, epics, madrigals, pastorals, sonnets, and even tragedies. Strict orders were given to the servants not to disturb the poet on any

account, but to take whatever food he might require—if
requiring food at all—to an adjoining room. The whole of
these excellent measures having been executed with great
precision, Mrs. Marsh left the palace, to complete the further
arrangements in connexion with the exhibition of her new
lion.

John Clare, being left alone in his little chamber, felt very
dull. He had no idea as to whether the way he was treated
was a special honour, or part of the general routine of episcopal existence. However, he concluded that, special or
general, his surroundings were of somewhat gloomy aspect.
There were certainly plenty of writing materials; but what
he wanted far more for the moment was a cup of tea, or
coffee, with a slice or two of bread and butter. After vainly
trying to make himself heard, he attempted to open the door
of his chamber, and found that it was not locked. But there
was no soul in the next room, nor in the farther passage, and
the whole mansion appeared to be silent like the grave. Up
another passage, and down a pair of stairs did not lead him
from the regions of silence; a little maid-servant, visible far
off, started away like a frightened hind on beholding the
poet. Mrs. Marsh evidently was well obeyed in her own
house. But Clare now began to feel rather uncomfortable,
and resolved to get somewhere, if not to human beings, at
least to bread and butter. So he marched down a final pair
of stairs, and through a small door out into the garden.
There was a porter at the outer garden gate; but he, too,
bowed in silence, and in another minute Clare found himself
in the streets of Peterborough. The doors of the 'Red Lion'
stood hospitably open, and feeling nigh starved, he went in to
get some refreshments. No tea and coffee, however, were to
be had at the 'Red Lion;' only ale and porter, brandy and
whiskey. Clare took some bread, with a glass of ale, and
felt very faint immediately after. Not having tasted any
alcoholic drink for a long time, the ale produced a sort of

stupefaction, from which he did not recover till late in the day. In the meantime, Mrs. Marsh returned to the episcopal palace, and at once inquired for her poet. He was not to be found anywhere, and it was discovered at last that he had escaped into the city. Messengers were despatched forthwith, and while they scoured the streets, John Clare ran right against them, coming from the 'Red Lion,' and feeling still somewhat drowsy. He was secured immediately, and taken in triumph before Mrs. Marsh. The lady, against his expectation, received him most graciously, ascribing his bewildered state to high poetic musings. She was sorry only that he had not been able to make use of her paper and ink in the chamber of genius; but trusted he would write all the more the next day, which, as she hinted, would be a day of great importance.

Clare went to bed, with the 'day of great importance' tingling in his ears. He could not go to sleep for reflections on the subject, and even after shutting his eyes it hovered over him in ghastly dreams. There was an immense table in an immense hall, with ten thousand parsons on the one side, and ten thousand old maids on the other. At the head presided Mrs. Marsh, with the bishop in waiting behind; while he himself was sitting in an arm-chair, suspended by ropes from the ceiling. Then Mrs. Marsh called upon him to make a speech, and while he was rising, down came the arm-chair, ropes and all. It was a hard bump, and Clare felt aching all over. Before he could rise, a man-servant rushed into the room. 'Good heavens, Sir, you have fallen out of bed,' he cried; 'I hope you are not hurt.' 'No, not much,' said Clare; 'but I should be glad to have a cup of tea.' The tea was brought, and with it some useful information. They were to have a grand party in the afternoon, said the man; he, that is, his mistress, having invited all the notabilities of Peterborough, with the dean, the archdeacon, and the canons. Clare shuddered. 'At what time will the entertainment commence ?' he inquired. ' At four,' was the reply. Nothing more was said; Clare sipped his tea, and, the servant gone, commenced making up his little bundle of clothes. Part of the contents he was able to stuff into his pockets; the rest formed a parcel not much larger than a couple of books. Once more he made his way down the broad flight of stairs, passed the silent porter at the gate, and a minute after stood in the High Street, opposite the Angel Inn. The coach for London, he was told, would start in half an hour. Clare took his seat inside, hiding his face, as best he could, under a handkerchief, and drawing a long breath when the horses were whipped into a gallop and sprang away southward. It was late at night when the Peterborough coach discharged its passengers at the ' Bell and Crown,' Holborn. Clare hurried up to Stratford Place, and was glad to find Mrs. Emmerson at home. The lady shook hands with the greatest cordiality, called him her dearest friend, and praised his verses in terms which made him blush. With all his bitter experiences, he was once more ready to fall in love—Platonic or otherwise.

One of Clare's first visits in London was to Allan Cunningham. He was received as a brother by the warm-hearted Scotchman, and encouraged to unburthen his whole heart. Allan now heard for the first time that his friend was in great pecuniary distress, and that his poetry, so far from bringing him a competence, as he had been led to believe, met with but the most trifling remuneration. Filled with compassion, Allan offered his friend assistance ; but this was proudly refused. He next advised Clare to go to Mr. Taylor, and request, politely but firmly, a statement of the whole of the transactions between them, including an account of the profits made by the sale of the ' Shepherd's Calendar,' the ' Village Minstrel,' and the ' Rural Poems.' Clare promised to do so, and the next day went to Mr. Taylor's residence, Percy Street, near Rathbone Place. The publisher received him in his ordinary friendly, though somewhat stiff and formal

manner. Clare was on the point of delivering his precon-
certed speech, when Mr. Taylor interrupted him with an unexpected communication. He told him frankly that he had
not been able hitherto to give much attention to the sale
of the 'Shepherd's Calendar,' and that this, probably, was
the reason why but few copies had been disposed of. As a
compensation, Mr. Taylor offered Clare to let him have as
many volumes of his new work as he liked at cost price, that
he might sell them in his own neighbourhood. The project
of becoming a perambulating bookseller, hawker of his own
poetical ware, came upon Clare in a startling manner. He
did not know what to reply to the proposal made to him,
and asked time for reflection. Mr. Taylor had no objection to
this, and told his friend to come again in a few days. Thereupon Clare went away, not saying a word on the financial
subject which he had come to discuss.

There was much fluctuating advice among Clare's friends
as to the propriety of his turning poetical bagman. Mrs.
Emmerson at first was greatly opposed to the scheme, but
afterwards changed her opinion, on the ground that the exercise and change of air might prove beneficial to his health.
Allan Cunningham, however, would not hear of Mr. Taylor's
scheme for a moment. He said it was disgraceful that such
a proposal should have been made, and exhorted his friend
not to think for a moment of accepting it. 'God knows,'
Allan exclaimed passionately, 'poetry has sunk low enough
already; but do not you haul it lower still by dragging the
muse along the muddy roads in a pedlar's bag.' Clare was
much impressed by these words, and promised further reflection, which, however, tended only to lead him in an opposite
direction to that proposed by his noble friend Allan. The
thought of being able to acquire a little capital; of getting
out of debt; of purchasing a small farm; and of giving his
children a good education, carried everything before it, and
he finally resolved to risk all else, even obloquy, to gain

these ends. Talking the subject over once more with Mrs. Emmerson, as happily ignorant as himself in the matter, the conclusion was arrived at that it would be easy to gain five hundred a year by the sale of his books. It seemed not necessary, therefore, that he should continue his new occupation longer than a few years, when he would be enabled to retire from business and spend the rest of his days in comfort and ease. Thus the poet kept on building his castles in the air, until they reached to the very clouds. When meeting Mr. Taylor at the appointed time, Clare told him that he accepted his kind offer, and would do his best to carry out the scheme with all possible energy. Thereupon the poet and his publisher parted—parted never to meet again, although to each life had scarce run half its course.

Clare remained in London till towards the end of March, lionising a little and making a few new acquaintances. Frequently, when walking along the streets, he found himself addressed by strangers, who recognised him at once from Hilton's exceedingly faithful picture, which hung in Mr. Taylor's parlour, and was reproduced in the portrait prefixed to the 'Village Minstrel.' Thus he ran one day in Russell Square against Alaric Watts, who, though never having met him before, addressed him without hesitation as a brother poet, and insisted upon remaining in his company for some time. In the same manner, too, he met Henry Behnes, the sculptor, who showed himself so delighted with his acquaintance that he would not let him go till he had promised to sit for his bust. Clare did sit, and Behnes produced an admirable work of art, which, like Hilton's picture, was paid for and kept by Mr. Taylor.* Mrs. Emmerson took

* Both the bust by Behnes, and Hilton's oil-painting of Clare, remained in Mr. Taylor's hands during his lifetime, and after his death (1864) were sold by public auction, at Messrs. Christie, Manson, and Woods, March 17, 1865, when they came into the possession of the author of this work.

advantage of the modelling of the bust by celebrating it
as a notable event, and inviting to her house a distinguished
party of artists and patrons of art, to whom she wished to
present her poet, together with 'his painter,' and 'his
sculptor.' As always on such occasions, Clare felt exceedingly uncomfortable, and had no sooner entered the bril-
liantly lighted-up saloon when he resolved to run away.
He communicated his intention to the other two heroes of
the evening, who at once expressed their wish to be the
companions of his flight. William Hilton, like Clare, was
averse to lionship, and glad enough to escape from any
crowd, whether in satin or rags ; and as for Henry Behnes,
he had become so fond of his 'Northamptonshire Peasant,'
that he declared himself ready to travel with him to the ends
of the world. The friends did not go quite as far on this
occasion, but only to a neighbouring tavern. Here the
happy trio, poet, painter, and sculptor, sat down to a supper
of bread and cheese, seasoned with pale ale, and the flow
of unrestrained thought. They talked of all the noblest
subjects that stir the human breast ; of all the unutterable
longings that fill the heart of genius. At last they talked
of each other, their hopes, aims, and aspirations, building
golden castles high up into the clouds. They saw fame
before them with outstretched arms ; wealth following in
its course ; and of love and happiness a bountiful reward.
These were lofty dreams : too lofty, alas ! for the flight of
helpless genius—genius not understanding the first of all
earthly arts, that of making money. William Hilton,
though a famous painter and Royal Academician, was left to
die in poverty, the greater part of his pictures remaining
on his hands unsold. Henry Behnes, noblest of sculptors,
went to perish in an hospital ; and John Clare . . . .
The reader may fill the blank.

Mrs. Emmerson was very angry with her guest when he
came back to her house a little after midnight, having been

kept so long in the delightful interchange of thoughts with
his two artist friends. Clare took very little notice of the
remarks of his fair host about want of courtesy and the
disappointment of distinguished visitors, his mind being full
of reflections engendered by the evening's conversation. He
inwardly resolved to enjoy, if possible, many more such
evenings ; but changed his determination the next day. It
was a beautiful day of spring, the warm sunlit air wafting in
soft breezes from over the green fields with its first blossoms,
into the crowded streets of the town. Clare took a long
walk through Regent's Park and past Primrose Hill towards
Hampstead, on the slopes of which he discovered some early
violets. The sight fairly made him home-sick. He ran back
to Stratford Place, and quite startled Mrs. Emmerson by
crying, 'I must go !' And go he did, twenty hours after ;
in such a haste as not even to find time to bid farewell
to Allan Cunningham, warmest of friends. But he left
a letter for Allan, 'a shake of the hand on paper,' which,
coming down to the present time, may be found still
interesting. The letter ran :—

'*Stratford Place, March* 21, 1828.

My Dear Cunningham—I wholly intended to see you,
but now I fear I cannot, as my stay is grown so short ; so, if
I cannot, here is a "good bye," and God bless you, and as
you are aware of my ignorance in travelling about your
great Babel, being insufficient to do so in most cases without a guide, which is not always to be procured, you must
allow me to make up for the omission by a shake of the
hand on paper, as hearty as your imagination can feel it.
If you had not been a poet I would not have made such
a bull, but it is an English one ; it has not a cold meaning.
Therefore accept it in lieu of a better. Pray give my kind
remembrances to Mrs. Cunningham, and if I could utter
compliments as well as I feel gratification in the society

of kind and warm-hearted people, I should grow eloquent
in her praise. But you well know I am not Ovid, and I as
well know I am no orator, so if I am unable to pay ladies
deserving compliments, if she will accept the plain respects
of a plain fellow, and allow them as nothing more, it will
please me much better. Once again, "good bye."

Now I am going to say last what would have been a
compliment to have said first, perhaps, and that is that Mrs.
Emmerson feels much gratified at your commendation of her
poem ["The Return," in Allan Cunningham's Annual, "The
Anniversary"], and much more so, as that commendation
came from a poet. Now comes the cut to my vanity, a sad
confession, but perhaps better "in the breach than the performance." (Allow me to misquote to suit my purpose.)
You ask me for a prose tale, and you imagine I have written
one. Good faith, my dear Allan, I have not, neither dare I,
for I know not what to say; excuses I might have for
writing it badly, but whether I could find excuses for
writing it at all I cannot say. I should be somewhat in
the case of the lady, who excused her faulty book before the
rude Dr. Johnson by saying that she had so many irons in
the fire that she had not time to write it better. You may
know his reply from my inability in the like. "Then I
advise you, madam," said he, "to put your book where your
irons are." Such I fear would be the deserving meed. of
a prose composition of mine, though your proposition goes a
good way to urge me, if I dare.—Farewell, my dear Allan,
and believe me your sincere friend and highly gratified
brother in the muses,

JOHN CLARE.'

The day after writing this letter, Clare was on his way
back to Helpston. He rejoiced inwardly when passing the
hill of Highgate, looking back over the vast world of bricks
and smoke behind, and beholding the sunny fields, fragrant

with the first blossoms of spring, in front. More than ever
he felt that he could not exist within the big metropolis,
even its large intellectual life offering no compensation for
the bounteous joys of nature. He almost shuddered when
glancing at the huge black vault for the last time, at the
turn of the Highgate Road. But he did not know it was
the last time that his eyes rested upon London.

THE POET AS PEDLAR.

Returned to Helpston, Clare made immediate preparations
for carrying out Mr. Taylor's project to become a hawker.
He sorted the little parcel of books which he had brought
from London, and having divided the volumes into sets, each
containing the 'Rural Poems,' 'Village Minstrel,' and 'Shepherd's Calendar,' he set out in regular pedlar fashion. By
dint of complex reasoning he had persuaded himself, to his
own entire satisfaction, that the profession of selling would
be fully as honourable as that of writing books; nay,
that there was greater merit in being the distributor than
the author, and consequently, that the highest vocation was
that of being both together. He therefore resolved to devote
himself with the greatest energy to his new business, and to
leave no stone unturned to succeed in it. As to his attempt
at farming, carried on during the past year in a very unprofitable manner, he had already come to the conclusion
to abandon it, by letting the land fall back to the original
tenant. Though in reality more attached to field labour than
any other kind of work, his love of it was for the moment
all obscured by the vision of the brilliant prospects open in
the new career as bookseller. His sufferings from poverty
had been so fearful, that the one all-absorbing aim to him
now was that of amassing a small capital and getting out of
debt.

It was on one of the first days in April when Clare commenced his trade as pedlar. With a dozen volumes of his poems in a canvas bag, slung by a strap over his shoulders, he bravely issued forth from his little hut, taking the road to Market Deeping. The people of the village, well acquainted with all his doings, peeped at him from out of doors and windows, shaking their heads in wonder at the strange sight. To his Helpston countrymen, Clare's new calling did not seem at all degrading, but, on the contrary, too ambitious. They looked upon a bagman as a person of superior social rank—decidedly higher than a poet. Their conclusions were fully justified from their own point of view, in a material sense. The hawkers who passed through Helpston were mostly men of substance, putting-up at the 'Blue Bell,' and ordering the best of everything from kitchen and cellar; while the poet among them was a starving wretch, over head and ears in debt, and with one foot in the workhouse. When Clare set out as a pedlar, therefore, they all declared that his ambition was carrying him too high. 'Pride comes before the fall,' said the old ones, tottering to the door, and stretching their necks to get a sight of neighbour John. He took no heed of all the signs of curiosity, but walked briskly up the road towards the north. The sun shone bright when he started; but before long it began to rain heavily, so that he was wet all through when arrived at Market Deeping. According to his carefully-arranged plan, he first called upon the rector. The reverend gentleman was at home, and condescended to see the poet. But his brow darkened when learning the errand of his visitor. He told Clare sharply that he did not intend buying his poems, and that, moreover, he held it unbecoming to see them hawked about in this manner. Having said this, he bowed his visitor out of the room, perceiving that his clothes were dripping wet, and likely to spoil his carpet. The poor pedlar-poet left the house with an ill-suppressed tear in his eye.

It still rained heavily, and Clare took refuge in a covered

yard attached to an inn. There were some horse-dealers lolling about, talking of the state of the weather and the forthcoming races. One of them, a jolly-looking man with red hair and a red nose, after scanning Clare for a while, engaged him in conversation. ' You have got something to sell there : what is it?' The answer was, ' Books.'—' Whose books?'—' My own.'—' Yes, I know they are your own ; or at least I suppose so. But what kind of books, and by what author?' — ' Poems, written by myself.' The horse-dealer stared. He looked fixedly at Clare, who was sitting on a stone, utterly dejected, and scarcely noticing his interlocutor. The latter seemed to feel stirred by sympathy, and in a more respectful tone than before exclaimed, ' May I ask your name ?'—' My name is John Clare,' was the reply, pronounced in a faint voice. But the words were no sooner uttered, when the jolly man with the red nose seized Clare by both hands. ' Well, I am really glad to meet you,' he cried ; ' I often heard of you, and many a time thought of calling at Helpston, but couldn't manage it.' Then, shouting at the top of his voice to some friends at the farther end of the yard, he ejaculated, ' Here's John Clare : I've got John Clare.' The appeal brought a score of horse-jobbers up in a moment. They took hold of the poet without ceremony, dragged him off his stone, and round the yard into the back entrance of the inn. ' Brandy hot, or cold ?' inquired the eldest of Clare's friends. There was a refusal under both heads, coupled with the remark that a cup of tea would be acceptable. An order for it was given at once, and after a good breakfast, and a long conversation with his new acquaintances, Clare left the inn, delighted with the reception he had met with. He had sold all his books, and received for them more than the full price, several of his customers refusing to take change. It altogether seemed a good beginning of a good trade.

Nevertheless Clare was uneasy in his mind. Not all the

kindness of his friends at the inn could compensate him for the
harsh words he had heard at the rectory. Clare asked himself
whether, supposing Market Deeping to be a fair sample of the
towns which he was going to visit, he would be able to bear
such treatment. And then the words of Allan Cunningham
recurred to his mind, and his noble scorn of the career in
which he was embarking. However, it seemed too late now
to repent, having gone beyond the starting point. The next
day, therefore, Clare once more slung his pack across his
shoulders, and sallied forth towards Stamford. He did not
expect to sell any of his books within the town, the market
having been abundantly supplied by Mr. Drury; but he had
hopes to meet with some success among the residents in the
neighbourhood, to many of whom he was personally known.
But his hopes were doomed to entire disappointment. He
went to numerous farmhouses, mansions, and parsonages, and
everywhere encountered refusal to purchase his ware. Some
persons upon whom he called treated him politely; others
with marked rudeness; and the great majority with indifference. Nearly all knew him by name, and had heard of his
poems; and nearly all, too, like the rector of Market Deeping, expressed their surprise that an author should retail his
own productions. One irascible old gentleman, living close
to the village of Easton, told Clare, after some conversation,
that he ought to be ashamed to go through the country with
a bundle on his back. The poet mildly suggested that to go
with a bundle might be better than to go to the workhouse
—the possible other alternative. There was huge astonishment depicted in the countenance of the old gentleman, and
he furtively left the room, evidently frightened at having
talked with a man likely to go to the workhouse.

It was late at night when Clare arrived home. He felt
footsore, and fainting almost from hunger and thirst, not one
of all the persons whom he had seen during sixteen hours
having offered him as much as a crust of bread or a glass of

water. The next day and the day after he was too ill to leave home, and remained on his couch, pondering on the subject uppermost in his mind. A fresh resolve to make still greater efforts to succeed was the result, come to after anxious consideration. As soon as recovered, he started again, this time to Peterborough. Though somewhat afraid of the inmates of the episcopal palace, he was in hopes of discovering a few friends in the city, having met with several people who knew his name and admired his writings during his previous short stay at the 'Red Lion.' Clare, therefore, once more visited this hospitable tavern, as well as the 'Angel,' but with no result whatever, as far as the sale of his books was concerned. The people were quite willing to talk with him for whole hours, and were willing even to pay for such slight refreshments as he might require; but they would not buy his books. They did not want poetry, they said; or they did not care for poetry; or they were not in the habit of reading poetry. Clare felt very depressed and sad at heart when starting on his homeward journey, after a day's ineffectual labour. He had left the 'Angel' inn, and was passing near the western front of the cathedral, when all on a sudden he found himself face to face with Mrs. Marsh. The active lady was bustling along in great haste, but recognised her poet at once. Escape being utterly impossible, he awaited his fate with resignation. But contrary to his anticipation, the bishop's wife was not in the least angry or resentful; she smiled upon him as benignly as if he had never escaped from her custody at a most trying moment. Clare did not know it at the time, but discovered afterwards, that Mrs. Marsh was pleased to allow him the privilege of unlimited eccentricity. That a poet should be playing fantastic tricks seemed to her the most natural thing in the world; perhaps she would not have held a man to be a true poet unless invested with this peculiar gift. Therefore, when Clare ran away in fear of her grand party, she did not wonder

much; only she blamed her servants for permitting him to
run away. That he had taken the coach to London she knew
an hour after he had started; but it was too late to follow
him, and too difficult to look for a single eccentric poet in
the streets of the metropolis. Great now was the joy of
Mrs. Marsh that accident threw him again into her way.

Being questioned as to his present movements, Clare was
simple enough, from a feeling of both diffidence and pride,
to hide his actual occupation. It was the greatest fault he
committed in his whole career of perambulating bookseller,
and fatal, in a sense, to his future prospects. With a better
acquaintance of the world and the human heart, he might
have known that Mrs. Marsh would have assisted him in
selling ten times as many books as he could ever hope to do
in his whole life; that she would have spread his 'Shepherd's Calendar,' like the Catechism, through the whole
diocese of Peterborough, and would have made every clerk
in holy orders, down to the lowest curate, buy the 'Village
Minstrel.' But Clare had no idea how active a friend he
possessed in Mrs. Marsh, and thereby lost the finest opportunity he ever had of succeeding in his career as a bagman.
He left the bishop's wife somewhat abruptly, on her renewed
invitation to pay a visit to the palace, and stay a week or
two in the chamber of genius. Hurrying home, very low
in spirits, Clare found the inmates of his little hut all in
trouble and consternation. A doctor was urgently needed
to attend to Patty, she having been suddenly seized with
the pains of labour. Though fearfully tired with his day's
march, he trotted back to Peterborough to fetch the medical
man. His assistance proved to be superfluous, for when
Clare returned he found that another member had meanwhile
been added to his household : a little son, who was christened
William Parker on the 4th of May, 1828. The poet's family
was increasing rapidly—too rapidly, alas, for his slender
means. Little William Parker was the third son and fifth

child, and there were now nine living beings within the
narrow hut depending upon Clare for bread. His head
throbbed in terrible anxiety when thinking that he might
not always be able to give them bread.

There was not much progress made in the bookselling
business during the next six months. Clare tried all possible
means to secure a sale of his works, walking not unfrequently
twenty and even thirty miles a day in all directions, through
Northamptonshire, Lincolnshire, and Rutland ; but meeting
with scarcely any success whatever. Sometimes, when most
fortunate, he sold two or three volumes a week, but oftener
did not find a single purchaser. Kindness, too, he met but
little, most of the people treating him as a pauper or a
vagrant. Many advised him to try the sale of trinkets and
drapery, or of pills and ' patent medicines,' instead of poetry ;
while others went so far as to recommend him to become an
itinerant musician. Having traversed the country in all
directions, suffering from want and fatigue, and, more still,
from insults, and not gaining enough to purchase the coarsest
food, he at last began to see the utter uselessness of perse-
vering further in his new occupation. However, as a last
attempt to succeed, he inserted a few advertisements in the
' Stamford News,' informing the public that he was selling
his own poems at his cottage at Helpston. This step was
taken by Mr. Taylor's advice, Clare having informed his
publisher of the failure of all his former operations. The
announcement in the ' Stamford News' did not remain
altogether without result, though its immediate effect was
rather unprofitable, the poet being visited by a number of
strangers, chiefly elderly ladies from the neighbouring towns,
who were kind enough to take his books upon credit, and
never ceased being creditors.

However, in spite of these constant disappointments,
Clare did not give up all hope of ultimately prospering as
a hawker of books. 'Though I have not as yet opened

Q 2

any prospect of success respecting my becoming a book-seller,' he wrote to Mr. Taylor, under date August 3d, 1828, ' yet I still think there is some hopes of selling an odd set now and then, and as you are so kind as to let me have them at a reduced rate, when I do sell them I shall make something, if only a trifle. I thought of more in my days of better dreams, but now even trifles are acceptable. For I do assure you I have been in great difficulties, and though I remained silent under them, I felt them oppress my spirits to such a degree that I almost sunk under them. Those two fellows of Peterborough in the character of doctors have annoyed and dunned me most horribly, and though their claims are unjust, I cannot get over them by any other method than paying.' The ' two fellows from Peterborough in the character of doctors ' were quacks into whose hands Clare, or rather his old father, had unfortunately fallen. They promised to cure the poor invalid of his lameness and all other ailings, and after nearly killing him with noxious drugs, made an exorbitant demand for ' professional assistance.' The demand was reduced ultimately, when they became aware of the utter poverty of Clare, to less than a tenth, which they extracted in small instalments, often taking the last penny from his pocket. For the present, Clare had hopes to pay ' those two fellows ' out of the income from ' annuals ' to which he was contributing. ' I am going to write for the Spirit of the Age,' he informed Mr. Taylor, ' for which I am to have a pound a page, and more when it becomes established. But promises, though they produce a good seedtime, generally turn out a bad harvest. Yet be it as it will, I am prepared for the worst. I have long felt a dislike to these things, but necessity leaves no choice.' Considering what Clare got for his other writings, the ' pound a page ' from the ' Spirit of the Age ' was no bad pay. But the poet's unqualified disgust of ' these things,' the annuals, was so great as often to counter-balance even his desire to gain a living by his pen. He not

unfrequently refused to write for the 'Souvenir' and 'Keepsake' family, and the only annual to which he contributed
with real pleasure was that under the editorship of Allan
Cunningham.

The advertisement in the 'Stamford News' brought some
curious letters to Helpston at the beginning of the autumn.
A few of the papers having been wafted into the eastern
parts of Lincolnshire, there came invitations from several
places for John Clare to show himself to the natives.   Feeling naturally dull in the Fens, they thought the sight of a
live poet, being a pedlar in the bargain, might be productive
of a mild kind of excitement, highly moral, and very cheap.
The mayor of Boston was the first to be struck with this
idea, which he communicated to the more distinguished of
his townsmen, and finally embodied in a most polite note of
invitation.   Clare felt exceedingly flattered by the compliments of the mayor of Boston, and in reply stated that he
would be happy to pay a visit to the ancient borough.   The
answer had no sooner been sent when there came summonses
from other places within the counties of Lincolnshire and
Norfolk.   At Grantham, too, they wanted to see John Clare,
as well as at Tattershall, at Spalding, and at Lynn Regis.
There seemed to be a slow poetic fever raging among the
people of the Fens.   Clare sent polite replies to all the courteous invitations, and having procured a small parcel of books
from Mr. Taylor, started for Boston at the end of September.
He walked all the way, and arriving in the evening of a
beautiful day, ascended the steeple of the old church, just
when the sun was sending his last rays over the surging
billows of the North Sea.   The view threw Clare into rapturous delight.   He had never before seen the ocean, and felt
completely overwhelmed at the majestic view which met his
eyes.   So deep was the impression left on his mind that it
kept him awake all night; and when he fell asleep, towards
the morning, the white-crested waves of the sea, stretching

away into infinite space, hovered in new images over his dreams.

The few days which he remained at Boston turned out a continual round of excitement. The worthy mayor called upon him at the 'White Hart,' the morning after his arrival, and insisted that he should be present at a grand dinner-party the same day. Finding all resistance useless, Clare submitted to his fate. The consequences he related to Mr. Taylor, in a letter written some time after. 'The mayor of the town,' Clare informed his publisher, 'was a very jolly companion, and made me so welcome, while a lady at the table talked so sweetly of the poets, that I drank off my glass very often, almost without knowing it, and he as quickly filled it—but with no other intention than that of hospitality —that I felt rather queer. It was strong wine, and I was not used to it.' After years of almost total abstinence from intoxicating drink, the effect was disastrous. For a whole day, the poet was confined to his little room at the inn, feeling very ill, and wishing himself back at Helpston. But the men of Boston had not yet done with him, and seemed determined to have as much lionizing as the occasion allowed. The mayor was preparing another dinner; and the lady who 'talked so sweetly of the poets' made strong attempts to get up a poetical conversazione, with sandwiches and lemonade; while some lively youths went so far as to order a supper at Clare's inn, thinking to make sure of their lion in this way. But he was not to be so easily caught, and, with some pride, let Mr. Taylor know how he escaped the ordeal. 'Several young men,' he informed his patron, 'had made it up among themselves to give me a supper, when I was to have made a speech. But as soon as I heard of it, I declined it, telling them if they expected a speech from me they need prepare no supper, for that would serve me for everything. And so I got off.' To which the pedlar-poet appended some moralizings, exclaiming, 'Really this speechifying is a sore humbug, and

the sooner it is out of fashion the better.' It was strange
how little John Clare understood the world in which he lived.

The visit to Boston was to have been followed by a trip to
other places in the eastern counties, but Clare felt unequal to
the task. A three days' sojourn at the 'White Hart' gave
him an insight into the nature of the work required from a
travelling provincial lion, and he became conscious that he
was not fitted for the calling. So he hurried home in great
haste, after having sold his little stock of books. The 'jolly
mayor' was kind enough to purchase two sets of the poetical
works, on the condition of getting the author's autograph,
together with his own name at full length, in every volume.
But the lady who talked so sweetly of the poets, refused to
buy anything, pleading that her bookcase was quite full
already. The truly liberal among the people of Boston were
the young men whose supper Clare refused. They made a
collection among themselves, and, unknown to the poet, put
ten pounds into his little wallet. He did not find the gift
of his unknown friends till he returned to Helpston, and the
discovery affected him to tears. For the first time in his life
he regretted not having made a speech, even at the risk of
breaking down in the middle of it.

CLOUDS AND SUNSHINE.

The journey to Boston was followed by a three months'
illness. A low fever, of the typhoid kind, was part of the
result of his trip into the fen country, and of the sudden
change of his diet, to which he had been driven in the intercourse with the hospitable mayor and his friends. The
disease spread through his whole family, attacking each
member in turn, and for a moment threatening to be fatal to
the youngest child. However, all recovered in the end,
though very gradually, it being not till towards the spring
of 1829 that the doctor's visits to the little hut came to

an end. The consequences of the illness did not end so soon.
Having been unable to do any work for months, and incurred,
moreover, great expenses for medical assistance and other
items connected therewith, Clare found himself now deeper
than ever in debt, and with scarcely any prospects of raising
himself from his abject state of poverty. Nevertheless, he
struggled on bravely, once more trusting to his pen and
poetical inspiration. That book-hawking would not open
the road to success, but, if anything, lead him into an
opposite direction, had become clear to him by this time,
and he resolved, therefore, to put himself once more into
communication with the editors of the annuals, so as to earn
a few shillings in writing poetry by the yard. In order to
extend the circle of his editorial acquaintances, he wrote
letters to several of his friends in London, notably to Mr.
John Taylor and Allan Cunningham. In the note to his
publisher, the old grievance of Clare came at length to be
touched upon by him in an almost piteous manner. The
poor poet's inexperience of the world was strikingly shown
in the tone as well as contents of this letter, bearing date
April 3d, 1829, and traced apparently in a trembling hand.

After referring to his continued efforts to dispose of his books
by means of advertisements in the 'Stamford News,' with
the appended doleful remark : ' If I succeed in selling them,
all well and good ; if not, it will not be the first disappointment I have met with,' Clare continues :—' And now, my
dear Taylor, I will, as a man of business, say what I have
long neglected to tell you. I never liked to refer to it ; but
it is a thing to be done, and, be it as it may, it will never
interfere in our friendship. So I should like to know at
your leisure how I stand with you in my accounts, and my
mind will be set at rest on that score at once. For if there
is anything owing to me it will be acceptable at any time,
and if there is nothing, I shall be content. The number
printed of the first three volumes I have known a long

while by Drury's account ; but whether I have overrun the
constable or not since then, I cannot tell, and that is what
I should like to know at the first opportunity.   I hope you
will not feel offended at my mentioning the matter, as I do
it with no other wish than to make us greater and better
friends, if possible.'   Notwithstanding this extreme humility
of tone, Mr. John Taylor felt offended at the letter of his
' Northamptonshire Peasant,'—and ' man of business ' to
boot.   He told the ' man of business ' that he was asking
indiscreet questions, and recommended him once more to try
success as a bagman, and to write for the annuals in his
spare hours.   To assist him in the latter object, Mr. Taylor
was kind enough to recommend his poet to a Monsieur
Ventouillac, ' 14, Cumming Street, Pentonville ; ' an enter-
prising professor of French, who was about entering upon
the Souvenir and Keepsake speculation.   John Clare, all
eagerness, wrote at once to Monsieur Ventouillac, and was
informed in return that the new annual, to be called ' The
Iris,' would be published in the autumn, and that his ' offer-
ings ' would be welcome.   Thereupon he sat down to write at
once a poem of twenty-five verses, entitled, ' The Triumph
of Time,' and sent it off in great haste to 14, Cumming
Street, Pentonville, with a request to forward ' the amount
for the trifle inserted ' at the earliest convenience.   The
' Iris ' made its appearance at the appointed time, as adver-
tised, ' bound in silk,' with numerous ' embellishments ' got
up regardless of expense.   But John Clare's ' Triumph of
Time ' was not in the ' Iris,' the able editor having placed it
among his waste papers, with a pencil note, ' to be shortened
one-half next year.'   The old MS. brown with age, has
survived the wreck of a thousand other manuscripts, and
remains in the world, melancholy to look at as a memorial
of the fate of poetry and poets.

Clare's success with the annuals, now as formerly, was
of a most unsatisfactory nature.   Acting upon Mr. Taylor's

advice, he continued sending verses to the wonderful periodicals, bound in silk, and got up regardless of expense,
but seldom received any money in return. Some took his
verses, and some did not; and nearly all forgot the fact of
other acknowledgment being due besides complimentary letters. Even Mr. Alaric Watts, who had made Clare's personal
acquaintance the year previous, forgot his promise to insert
one of his poems in the 'Literary Souvenir,' preferring
jingling rhyme manufactured to suit the 'embellishments.'
Almost the only one who took Clare's verses, as well as
paid for them, was brave Allan Cunningham, who stood fast
to his friend amidst all the deluge of silk-bound volumes.
During the present summer, as in former years, Clare continued his contributions, consisting, in this instance, of
several pastorals and sonnets, among them some verses dedicated to Mrs. Emmerson. But, owing to Clare's rather illegible handwriting, Mr. Cunningham misread the address
of these lines, which so much affected the poet that he wrote
a long and curious note of explanation to Mrs. Emmerson.
'My dear Eliza,' the note ran : 'I got a letter from friend
Cunningham yesterday, who tells me that my trifles suit
him. Among them are the verses to E. L. E. of which he
makes a strange mistake by fancying they are written to Miss
Landon, and flatters me much by praising them, and also by
thinking them "worthy of the poetess." So I wish that
the first opportunity you have you would correct the mistake,
and if you feel the matter too delicate to write upon, you can
tell the Miss Frickers when they next call upon you. For
he will most likely change the E. L. E. to L. E. L. which I
shall not be able to rectify if he does not send me a proof
sheet, and I would much rather that they should stand as
written. Proud as I am of brother Allan's commendation,
and proud as I should be of Miss Landon's commendation
also, I feel much prouder to know that they were deemed
worthy the acceptance of yourself, to whom they were dedi-

cated. I will give you the quotation from Allan's letter relating to the verses :—" I have placed your contributions in the approved box, marked with my hearty approbation. Your verses to Miss Landon are the very best you ever composed. After all, a flesh and blood muse is best, and Miss Landon I must say is a very beautiful substitute for these aerial mistresses. I shall show it to her." How Allan should mistake E. L. E. for L. E. L., I cannot say ; but in his hurry he must have overlooked it, and I hope you will rectify the error. I did not tell him to whom the verses were written, because I thought is was not necessary, but I wish I had now power to prevent the mistake that may get into the proof-sheet, and remain there if not corrected—.' To judge by the earnestness with which he dwells upon the subject, these little troubles of authorship had nearly as deep an effect upon Clare's sensitive mind as some of his real life-sorrows.

When Clare came to make up the account of his income derived from the annuals, he found that his labours in this direction were less remunerative than stone-breaking on the road would have been. He thereupon determined to break his connexion with the silk-bound periodicals, with the exception of two or three of the class, Allan Cunningham's ' Anniversary' among the number. But with Allan, too, he had occasion to find fault ; not indeed for paying him too little, but too highly. 'I do not,' he wrote to him, in 1829, ' expect pay by the foot or page, but I like to give good measure and throw in an extra gratis. You gave me too much for my last, and I hope you will keep that in mind next year and not do so ; for I never feel the loss of independence worse than when I cannot serve a friend without knowing that I receive a recompense in return far more than the labour is entitled to.' Allan Cunningham responded nobly to this disinterested communication. He told his friend that, though his poetry was of the highest excellence, he was a writer altogether unfit for the annuals, and the great world of printers and publishers. In half-playful and half-serious mood, he advised him to try his hand again at farming, offering some assistance for the purpose. Clare hesitated for a while; but having carefully considered the matter, accepted the kindly help tendered by his friend. His chief hope was in the expectation that he should be able to profit by past experience, and, avoiding former errors, convert failure into success. So he took again a small plot of land, for farming purposes, in the autumn of 1829.

There did not seem at first much prospect of good fortune in the new speculation; nevertheless it turned out remarkably well in the end. Clare had no sooner returned to his old labours in the field than his health improved visibly; his mind became more cheerful, and everything around him seemed to assume a bright and sunny look. His pecuniary circumstances, too, improved considerably; small sums sufficient to pay the most pressing of his debts, came in payment for his books; and even the proprietor of a London annual had the extreme generosity to pay for contributions sent to him three years previously. Best of all, he got some regular employment on a farm belonging to Earl Fitzwilliam, which, together with the cultivation of his own little plot of land, served to fill up his whole time, leaving him no leisure for writing, but adding a fair sum to his income. This enforced rest from his poetical labours proved of the greatest benefit to Clare. The immense mass of verses which he had produced within the last few years threatened to be highly detrimental to his genius, in exhausting his mind, and destroying the very sap of his poetical imagination. He required mental rest, more than anything else; and this being not only given, but enforced in his new occupation as both cottage-farmer and agricultural labourer, he found himself almost suddenly a better, wiser, and more prosperous man. Clare never spent a happier Christmas than that of 1829. With his little baby-boy, now eighteen months old, on his knees, his Patty and four eldest children around the table, and his aged parents seated comfortably at the place of honour near the fireside, he thought himself truly blessed, and on the very zenith of earthly joys. There was scarcely a wish of his heart left for fulfilment, save, perhaps, the old dream to possess a little strip of the surface of mother earth, and be a king on his own land, instead of a serf labouring for others. It was the one lasting dream of his life—a dream unfortunately never destined to be realized.

The next twelve months of Clare's life were uneventful. He worked hard and wrote little; and, with increasing bodily and mental health, got more and more at ease in his worldly circumstances. Even his little attempt at farming was not altogether unsuccessful, for though it did not bring much direct gain, it secured to him the esteem of his neighbours, and a feeling of self-dependence which he had never before known. When Patty presented him with another baby —sixth in the list; baptized Sophia, on the 3d of October, 1830—he felt by no means despondent as on a former occasion, but joyful in the extreme. The dread vision of poverty, so long before his eyes, had suddenly vanished, giving way to fancies of roseate hue. He almost wondered why he had ever despaired—happiness, after all, seemed so cheap and within such easy reach. There was wealth and health sufficient springing from his daily labour, and abundant joy in the constant sight of green fields, rippling brooks, and the smiling faces of his little ones at home. And there was joy scarce ever known when sitting down, at rare intervals, to the inspiration of the muse. Here was the supreme bliss of existence. Clare knew that the poetry, offspring of these happy hours, was far superior to anything that had ever flown from his pen. He almost felt as if now, and now only, he was becoming a true poet.

In truth, Clare never was a writer of perfect melodious verse till this time. A poet he had always been—had been from the day when, a tottering child, with senses scarce awakened, he thought to discover at the faint outline of the distant horizon, the touch of heaven and earth. But hitherto, and up to this period, the tumultuous inspiration of his soul had never found vent in soft and even flow of language : the poet had never been completely able to clothe noble thoughts into noble form. Want of early training, with grief and care, and unceasing mental agitation, had hemmed in on all sides the fair stream of his imagination, and the bright flash of genius was hidden under more or less rugged form. It was only now, that, having nursed his mind at the source of the great masters of poetry, and enjoying harmonious peace and rest from cares in the calm life of labour, that the outward form came to be mastered by the inward spirit, as clay in the hands of the sculptor. The poet himself was surprised at this momentous change, which came upon him with a suddenness almost startling in its intensity. He had left off writing verses for many months, devoting every moment of leisure to calm study, and happy wanderings through woods and fields, when one evening, with the setting sun before his eyes, he felt a powerful longing to make one more attempt in poetical composition. Full of this feeling, he sat down at the borders of Helpston Heath, lost in heavenly visions, and as he sat there the verses came flowing from his pen :—

> 'Muse of the fields ! Oft have I said farewell
> To thee, my boon companion, loved so long,
> And hung thy sweet harp in the bushy dell
> For abler hands to wake an abler song—
>
> .   .   .   .
>
> Aye, I have heard thee in the summer wind,
> As if commanding what I sung to thee ;
> Aye, I have seen thee on a cloud reclined,
> Kindling my fancies into poesy ;

I saw thee smile, and took the praise to me.
In beauties, past all beauty, thou wert drest :
I thought the very clouds around thee knelt,
I saw the sun did linger in the West
Paying thee worship ; and as eve did melt
In dews, they seemed thy tears for sorrows I had felt.

Sweeter than flowers on beauty's bosom hung,
Sweeter than dreams of happiness above,
Sweeter than themes by lips of beauty sung,
Are the young fancies of a poet's love.'

. . . .

When Clare had written his song ' To the Rural Muse,' he
went home and kissed his children, and, it being full moon,
kept working in his garden for another couple of hours.
And the next day, and for days after, he kept on digging
and planting, hoeing and ploughing, without ever touching
a pen. It was thus a great and noble poet grew out of the
' Northamptonshire Peasant.'

FRIENDS IN NEED.

The short summer was followed by a long winter. Again
Clare fell ill ; and with suffering and disease there came a
train of misfortune completely overwhelming the frail life of
the poet. The year 1831 proved very unfavourable to his
farming operations, and, having no capital whatever to fall
back upon, he at once relapsed into his former state of indi-
gence. It was in vain that he attempted to make up for his
losses by increased exertions as a labourer. Working fifteen
and sixteen hours a day during harvest time, and not unfrequently standing up to his knees in mud in the undrained
fields, his health gave way before long, and then there was
an end of all work. He was confined to his bed for longer

than a month, and gaunt poverty now again made its appearance at the little hut. There were ten persons to be clothed
and fed, and no money incoming save the small quarterly
stipend settled upon the poet, which was scarce sufficient to
pay off the debts incurred by the unsuccessful farming of
the year. When Clare saw that his children were wanting
bread, his heart trembled in agony of despair. He rushed
forth once more to labour in the fields, but had to be carried
home by his fellow workmen; a mere look at his feverish
ague-stricken frame being sufficient to show them that he was
utterly unfit to be out of doors. So he had to lay his head
again on his couch, happily unconscious for a time of what
was passing around him. There was deep sorrow and lamentation in the little hut of the poet.

When everything was at the worst, kind friends came to
the rescue. The Rev. Mr. Mossop, vicar of Helpston, and
his kind-hearted sister, who had often before assisted Clare
and his family, gave once more active aid and succour;
and from Milton Park, too, there came valuable presents of
food and medicine. Thus when the poet was able again to
leave his bed, he found a much brighter outlook around him.
Nevertheless, though there was no more absolute want of
the necessaries of life, grim poverty was still standing at
the threshold. The baker threatened to stop the supply of
bread if his debt should long remain unpaid, and even the
owner of the little ruinous dwelling, fourth part of a hut, in
which Clare lived, hinted that the inmates would be driven
out, unless the arrears of rent were discharged. This last
menace almost drove the poet wild with excitement. Narrow
and dark as it was, he dearly loved the little hut in which he
was born, and the thought of leaving it, with, perhaps, the
ultimate prospect of going to the workhouse for shelter, was
to him blank despair. Agitated beyond measure, he ran to
his friends at Milton Park, imploring aid and advice. Mr.
Edward Artis was, as usual, away on his antiquarian rambles,

intending to leave the service of Earl Fitzwilliam altogether, and devote himself to authorship on Durobrivæ and Roman pottery. But Henderson was at home, and to him Clare poured out his tale of woe. While talking in the garden, the earl happened to come near, and kindly addressed Clare. The latter, in his excitement, found courage to speak of all his troubles, and his fear of having to quit his little home, with no place in the world where to lay his head. His lordship was struck with the intensity of feeling exhibited by the poet. He told him that he would attend to his wants, and provide a little cottage for him somewhere in the neighbourhood. Clare was astonished; the offer seemed to him so excessively generous that he scarce knew how to express his thanks. Seeing his confusion, the earl turned to other subjects, asking Clare whether he intended to bring out a new volume of poems, and being answered in the negative, earnestly advised him to do so. The counsel of the noble lord, no doubt, was well meant, but nevertheless very injudicious. The grant of a few acres of land, in a healthy district and at a moderate rent, would have been more beneficial to him than all the fame he could ever hope to gain from book-making.

Clare returned to his cottage with a joyful heart, brimful of pleasant visions of the future. The next day he was visited by Dr. Smith, a physician of Peterborough, who came in consequence of orders received from the noble owner of Milton Park. Earl Fitzwilliam, in his interview with Clare, perceived, or fancied he perceived, a certain wildness of looks about him, and not knowing what to think of it, was anxious to get the opinion of a medical man, well known for his successful treatment of mental diseases. The poet was not at all pleased with the visit of Dr. Smith; however, in gratitude to his benefactor, he willingly submitted to a lengthened examination. It had for result a report by the Peterborough physician to Earl Fitzwilliam, stating that there was

no mental derangement whatever visible in Clare; but that
his brain, developed to an unusual degree, was liable to great
and sudden fits of excitement, from which it ought to be
guarded by constant employment and a fair share of physical
labour.   Here was useful advice; but which, unfortunately,
was misunderstood by his lordship.   The earl quite agreed
with the counsel of giving employment; but fancied the most
natural work for a poet was that of writing poetry, at almost
any time, and to any extent.   In consequence, he sent for
Clare, and, repeating his promise of giving him a neat little
cottage with garden for occupation, urged him strongly not
to neglect writing poetry, and to publish his new volume as
soon as possible.   Clare was but too willing to follow the
advice of the noble lord.

The visits of Dr. Smith to Helpston did not cease with
the first.   Having been very favourably impressed with the
character of the poet, the Peterborough physician took a
great liking to him, and lost no occasion for friendly intercourse.   Clare being devoted anew to writing poetry, some
of the verses fell under the notice of the doctor, who expressed his approbation of them in rapturous terms.   This
naturally won the heart of the author, and, being urgently
pressed, he consented to pay a visit to his medical friend at
Peterborough, and stay a few days at his house.   The visit
took place in the spring of 1832, and led to some not un-
important results.   Having communicated to his friend his
former unfavourable attempts of book-publishing, and how
the four volumes which had been issued had brought him
nothing more substantial than fame, Dr. Smith felt moved
by compassion, and began earnestly to reflect upon the great
problem of converting poetry into cash.   The result of these
meditations came out in the shape of strong advice to Clare
to fall back upon the old plan he had once entertained of
publishing his verses by subscription.   This was coupled
with the promise that he would do his best to procure sub-

scribers, and otherwise assist in the matter. Clare joyfully entered into the scheme, and, before leaving Peterborough, made arrangements with a Mr. Nell, a bookseller, to be his local agent for getting subscriptions, as well as to make arrangements with a London publisher to bring out the new volume of poems as soon as sufficient subscribers had ensured the success of the work. Mr. Nell promised his most energetic support, and being on the point of undertaking a visit to the metropolis, Clare furnished him with the following note to his friend Allan Cunningham :—

Angel Inn, Peterborough.

MY DEAR ALLAN,

Here is a friend of mine, a Mr. Nell, a very hearty fellow, and one who is very desirous of seeing you—a poet, and, as I have convinced him, as hearty a fellow as himself. Therefore I have taken the liberty of introducing a stranger without any apology, feeling that such an introduction was not needed. He will be particularly gratified in seeing what you can show him of the immortal specimens of Chantrey's genius, and any other matters that can interest a literary man ; for his profession, that of a bookseller, is not his only recommendation, he being a man of no common taste, and also a great admirer of painting and sculpture, and a lover of the muses.

Here ends my introduction of my friend Mr. Nell. And now, my dear Allan, how are you? How is Mrs. Cunningham and your family, and our old friend George Darley? As for myself, I am as dull as a fog in November, and as far removed from all news of literary matters as the man in the moon ; therefore I hope you will excuse this dull scrawl, and believe me, as I really am,

Yours heartily and affectionately,

JOHN CLARE.

Has Hogg visited London yet? When he does tell me,

and I'll see if I don't muster up every atom of my strength to have a sight of him.

Having left your address at Helpston, I am obliged to trust this letter and my friend to Providence to find you, which I trust he will readily.   Your

J. C.

Allan Cuningham, Esq. London.
Favoured by my friend, Mr. Nell.'

Although 'as dull as a fog in November,' Clare was in a hopeful mood at this time. Sanguine as ever, and more than ever imbued with the consciousness of his poetical power, he dreamt that his new publication would be a success, and that his verses at last would gain a sufficient circle of admirers to encourage him in writing more, and thus securing independence for the rest of his days. This hopefulness was somewhat disturbed after a while by news from his friends at Peterborough, who told him that sub-scribers were coming in but very slowly. These unfavour-able tidings he communicated to Mr. Artis, in a note dated May, 1832, in which he said : 'I want to get out a new volume ; but the way in which I have started is not very practicable, for I want to make it a source of benefit.' The words bear a striking melancholy sound. Evidently the poor poet, deeply impressed with his sad experience of the past, scarcely dared to expect the golden millennium when his verses should actually prove 'a source of profit' to him as well as to the booksellers. There probably never lived a poet—a printing and publishing poet—full of more sublime meekness and resignation.

NORTHBOROUGH.

Earl Fitzwilliam punctually kept his promise to assign a new dwelling to Clare. The latter received notice at the beginning of May that he might remove in the course of the month to a pretty and substantial cottage which his lordship had erected for him 'at the hamlet of Northborough, three miles from Helpston, nearer to the Peterborough Great Fen. The news did not bring joy to the poet, but bitter sorrow. His heart was full of anguish at the thought of quitting the little hut where he was born, the village which he so dearly loved, and all the familiar scenes and objects amidst which the quiet course of his existence had rolled on for nearly forty years. He went over to Northborough, and saw the neat dwelling which the kindness of Earl Fitzwilliam had prepared for him; and though he liked the place, he could no more than before reconcile his mind to the thought of leaving his dear old home and all its cherished associations. The noble earl had fixed upon Northborough as the residence of the poet on account of the thoroughly sylvan scenery all around, the little hamlet lying hidden in a very sea of flowers, trees, and evergreens. The spot indeed was beautiful enough; yet to Clare it did not appear half so beautiful as the bare and bleak environs of his native village. Here he knew every shrub and every inch of ground, and, through many years' converse with nature, had come to look upon the most minute objects with intense feelings of love. Though strangers might see nothing but a barren landscape all around, to him it was a Garden of Eden, animated with living thought, and full of soul-inspiring beauty. The mere thought of quitting this Eden filled his mind with terror.

The terror increased when the time came near that he was actually to leave. More than once he was on the point of requesting an audience at Milton Park, for the purpose of imploring the noble earl to take back his kind gift and leave him in his little hut. But his friends at Milton Park, Artis and Henderson, would not hear of this resolution, and got quite angry at the mere mentioning of the subject. They represented to Clare that it would be black ingratitude on his part not to accept the generous benefaction of his lordship, who had taken all along the greatest interest in his welfare, and in this very choice of a residence in the evergreen vale of Northborough had shown the most delicate taste and appreciation of his poetical genius. Clare could not deny the force of these arguments, and, after another inward struggle, decided to go to Northborough, at any sacrifice to his feelings. Yet even after this firm determination of his mind, he could scarcely bring himself to the execution of the task. Patty, radiant with joy to get away from the miserable little hut into a beautiful roomy cottage, a palace in comparison with the old dwelling, had all things ready for moving at the beginning of June, yet could not persuade her husband to give his consent to the final start. Day after day he postponed it, offering no excuse save that he could not bear to part from his old home. Day after day he kept walking through fields and woods among his old haunts, with wild haggard look, muttering incoherent language. The people of the village began to whisper that he was going mad. At Milton Park they heard of it, and Artis and Henderson hurried to Helpston to look after their friend. They found him sitting on a moss-grown stone, at the end of the village nearest the heath. Gently they took him by the arm, and, leading him back to the hut, told Mrs. Clare that it would be best to start at once to Northborough, the earl being dissatisfied that the removal had not taken place. Patty's little caravan was soon ready, and the poet, guided by his friends, followed in the rear, walking mechanically, with eyes half shut, as if in a dream.

His look brightened for a moment when entering his new dwelling place, a truly beautiful cottage, with thatched roof, casemented windows, wild roses over the porch, and flowery hedges all around. Yet, before many hours were over, he fell back into deep melancholy, from which he was relieved only by a new burst of song. His feelings found vent in the verses :—

'I've left my own old Home of Homes,
    Green fields, and every pleasant place ;
The summer like a stranger comes,
    I pause—and hardly know her face.

. . . . .

I miss the heath, its yellow furze,
    Mole-hills and rabbit-tracks, that lead
Through besom-ling and teasel burrs
    That spread a wilderness indeed :
The woodland oaks, and all below
    That their white powder'd branches shield,
The mossy paths—the very crow
    Croaks music in my native field.

I sit me in my corner chair,
    That seems to feel itself alone ;
I hear fond music—here and there
    From hawthorn-hedge and orchard come.
I hear—but all is strange and new :
    I sat on my old bench last June,
The sailing puddock's shrill " pee-lew,"
    O'er Royce Wood seemed a sweeter tune.

I walk adown the narrow close,
    The nightingale is singing now ;
But like to me she seems at loss
    For Royce Wood and its shielding bough.
I lean upon the window sill,
    The trees and summer happy seem,—
Green, sunny green they shine—but still
    My heart goes far away to dream

Of happiness—and thoughts arise
    With home-bred pictures many a one—
Green lanes that shut out burning skies,
    And old crook'd stiles to rest upon.

  . . . . .

I dwell on trifles like a child—
    I feel as ill becomes a man ;
And yet my thoughts like weedlings wild
    Grow up and blossom where they can.'—

' Northborough, June 20, 1832,' these lines were written.
They formed the beginning of a new era in the life of the
sorrowing poet.

Happiness never came to Clare in his rose-enshrined cottage
at Northborough. His poetical powers culminated at this
period ; but his mind gradually gave way under a burthen
of sorrows and cares. Perhaps some of them were fanciful,
and such ' as ill become a man ;' but the bulk had their
roots in bitter reality. Clare now had a pretty cottage to
live in ; yet, for all that, remained as poor as ever. In truth,
he was, if anything, poorer ; for having left his old neighbourhood, and come to dwell among strangers, he had lost
his chances of finding work as a farm-labourer. His little
garden, it was true, yielded a few fruits and vegetables for his
family ; yet there was not a tithe enough for their support,
and dire want was standing at the door with as grim aspect
as ever. Then there came new expenses for keeping the
larger cottage in repair, and for fitting it with appropriate
furniture, and a mountain of fresh debt was added to the
old liabilities which so sorely pressed upon the poor poet.
It was a pressure nigh overwhelming to a tenderly susceptible
mind.

Clare's removal to Northborough had the immediate effect,
not desirable by any means, of drawing upon him the attention of a number of persons more or less acquainted with

his works, but by whom he had been forgotten. As usual, public rumour magnified to an enormous extent the nature of the bounty conferred by Earl Fitzwilliam ; and while the most moderate statement was that the poet had an annual allowance of two hundred pounds a year from his lordship, besides a fine house to live in, others went so far as to raise the two hundred to a thousand, and the house to a mansion. Local newspapers busily printed these attractive items of public intelligence, and the consequence was that the cottage at Northborough was for some months quite besieged with visitors, all come to congratulate. Clare felt in no mood to give or receive compliments, and positively refused to enter-tain the stream of kind friends of whose friendships he had never before been aware. With a few of the visitors, how-ever, with whom he had been previously acquainted, he entered into conversation, speaking frankly of his actual circumstances, and of the entire untruth of the rumours which assserted his sudden wealth. Among the friends who gained his confidence to this extent was a Mr. Clark, editor of a literary magazine, who, with the view of making a little article out of his visit, questioned and cross-questioned Clare in the most minute way as to his financial circumstances, and the number of his patrons. John Clare, as to all men, so here to this supposed friend, spoke in a frank and con-fiding manner, not hiding the fact that his poetry had never been remunerative, nor that, though having many patrons left, he was on the very brink of starvation. This was interesting news to Mr. Clark ; and the matter being emi-nently fit for raising the old discussion about poets and their patrons, he spun it into a flaming article, duly painted and coloured, which was printed in the literary magazine.

The poet was immensely astonished when, at the beginning of October, he received a paper containing an account of himself and his troubles. It was stated that his publishers had robbed him of the profits of his works ; that some noble patrons, alluded to in no complimentary terms, kept feeding him with compliments, but left him to starve; and much more to the same effect.   The whole account deeply hurt his feelings, and he at once sent a letter to a friend at Stamford, contributor to Mr. Clark's magazine.   The letter ran: ' My dear friend,—I am obliged to write to you to contradict the misrepresentations in your paper of October the 5th, which I received on Saturday.   As long as my own affairs are misrepresented, I care nothing about it ; but such falsehoods as are bandied about in this article not only hurt my feelings but injure me.   Mr. Clark in making these statements must have known that he was giving circulation to lies ; and had I been aware of his intentions to meddle in my affairs, I should most assuredly have treated him as a foe in disguise. For enemies I care nothing ; from friends I have much to fear, it seems.   There never was a more scandalous insult to my feelings than this officious misstatement . . . .   I am no beggar ; for my income is £36, and though I have had no final settlement with Taylor, I expect to have one directly.' The letter, after going into the details of his commercial transactions both with Mr. Drury and Mr. Taylor, not altogether complimentary to the former, ended with a positive demand that the statements made in the magazine should be retracted.

But no attention was paid to this demand.   The result was that Clare got more gloomy and melancholy than ever, hiding himself for whole days in the neighbouring woods, and refusing to see even the most intimate of his friends. The publication of the unfortunate magazine article and ' officious misstatement,' of which there appeared no public contradiction, was likewise not without effect upon the demeanour of Clare's patrons.   Earl Fitzwilliam, after providing him with a suitable dwelling in an unexpectedly generous manner, subsequently left him to his fate.   Thus the poet sank deeper and deeper into poverty and wretchedness, until he could sink no further.

ALONE.

The publication of the new volume of verses made little progress for a long time to come. Notwithstanding the strenuous exertions of Dr. Smith and other friends, the desired subscribers were very slow in presenting themselves, poetry being evidently at a discount at the border of the fen regions. In the spring of 1833, Clare informed his kind friend, the Vicar of Helpston, who continued to assist him in his needs, that he had secured 'subscribers for forty-nine copies' of his intended new volume; adding, however, the dismal fact of eighteen among them being 'rather doubtful.' Thus a poet, whose fame the leading organ of criticism, the 'Quarterly Review,' had proclaimed a dozen years before, and who was now at the very zenith of his power, was actually unable to find more than thirty persons in his own neighbourhood, where he was best known, who would support him to the extent of a few pence. Nor was Clare more fortunate in his endeavours to find patronage among the great publishers of the metropolis. Although he sent specimens of some exquisite songs and ballads to many of the best-known dealers in poetical ware, they declined publishing them without having the previous signatures of a certain number of purchasers. One of the specimen poems thus sent to London was the following song, entitled 'Woman's Love:'—

'O the voice of woman's love!
What a bosom stirring word!
Was a sweeter ever uttered,
Was a dearer ever heard,
Than woman's love?

How it melts upon the ear !
How it nourishes the heart !
Cold, cold must his appear
Who has never shared a part
Of woman's love.

'Tis pleasure to the mourner,
'Tis freedom to the thrall ;
The pilgrimage of many,
And the resting place of all,
Is woman's love.

'Tis the gem of beauty's birth,
It competes with joys above ;
What were angels upon earth
If without woman's love ?
A woman's love.'

It did not seem to strike the publishers, to whom this poem, with many similar ones, was submitted, that there was anything beautiful in it; and after having travelled up and down Paternoster Row, the verses were returned to the author, 'with thanks.' One bookseller, indeed, offered to bring out the volume, but on condition that Clare was to advance one hundred pounds, to be spent in steel engravings and other 'embellishments.' Without embellishments, he told his correspondent, the verses would never attract public attention, the taste of the day being all for high art, as exhibited in the annuals. Clare wrote an angry note in return, deeming it an insult that a man should ask him to spend a hundred pounds upon steel engravings, when he was in want of bread.

The winter of 1832-3 proved the greatest trial the unhappy poet had yet undergone. With scarcely food for his children; with not money enough to satisfy even a fraction of the claims of his most importunate creditors ; and with no expectations of earning anything, either by work in the fields or by the publication of his new volume of verses, he saw nothing but the dreariest prospect of misery staring him in the face. He wept bitterly when, on the 4th of January, 1833, his wife brought him another boy, his seventh child. Passionately fond of his little ones, and devoted to them heart and soul, he could not bear the thought of the coming day when he might have no bread to give them. The mere idea made him feel faint and giddy, and he rushed forth into the fields to cool his throbbing head. Not returning in time for the evening meal, his eldest daughter went in search through all the neighbourhood. After long inquiries and searching, she found her father lying on an embankment, close to a footpath leading from Northborough to the village of Etton. He looked deadly pale, and being quite insensible, had to be carried home on the shoulders of some labourers, who were called for assistance. Consciousness did not return till some hours after, and for nearly a month he was unable to leave his bed. The parish doctor, when called in, shook his head, talked something of ague and fever, and ended by sending some bottles full of yellowish stuff, which Clare refused to take. He knew, better than the doctor, that something else than medicine was required to restore his health—health of the mind, as well as of the body.

When the spring came, Clare had gathered sufficient strength to be able to leave the house. But he now, to the infinite surprise of his family, refused to leave it. He seemed to have lost, all at once, his old love for flowers, sunshine, and green trees, and kept sitting in his little study, silently writing verses, or poring over his books. In vain his children begged him to go with them into the smiling fields, spread out temptingly on all sides around their pretty cottage. He went, now and then, as far as the garden ; but quickly returned, sitting down again to his books and papers. Some theological works in his collection, which had been presented

to him years ago, but at which he had scarcely ever looked
before, now chiefly engrossed his attention. He sat reading
them all day long, and often till late at night, neglecting
food and rest over the perusal of these works. Sometimes
he ceased reading for a few hours, and took to writing religious
verses, attempting paraphrases of the Psalms, the Proverbs,
and the Book of Job. Visitors he now altogether refused to
see, and even to his wife and children he spoke but little.
Thus the news of his illness did not spread beyond the village, and remained unknown even to his friends at Milton
Park. It was quite accidentally that Dr. Smith looked in
upon his friend one day, and was admitted after some difficulty. The doctor was startled on seeing the pale and haggard face of Clare, and the fixed stare of his eyes. But a
short examination of his friend went far to reassure the
physician, for he found that Clare talked not only quite
rationally, but with more than usual good sense and apparent
firmness of purpose. He informed his visitor that, as his
former productions had not been as favourably received as
he hoped they would be, he had bethought himself of writing
a volume of religious poetry; not controversial, but simple
expositions of the truth proclaimed in the Bible. To show
the work he was doing, Clare read two of his renderings of
the Psalms, which pleased the doctor so much that he broke
out into rapturous applause. He promised at the same time
that he would leave no stone unturned to get subscribers
both for the book of ballads and sonnets previously planned,
and for the new volume of religious verse. The poet, usually
so sensitive to words of kindness, received both the praise
and the promise with great coldness. This again surprised
the Peterborough physician.

Dr. Smith kept word in regard to the beating-up of subscribers. After indefatigable exertions, and by almost forcing
his poor patients, lay and clerical, to take a poetical prospectus
together with their pills, he succeeded in getting a couple of

hundred names to the subscription list. He carried the paper in triumph to Northborough; but was again received in a cold and apathetic manner. Clare expressed no pleasure whatever on hearing that there was now a good prospect of bringing out his new volume. He scarcely listened to what the doctor said, and kept on interrupting him every minute with remarks of his own on biblical subjects. 'Is not this Book of Job a wonderful poem—one of the most wonderful elegies ever written?' he asked again and again. Dr. Smith was somewhat surprised; the man of science had never been thinking much about the Book of Job, and, perhaps, knew it only by repute. He looked Clare steadfastly in the face; but the latter averted the glance, bending over the papers before him. 'Shall I read to you some of my verses?' he inquired, after a pause. The doctor willingly consented, and Clare began declaiming his paraphrase of the 38th chapter of Job:—

'Then God, half angered, answered Job aright,
    Out of the whirlwind and the darkening storm—'

When he had finished reading, with tremulous voice, the last lines, scarcely altered from the text:—

'And who provides
The raven with his food—His young ones cry
To God, and wander forth for lack of meat'—

Clare burst out crying, hiding his face in his hands. The medical man got alarmed, and went out to see Mrs. Clare. He asked her whether she had observed anything unusual about her husband of late; in fact, words or doings betoking mental disorder. She replied that she had not noticed anything, except his being unusually silent and reserved, and utterly disinclined to leave the house. Thereupon both went into Clare's room, and found that he had overcome his sudden

burst of grief, and was looking out of the window. He now
entered freely into conversation with the doctor, betraying
not the slightest sign of incoherent thought or reflection.
Thanking his friend for all his kindness in getting subscribers for the intended volume of poems, he told him
that he was going to write immediately to London, and
make arrangements for the publication of the book. The
doctor then left, promising to call again.

He often called, and invariably met Clare in the same
mood. Though somewhat reserved in manner, he was
cheerful, and his talk completely rational; so that Dr.
Smith almost reproached himself for having harboured suspicions about the mental condition of his friend. What
dispelled the last remnant of these suspicions, was the
character of some of the poems which Clare was writing
in his presence, and afterwards reading aloud. The doctor
was a fair judge of verses, and he confessed to himself that
those which his friend was now composing were more exquisite in form than any which had ever before come from
his pen. When visiting Clare early one morning, he found
him in a happier mood than usual, and learned that he had
just written some lines in praise of an old sweetheart, whom
he had seen the day before from his window, when she was
walking along the road. The poet, being asked to do so,
willingly read the verses to his friend. But his voice
quivered with emotion, when commencing :—

> ' First love will with the heart remain
>   When all its hopes are bye,
> As frail rose-blossoms still retain
>   Their fragrance when they die ;
> And joy's first dreams will haunt the mind
>   With shades from whence they sprung,
> As summer leaves the stems behind
>   On which spring's blossoms hung.

Mary! I dare not call thee dear,
 I've lost that right so long;
Yet once again I vex thine ear
 With memory's idle song.
Had time and change not blotted out
 The love of former days,
Thou wert the last that I should doubt
 Of pleasing with my praise.'

The doctor highly praised these and the following verses addressed to ' Mary ;' and, on proffering the wish, was promised a copy of them. The poem seemed to him a convincing proof that, whatever Clare's sufferings had been, they had left no effect upon his mind. Had the man of science been aware of all the facts, he would have known that these very verses were indications of a partial disturbance of reason. Sweet 'Mary,' to whom Clare's verses were addressed, and whom he fancied to have seen in the road the day before, had long been lying in her grave.

THE LAST STRUGGLE.

Being under the impression that his friend was perfectly well, Dr. Smith soon discontinued his visits, and, not being called upon, never saw him again. But just at this time the poet's condition got rapidly worse, and the first tokens of insanity began to show themselves. Morbidly occupied with one set of thoughts, he had now lost the consciousness of his own identity, and addressed his wife and children as strangers. When the former first heard her husband speaking of 'John Clare' as a third person, she became terribly frightened; but thinking he might recover from his mental aberration by being carefully nursed and kept as quiet as possible, she resolved to do her own duty independent of the world. She was successful, to some extent; for after a

while the clouds began to disappear, and the poet again
spoke in a rational manner. He seemed to feel as if awakening from a heavy, oppressive dream; his thoughts perfectly
clear, yet with a conscious remembrance that his reason had
been disturbed, and an infinite dread that the same calamity
might happen again. Full of this apprehension, and in
terrible anxiety to shield himself against the coming danger,
he resolved to consult his friend, Mr. John Taylor, from
whom he had not heard for a long time. He wrote a first
note at the beginning of July, 1834; but, not getting an
immediate reply, despatched a second letter. It ran :—

' Northborough, July 10, 1834.

My dear Taylor,—I am in such a state that I cannot
help feeling some alarm that I may be as I have been. You
must excuse my writing; but I feel if I do not write now I
shall not be able. What I wish is to get under Dr. Darling's
advice, or to have his advice to go somewhere; for I have
not been from home this twelvemonth, and cannot get anywhere. Yet I know if I could reach London I should be
better, or else get to salt water. Whatever Dr. Darling ad-
vises I will do if I can.

Mrs. Emmerson, I think, has forsaken me. I do not feel
neglect now as I have done : I feel only very anxious to get
better. I cannot describe my feelings; perhaps in a day or
two I shall not be able to do anything, or get anywhere.
Write, dear Taylor, and believe me,

Yours sincerely,   John Clare.'

The reply to this note was an invitation to come to London
at once, and consult Dr. Darling, who would be glad to see
his old friend and patient. But the advice was easier than
its execution. There was such dire poverty within the pretty
cottage at Northborough, that many a day its inmates had to
go without a dinner; and to raise the money for paying the

journey to London and back seemed sheer impossibility. Clare had made arrangements, some time previous, for the printing of his new volume of poems; but this, too, had not yet proved a remunerative affair. The publishers who had undertaken the task, Messrs. Whittaker and Co. of Ave Maria Lane, informed him that, before sending any remuneration for the book, they must see how it would sell; clearly hinting that, if not successful, there would be no payment. Thus the poor poet was again baffled in his endeavours to extricate himself from his dire misery by the want of a few pounds. Probably, could he but have raised at this moment sufficient money to pay for his journey to London and consult Dr. Darling, his life, and what was more than his life, might yet have been saved. But, again and again, there was not a hand stretched forth from among the host of high friends and patrons to save a glorious soul from perdition.

A last appeal for help and assistance issued forth from the cottage at Northborough at the beginning of August. Clare once more informed his friend Taylor that he felt terribly anxious to consult Dr. Darling, but could not undertake the journey for want of means. ‘If I could but go to London,’ he wrote, ‘I think I should get better. How would you advise me to come? I dare not come up by myself. Do you think one of my children might go with me? Write to me as soon as you can. God bless you! Excuse the short letter, for I am not able to say more. Thank God, my wife and children are all well.’ There was no answer to this note, nor to a final still more piercing cry for help. After that, all was quiet at the pretty cottage at Northborough. The last struggle was over.

Months and months passed, and no change took place in the mental condition of the poet. He kept reading and writing all day long; spoke but little, and seemed averse to the society of even his wife and children. At times, and for long consecutive periods, his remarks to his family, and some few neighbours or visitors who were admitted to the house, were quite rational; but again at other times his language betrayed the sad aberration of a noble intellect. At such moments he always spoke of himself as a stranger, in the third person, alternately praising and condemning the sayings and doings of the man John Clare. He was fond, too, of appealing to some invisible 'Mary,' as his wife, quite ignoring the faithful spouse at his side, and treating her with utter indifference. Throughout, however, he was calm and quiet; never complaining of anything, nor possessing, to all appearance, any other desire than that of being left alone in his little room, among his books and papers. Thus the winter passed, and the spring made its appearance—the spring of 1835. At the approach of it the dark clouds seemed to vanish once more for a short time. Throughout March and April, he did not show the least sign of mental derangement, and on there coming a letter from his publishers, asking him to write a preface to his little book of poems, just on the point of being issued, he did so without hesitation. This preface, dated 'Northborough, May 9, 1835'—containing nothing remarkable, except a melancholy allusion to 'old friends' long vanished from the scene, and to 'ill health,' which had left the writer 'incapable of doing anything,'— was duly issued with the new book in the month of June.

The book was entitled 'The Rural Muse,' and, by desire of the publishers, was dedicated to Earl Fitzwilliam. It was but a small volume of 175 pages, comprising some forty-four ballads and songs, together with eighty-six sonnets. Messrs. Whittaker and Co. fearful of risking money in printing too large a quantity of rural verse, so much out of fashion for the time, had picked these short pieces from about five times as many poems, furnished to them by the author. The pieces, however, were well chosen; and were likewise tastefully printed, besides being illustrated with the inevitable steel engravings — pictures of Clare's cottage and of the church at Northborough. Short as most of the poems were, it was on the whole a splendid collection of exquisite verse, such as had not been published for many a day. The 'Rural Muse,' compared to Clare's first book, the 'Poems of Rural Life,' was as much higher in thought as the works of the master are to those of the apprentice, and as much more beautiful in outward form as the butterfly is to the chrysalis. Nevertheless, the new volume, so far from passing, like the first, through four editions, and being praised by 'Quarterly Reviews' and other high organs of criticism, proved thoroughly unsuccessful. The reviewers refused to notice, and the public to buy, the 'Rural Muse.' There was no critic in all England to say one word in its recommendation ; nor one of all the old friends and patrons who sent a cheering note of praise to the author. Of the ill success of his book Clare, however, heard soon enough. The publishers let him know that he could expect no remuneration, the entire receipts being insufficient to pay the expenses, including the cost of the much-admired steel engravings. Clare received the information very calmly. His soul, once more, was beyond the strife of hopes and fears.

Though there was no literary review in England to say a word in favour of the forgotten poet at Northborough, there was one in Scotland. Professor Wilson, of Edinburgh, had no sooner seen the new book when he broke forth in eloquent praise of it in 'Blackwood's Magazine.' In the number for August, 1835, he gave an article of sixteen pages, headed 'Clare's Rural Muse,' containing not a few strong honest words about the poet and the unjust neglect under which he was suffering. After comparing Clare with Burns, and setting him, at the same time, far above Bloomfield, Professor Wilson broke forth in indignant strain :—

'Our well-beloved brethren, the English—who, genteel as they are, have a vulgar habit of calling us the Scotch—never lose an opportunity of declaiming on the national disgrace incurred by our treatment of Burns. We confess that the people of that day were not blameless—nor was the bard whom now all the nations honour. There was some reason for sorrow, and perhaps for shame; and there was avowed repentance. Scotland stands where it did in the world's esteem. The widow outlived her husband nearly forty years; she wanted nothing, and was happy. The sons are prosperous, or with a competence; all along with that family all has been right. England never had a Burns. We cannot know how she would have treated him had he " walked in glory and in joy " upon *her* mountain-side. But we do know how she treated her Bloomfield. She let him starve. Humanly speaking, we may say that but for his imprisonment— his exclusion from light and air—he would now have been alive. As it was, the patronage he received served but to prolong a feeble, a desponding, a melancholy existence; cheered at times but by short visits from the Muse, who was scared from that dim abode, and fain would have wafted him with her to the fresh fields and the breezy downs. But his lot forbad—and generous England. There was some talk of a subscription, and Southey, with hand "open as day to melting charity," was foremost among the poets. But somehow or other it fell through, and was never more heard of—and meanwhile Bloomfield died. Hush then about Burns.'

When brave Christopher North wrote these lines in ' Blackwood,' he probably knew nothing about the actual position of Clare, except the general rumour that he was not very well off, though not absolutely poor. He therefore thought to do enough in inviting all the admirers of genuine poetry to purchase the ' Rural Muse,' in order that ' the poet's family be provided with additional comforts.' That some ' comforts ' were theirs already, Professor Wilson judged from the elaborate steel engraving of Clare's dwelling, prefixed to the new volume. ' The creeping plants,' he said, ' look pretty in front of the poet's cottage, but they bear no fruit. There is, however, a little garden attached, and in it may he dig without anxiety, nor need to grudge among the esculents the gadding flowers. . . . . Clare is contented, and his Patty has her handful for the beggar at the door, her heartful for a sick neighbour.'

Alas! had but Professor Wilson known the bitter actual truth, the frightful condition of another Burns, it might have been time yet to rouse with thunder voice the heart of England—of England and of Scotland—to prevent another ' national disgrace.'

BURST OF INSANITY.

The article in ' Blackwood's Magazine' occasioned some talk in the literary world of London; but on the whole made little impression, and probably did not contribute much to the sale of the ' Rural Muse.' The old patrons of Clare were glad to learn, on the authority of a great writer, that he was tolerably comfortable and ' contented,' with something to spare for ' the beggar at the door,' and for the rest people did not trouble themselves much about ' national disgrace,' engendered by the treatment of rural poets. Three months after the publication of his ' Rural Muse,' Clare was as much forgotten as ever; his name never mentioned in polite society; and the copies of his book lying unsold on the shelves of Messrs. Whittaker and Co. in Ave Maria Lane. The poet himself was not affected by it, for he had ceased to suffer from the neglect of the world and the rude buffetings of poverty and misery. Like Hamlet—

> ' He, repulsed,
> Fell into sadness, then into a fast,
> Thence to a watch, thence into a weakness,
> Thence to a lightness; and, by this declension,
> Into the madness wherein now he raves.'

In the winter of 1835-6 the poet's mental state became alarming. His ordinarily quiet behaviour gave way at times to fits of excitement, during which he would talk in a violent manner to those around him. However, his wife and children were as yet almost the only people who knew of his mental derangement, the world being still entirely ignorant that the 'Northamptonshire Peasant,' who had just issued a new book of poetry, was a madman. Even Clare's own neighbours knew little of his state; to them he always was an inexplicable, erratic being, with words and actions not to be measured by the ordinary standard, and they, therefore, took little notice of occasional strange scenes which they witnessed. This was fortunate, in so far as it contributed to put poor Mrs. Clare more at her ease. She rightly judged that if she could but induce her husband to leave his narrow room and his books, and enjoy again as of old the sight of flowers, trees, and green fields, his health would be greatly improved. With this constant aim in view, she succeeded at last in drawing her unhappy partner from his gloomy retirement. The spring of 1836 was unusually fine, and when nature had put on her first smiling green, and the whole little village was wrapped in a belt of fragrant blossoms and flowers, Patty instructed her two eldest daughters to lead their father for a short walk through the neighbourhood. The poet, this time, made no resistance whatever, but allowed himself to be guided by his children. He returned much pleased with his excursion, expressing a wish to go again the next day. From the second walk he came back still more delighted, and the daily rambles continuing for more than a month, Clare at last seemed almost recovered from his malady. Except at rare intervals, when his speech would become somewhat wild and incoherent, his behaviour showed not the least signs of eccentricity, and though more quiet and subdued than formerly, the conversation he carried on seemed perfectly judicious and rational.

Once more, Patty fervently hoped Heaven would restore her husband.

It was not long before Clare's old love of nature came back with such renewed ardour that he could not be made to stop a single day at home. Whenever the weather was moderately fine, he sallied forth, mostly unaccompanied by any one, and seldom returned before the sun had set. He extended his excursions as far as Helpston Heath on the one side, and Peterborough on the other, seemingly as much as ever acquainted with every nook and piece of ground for miles around the neighbourhood of his ancient haunts. One day, when rambling about on the confines of the cathedral city, he met and was recognised by Mrs. Marsh. The good old lady was delighted to see her poet again, and insisted that he should make up for his former neglect by accompanying her at once, and staying a few days at the episcopal mansion. Clare said he was expected home by his wife, and could not go the same day; but promised to pay a visit to Peterborough in the course of a week. He kept his word, and on the appointed time presented himself before Mrs. Marsh. She was exceedingly pleased, and to prevent her poet from running away again, kept him constantly in her company. Conversing with him on all subjects, Mrs. Marsh at times thought his remarks rather singular; while his sudden swerving from one topic to another often astonished her not a little. But all this the good lady held to be perfectly natural in a poet and a man of genius. To her a poet was nothing if not eccentric.

Clare remained for several days a guest at the residence of the bishop, and on the last evening of his visit was taken by Mrs. Marsh to the theatre. A select band of roving tragedians had taken possession of the Peterborough stage— converted, by a more prosaic living generation, into a corn-exchange—and were delighting the inhabitants of the episcopal city with Shakespeare, and the latest French melodramas.

On the evening when Clare went to the theatre in company with Mrs. Marsh, the ' Merchant of Venice ' was performed. Clare sat and listened quietly while the first three acts were being played, not even replying to the questions as to how he liked the piece, addressed to him by Mrs. Marsh. But at the commencement of the fourth act, he got restless and evidently excited, and in the scene where Portia delivered judgment, he suddenly sprang up on his seat, and began addressing the actor who performed the part of Shylock. Great was the astonishment of all the good citizens of Peterborough, when a shrill voice, coming from the box reserved to the wife of the Lord Bishop, exclaimed, ' You villain, you murderous villain ! ' Such an utter breach of decorum was never heard of within the walls of the episcopal city. It was in vain that those nearest to Clare tried to keep him on his seat and induce him to be quiet ; he kept shouting, louder than ever, and ended by making attempts to get upon the stage. At last, the performance had to be suspended, and Mrs. Marsh, after some difficulty, got away with her guest. The old lady, in her innocence, even now did not apprehend the real cause of the exciting scene which she had witnessed, but, as before, attributed the behaviour of her unfortunate visitor to poetic eccentricity. But she began thinking that he was almost too eccentric.

The next morning, Clare went back to Northborough, having received an intimation from Mrs. Marsh that it would be best he should go home at once. He wandered forth from the city in a dreamy mood, and lost his way before he had gone far. Some acquaintances found him sitting in a meadow, near the hamlet of Gunthorpe, and seeing his wild haggard looks and strange manners, they took him by the arm, and led him back to Peterborough, delivering him over to the porter at the episcopal mansion. Mrs. Marsh, on hearing that her poet had again made his appearance, was somewhat alarmed ; her guest had ceased to be ornamental to her establishment, and her chief object now was to get rid of him as soon as possible. She therefore ordered a servant to take charge of Clare and deliver him up to his wife, with instructions not to let him go, under any pretence, to Peterborough. The order was duly obeyed, and the poet soon found himself in his little cottage. Patty was frightened to see what a sad change the few days' absence had wrought in her husband. He no longer talked sensibly as before, but addressed her and the children in an abrupt manner, asking for his 'Mary,' and complaining that all his friends had left him. The poor wife soothed him as best she could, and after some efforts succeeded in calming his mind. At the end of a few days, Clare seemed again sufficiently well to leave the house, and renewed his daily walks in company with one or the other of his children. The inhabitants of the village, together with most of his acquaintances in the neighbourhood, were still ignorant that the poet whom they saw daily roving through the fields was a madman.

The ignorance was so general as to be shared by most of Clare's friends and patrons. One of the latter, the Rev. Mr. Mossop, Vicar of Helpston, had frequent occasions of seeing him, but never detected the slightest sign of mental derangement. Thus one morning, soon after the poet's return from Peterborough, he invited him to his house, to meet a friend who wished to make the acquaintance of the author of the ' Rural Muse.' Mrs. Clare was rather unwilling to let her husband depart ; but had not the courage to detain him, remembering the exceeding kindness always shown to her family by the vicar and his sister. The poet accordingly made his appearance at Mr. Mossop's house ; but had not been long there before he showed unmistakeable signs of a wandering intellect. In the midst of an animated conversation, he suddenly broke off, and pointing to the ceiling, cried that he saw figures moving up and down. Surprised as the host and hostess were at this exclamation, they at once perceived the real condition of their unhappy visitor. The reverend gentleman, without loss of time, hurried off to get medical assistance, while his sister, Miss Jane Mossop, did her best to quiet the poet by conversing with him on his favourite topics, and drawing his attention to the plants and flowers in the garden. It was not long before a surgeon arrived, in the person of a Mr. Skrimshaw, resident at Market Deeping. He pronounced at once—what, indeed, was obvious to all the persons in the house—that the poor poet was a lunatic. The kind-hearted vicar thereupon had Clare carefully conveyed back to his own home, making further arrangements for his comfort and safety.

Through Mr. Mossop, the Earl Fitzwilliam and other patrons of Clare were made acquainted with the mental state of the poet, of which they had been so long ignorant. The earl at once proposed to send the poet to the county lunatic asylum, at Northampton, where he would be kept under safe restraint; but this scheme met with some opposition on the part of Mrs. Clare, who thought that her husband might yet recover by being left quietly at home. For a short time, indeed, it seemed as if this was the case. During the next four or five months, and up to the spring of 1837, the cottage at Northborough bore as quiet an aspect as if disease and misery had never entered it. Clare kept working in his garden, and reading in his little study, week after week, speaking to his family in the most rational manner, and occasionally writing verses as sweet and beautiful as any that had ever come from his pen. But with the warm days of summer, his mind seemed again to get distracted, and the report reaching Milton Park, imprisonment at the Northampton asylum was once more advised, or ordered. By desire of the noble earl, negotiations were entered into with the authorities at the county establishment to receive Clare, against payment of a small weekly sum, at a somewhat better footing than the ordinary paupers; but while these

were pending, there came letters from London offering to do
a little more for the unhappy poet. Mr. John Taylor and
other old friends and patrons, having now become fully
acquainted with the condition of Clare, proposed to place
him in a private lunatic asylum, near the metropolis, discharging all the expenses of his maintenance there. The
earl, being a clear gainer by this new arrangement, had no
objection whatever to make against it, and signified his
desire of having his pensioner at Northborough at once
removed to the new place of safety. This was done without
loss of time. Early on the morning of the 16th of July,
1837, Clare was led away from his wife and children, by two
stern-looking men, who placed him in a small carriage and
drove rapidly away southward. Late the same day, the
poet found himself an inmate of Dr. Allen's private lunatic
asylum, at Fair Mead House, High Beech, in the centre of
Epping Forest.

GLIMMERS OF COUNTY PATRONAGE.

The news that Clare had been taken to a lunatic asylum
did not become generally known till many months after the
event had taken place. In the meanwhile, however, the few
persons who still took an interest in the 'Northamptonshire Peasant' heard vague rumours that he was living at
home in a state of extreme destitution, productive at times
of mental derangement, and on the initiative of the most
energetic of these old friends another appeal was made to
the public for pecuniary aid. Allan Cunningham was the
first to call upon the admirers of Clare to help him in his
distress, and the editors of various more or less fashionable annuals, published in the autumn of 1837, followed
the example. Though it did not lead to the desired result,
the movement thus set on foot was curious, as showing the
estimation in which the poet was held by some of those who

wished to figure as his patrons. Among them was the Marquis of Northampton, a nobleman who, though never having in the least assisted Clare, fancied himself a sort of protector of the poet, for the sole reason that he was living in the county. This sort of county-property feeling, common to not a few of Clare's noble patrons, was expressed to a notable degree in a letter which the marquis wrote in reply to one of the appeals in favour of the 'Northamptonshire Peasant.'

The appeal in question appeared in the 'Book of Gems,' an annual edited by Mr. S. C. Hall. The writer, after stating that Clare had 'for many years existed in a state of poverty, as utter and hopeless as that in which he passed his youth;' that he had 'a wife and a very large family;' and that 'at times his mind is giving way under the sickness of hope deferred,' finished with an eloquent address to some noble-minded patron of poetry to come forward and help Clare. 'It is not yet too late,' the writer exclaimed, 'for a hand to reach him : a very envied celebrity may be obtained by some wealthy and good Samaritan. Strawberry Hill might be gladly sacrificed for the fame of having saved Chatterton.' The Marquis of Northampton replied to this address. His lordship evidently was hankering after the 'envied celebrity,' but wished to get it as cheap as possible. So he wrote a long letter to the editor of the 'Book of Gems,' making his bid for fame, and expressing at the same time his opinion about one whom he considered a 'county poet.' His lordship's letter—in which, it will be noticed, the county predominates over all heavenly and earthly things — ran as follows :—

'Castle Ashby, Northampton, Oct. 17th, 1837.

Sir,—Though an utter stranger, I think you will excuse my troubling you with this present letter: but I will not waste your time with a lengthened apology. I was this morning reading the collection of poetry which you have lately published—"The Book of Gems, 1838,"—and I was

at the same time struck and shocked by what you say on the
subject of our county poet, Clare. I must confess that I
am not of his exceeding admirers, and should by no means
be disposed to place him in the same rank with Hogg, or
even with Bloomfield and Crockford. Still he is undoubtedly
a great credit to our county, and it would, I think, be a great
disgrace to it if Clare was left in the state in which you
mention him to be. Now it appears to me that the most
feasible means of relieving him would be for him to publish
a collection of all his poems in a volume by subscription.
Probably there would be found a good many persons in this
county who would subscribe for five or ten copies each.
Northamptonshire is not a large county, nor is it either
wealthy from manufactures or from a dense population. It
has, however, some considerable source of wealth. Many
of its resident nobility and gentry have considerable proper-
ties elsewhere, as for instance the Dukes of Buccleuch and
Grafton, and Lords Spencer, Fitzwilliam, Winchelsea; and
you will see that the resources of the county are really in
that sense larger than they appear. However, I must confess that I do not think that we are very literary, and probably such a speculation would hardly succeed unless in
addition to the copies taken here there were hopes of a sale
elsewhere. On this subject you are far better able to judge
than I can be. You know also more exactly how Clare is
situated, at least you could find out. If Her Majesty would
allow the book to be dedicated to her that would probably
be a considerable advantage, and through Lord Lilford, who,
I think, is a Lord of the Bedchamber, permission might be
obtained. But in this I speak at random. If such a plan
was taken up, I should myself be willing to subscribe for
ten or twenty copies, and I have no doubt that I could
obtain subscriptions from others. But I could not myself
do more for this scheme. In fact I should not be able to
do quite so much now in this way in consequence of a late

publication of mine, as I could not in general apply to the same subscribers. Still I could apply to many on the ground of it being a county question. But still, as I said before, the question is whether the public in general would be likely to join the effort. Pray let me know what you think of the matter. If a direct subscription for Clare should be proposed in lieu of the publication I should be happy to contribute towards it, but I should doubt its being as productive as the book. It would be probably well if there were some new poems in the book in addition to the old ones. Perhaps there may be a difficulty to get the copyright if he has sold it to a bookseller.

I am, Sir, your humble servant
NORTHAMPTON.'

The philanthropic scheme of the Marquis of Northampton in favour of ' our county poet ' was destined not to be realized. Whether the failure was owing to the mysterious ' Lord of the Bedchamber,' or to differences of opinion in respect to Clare being ' a great credit to our county,' and his relief ' a county question,' so much is certain, the not ' *very* literary ' county subscribers declined to come forward, although a number of prospectuses were printed and issued to them. Thus there remained the ' great disgrace.' To Professor Wilson it simply was a ' national disgrace ;' but the most honourable the Marquis of Northampton undoubtedly felt it deeper by declaring it to be a ' disgrace to our county.'

DR. ALLEN'S ASYLUM.

Dr. Matthew Allen, of Fair Mead House, into whose asylum Clare had been taken, was among the first reformers who adopted the mild system of treatment for the insane, both on medical and philanthropic grounds. He argued, in the teeth of a whole legion of irate professional brethren, that kindness would be more powerful than cruelty in curing human beings deranged in intellect, and that, even if incurable, the poor creatures whom God had afflicted did not deserve being laid in fetters and treated like savage animals. The doctor necessarily made a great many enemies by preaching this new doctrine ; but he likewise was fortunate enough to gain a few friends, who advocated his cause and rendered active aid in carrying it into practice. It was with the help of these friends that Dr. Allen was enabled to set up a large private asylum in the centre of Epping Forest, the establishment consisting of half-a-dozen houses, connected together, and surrounded by large gardens. Here the unhappy sufferers from mental derangement were kept under no more restraint than was absolutely necessary for their own safety and that of others ; and, while under the best medical care and attention, were allowed an abundant amount of indoor recreation as well as out-door exercise. When Clare arrived, there were about fifty inmates at Fair Mead House, all of them belonging to the middle and upper classes. Feeling deep sympathy with the unfortunate position of the poet, Dr. Allen admitted him at a mere nominal rate of payment, treating him nevertheless exactly on the same footing as the most favoured of his patients.

The poet's existence at Fair Mead House for several years flowed on monotonous enough ; even more so than that of the other inmates of the asylum. He longed to see his family, to meet familiar faces, and to read and write poetry ; but neither wife, nor children, nor any friends ever came to visit him, and the supply of books was necessarily scant and not altogether to his taste. Dr. Allen's treatment of his patients was based on the principle of giving them as much physical labour and exercise as possible, so as to destroy all tendency to a morbid concentration of thought ; and thus Clare was kept away from books and paper, and made to go into the garden, to plant, and dig, and water the flowers.

T

He seemed to fret at first on being deprived of the solace of his poetry, and eagerly seized every occasion to scribble verses upon odd slips of paper, or with chalk against the wall. But as the months passed on, his new forced habits grew upon him, and he left off writing to a great extent, and was foremost among the workers in the fields and garden. His mental state, however, did not improve, although his physical strength appeared to gain by this change. He got stout and robust, and able to go through a greater amount of physical labour than in former days. What seemed to contribute to sooth and quiet—or, perhaps, deaden—his mental energies, was the habit of smoking, which he acquired from his companions. He would smoke for whole days and weeks, either working in the garden, or sitting on the stump of a tree in Epping Forest, without uttering a word.

Yet notwithstanding the visible and increasing derangement of his mental faculties, Clare's poetical powers seemed to be nearly as great and as brilliant as ever. Rare as were the opportunities when he was allowed to indulge in the luxury of writing verses, whenever they offered, the stream of poetry came flowing on swiftly and sweetly. Some accidental visitors to Fair Mead House one day offered him a pencil and sheet of paper, when he sat down on a bench in the garden, and without further musing wrote the following lines :—

> ' By a cottage near the wood
>   Where lark and thrushes sing,
>   In dreaming hours I stood,
>   Through summer and through spring :
>   There dwells a lovely maiden
>   Whose name I sought in vain—
>   Some call her pretty Lucy,
>   And others honest Jane.

By that cottage near a wood
　　I often stood alone
In sad or happy mood,
　　And wished she was my own.
The birds kept sweetly singing,
　　But nature pleased in vain ;
For the dark and lovely maiden
　　I never saw again.

By the cottage near the wood
　　I wished in peace to be :
The blossoms where she stood
　　Were more than gems to me.
More fair or sweeter blossoms
　　My rambles sought in vain ;
But the dark and lovely maiden
　　I never found again.

By that cottage near a wood
　　The children held her gown,
And on the turf before her
　　Ran laughing up and down.
They played around her beauty,
　　While I sought joys in vain ;
She fled—the lovely maiden
　　I could not find again.

By that cottage near the wood,
　　Where children used to play,
Spring often burst the bud,
　　And as often passed away.
And with them passed my visions
　　Of her whom I adore ;
For the dark and lovely maiden,
　　I love her evermore.'

When Clare had been above a year at the asylum, and it was found that he was perfectly harmless and inoffensive, he was allowed to roam at his will all over the neighbourhood and through the whole of the forest. This freedom he greatly enjoyed, and not a day passed without his taking long excursions in all directions. In these wanderings he was mostly accompanied by T. Campbell, the only son of the author of 'The Pleasures of Hope,' with whom he had come to form an intimate acquaintance. Clare wrote a sketch of his forest promenades in a sonnet which he handed to Dr. Allen. It ran :—

> 'I love the forest and its airy bounds,
> Where friendly Campbell takes his daily rounds ;
> I love the break-neck hills, that headlong go,
> And leave me high, and half the world below.
>
> I love to see the Beech Hill mounting high,
> The brook without a bridge, and nearly dry.
> There's Bucket's Hill, a place of furze and clouds,
> Which evening in a golden blaze enshrouds :
>
> I hear the cows go home with tinkling bell,
> And see the woodman in the forest dwell,
> Whose dog runs eager where the rabbit's gone ;
> He eats the grass, then kicks and hurries on ;
> Then scrapes for hoarded bone, and tries to play,
> And barks at larger dogs and runs away.

His acquaintance with young Thomas Campbell brought to Clare occasional presents, and now and then the pleasant face of a visitor. Among them was Mr. Cyrus Redding, who left a record of his visit in the 'English Journal.' Describing Dr. Allen's asylum, he says :—'The situation is lofty ; and the patients inhabit several houses at some distance from each other. These houses stand in the midst of gardens, where the invalids may be seen walking about, or cultivating the flowers, just as they feel inclined.'

The visitor, who was accompanied by a friend who had known Clare previously, found him working in a field, ' apart from his companions, busily engaged with a hoe, and smoking. On being called, he came at once, and very readily entered into conversation. Our friend was surprised to see how much the poet was changed in personal appearance, having gained flesh, and being no longer, as he was formerly, attenuated and pale of complexion. We found a little man, of muscular frame and firmly set, his complexion fresh and forehead high, a nose somewhat aquiline, and long full chin. The expression of his countenance was more pleasing but somewhat less intellectual than that in the engraved portrait prefixed to his works in the edition of " The Village Minstrel," published in 1821. He was communicative, and answered every question put to him in a manner perfectly unembarrassed. He spoke of the quality of the ground which he was amusing himself by hoeing, and the probability of its giving an increased crop the present year, a continued smile playing upon his lips. He made some remarks illustrative of the difference between the aspect of the country at High Beech and that in the fens from whence he had come— alluded to Northborough and Peterborough—and spoke of his loneliness away from his wife, expressing a great desire to go home, and to have the society of women. He said his solace was his pipe—he had no other : he wanted books. On being asked what books, he said Byron ; and we promised to send that poet's works to him.

' The principal token of his mental eccentricity was the introduction of prize-fighting, in which he seemed to imagine he was to engage ; but the allusion to it was made in the way of interpolation in the middle of the subject on which he was discoursing, brought in abruptly, and abandoned with equal suddenness, and an utter want of connexion with any association of ideas which it could be thought might lead to the subject at the time ; as if the machinery of thought were dislocated, so that one part of it got off its pivot, and protruded into the regular workings ; or as if a note had got into a piece of music which had no business there. This was the only symptom of aberration of mind we observed about Clare ; though, being strangers to him, there might be something else in his manner which those who knew him well could have pointed out. To our seeming, his affection was slight ; and it is not at all improbable that a relief from mental anxiety might completely restore him. The finer organization of such a humanity, if more easily put out of order than that of a more obtuse character, is in all probability more likely to re-tune itself, the evil cause being removed.'

Mr. Cyrus Redding was mistaken in the anticipation that Clare's 'machinery of thought' would ever get again 'into the regular workings.' At the very time when the visit described here took place, the poet's mental state was worse than before, and there seemed less chance than ever of restoring ' the finer organization of such a humanity.' Clare was haunted now, wherever he went, by the vision of his first ideal love, his ever-sought 'Mary.' He fancied that she was his wife, torn from him by evil spirits, and that he was bound to seek her all over the earth. In his wild hallucinations, he confounded his real with his ideal spouse, addressing the latter in language wonderfully sweet, though exhibiting strange flights of imagination. On one occasion, the poet handed to Dr. Allen the following piece of poetry, which he called ' A Sonnet,' with the remark that it should be sent to his wife :—

> ' Maid of Walkherd, meet again,
> By the wilding in the glen ;
> By the oak against the door,
> Where we often met before.
> By thy bosom's heaving snow,
> By thy fondness none shall know ;

Maid of Walkherd, meet again,
By the wilding in the glen.

By thy hand of slender make,
By thy love I'll ne'er forsake,
By thy heart I'll ne'er betray,
Let me kiss thy fears away !
I will live and love thee ever,
Leave thee and forsake thee never !
Though far in other lands to be,
Yet never far from love and thee.'

Dr. Allen told his patient that he thought his verses very beautiful, at which Clare seemed pleased, and expressed his intention to take them home to his wife, his 'Mary.' The doctor paid little heed to this remark, which, however, was seriously meant. To see his beloved Mary again, now became the one all-absorbing thought of the poet's mind. He appeared to have a vague notion that she was far away ; but determined, nevertheless, to seek her, even at the risk of his life. In the spring of 1841—having been nearly four years at Fair Mead House—he made several attempts to escape, but was frustrated each time, being brought back by people who met him wandering at a distance. Dr. Allen, notwithstanding these warnings, continued to allow full liberty to his patient, ascribing his occasional flights to a mere propensity for roaming about. Clare, as before, took his daily excursions, sometimes in company with his friend Campbell, but oftener alone. One day, in the middle of July, 1841, he stayed away unusually long. When the sun had set without his returning home, attendants were despatched in all directions ; but after a long and minute search over the whole neighbourhood, they came back, late at night, reporting that they had been unsuccessful in tracing the lost patient. Some persons who knew him by sight had seen him passing through Enfield in a northerly direction; but beyond this fact nothing could be ascertained. Dr. Allen felt very uneasy at this mysterious disappearance, and the next day despatched two horsemen in search of Clare. But even they could discover no trace of him beyond Enfield. John Clare was never seen again at Fair Mead House, Epping Forest.

ESCAPE FROM THE ASYLUM.

Clare's flight from Dr. Allen's custody was accomplished by dint of extraordinary perseverance, involving an amount of physical suffering almost unexampled, and approaching starvation and the most horrible of deaths. The poet started early on the morning of the 20th of July, with not a penny in his pocket, and no other knowledge of the road than that given to him by a gipsy whom he had met a few days before. This gipsy at first promised more active assistance in his flight; but did not keep his word, owing, probably, to the inability of the poor lunatic to procure any tangible reward. However, urged onward by his intense desire to see his ' Mary ' again, Clare did not hesitate to start alone on his unknown journey, and, groping his way along, like one wrapt in blindness, he at once succeeded so far as to get into the right track homewards. The first day he walked above twenty miles, to Stevenage, in Hertfordshire, where he arrived late at night, footsore and faint, having been without any refreshment the whole day. He rested for the night in an old barn, on some trusses of clover, taking the singular precaution, before lying down, of placing his head towards the north, so as to know in which direction to start the next morning. This day, the 21st of July, he rose early, pursuing his way northward, and crawling more than walking along the road. A man threw him a penny which he used to get a glass of ale ; but beyond this he had again no refreshment. After a second night, spent in the open air, he rose once more to crawl onward, slowly but steadily. To stille the torments of hunger, he now took to the frightful expedient of eating grass with the beasts in the field. The grass served to appease the dreadful pains of his stomach, yet left him in the same drowsy condition in which he was before. His feet were bleeding, the dry gravel of the road having penetrated his old worn-out shoes ; but he heeded it not, and stedfastly pursued his way northward. Alternately sleeping and walking, sometimes wandering about in a circle, lying down in ditches at the roadside, and continuing to eat grass, together with a few bits of tobacco which he found in his pocket, he at length reached the neighbourhood of Peterborough and scenes familiar to his eye. But he was now fast breaking down under hunger and fatigue, having had no food for more than ninety hours. Nearing the well-known place, he could get no further, but sank down on the road, more dead than alive. A great many people passed—people rich and poor, on foot and in carriages, in clerical habit and in broadcloth ; but not one gave alms, or even noticed, or had a kind word for the dying man at the roadside. There was not one good Samaritan among all the wayfarers from the rich episcopal city.

At last there passed a cart, containing some persons from Helpston. They recognised their old neighbour, although he was terribly altered, with the livid signs of starvation impressed upon his face. The wanderer, in a faint voice, told those friends his tale of woe ; but even they were not Christians enough to lift him into their vehicle and take him home. All that they did was to give him a few pence ; not even placing the money in his hand, with, perhaps, a kindly greeting, but throwing it at him from their cart. The wretched poet crept along the road to gather the coppers, and then crawled a little farther on to a public-house, where he procured some refreshment. The food—the first he had taken for nigh four days—enabled him to pursue his journey slowly, and he hobbled on through Peterborough, the blood still trickling from his wounded feet. At every stone-heap at the roadside he rested himself, until he came to the hamlet of Werrington, where a cart ran up against him, out of which sprang a woman who took him in her arms. It was Patty, who had heard from the charitable Helpston people that her husband was lying on the road, and had come in search of him. But Clare did not know her. He refused even to take a seat at her side, until he was told that she was his 'second wife.' Then he allowed himself to be taken to Northborough, where he arrived in the evening of the 23d of July, utterly exhausted, and in a state bordering upon delirium.

But already the next day he felt considerably better, and at once asked for writing materials. Having obtained pen and ink, together with an old blank ledger, in which he formerly entered his poems, he sat down to write an account of his 'Journey from Essex.' Such another account, probably, was never written before. Here it stands, unaltered from the original, save in slight attempts at punctuation. The paper commences :—

'*July 24th*, 1841.—Returned home out of Essex, and found no Mary. Her and her family are nothing to me now, though she herself was once the dearest of all. And how can I forget !'

After this entry begins what is headed the 'Journal':—

'*July* 18, 1841, *Sunday*.—Felt very melancholy. Went for a walk in the forest in the afternoon. Fell in with some gypsies, one of whom offered to assist in my escape from the madhouse by hiding me in his camp, to which I almost agreed. But I told him I had no money to start with ; but if he would do so, I would promise him fifty pounds, and he agreed to do so before Saturday. On Friday I went again, but he did not seem so willing, so I said little about it. On Sunday I went and they were all gone. An old wide-awake hat and an old straw bonnet, of the plum-pudding sort, was left behind, and I put the hat in my pocket, thinking it might be useful for another opportunity. As good luck would have it, it turned out to be so.

July 19, *Monday.*—Did nothing.

July 20, *Tuesday.*—Reconnoitred the road the gypsey had taken, and found it a legible (!) one to make a movement; and having only honest courage and myself in my army, I led the way and my troops soon followed. But being careless in mapping down the road as the gypsey told me, I missed the lane to Enfield Town, and was going down Enfield Highway, till I passed the " Labour-in-vain " public-house, where a person who came out of the door told me the way. I walked down the lane gently, and was soon in Enfield Town, and by and by on the great York Road, where it was all plain sailing. Steering ahead, meeting no enemy and fearing none, I reached Stevenage, where, being night, I got over a gate, and crossed the corner of a green paddock. Seeing a pond or hollow in the corner, I was forced to stay off a respectable distance to keep from falling into it. My legs were nearly knocked up and began to stagger. I scaled over some old rotten palings into the yard, and then had higher palings to clamber over, to get into. the shed or hovel; which I did with difficulty, being rather weak. To my good luck, I found some trusses of clover piled up, about six or more feet square, which I gladly mounted and slept on. There were some drags in the hovel, on which I could have reposed had I not found a better bed. I slept soundly, but had a very uneasy dream. I thought my first wife lay on my left arm, and somebody took her away from my side, which made me wake up rather unhappy. I thought as I awoke somebody said " Mary ;" but nobody was near. I lay down with my head towards the north, to show myself the steering point in the morning.

July 21.—Daylight was looking in on every side, and fearing my garrison might be taken by storm, and myself be made prisoner, I left my lodging by the way I got in, and thanked God for His kindness in procuring it. For anything in a famine is better than nothing, and any place that giveth the weary rest is a blessing. I gained the North Road again, and steered due north. On the left hand side, the road under the bank was like a cave; I saw a man and boy coiled up asleep, whom I hailed, and they awoke to tell me the name of the next village. Somewhere on the London side, near the "Plough" public-house, a man passed me on horseback, in a slop frock, and said, "Here's another of the broken-down haymakers," and threw me a penny to get a half pint of beer, which I picked up, and thanked him for, and when I got to the "Plough," I called for a half pint and drank it. I got a rest, and escaped a very heavy shower in the bargain, by having a shelter till it was over. Afterwards I would have begged a penny of two drovers, but they were very saucy; so I begged no more of anybody.

Having passed a lodge on the left hand, within a mile and a half, or less, of a town—I think it might be St. Ives, or it was St. Neot's, but I forget the name—I sat down to rest on a flint heap, for half an hour or more. While sitting here, I saw a tall gypsey come out of the lodge gate, and make down the road to where I was. When she got up to me, I saw she was a young woman, with a honest-looking countenance, and rather handsome. I spoke to her, and asked her a few questions, which she answered readily and with evident good humour. So I got up, and went on to the next town with her. She cautioned me on the way to put something in my hat to keep the crown up, and said in a lower tone, "You'll be noticed." But not knowing at what she hinted, I took no notice and made no reply. At length she pointed to a small church tower, which she called Shefford Church, and advised me to go on a footway, which would take me direct to it, and would shorten my journey fifteen (!) miles by doing so. I would gladly have taken the young woman's advice, feeling that it was honest, and a nigh guess towards the truth; but fearing I might lose my way, and not be able

to find the North Road again, I thanked her, and told her I
should keep to the road. She then bid me "good day," and
went into a house or shop on the left hand side of the road.

Next I passed three or four good built houses on a hill,
and a public-house on the roadside in the hollow below them.
I seemed to pass the milestones very quick in the morning,
but towards night they seemed to be stretched further
asunder. I now got to a village of which I forget the
name. The road on the left hand was quite overshadowed
by trees, and quite dry. So I sat down half an hour, and
made a good many wishes for breakfast. But wishes were
no meal; so I got up as hungry as I sat down. I forget here
the names of the villages I passed through, but recollect
at late evening going through Potton, in Bedfordshire, where
I called in a house to light my pipe. There was a civil old
woman, and a country wench making lace on a cushion as
round as a globe, and a young fellow; all civil people. I
asked them a few questions as to the way, and where the
clergyman and overseer lived; but they scarcely heard me,
and gave no answer. I then went through Potton, and
happened to meet with a kind-talking countryman, who told
me the parson lived a good way from where I was. So I
went on hopping with a crippled foot; for the gravel had
got into my old shoes, one of which had now nearly lost the
sole. Had I found the overseer's house at hand, or the
parson's, I should have given my name, and begged for a
shilling to carry me home; but I was forced to brush on
penniless, and be thankful I had a leg to move on. I then
asked him whether he could tell me of a farmyard anywhere
on the road, where I could find a shed and some dry straw,
and he said, " Yes, if you will go with me, I will show you
the place; it is a public-house on the left hand side of the
road, at the sign of the Ram." But seeing a stone heap, I
longed to rest, as one of my feet was very painful. So I
thanked him for his kindness, and bid him go on. But the

good-natured fellow lingered awhile, as if wishing to conduct me ; but suddenly recollecting that he had a hamper on his shoulder, and a lock-up bag in his hand, to meet the coach, he started hastily, and was soon out of sight.

I followed, looking in vain for the countryman's straw bed. Not being able to find it, I laid down by the wayside, under some elm trees. Between the wall and the trees there was a thick row, planted some five or six feet from the buildings. I laid there and tried to sleep ; but the wind came in between the trees so cold that I quaked like having the ague, and I quitted this lodging to seek another at the " Ram," which I scarcely hoped to find. It now began to grow dark apace, and the odd houses on the road began to light up, and show the inside lot very comfortable, and my outside lot very uncomfortable and wretched. Still I hobbled forward as well as I could, and at last came the " Ram." The shutters were not closed, and the lighted window looked very cheering ; but I had no money, and did not like to go in. There was a sort of shed, or gig-house, at the end ; but I did not like to lie there, as the people were up ; so I still travelled on. The road was very lonely and dark, being overshaded with trees. At length I came to a place where the road branched off into two turnpikes, one to the right about, and the other straight forward. On going by, I saw a milestone standing under the hedge, and I turned back to read it, to see where the other road led to. I found it led to London. I then suddenly forgot which was north or south, and though I narrowly examined both ways, I could see no tree, or bush, or stone heap that I could recollect having passed.

I went on mile after mile, almost convinced I was going the same way I had come. These thoughts were so strong upon me, and doubts and hopelessness made me turn so feeble, that I was scarcely able to walk. Yet I could not sit down or give up, but shuffled along till I saw a lamp shining

as bright as the moon, which, on nearing, I found was suspended over a tollgate. Before I got through, the man came
out with a candle, and eyed me narrowly; but having no
fear I stopped to ask him whether I was going northward.
He said, "When you get through the gate you are." I
thanked him, and went through to the other side, and
gathered my old strength as my doubts vanished. I soon
cheered up, and hummed the air of "Highland Mary" as I
went on. I at length came to an odd house, all alone, near
a wood; but I could not see what the sign was, though
it seemed to stand, oddly enough, in a sort of trough, or
spout. There was a large porch over the door, and being
weary I crept in, and was glad enough to find I could lie
with my legs straight. The inmates were all gone to rest,
for I could hear them turn over in bed, while I lay at full
length on the stones in the porch. I slept here till daylight,
and felt very much refreshed. I blest my two wives and
both their families when I laid down and when I got up in
the morning.

I have but a slight recollection of my journey between
here and Stilton, for I was knocked up, and noticed little
or nothing. One night I laid in a dyke-bottom, sheltered
from the wind, and went asleep for half an hour. When I
awoke, I found one side wet through from the water; so
I got out and went on. I remember going down a very
dark road, hung over on both sides with thick trees; it
seemed to extend a mile or two. I then entered a town,
where some of the chamber windows had lights shining in
them. I felt so weak here that I was forced to sit on the
ground to rest myself, and while I sat here a coach that
seemed heavily laden came rattling up, and splashing the
mud in my face wakened me from a doze. When I had
knocked the gravel out of my shoes I started again. There
was little to notice, for the road very often looked as stupid
as myself. I was often half asleep as I went on.

The third day I satisfied my hunger by eating the grass on the roadside, which seemed to taste something like bread. I was hungry, and eat heartily till I was satisfied; in fact, the meal seemed to do me good. The next and last day I remembered that I had some tobacco, and my box of lucifers being exhausted, I could not light my pipe. So I took to chewing tobacco all day, and eat it when I had done. I was never hungry afterwards. I remember passing through Buckden, and going a length of road afterwards; but I do not recollect the name of any place until I came to Stilton, where I was completely footsore, bleeding, and broken down. When I had got about half way through the town, a gravel causeway invited me to rest myself; so I laid down and nearly went to sleep. A young woman, as I guessed by the voice, came out of a house, and said, " Poor creature ; " and another more elderly said, " Oh, he shams." But when I got up the latter said, " Oh no, he don't," as I hobbled along very lame. I heard the voices, but never looked back to see where they came from. When I got near the inn at the end of the gravel walk, I met two young women, and asked one of them whether the road branching to the right by the inn did not lead to Peterborough. She said, " Yes." As soon as ever I was on it, I felt myself on the way home, and went on rather more cheerful, though I was forced to rest oftener than usual.

Before I got to Peterborough, a man and woman passed in a cart; and on hailing me as they passed, I found they were neighbours from Helpston, where I used to live. I told them I was knocked-up, which they could easily see, and that I had neither food nor drink since I left Essex. When I had told my story they clubbed together and threw me fivepence out of the cart. I picked it up, and called at a small public-house near the bridge, where I had two half pints of ale, and twopennyworth of bread and cheese. When I had done, I started quite refreshed ; only my feet were more crippled than ever, and I could scarcely bear to walk over the stones. Yet I was half ashamed to sit down in the street, and forced myself to keep on the move.

I got through Peterborough better than I expected. When I came to the high road, I rested on the stone-heaps, till I was able to go on afresh. By-and-by I passed Walton, and soon reached Werrington. I was making for the "Beehive" as fast as I could when a cart met me, with a man, a woman, and a boy in it. When nearing me the woman jumped out, and caught fast hold of my hands, and wished me to get into the cart. But I refused; I thought her either drunk or mad. But when I was told it was my second wife, Patty, I got in, and was soon at Northborough. But Mary was not there; neither could I get any information about her, further than the old story of her having died six years ago. But I took no notice of the lie, having seen her myself twelve months ago, alive and well, and as young as ever. So here I am hopeless at home.'

This wonderfully graphic narrative—extraordinary compound of facts and dreams, illuminated by the lurid flame of a marvellous imagination—Clare accompanied by a letter to his visionary spouse. The letter, addressed, 'To Mary Clare, Glinton,' and dated 'Northborough, July 27, 1841,' ran as follows :—

'MY DEAR WIFE,—I have written an account of my journey, or rather escape, from Essex, for your amusement. I hope it may divert your leisure hours. I would have told you before that I got here to Northborough last Friday night; but not being able to see you, or to hear where you were, I soon began to feel homeless at home, and shall by and by be nearly hopeless. But I am not so lonely as I was in Essex; for here I can see Glinton Church, and feeling that my Mary is safe, if not happy, I am gratified. Though

U

my home is no home to me, my hopes are not entirely hope-less while even the memory of Mary lives so near me. God bless you, my dear Mary ! Give my love to our dear beautiful family and to your mother, and believe me, as ever I have been and ever shall be,

My dearest Mary,

Your affectionate husband,

JOHN CLARE.'

The poet's glorious intellect was gone ; he sat there bereft of reason ; body and soul alike shattered and broken to pieces. Yet on the wreck and ruins of all this mass of marvellous life, there still sat enthroned the memory of his First Love. 'For Love is strong as Death,' says the Song of Songs.

FINIS.

Happy for Clare if his weary life had been allowed to end here, in dreams of his first, his purest love. But it was ordained otherwise, and he had yet to drag a miserable course of earthly existence for more than twenty years. The period was one of great physical and mental suffering. Much of it might have been, if not prevented, at least softened and alleviated, but for the fresh interference of troublesome foes and ignorant friends. There was clearly no harm in leaving the poet in his little cottage at Northborough, allowing him to tend his flowers, to listen to the song of birds, and to write verses to his Mary in heaven. Now as ever, he was as harmless and guileless as a child ; he would not hurt the worm under his feet, and even in his most excited moods not an unkind word to those around him escaped his lips. A little additional assistance—if only from the 'county,' of which a noble earl held him to be 'a great credit'—might have made his own and his wife's existence perfectly free from cares, and softened the evening of their lives. But the great patrons would have it otherwise. Clare had no more books to dedicate to Honourables and Most Honourables, and they thought that the best thing to be done was to get such a useless 'county poet' out of the way and out of sight.

Clare had not been many weeks at his little home, resting from his fatigue, and enjoying the caresses of his children, when he was visited by the Mr. Skrimshaw, of Market Deeping, who had attended him on a former occasion. This person, who called himself a doctor, had a notion that poets were always and naturally insane, and that the very fact of a man being given to write verses was decisive proof of his madness. Mr. Skrimshaw, therefore, had little trouble in consigning Clare to another lunatic asylum. All that was necessary was to engage the help of a brother-doctor to go through a slight legal formality. This was soon done, and 'Fenwick Skrimshaw,' together with 'William Page,' both of Market Deeping, signed the due certificate that John Clare was to be kept under restraint at a madhouse, for the definitely stated reason of having written poetry, or, as literally given by the doctors :—

'After years addicted to poetical prosings.'

On the ground of this new crime, punishable, according to the wise men of Market Deeping, with life-long imprisonment, Clare was torn away from his wife and children, and carried off to the madhouse. He struggled hard when the keepers came to fetch him, imploring them, with tears in his eyes, to leave him at his little cottage, and seeing all resistance fruitless, declaring his intention to die rather than to go to such another prison as that from which he had escaped. Of course, it was all in vain. The magic handwriting of Messrs. Fenwick Skrimshaw and William Page, backed by all the power of English law, soon got the upper hand, and the criminal 'addicted to poetical prosings' was led away, and thrust into the gaol for insane at Northampton.

It was, perhaps, with some regard to Clare being considered, on high authority, 'our county poet,' that he was consigned to the county lunatic asylum at Northampton, instead of being taken back to the more respectable refuge of Dr. Allen, who was anxious to see him again under his charge, and even expressed strong hopes of an ultimate cure. The change was not a hopeful one; though, as far as the patient's physical comforts were concerned, there was no suffering attached to it. During the whole of his long sojourn at Northampton, the poet was treated with a kindness and consideration beyond all praise, and which, indeed, he had scarcely a right to expect from his position. Earl Fitzwilliam, who had taken him under his charge, only allowed eleven shillings a week for his maintenance, which small sum entitled Clare to little better than pauper treatment. Nevertheless, the authorities at Northampton, with a noble disregard for conventionalities, placed Clare in the best ward, among the private patients, paying honour to him as well as themselves by recognising the poet even in the pauper.

The Northampton General Lunatic Asylum stands at a little distance from the town, on the brow of a hill, in a very beautiful position, overlooking the smiling plain traversed by the River Nene. It is a large establishment, containing, on the average, some four hundred patients, the great majority of them paupers. The private patients have to themselves a large sitting-room, somewhat similar to a gentleman's library, the windows of which overlook the front garden, the valley of the Nene, and the town of Northampton. In the recess of one of these windows, Clare spent the greater part of his time during the twenty-two years that he was an inmate of the asylum. Very melancholy at first, and ever yearning after his 'Mary,' he became gradually resigned to his fate, and after that never a murmur escaped his lips. He saw that the world had left him; and was quite prepared himself to leave the world. During the whole twenty-two years, not one of all his former friends and admirers, not one of his great or little patrons ever visited him. This he bore quietly, though he seemed to feel it with deep sorrow that even the members of his own family kept aloof from him. 'Patty' never once showed herself in the twenty-two years; nor any of her children, except the youngest son, who came to see his father once. The neglect thus shown long preyed upon his mind, till it found vent at last in a sublime burst of poetry : —

'I am! yet what I am who cares, or knows?
    My friends forsake me like a memory lost.
I am the self-consumer of my woes,
    They rise and vanish, an oblivious host,
Shadows of life, whose very soul is lost.
And yet I am—I live—though I am toss'd

Into the nothingness of scorn and noise,
    Into the living sea of waking dream,
Where there is neither sense of life, nor joys,
    But the huge shipwreck of my own esteem
And all that's dear. Even those I loved the best
Are strange—nay, they are stranger than the rest.

I long for scenes where man has never trod,
    For scenes where woman never smiled or wept;
There to abide with my Creator, God,
    And sleep as I in childhood sweetly slept
Full of high thoughts, unborn. So let me lie,
The grass below; above the vaulted sky.'

This was the last poem which Clare wrote—the last, and, we think, the noblest of all his poems. Clare's swan-song, we fervently hope, will live as long as the English language.

For the last ten or twelve years of his existence the poet suffered much from physical infirmities. Previously he was allowed to go almost daily into the town of Northampton, where he used to sit under the portico of All Saints' Church, watching the gambols of the children around him, and the fleeting clouds high up in the sky. When these excursions came to be forbidden, he retired to his window-recess in the asylum, reading little and speaking little; dreaming unutterable dreams of another world. Sometimes his face would brighten up as if illuminated by an inward sun, over-whelming in its glory and beauty. This life of contempla-tion, extending over many years, was followed by a singular change in the physical constitution. The head seemed to expand vastly; the bushy eyebrows grew downward until they almost obscured the eyes, and the abundant hair, white as snow, came to fall in long curls over the massive shoulders. In outward appearance the poet became the patriarch.

The inmates of the asylum treated Clare with the greatest respect—far greater than that previously allotted to him by the world without. To his fellow-sufferers he always was John Clare the poet; never Clare the farm-labourer or the lime-burner. An artist among the patients was indefatigable in painting his portrait, in all possible attitudes; others never wearied of waiting upon him, or rendering him some slight service. The poet accepted the homage thus rendered, quietly and unaffectedly, as a king would that of his subjects. He gave little utterance to his thoughts, or dreams, whatever they were, and only smiled upon his companions now and then. When he became very weak and infirm, they put

him into a chair, and wheeled him about in the garden.
The last day he was thus taken out, and enjoyed the fresh
air and the golden sunshine, was on Good Friday, 1864.
He was too helpless to be moved afterwards; yet would
still creep, now and then, from his bed to the window, looking down upon the ever-beautiful world, which he knew he
was leaving now, and which he was not loth to leave, though
he loved it so much.

Towards noon on the 20th of May, the poet closed his
eyes for ever. His last words were, 'I want to go home.'
So gentle was his end that the bystanders scarcely knew
when he had ceased to breathe. God took his soul away
without a struggle.

Clare had always expressed a wish to sleep his last sleep
in the churchyard of his native village, close to his ' own
old home of homes.' In the very first poem of his earliest
published book of verses, he summed up all his aspirations
in the one that he should—

'As reward for countless troubles past,
  Find one hope true : to die at home at last.'

Accordingly, when the poet's spirit had fled, the superin-
tendent of the Northampton asylum wrote to his patron,
Earl Fitzwilliam, asking for a grant of the small sum necessary to carry the wish of the deceased into effect. The noble
patron replied by a refusal, advising the burial of the poet
as a pauper at Northampton.

But this lasting disgrace, fortunately, was not to be.
Through the active exertions of some true Christian souls,
real friends of poetry, the requisite burial fund was raised
in a few days, and the poet's body, having been conveyed
to Helpston, was reverently interred there on Wednesday,
the 25th of May, 1864. There now lies, under the shade

FINIS.

of a sycamore-tree, with nothing above but the green grass and the eternal vault of heaven, all that earth has to keep of John Clare, one of the sweetest singers of nature ever born within the fair realm of dear old England—of dear old England, so proud of its galaxy of noble poets, and so wasteful of their lives.

———————

INDEX.

THE END.

LONDON :

R. CLAY, SON, AND TAYLOR, PRINTERS,

BREAD STREET HILL.